Alison Joseph was born in North London and educated at Leeds University. After graduating, she worked as a presenter on a local radio station in West Yorkshire, then, moving back to London, for Channel 4. She later became a partner in an independent production company and one of its commissions was a series about women and religion, the book of which was published by SPCK. She has since worked as a reader and abridger for BBC Radio Drama. Alison, who has three children, now lives in London. Her first four novels featuring Sister Agnes Bourdillon are available from Headline.

Also by Alison Joseph

Sacred Hearts
The Hour of Our Death
The Quick and the Dead
A Dark and Sinful Death

The Dying Light

Alison Joseph

HEADLINE

First published in 1999
by HEADLINE BOOK PUBLISHING

First published in paperback in 1999
by HEADLINE BOOK PUBLISHING

10 9 8 7 6 5 4 3 2 1

ISBN 0 7472 5944 5

Typeset by Avon Dataset Ltd, Bidford-on-Avon, Warks

Printed and bound in Great Britain by
Clays Ltd, St Ives plc

HEADLINE BOOK PUBLISHING
A division of the Hodder Headline Group
338 Euston Road
London NW1 3BH

www.headline.co.uk
www.hodderheadline.com

I wish to thank Joe and Jane Thubron, the Governor and staff of HMP Bullwood Hall, and the Chaplain, Governor and staff of HMP Drake Hall. I also wish to thank the staff of London Transport and the Jubilee Line extension for all their help with my research.

Chapter One

The candles flickered in their bowl in front of the altar, bright against the darkness of the prison chapel. The young woman bent over them, and for a moment her thin features were radiant with light.

'What's she doin' here?' The voice was a raucous whisper, and came from the back of the chapel. 'We don't want no trash in here,' the voice continued.

The young woman murmured a few words over the candles.

'She's out, she is,' the voice said.

'Leave her alone, Janette,' someone else whispered.

Agnes looked towards Janette where she slouched in her seat, her large form draped with uneven layers of cardigans.

Janette faced her. 'Sister, she shouldn't be here, should she? Not after what she's done.' Her voice was now a pleading whine.

The young woman stood up and went back to her place, not raising her eyes.

'Anyone else?' Agnes asked, ignoring Janette. A thin, grey-haired woman went forward and lit a candle, knelt quietly for a moment, then returned to her place. Agnes waited in the silence, then said the closing words of the intercession. 'Father, in mercy and love unite all your children wherever they may be.' As she looked up, she saw Janette directing some kind of venomous gesture towards the young woman, who sat quite still, staring at the floor.

1

* * *

'How did it go?' Sister Imelda looked up from her desk in the office she shared with Agnes in the prison Roman Catholic chaplaincy.

Agnes sighed. 'Why can't we ban Janette from the services?'

'It would cause more trouble than it's worth.'

'I can't bear it. I've tried, but really . . .'

'Who this time?'

'Amy, again.'

'It's always Amy now. While you were away in France they put her on segregation, for her own safety.'

'But just because of what she's done—'

'It's not that,' Imelda said. 'I think Janette's anger is universal. Whoever's nearest gets it.'

'So her husband just happened to be in the way?'

A brief smile touched Imelda's face, lightening its customary seriousness. 'And Janette was holding the carving knife by accident.' She shook her head. 'Four years for GBH – that's hardly an accident. Mind you, she's done most of her time; her release date is due very soon.'

'Thank goodness.' Agnes riffled through some papers on her desk. 'Cally wasn't in chapel today.'

'No, I saw her earlier. She said she wanted to speak to you.'

'To me?'

'You're newer than me. Novelty value. They've all fallen out with me.' Imelda turned back to her desk, straight-backed and placid.

Agnes walked along the prison corridor. From the cells came loud shouts, swearing, laughter. Radios were being played at high volume. She touched the heavy keyring that hung at her waist. She selected a key and unlocked the door in front of her. It swung shut behind her and she locked it again. Ahead of her stretched a corridor, dim and shabby, as if what light there was had long ago been absorbed into the beige gloss paint. She set off along it, her keys making a loud, discordant jangling. She thought about Sister Imelda, about her calm acceptance of her vocation. She must be about fifty, Agnes thought, although sometimes she looks much older. She has that air of gravity about her, that lined face. But I've never seen her upset or angry. Perhaps that's what it is to be a good nun, Agnes thought, unlocking the door to C wing and locking it behind her.

She paused by a cell door and knocked, then unlocked it and walked in. In the tiny space two young women were sitting on two identical beds. One was reading a magazine. The other sat, staring at her hands in her lap.

Agnes locked the door behind her. 'You asked to see me, Cally,' she said.

'Did I?'

'You know you did. Sister Imelda told me.'

'She's always making stuff up about me. Bad as the screws, that cow.'

Agnes looked at her. She was pale, and hollow-eyed, and her fingers picked nervously at each other. Her hair had once been bleached, but was now a ragged mix of blonde and mouse.

'I'll go then,' Agnes said.

'Fine by me.'

Agnes hesitated. The ceiling flickered with gold, as the sun defied the narrow strip of glass that served as a window. The girl on the next bed sighed, stretched and closed her magazine. 'She had a dream, Sister,' she said.

Cally stirred. 'Leave it, Nita.' Her voice was barely audible.

'She said it was a what's-it – you know, like when you tell the future.'

'Shut your fuckin' gob, Nita.'

Agnes spoke firmly. 'Perhaps one day she'll tell me herself.' She turned to go.

'She's done it before, ain't you, Cal? Dreamt the future.' Nita turned back to her magazine. 'Mind you,' she added, 'I've done it too. The night before my court hearing, and there's my brief saying, don't worry, girl, you'll get probation at worst, haven't packed a nightie or nothing – and I dreamt about a songbird in a cage.'

'A budgie, you said it was.' Cally started to giggle.

'Well, they sing, don't they?'

'Your nan's mangy old budgie, you said.' Cally was still laughing.

'Same bleedin' difference.'

'No, it ain't.' Cally's smile vanished. 'Nothin' like what I dreamt last night. What happened to me last night, it was like I were awake, right, but not really conscious, and I saw . . .'

'Saw what?' Agnes prompted, gently.

Cally looked up at her, then looked back at her hands and started pulling at her fingers again. 'Nothing,' she murmured.

'But you asked for me—' Agnes began.

'She was that upset this morning,' Nita said.

'And now?'

Cally looked away.

Agnes turned to the door and unlocked it. Behind her she heard Cally say, 'I just know something terrible's going to happen.'

Agnes turned and glanced at her. Cally was staring at the wall, tracing the angles of the bricks with her finger. Agnes went out through the door and locked it behind her.

Imelda was in the staff kitchen. 'So she wouldn't tell you?'

Agnes shook her head.

'Coffee?' Imelda offered.

'Just a quick one, thanks. I'm about to have lunch with Father Julius. I haven't seen him since I got back from France.'

'Going somewhere nice, then?'

Agnes shook her head. 'He's always in his church. He has an office there.'

'You're old friends, aren't you?'

'Yes. We go back years. He rescued me from my violent ex-husband. In France. About twenty years ago.' She took the mug of coffee that Imelda handed her.

'Yes.' Imelda stirred some milk into her mug, her apparent lack of interest betraying the fact that all the sisters knew everything about each other without anyone actually having to be told. Even though Agnes lived separately, in a small flat of her own, the details of her past still seemed to belong to the communal life of the order. Everyone knew about Agnes's privileged French childhood, the house in Provence, the wealthy parents, the ponies and governesses; everyone knew about her early marriage to a man whose violence had almost cost Agnes her life. And although the details were a little obscure, everyone knew that it was Father Julius who'd arranged for her to escape from France to England, all those years ago, and who'd managed to get a special dispensation to annul the marriage. Everyone knew everything about everyone.

Agnes looked at Imelda as she busied herself tidying away other people's mugs, thin and upright, a wisp of grey hair brushing her cheek. Except Imelda, Agnes thought. No one seems to know anything about her at all.

'You seem happy here,' Imelda said suddenly.

'I like it.'

'Like it?'

'Shouldn't I?'

'Some people find it very difficult. The noise, the endless locking and unlocking of doors, the constant tension amongst

5

the women, the general hysteria, alarms going off – a lot of sisters haven't lasted.'

'Listen, I've just been moved from our privileged convent boarding school in Yorkshire. Compared to that, this is a doddle.'

Imelda smiled, and sat down on one of the chairs. 'Eleanor's very pleased that we're job-sharing now. She said that in all her years as governor here at Silworth she's never known so many of the women to be religious.'

'It's still a minority of inmates, isn't it?'

'Not if you count the Anglicans as well. Sarah gets a good turnout these days at her services.'

'And there's the other faiths too.'

'And the anger management, and the counselling . . . in fact, everyone here is probably much more spiritually advanced than anyone on the outside.' Imelda laughed. 'And what did Cally want, then?'

'I'm not quite sure. She'd had a premonitory dream, apparently. But she wouldn't tell me what it was.'

'She's a manipulative little thing, isn't she? It's like all that performance about having to see her father, all that tearful pleading, and then when I did ask him to come in she refused to see him.'

'Is that why she's angry with you?'

Imelda shrugged. 'That or something else. We can't afford to care what they think of us, can we?' Her face looked harsh under the fluorescent light. 'They're all the same. Their lives governed by who they can get favours from, who they can get drugs from . . . and if it's not drugs, it's all that fixation about their children.'

'Imelda – you can hardly blame them. They only get to see their children on visits. It's terrible for them—'

'They play it up, though, don't they? It's part of the attention seeking.'

'But we can't know how it feels.'

Imelda's face looked grey in the bright white light. 'No,' she said. 'We can't.'

Agnes glanced at her. 'By the way,' she said. 'Amy Kearney. I wanted to ask you—'

Imelda blinked at the name. She looked up at Agnes, and there was a tension around her eyes. 'I don't know,' she said. 'I don't know anything about her. I'd – I'd better get back to the office now.' She stood up, picked up her coffee mug and went out of the door.

Agnes stared after her. It was midday. Somewhere in the prison an alarm was sounding, a loud siren drowning out the blaring radios, followed by the hammering of feet as officers raced to the scene. Agnes wondered briefly if it was serious. She gathered up her coat and bag and left the prison.

'Well, this is just like old times.' Julius took the bagel that Agnes offered him, and arranged it neatly on his desk on its paper serviette.

'It was only two weeks.'

'You'll remember how to make the coffee, then.'

Agnes went over to the kettle and switched it on.

'And how was France?' Julius went on.

'Fine.' Agnes searched for the coffee tin on the shelf above the kettle.

'Good.' Julius watched her as she spooned coffee grounds into the cafetière. 'Only—'

'Only what?'

'I thought it might be rather difficult. You seeing your mother, and her being so old, and—'

'It was fine.'

'Right.'

Agnes poured boiling water into the cafetière.

'Have you seen Athena?' Julius asked.

'I'm having a drink with her tonight.'

'She'll have missed you.'

Agnes smiled at him. 'It's not like you to be concerned for Athena.'

'Of course it is. Any friend of yours . . .'

Agnes laughed.

'And will she be in Armani? Or Nicole Farhi?'

'Good heavens, Julius, you do listen after all. It's all Jaeger for her at the moment.'

'Well, don't you go getting ideas.'

'Julius, any ideas of that nature that I might have are all my own and owe nothing to Athena.' She poured their coffee and sat down opposite Julius. She unwrapped her bagel from its paper bag.

After a while he said, 'It's really nice to see you again.'

'You too.'

'So – um, France was fine?'

'France was wonderful, Julius. Fantastic. Great weather, wonderful food, lovely beaches. And speaking my other language again. Wonderful. And then I come back to a London November. I should just stay there, really, and find a nice comfortable order of nuns, maybe with its own vineyard. What do you think?' She looked up and caught Julius's expression. 'It's all right, I'm not serious. Look, I brought you a present,' she said, jumping up and rummaging through her bag. 'There's a tiny church in the next village that has these wonderful paintings. Look, I got postcards of this one, the Madonna. Isn't it lovely? So simple . . . People light candles in front of it. I got one for you and one for me.'

She went to him and handed him the card. 'Look, it's so natural, and the baby's looking all grumpy, and the mother's so radiant. I thought it summed something up, about God's love being all-encompassing.'

Julius took the card. 'Like a mother's love?'

Agnes went and sat down again, and sipped her coffee.

After a while Julius said, 'She must be very frail now.'

'Yes.'

'Was she pleased to see you?'

'Julius, it went all right. Okay? It was never going to be a tearful reunion. We never had that mother-daughter thing; we're not going to start now. Okay? She's not that well, no, she's very old, it was a good idea that I went to see her, but in the end – we've never had very much between us. I didn't feel . . .' She stood up and went over to the window. She traced the lines of lead around the panes of glass. 'She's not someone I . . . I don't have to . . .' She shrugged, and went over to him, and put her hands on his shoulders where he sat. He reached up and patted one of her hands. He picked up the postcard with his other hand and turned it over in his fingers.

'I'm glad you're back,' he said.

Walking back along Borough High Street to the prison, Agnes found she was blinking back tears. She picked her way across a building site. What else was there to say? she thought. Nothing. There was nothing to be said. Not even to Julius.

Back in her office she checked the rota. She went to join D wing on association.

Janette patted the seat next to hers, and grinned at Agnes.

'Come and sit down, Sister.' She laughed, exchanging a toothy grin with her friend across the table.

Agnes took the seat next to her and waited.

'Well, what you got to say for yerself, eh?' Janette said, and her friend started to laugh.

'What would you like me to say?' Agnes felt outnumbered.

'I dunno, do I?'

'Last time we spoke, you said you didn't believe in God.'

'I never. I never said that, did I, Tils? I wouldn't have said that, not me – I were brought up God-fearing. Me Mum, God rest her soul, she'd be turning in her grave if she thought I'd said I didn't believe. You're just a lyin' bitch, you are, a great big liar. You're just saying that to wind me up. You're as bad as the rest of them, you are. Clear off out of here. We were havin' a laugh before you poked your bleedin' nose in, weren't we, Tils? You saw her didn't you, comin' here to wind me up? Clear off I said, before someone gets damaged, and it won't be me.'

She pushed her face up close to Agnes. Agnes was aware of bad teeth, the stale smell of cigarettes, a sensation of heat from the fleshy body that pressed against her. Agnes stood up and left without a word.

She found Cally in her cell.

'It was about my dad,' Cally said, looking up as Agnes came in. 'My dream.'

Agnes sat on Nita's bed and waited.

'Someone killed him,' Cally said, 'Shot him.'

'Who shot him?'

Cally started to say something, then stopped herself. 'You know how dreams are. People turn into other people.'

'Who was it?'

Cally shrugged, as if she'd suddenly lost all interest in the conversation. 'No one I knew.'

'And as for Cally—' Eleanor, the prison governor, sighed and sat down at her desk. 'She's another one.'

'Another what?' Agnes pulled up a chair opposite her. Eleanor had expressive grey eyes and even features. Her short brown hair was sprinkled with grey.

'Everyone's to blame but her,' Eleanor said.

'I wondered whether to talk to her personal officer.'

'You can try.' Eleanor doodled on a scrap of paper in front of her. 'Some of these officers are better than others. It's all a bit new, this personal relationship between screws and inmates. The old guard are finding it a bit difficult, I think. Let me see . . .' She pulled out a file. 'June. She's the screw for that wing.' Eleanor put the file away. 'You can try if you like.'

'In other words . . .' Agnes hesitated.

'Let's just say, if you can build up your own relationship with Cally without involving June, you might get further.'

Agnes smiled at her. 'I've brought you the chaplaincy rota,' Agnes said, passing her a sheet of paper.

Eleanor glanced at it. 'Thanks.' She looked up at Agnes. 'And how are you settling in here?'

Agnes noticed the concern in her expression. 'Fine, thanks. Really.'

'It takes a particular kind of person,' Eleanor said.

'I know.'

'We're very grateful to your order, for working with us like this. The Catholic chaplaincy at Silworth would be lost without you lot.' She smiled. 'And dear old Father Julius, too.'

'Yes. Dear old Julius.'

'We don't see him so often these days.'

'He leaves us to it,' Agnes laughed. 'All he has to do is consecrate the host for communion – a minor theological point, to do with Christ reserving the priesthood solely for men.'

Eleanor met her eyes. 'Doesn't that annoy you?'

Agnes thought for a moment. 'I think I've been a nun too long to mind.'

'Sweetie, how can you enjoy your new job so much?' Athena

tasted her glass of wine. Her black hair was piled on top of her head, and she was wearing large silver earrings. 'I mean, working with people like that – we need fizzy water too, don't we, poppet?' She gestured madly to someone by the bar, then turned back to Agnes.

'I like it,' Agnes said.

'So you're happy, poppet?'

'Happy?'

'No excuse to run away this time?'

'Athena, I've got nowhere left to run. The order, for once, has respected my wishes. I was allowed to leave the school; I was allowed to return to London, back to you lot, to do a job I'm really well suited for – is that new, that black jumper?'

'Cashmere. A bargain, it was. Why are you laughing?'

Agnes shook her head. 'Julius said I wasn't to go getting ideas.'

'Better to have the ideas than the thing itself. At least ideas don't cost ninety quid.'

'You said it was a bargain.'

'It was.'

Agnes topped up her wine glass.

Athena glanced at her, then frowned. 'Are you sure you're happy?'

'Of course I am.'

'What is it?' Athena was studying her carefully.

Agnes looked at Athena. 'Nothing, honestly.'

'You don't mean that, sweetie. You know very well. What you mean is, you wish you could tell me.'

'It's not—'

'Yes it is. You trust old Julius with your doubts and uncertainties, because you go back such a long way—'

'But—'

'Precisely, because he believes. He has a God, like you do.

And you don't confide those things in me because I'm just silly old Athena, and good for a spot of shopping and Chardonnay and eyeing up tasty geezers—'

'Athena, that's really not—'

'Will you let me finish? What I'm saying is, I know why you're unhappy. It's about your mother, isn't it? You keep saying it was fine when you went to see her, but it wasn't, was it? I bet you've told Julius all about it.'

'Athena, there's nothing to tell.'

'How long did you spend with her, then?'

'Oh, you know—'

'How many times did you visit her in the fortnight?'

'Oh, most days . . .'

'Agnes, you're such a hopeless liar. I bet she didn't even recognise you – and I bet you think she did it on purpose. No doubt you told Julius all about it.'

'Really, Athena—' Agnes felt her eyes well with tears.

Athena looked up. 'Oh, God, I'm sorry. I didn't mean – I've upset you. Something I said – I'm such an idiot. I'm so sorry, sweetie . . .'

Agnes fumbled for a handkerchief. Athena passed her a packet of tissues, and she dried her eyes.

'I'm sorry,' Athena said again.

'You're right, it was awful in France.'

'I know.'

Agnes filled up both their glasses, then peered at the empty wine bottle. 'You don't get much of this to the pint, do you?'

The phone rang, a persistent urgent ringing that drilled into her sleep. Agnes reached out an arm and picked up the receiver.

'Hello?'

'Agnes – it's Eleanor.'

Agnes struggled to sit up. Her head seemed to be in a

pounding fog. 'What time – am I late?' Her mind tried to sift through the fog to find reasons why the prison governor should be phoning her.

'It's only seven. I just thought I'd better tell you – Cally's father was found dead, early this morning. Shot. I thought you should know, that's all. It's probably drug-related – the police think so, anyway. He was in his flat; there were no signs of a break-in. But Cally will be in a state about it. I just thought I'd warn you.' She rang off.

Agnes got up slowly, clutching her head. Surely two bottles of wine between two people wasn't excessive?

She dissolved two headache tablets in a glass of water. She watched them fizzing, and remembered what Cally had said about her dream, her dream which foretold the future. Her dream, in which someone shot her father.

How odd, Agnes thought, feeling her headache clear, watching the steam rise from the kettle as she made a pot of tea. It was only after she'd had her shower and was getting dressed that she remembered that she, too, had been dreaming. It was a dream about her mother, who was younger, and beautiful, and she was holding a candle. Agnes had been looking at her, and admiring the tones of her skin in the candle's glow. And her mother had turned to Agnes, but it was as if she couldn't see her. Agnes wanted her to keep the candle alight, but then her mother had blown out the candle, and Agnes was angry with her.

I was angry with her, Agnes thought. In my dream. She went to her wardrobe to find a sweater. She glanced out of the window at the dark grey sky, barely lightened with the dawn; at the frost on the rooftops of the housing estate opposite. She chose her warmest jumper, put on her heavy winter coat and left for the prison.

Chapter Two

On the corner of the street, Agnes stopped. The blank concrete face of the block of flats rose up before her. There was a stilted silence, broken only by the distant rumble of a car, as the wind whipped the litter into dirty circles across the tarmac. She'd expected to see a police cordon; there was nothing apart from one deserted police car parked outside the furthest entrance. She walked towards the doorway, checking the address that she'd written down earlier that morning from Cally's file.

The door was wedged open with a chunk of concrete. The security intercom had been pulled out of the wall. Agnes walked in, crunching broken glass underfoot, trying not to breathe the dank stench. On the third floor she turned right and started down the corridor. At the end she could see a door open, people coming and going, doors slamming, raised voices.

'You coppers are the bleedin' limit,' she heard, a shrill, female voice. 'We told you, all of us here, we said that family was nothing but trouble. Don't you go calling me madam – you should've done something about him when he moved in. It's too late now, innit? Still, at least we might have some peace and quiet now . . .'

There was more shouting, then quieter, male voices. Agnes approached the door, which was open but sealed with police tape. A policeman crossed the hall, saw her and came to the door.

'Can I help you?'

'I'm – um – I'm Sister Agnes. I'm a nun. I know the family.' Behind him she could see two men in civilian clothes. From next door she could still hear the neighbour complaining.

The police officer eyed her clothes, and Agnes regretted the passing of the habit. 'If you have any information, you should phone our incident room.'

'Well, I don't really, um—'

The policeman scribbled a phone number on a piece of paper. 'Here you are, madam – I mean, Sister. All information is dealt with in confidence, of course.'

'Yes. Thank you. Um, goodbye.'

Agnes descended the stinking staircase again, wondering why she'd come.

Back at the prison, she knocked on Eleanor's door.

'Come in – hello, Agnes.'

'I went to the flat. Cally's father's place. Just now.'

'Whatever for?'

'I don't know. I just thought, if I'm going to talk to Cally about it, I should find out as much as possible. How is she?'

Eleanor sighed. 'She's heavily sedated. The police want to question her later. The thing is, and this is strictly in confidence, they think it's her boyfriend who did it.'

'Why do they think that?' Agnes was about to mention Cally's dream but thought better of it.

'Mal, he's called. They've had their eye on him and Cliff, Cally's father, for some time. They were both involved in some suspicious business to do with getting street drugs from the coast, somewhere in Kent, apparently.'

'And why do they think—'

'Because of the bullet. It's from a particular kind of gun, commonly associated with drug-related shootings. That's what

16

they told me, anyway. They haven't found the gun yet.'

'Cally's boyfriend and Cally's father – both working together? It seems unlikely.'

'Why?'

'Because Cally adores Mal. And hates her dad.'

Eleanor smiled. 'You know Cally. It's all show, with her. Who knows what she really thinks underneath all that?'

'Does she know that the police are after Mal?'

'At the moment she doesn't even know what day it is. She's over in Healthcare, on the ward there.'

'What about the funeral?'

'It won't be for ages. She might be out by then – she's only in for shoplifting after all. Do you fancy a coffee? I was just going to the machine.' She got up and left the room.

Agnes sat in the chair by her desk. On one corner was a vase of pink carnations. Agnes fingered their petals and was surprised to find they were real. She wondered where they came from, imagining someone buying them for Eleanor; it seemed unlikely, somehow, and Agnes found herself thinking of Eleanor buying herself a small bunch of flowers from time to time for her own desk. Next to the flowers was a photo, of a young man. She remembered that Eleanor had a son, and wondered whether he lived near by, whether they had a good relationship, what his father was like.

Eleanor came back into the room.

'Thanks,' Agnes said, taking the plastic cup of coffee. Eleanor too had glanced at the photo, and Agnes saw a shadow pass across her face. Then she brightened again, and sat down at her desk.

'I needed to talk to you about Amy, too. Amy Kearney.'

'Oh, yes.'

'Imelda said that as she's a Catholic she might qualify for housing. Your order has some kind of hostel, apparently. And she said, as you're now dealing with it—'

'When did she say that?'

'This morning.'

'Oh. Right.'

'She said you'd sort out the relevant documentation for Amy to apply for a place.'

Agnes turned her coffee cup around in her hands. 'Sure.'

'You see, Amy may be here for some time.'

'She's on remand.'

'But it's a serious charge.' Eleanor doodled on a slip of paper in front of her. 'Have you met her?'

'Not properly. She comes to mass, but she never wants to talk.'

'You know what she's charged with, of course.'

'Yes.'

'Even if she gets manslaughter, it'll be custodial.'

'But to do what she did, she must be – they must see she's not in her right mind.'

'It's still murder.' Eleanor smoothed the corner of a piece of paper on her desk.

'Her partner was abusive, I gather.'

'It's not him she killed.' Eleanor was now fiddling with the photograph on her desk. She looked up. 'Three months old, the baby was. A little girl. Suffocated her. Her own child.'

'I know.'

'She needs psychiatric help. But whether she'll get it or not . . .' She replaced the photo neatly in its place. 'And even if she does – what difference will it make, long term?'

'This boyfriend – was he the father?'

'Oh yes.'

'And he was violent?'

Eleanor nodded. 'Apparently he was threatening to take the baby away.'

'Is he still around?'

'Somewhere, I expect. They usually are.' Eleanor stood up. 'Ian Marsden is her probation officer. You know him?'

'I've met him, yes.'

'He'll give you the details. If your people can show she'll be supported out in the world, that might help her.'

Agnes got up and picked up her bag. 'I'll keep you posted,' she said. She went to the door. As she went out, she glanced back. Eleanor had picked up the photo and was turning it over in her hands.

Out in the corridor, women were sitting in lines waiting for the prison shop to open. Agnes passed Nita, sitting quietly on her own at the front of the queue. She smiled briefly at Agnes, then looked away. Agnes could see Janette at the end of the line, slouching against the wall, laughing loudly. As Agnes passed the shop the shutter was lifted. The queue began to jostle, closing in to the counter. Agnes heard a loud voice.

'I think we was first, weren't we?'

Agnes turned to see that Janette and her friends had moved to the front of the queue and were now standing by the counter. Nita looked insubstantial next to them, but stood her ground. 'I been here for half an hour,' she said.

'So? You can wait another five minutes then, can't yer?'

Nita's voice was low. 'No.' She glanced at the queue for support, but none of her friends was there.

'What you buying anyway?' Janette moved a step closer to Nita.

'None of your business.'

Janette laughed, looking at her friends. 'Make-up? Won't make no difference to you, will it?' She laughed again, and her friends laughed too. 'Or hair dye? Nothing's going to improve this lot, is it?' She lunged forward and grabbed a handful of Nita's hair and pulled, hard. Nita screamed. 'Maybe you'd like to take your place in the queue now. Eh?'

Agnes looked at the prison officers behind the counter. She could see them calculating the risk, measuring Janette's weight against their own. She felt a rising tide of anger.

'I think perhaps you don't understand queueing,' she heard herself say, grabbing Janette's arm. With her other hand she forced Janette's fingers down so that they lost their grip on Nita's hair. Janette turned, her face blank with surprise. Janette's friends giggled nervously; Janette's eyes narrowed under their fleshy lids, and she fixed Agnes with a look of malevolence. Her voice made a harsh, rasping sound.

'I think you've made a bit of a mistake,' she said. 'Sister,' she added, loading the word with venom.

Nita was standing by the counter, rubbing the side of her head. One of the prison officers started to serve her, and the women in the queue formed an orderly line, their eyes fixed on Janette.

Agnes was still holding Janette's arm, but now she loosened her grip. Janette looked down at the place on her forearm where Agnes's fingers had been. She looked up to face the queue. 'I think she's going to regret that, don't you, girls?'

Most of the women in the queue looked uneasily away. Janette's friends exchanged glances.

Janette turned back to Agnes. 'See?'

Agnes looked at her levelly. 'See what?'

One of Janette's friends was lighting up a cigarette. Janette nudged her. 'Oi, Barney.'

Barney handed her the cigarette. Janette took a long draw on it, and slowly blew out the smoke in Agnes's face. 'There's rules, right,' she said. 'This lot here,' – she gestured to the queue – 'this lot here, they know the rules. Seems to me, lady, someone better teach you. Before you find yourself in deep shit.' She handed the cigarette back to Barney, turned away, and sauntered over to the counter. Nita had gone, and Janette and her friends took their place at the front of the queue, as the women there stood back to let them in.

Agnes unlocked the gate to the Healthcare wing. The sister in charge came out of her office, and nodded at her.

'I gather Cally's here – Cally Fisher?'

The sister led her through another locked door on to the ward. It had eight beds, but they were all empty, apart from one. At the far end of the room, under a high strip of barred window, lay a bundle of bedclothes, huddled, immobile.

'She's been like that all morning,' the nurse whispered. 'Best not to disturb her.'

Agnes walked back with the sister to the corridor.

'Amy Kearney's back with us now,' the nurse said.

'From segregation?'

The sister nodded. 'It was getting to her – she was self-harming. She's in one of the cells for now. We'll probably put her on the ward if she stays.' She led Agnes to a door, and slid back the hatch.

Agnes peered through the window. Amy was sitting on the narrow bed, cross-legged, unravelling a piece of knitting, her face expressionless.

Agnes walked out of the main gate on to the street, breathing in the London smog as if it was a sea breeze. So much hardship, she thought. So much anguish. And more than half the women inside were mothers.

Mothers, Agnes thought, waiting for the traffic lights to change.

She stood by the bus stop in the cold. A flash of memory, of a room in a nursing home in Provence, passed through her mind, but she pushed it away. The bus arrived, and she got on, grateful for its warmth.

The sisters gathering for evening mass greeted her, and enquired after her trip to France. The chapel seemed chilled in the winter's evening, its windows already dark, the shadows of the pillars lengthened by the sparse lighting.

Sister Madeleine stood to read the psalm. ' "Lord, you have searched me out and known me; you know my sitting down and my rising up; you discern my thoughts from afar . . ." '

Agnes felt the dim chapel suddenly invaded by sunlight, and she saw her mother's room, and her mother lying in bed, propped up on pillows. The light washed the room, picking out the detail of the fine linen pillowcases, the pale cream roses in a vase, the lace of her mother's nightdress. She tried to recall her mother's face, but it seemed bleached and faded in the coastal light.

Through it all she could hear Madeleine's voice. ' "If I take the wings of the morning, and dwell in the uttermost parts of the sea, even there your hand will lead me, and your right hand hold me fast . . ." '

'Hello, Maman, it's me,' she'd said.

Her mother had looked at her, screwing up her eyes. Then she'd turned to the nurse. 'Is this lady a visitor for me, Celine?' she'd asked sweetly.

'But – madame – it's your daughter,' the nurse had stuttered.

Agnes was standing at the end of the bed. Her mother had scanned her with piercing eyes, and Agnes felt a jumble of memories tumbling in her mind, while her mother's gaze passed over her and came to rest on her face.

'My daughter,' her mother had said, and turned to smile at Celine. 'How nice.'

' "Search me out, O God, and know my heart; try me and know my restless thoughts . . ." '

How dare she, thought Agnes. How dare she pretend not to recognise me. If only I'd gone with someone else, if only there'd been someone else there for me, then she'd have had to recognise me, she'd have had to admit I existed . . . Poor madame, the nurse had said, afterwards, she's losing her mind now. Physically she is fine, she is comfortable, but mentally, she is receding from us . . .

Receding from us. And there was another day, when her mother stared at her, and then began to complain about her stockings. Look, she said, pointing to her reclining legs, they're laddered, ruined – can't you see, mademoiselle? Where's that other girl? Run and fetch her, do; I need a new pair. These young women, it's a disgrace, her mother was saying, so lazy, so untrained, as she tugged clumsily at the stockings.

Agnes knelt in the chapel, remembering the misshapen, mottled legs, veined with purple; remembering her mother's bright, bright gaze. How dare she pretend, Agnes thought; how dare she look at me with such clarity and tell me that I don't exist?

Agnes opened her eyes. The nuns continued to murmur the responses; Madeleine finished the psalm and took her place, and the service proceeded. Agnes dabbed the tears from her eyes, checking to see that no one had noticed. But each sister was anonymous, unobserved, lost in her own private worship.

Chapter Three

The fine November afternoon seemed to have brought all London's tourists to the south bank of the Thames. The river shimmered with sunlight, and people congregated on the new riverside developments, shading their eyes to admire the view. It's all right for them, Agnes thought, hurrying through the dawdling crowds to get to her meeting at the probation service. All they've got to do is decide which charming little bistro they should choose for lunch.

She turned southwards, away from the river, weaving her way through grimy streets, past blocks of flats starkly anonymous after the high-tech glamour of the riverfront. She came out on to Borough High Street and just missed colliding with a skeletal and ancient woman wearing dressing gown and slippers, who walked straight across her path shouting incoherent abuse at the top of her voice. Agnes hurried on, gathering her scarf around her neck. All those bloody tourists, she thought; there they are thinking that everything in London is lovely. She heard a sudden screech of brakes behind her. She turned, chilled, to see that the old woman had somehow crossed to the other side of the road, still waving her fist in the air and shouting.

Ian showed her up to his office, which was a partitioned section of a large open-plan area. He had a loping gait and wide, innocent eyes that blinked out at her from behind gingery lashes. Agnes felt he reminded her of someone.

He stood by his desk, shifting from foot to foot. 'Thanks for coming, Sister – um—'

'Agnes.' Of course, she thought. It was Toby. That was who he reminded her of. Poor Toby, an Afghan puppy that her mother had acquired for a while, made a huge fuss over for some weeks, then passed to a neighbour when she got bored with him.

'Agnes. Um – coffee? Hang on, I'll find you a chair. That's the problem with this office – everyone moves the furniture around—No, don't sit on that one, it's got a dodgy foot. Hang on – um – milk? Sugar?'

'Just milk, please.'

He went off and returned with a chair, then disappeared again. Agnes sat down and waited. She wondered what had become of Toby. She wondered whether he'd suffered terrible trauma from being rejected. Although it was much more likely, she thought, that he was delighted to find he didn't have to live with us any more. She stared around the office, watching people come and go behind their partitions, listening to the indistinct buzz of conversations. On Ian's desk was a file, and she read the words 'Caroline Fisher' on the label. She was just about to reach out for it when he returned with two mugs of coffee.

'Stolen my colleague's mug for you, I'm afraid,' he laughed. 'Better drink up quickly before he misses it, or there'll be hell to pay.'

Agnes took the mug and sipped at the milky instant brew.

'Coffee all right for you?' Ian was looking at her, anxious to please.

'Lovely, thanks.'

'It's just you were looking a bit – um – you know . . .' he crossed his long legs, uncrossed them again.

'Ian, this file, Caroline – is that Cally who's in Silworth? G Wing?

'Yes, that's right.'

'Are you her probation officer?'

'Yes. Just inherited her from a colleague, actually. Why?'

'Oh, I just wondered, that's all.' Agnes took a large swig of coffee, then said, 'Her father's been murdered.'

'I know.'

'They're saying her boyfriend did it.'

Ian looked up from his mug. He nodded. 'So I heard.'

'What do you think?'

'What do I think? How long have you got?' He smiled. 'From what I gather, I imagine Cally's the sort to be none too clever about picking her boyfriends. Mal's a nice kid, but hopeless at avoiding trouble.' He smiled at Agnes, and she saw a slight sadness behind his gaze which made the resemblance to Toby even stronger. 'But obviously, it's not for me to say. Can I have your mug?'

Agnes handed it back, hoping he didn't notice it was still half full.

'Actually,' he said, 'can we adjourn to the coffee bar outside? I'm dying for a cigarette.'

Agnes ordered a large espresso. Ian sat opposite her, and lit a cigarette with obvious relief. He took a long pull on it, watching her as she tasted her coffee. 'You should have said,' he said.

'Said what?'

He smiled. 'The coffee. I didn't realise mine was so bad.'

Agnes felt her cheeks colour. 'It's just – I'm a foreigner, you see. I don't like instant coffee.' She smiled at him.

'Which part of Foreign are you from?'

'France. Sort of.'

He nodded. 'I wondered. You're – um – you're very different from Sister Imelda.'

'There's nothing uniform about nuns.'

'No, of course . . . It's just – I felt, there was something about Amy's case . . . I'm glad it's you now.' He smiled, awkward, as if perhaps he'd spoken out of turn.

'Have you always been a smoker, then?'

Ian watched the thin column of smoke rise from his cigarette. 'I'm trying to give up.'

'Why?'

'What do you mean, why? Because it's bad for you, of course.'

'Sometimes I wonder if that's sufficient reason not to do something,' Agnes said.

Ian smiled at her. 'These days I wonder that an awful lot.'

'I used to love smoking,' Agnes said, wistfully.

'But, see, even you gave up.'

'I'm not sure I did. I just don't do it very often, that's all.'

'I wish it were that easy.'

'You see—' Agnes gathered some spilled sugar into a little heap with her finger. 'Sometimes I think of prayer like that. Like smoking.'

'Praying's like smoking?' Ian stared at her.

'Yes. In a way. It's about the moment, isn't it? A kind of pause, a stillness. You think I'm mad, don't you?'

'No.'

'You were staring at me.'

'I was just thinking . . . You see, I've started going to this meditation class, sort of Buddhist. It's a bit like what you said about smoking. Just then. About the moment, about celebrating the moment.'

'Maybe I'll take it up again, as part of my spiritual path.'

Ian laughed. 'But it shortens your life.'

'But that's just part of it, isn't it? If you live in the present, and the present includes smoking a fag, just for the enjoyment of it, even if it's an act of self-destruction, then the very act of lighting it links you with your own mortality. It's like saying, in this moment, I accept the inevitability of death, and yet, in accepting that, I shall live this moment with joy, I shall make this moment perfect.'

Ian was staring at her again.

Agnes laughed. 'In fact,' she said, 'I'll definitely take it up again.'

'And here's me trying to give up. You're really no help.'

'I could found a whole order based on it. We'd be the only Order of Smoking Nuns in the whole Church.'

Ian was laughing. He shook his head. 'I'm not sure the argument works.'

'Why not?'

'Because something about lighting a cigarette is actually illusory. It's not an acceptance of the moment: it's trying to make something of the moment that doesn't actually exist.' He stubbed out his cigarette in the ashtray.

Agnes looked at him. She sighed. 'You're right. I suppose. What a bore. Hedonism always has its limits.' She reached for his packet of cigarettes, took one, picked up his lighter and lit it. 'Anyway,' she said. 'Amy Kearney.'

He sighed. 'Amy Kearney. If anyone can claim that life dealt them a bum hand, it's Amy. I've only met her boyfriend once and that was once too often. Violent, abusive . . . She didn't stand a chance. Didn't want to be pregnant, but when the baby came she made such a good job of being a mother, it was the making of her. You should have seen her. She worked out all her benefits, got herself decent accommodation, was trying to find a training scheme that had a crèche, and started standing up to her horrible boyfriend . . . which was the problem, really, because that just made him worse.'

'So what happened?'

'She won't talk about it. You've seen her – she's not really in this world at all at the moment. She'd thrown him out, and he broke in one night and gave her a beating. It happened after that. She pleaded guilty. She's on remand, awaiting trial and sentencing. If she's given a custodial sentence, which is most likely, she'll be sent to a secure unit, maybe miles away.'

'For how long?'

'I reckon two years. But' – Ian lit another cigarette – 'she's done six months on remand, before she came here. We can plead she's already served part of a sentence. We're going to recommend a twenty-eight-day hospital order in a secure unit, and then attendance locally at a psychiatric hospital. She's such a fragile person, locking her away could do her terrible damage. As it is, she shouldn't be in a dispersal prison at all. Apart from what it does to her, there's all the potential for violence from the other inmates.'

'Yes,' Agnes said, remembering Janette.

'I gather your order runs a hostel for women like her.'

'Did Imelda tell you?'

'No. Eleanor did.' Ian picked up his packet of cigarettes and turned it over in his hands. 'And then I happened to see Imelda and I tried to ask her about it, but . . . she didn't seem to want to discuss it.'

Agnes shrugged. 'How odd. Does Amy have family?'

'No one's interested in her. She ran away to London a couple of years ago and was probably working the streets. There's an aunt in Liverpool somewhere but no one can be bothered.'

'And she's a Catholic, Amy?'

'Technically, yes. A good Catholic girl; refuses to use contraception or have an abortion. Ironic, isn't it?' Agnes met his gaze, but said nothing. Ian passed his hand across his forehead. 'Sorry. Maybe you don't see it that way.'

Agnes smiled at him. 'Maybe I don't. Doesn't mean you can't.'

He looked at her. 'Are there many nuns like you?'

'I hope not. One of me's enough for any order.'

He laughed. 'Shall we go and see Amy? I'm due to have a meeting with her in a few minutes. I can introduce you properly.'

Amy glanced up at them as they came into her cell in Healthcare, then looked away and put her thumb in her mouth.

'This is Sister Agnes,' Ian said. Amy's eyes were very blue, unblinking, wide open. She seemed to be seeing nothing at all. 'Amy?' The girl turned slowly on her bed until she was facing them, her thumb still in her mouth. Ian sat down next to her. 'Amy, Agnes can help you. We're trying to get you out of here. Do you see?' Amy looked at him, with the same wide, unfocused stare.

'Amy?' Agnes tried.

Amy blinked and looked at Agnes. She shrugged, a tiny movement of her thin shoulders. She murmured something, so faint Agnes could only just hear. 'Don't care.'

'Amy, you must – you must care.' Ian leaned towards her.

Again the thin whisper. 'Makes no difference to me.' She put her thumb back into her mouth, and turned to face the wall.

They walked back towards the prison wings. 'I suppose I've seen worse,' Ian said, conversationally. 'Worse than Amy, I mean.'

'She's in a bad state.'

'She shouldn't be in a place like this. Bloody remand

system. There's something about her, isn't there? She kind of gets to you.'

'Amy?'

He nodded. 'She gets to me, anyway. She has a kind of light.'

'Must be all your Eastern religion.'

'Don't you start converting me.'

'Wouldn't dream of it.'

He checked his watch. 'I've got a meeting in ten minutes. I must go. See you soon.'

Agnes watched him disappear down the corridor, then turned back to Healthcare and went to find Cally.

The nursing sister opened the door for her. Cally was lying down, but turned to see who had come to see her. She gestured Agnes towards her with some urgency, and sat up. Her hair was uncombed, and her face was puffy.

'It ain't him,' she whispered to Agnes as soon as the nurse had gone. 'It ain't Mal – tell them. Why would he have done it?' She turned to Agnes. 'He ain't got nothing against him, see. There weren't no hard feelings between them two. When my sister said what she said—'

'Your sister?'

'Yeah, my twin. Claire.'

'What did she say?'

'She was bleedin' lying, though. Cow. She was just jealous.'

Agnes touched Cally's arm. 'Can we start at the beginning?'

Cally sighed. 'My sister tried to stir things up with Mal, 'cos she was jealous, right. She told me he was a gangster, and I'd end up in trouble.'

'When?'

'Some time ago. A few months ago. We don't see each other much. And then she told my dad, and he always took her side, so he believed that Mal was no good, and he tried to stop us seeing each other. And it was all her fault, stupid bitch. We've always hated each other . . .'

'But you said Mal and Cliff got on?'

'That was later, right? Even when my sister tried to stir things up, they ended up friends, see? So Mal wouldn't have done it, okay? That's what I'm telling you.' Cally was breathing heavily, chewing her lip.

Agnes took her hand to calm her. 'I know. I know he didn't. We'll sort it out, Cally. You try and rest now.'

Cally lay down again. 'Tell them, Sister. Won't you? Tell them it weren't him.' Agnes nodded, tucking the blankets around her. The nurse unlocked the room to let her out.

' "There was a man sent from God, whose name was John . . ." ' Agnes knelt with the other sisters in the chapel, listening to the reading. ' "The same came for a witness, to bear witness of the Light, that all men through him might believe . . ." '

Agnes thought about Cally. And Mal. And Claire, her twin. She wondered what Cally's twin was like.

' "He was not that Light, but was sent to bear witness of that Light . . ." '

She remembered Amy lighting candles in the chapel, her face illumined with their glow.

At tea she sat with Sister Madeleine, at the wide, pine table in the community kitchen.

'How's the prison?' Madeleine asked.

'Fine. How's your work?'

'I'm working with Father Julius again.'

'Lucky old you.' Agnes saw Imelda come into the kitchen and pour herself some tea.

32

'I'm sure he'd rather it was you.'

'Nonsense. And I'm sure you look after him as well as I can,' Agnes said to Madeleine. Imelda was standing by the window, staring out into the darkness of the garden.

'I'm not sure he needs looking after.' Madeleine laughed.

'Poor old man, of course he does.'

'Agnes, you'd have to look at Julius for quite some time before you were reminded of a poor old man. Anyway, he won't let anyone else look after him.'

'Julius is no more dependent on me than I am on him.'

Madeleine got up and went over to the sink to wash her cup. 'That's just what I mean,' she said. 'And now I'm late, and if I were to try to say it's your fault he wouldn't hear of it.' She squeezed Agnes's shoulder and hurried from the room.

The kitchen was quiet, apart from the hum from the fridge. Agnes glanced at Imelda. 'I met Amy today,' she said.

Imelda turned away from the windows. 'Oh.' She seemed tense and drawn.

'She's very upset, isn't she?'

Imelda stood as if frozen. 'I don't – I don't know.'

There was a silence.

'I'm sure—' Imelda began. 'I'm sure the Lord knows . . . knows what's best for us.' She walked stiffly to the door and shut it hard behind her.

Agnes stared after her, then remembered that she'd promised to cook dinner for Athena and there was nothing in her fridge.

Athena poured herself a glass of wine, and then stared at it distractedly.

Agnes brought a bowl of salad from the kitchen and put it on the table in front of her. 'So, what is it?' she said.

'What's what?'

'You've hardly tasted the wine you so kindly brought, and you've hardly said a word since you arrived.'

Athena smiled in a vague way, then broke off a piece of bread and fiddled with it.

'It can't be a man,' Agnes said.

Athena looked up. 'Why not?'

'I mean, like the old days.'

'Why can't it?'

'Because we're older. And wiser.' Agnes went into the kitchen.

Athena sighed. 'If only.'

Agnes came back into the room with a perfect cheese soufflé. She smiled. 'Okay then, who is he?'

'No one.'

'Right.'

'After all, there's Nic now.'

'Of course.'

'We're really settled. Nic wants us to live together – did I tell you?'

Agnes looked at her hard.

'I must have told you. We're just debating whose flat, or whether to buy one together. You see, his work has just taken off recently. He's really busy. There's so much demand for past life regression stuff – everyone's obviously much more interested in who they used to be rather than who they are now. I blame the millennium.'

'I'm not sure that's quite how it works, is it?'

'And so he's worried that we don't see enough of each other, and he thinks he needs more of a proper base to work from, and Ben, you know, his son, they're really close, even though Ben's grown up now, but he thought if we bought somewhere together, Ben would have a base there too . . . And it's not just that. We're good friends now, we're comfortable with each other, and it is really much more sensible, isn't it, sweetie?' Athena poured herself some more wine. Agnes waited. Then Athena said, 'Today, in the gallery, this man came in and started talking to me – why are you nodding like that?'

'I wasn't nodding.'

'You were, in a kind of "I know what you're going to say next" way.'

'I have absolutely no idea what you were going to say next.'

'Go on, say it. You do.'

'You really fancied him. This man who came in today.'

'I mean, really, poppet. At my age. When it would be much better to settle down with Nic. And I should be pleased that anyone wants to live with me, for God's sake, when I'm such an old crone, set in my ways, with all my anti-social habits. I should jump at the chance, as it's obviously the last one I'll ever get.'

'Instead of which?'

'I was blushing, sweetie. Me. He came in and wandered around a bit, and I was just looking at him really, and it's not as if he's anything special – Nic's much better looking. Then he came over and asked me something, and I kind of felt all hot, and I realised my cheeks had gone all pink, and he was asking me about these mobile sculpture things we've got in at the moment, sort of metalwork things, all balanced so they swing around, and I meant to say something clever about harmony and equilibrium, and instead I said you had to be careful where you put them because they were liable to clonk you on the head when you weren't looking— It's not that funny—'

'Athena, it's very funny—'

'All right, it's funny . . .' When they'd finished laughing,

Athena said, 'Of course, it's out of the question.'

'Of course.'

'I mean, I love Nic.'

'I know.'

'And I'm sure he's quite right that we should live together.'

'Mmm.'

'Isn't he?'

Agnes refilled their wine glasses. She sipped at hers. 'I seem to remember it's what you wanted a long time ago.'

'Did I?'

'Yes. You did. You were very disappointed when Nic insisted on keeping his own place.' She noticed Athena was drinking rather fast. 'Still,' Agnes said, 'if you could fit in with his plans then, there's no reason not to change to fit in with his plans now.' Athena was holding her wine glass, twirling it in her hands. 'It's all about commitment, isn't it,' Agnes said.

'Well, you know all about that,' Athena said.

Agnes took another sip of her drink. 'Except I always want to run away,' she said.

'Not any more,' Athena said, raising her glass. 'To Us. To Us being old and wise and not running away. What do you think?'

Agnes clinked her glass with Athena's. 'To not running away.'

They looked at each other. Athena shook her head. 'I mean, us, darling. What are the chances?'

'Changing our ways after all this time? Pretty slim, I'd say.'

Chapter Four

On her way to Healthcare next morning, Agnes stopped in the corridor. She could hear sobbing: terrible, heartfelt weeping. She came round the corner and saw Janette, leaning against the counter of the dispensary, which was closed. Agnes stood, watching her. Janette looked up, saw it was her, and carried on with her loud weeping. Agnes was unsure what to do. She moved towards the next door. She'd just put her keys in the lock when she heard Janette say, 'It ain't bleedin' fair.'

Agnes turned the key in the lock and opened it.

'After all I've done for 'im.'

Agnes sighed. She relocked the door and turned to Janette. 'Is there anything I can do?' she said. She realised, seeing her standing there, her face red and blotchy, how rare it was to see Janette on her own, without her group of friends. She was leaning clumsily against the wall, looking lost, and now she smiled at Agnes, a lopsided grimace of a smile.

'Should you be here?' Agnes said.

'Waiting for medication. That upset. Screws sent me over here.'

'Why are you upset?' Agnes said, knowing it was expected of her, wondering why she didn't just unlock the door and walk through it.

'Oh, Sister, it's me old man, right. He was supposed to visit today. I sent him the VO and everything, and then I just heard from the office, he ain't phoned up. He ain't booked to see

37

me. And they won't let him in on the gate if he ain't phoned up. I can't think what's happened. I'm that worried about him, I am, worried sick I am . . .' she burst into renewed sobbing, peeking at Agnes through her tears.

Agnes sighed. 'Perhaps he was busy,' she said. 'Or perhaps he forgot.' Perhaps, she thought, if someone had been sent down for four years for attempting to kill you, you wouldn't feel terribly like visiting them in prison either.

'Busy? Him?' The tears suddenly vanished, and Janette's face assumed a hostile sneer. Behind them someone unlocked the door, and one of the nursing sisters appeared, with Cally leaning on her arm. Cally looked pale, but managed a brief smile at Agnes. 'You ask anyone who knows him,' Janette said, as Cally passed. 'You ask anyone whether my old man has ever done a day's work in his life. Idle good-for-nothing sod, he is; always has been. And now he can't be fuckin' bothered to shift his fuckin' arse over here . . . soddin' bastard. And where's that fuckin' nurse gone? She was supposed to give me me pills – that's why I've been hanging around here all morning . . .' Her eyes were bright now, shining with their usual malevolence.

Agnes turned to follow Cally.

'Oh, Sister, don't go.' Janette dabbed at her eyes, which were completely dry. 'You have the key here, don't you? You can get me my pills, can't you? I'm that upset, I am . . .'

'No. I don't have the key.'

'I really need them pills, see. I'm in one of me states . . .' Her voice had a wheedling tone.

'Too bad.' Agnes went to the door.

'Sister, the other day, right, outside the shop – it weren't nothing personal, right. Don't take it personally, eh?'

Agnes faced her. Is that what you said to your husband? she wanted to say. It's nothing personal? When you inflicted on him the sort of injuries that land you in prison for four years, and then expect him to visit you? Is that what it means, that nothing's personal? Agnes felt a knot of anger tightening her breath. 'No,' she said, 'of course it's not personal, is it? It's universal. Just a universal, random brutality that lands on whoever happens to be the nearest. Not personal at all.' She turned the key in the lock, walked through the door and slammed it hard behind her.

She strode through the corridor to find Cally, breathing fast, trying to calm herself, to see clearly through the haze of anger.

Cally was back on her wing, the officers told her. Agnes unlocked the gate to C wing, and walked through the association area. Cally was sitting at the end of the landing, in one of the armchairs, alone. She looked up as Agnes came and sat next to her.

'How are you?' Agnes asked her.

She shrugged. 'They reckon I've got to go back to work tomorrow.'

'It's probably better than being stuck in Healthcare.'

Cally looked away. Her eyes seemed dulled, circled with dark rings.

'Such a bleedin' waste,' she said, suddenly. She turned back to Agnes. 'He was about to make a go of things. He'd got this job. Loads of money, more than you can ever imagine. I thought he'd got it wrong when he said, all the noughts in the wrong place, I thought, but it was straight up.'

'What kind of job?'

'On a building site. Tunnelling job. His mate Marky, he's been working sites for a while now, with his uncle, and they'd got a vacancy, he said. And Mal got the job. He said it would be the hardest work he'd ever known – that's why the money was so good.'

'Was it straight, do you think?'

'I think so, yeah.'

'They're saying it was a drug-related shooting.'

Cally chewed her lip. She shook her head. 'My dad? Mal? They don't know nothin', them pigs. I mean, my dad's a complete bastard, a stupid git, my dad, but even he ain't that stupid.'

'You mean, he wasn't dealing drugs?'

'He might have used, sure, but round us, it's all sewn up, right, everyone knows that. No one with any sense would try to break into it. And Mal, what does he need to do that for? Like this job he got, when he first told me, I thought someone was having him on. I mean, if a bloke in a pub offers you money, you think, hang on a minute, don't you? Like me dad – he was always one for coming a cropper that way . . .' Her eyes filled with tears. 'Don't suppose I'll ever get used to him being gone. Bastard.'

'Do you think—'

'Do I think what?'

'Mal—'

'Do I think he did it?' She turned to face Agnes, her eyes wide, her lashes wet with tears. 'No. I don't think he did it. Here, can you lend me a couple of quid? I've got a visitor coming this afternoon.'

Agnes shook her head. 'I don't have any money on me,' she said. There was a rattle of keys from the gate. 'Here's your officer taking you across to lunch.'

Agnes followed Cally out of the gate and across the courtyard. 'Who's your visitor?'

'My mate Steph.' Cally beamed. 'She's me best mate.'

Agnes found the staff room empty. She unwrapped a sandwich and sat in a corner, eating it.

Sarah, the Anglican chaplain, came in. 'Everyone on lunch duty?' She went to the coffee machine and punched a button. 'Visiting time this afternoon. Should be fun.'

'It usually is.'

'It's the children. It stirs them up, seeing their kids. Having to hand them back when time's up. I can't bear it, myself. Seeing the little things being searched as well . . . It's the only time I ever wish I worked in a men's prison.'

'Janette was expecting her husband.'

Sarah sighed. 'I'd take all that with a pinch of salt. Mind you, it's probably better if he does visit. Eleanor's told me she's due to be released next Wednesday. There's going to be no one else to take care of her. It might be better if he'd take an interest.'

'But – after what she did . . . ?'

Sarah smiled at her. 'Where else will she go?' She picked up her coffee and went back to her office.

Agnes unlocked her own office and sat at her desk. She wondered where Imelda was. It was usual practice for them both to be on duty on visiting days. To pick up the pieces, Agnes thought.

She jumped as the door opened.

'Oh. You're here.' Imelda seemed distracted.

'Hello.'

'I didn't realise it was both of us today.'

'I'm just going. I'll go and check the visitors' list.'

As she approached the main gate, she could hear something going on. Raised voices; a man shouting. She stood by the inner gate, waiting for the duty officer to let her out. He came over and unlocked the door. 'I wouldn't go out there, Sister,' he said. 'Not right now.'

'Why not?'

'Trouble, in't there? If you ask me, them visits cause more trouble than they're worth. Usual story: someone's pitched up without their VO – we can't let them in, can we?'

'I bet I know who that is.' Agnes could hear a male voice, rough and abusive, gaining in intensity. The officer let her out, and Agnes went outside. In the outer courtyard stood a man, flanked by prison officers, gesticulating with his fists, shouting.

'If I say I'm fuckin' goin' ter be here, then I am, right? I ain't gonna let no one down – you ask anyone. You can't keep me from seein' her. I know all about the tricks you fuckin' screws play, but let me tell you, no one plays them tricks on me, right? Where is she?'

The man had turned towards Agnes as she came out, and the last question seemed to be directed at her.

'Where's who?' Agnes took in his thick face, his dishevelled hair, his filthy jeans and expensive leather jacket. He was tall and broad, and his face had a strange discoloration down one side.

'Janette,' he said, as she'd known he would.

'She was hoping you'd come,' Agnes said.

'These fuckin' screws trying to keep me out—'

'Without your VO—' one of the officers began.

'I had my bleedin' VO—'

'You didn't phone to book.'

'I'm her fuckin' husband, ain't I?'

Agnes took a step towards him. 'Shall I phone the governor for you? See what I can do?'

He stared at her, unsteadily, his red face still puffed out with hostility. After a moment he nodded. 'Yeah. Okay.' The officers backed off. Agnes led him to the gate. 'Can he wait here?' she asked the duty officer.

He was allowed to stand by the gate, while she phoned up

to Eleanor. They spoke for a few minutes; then Agnes turned to him. 'She said you could see her. A special dispensation, as Janette's due to be released soon.'

The duty officer stamped the book, and gave him a pass.

'I'll escort him to the visitors' wing, shall I?' Agnes said.

The gate was unlocked, and they proceeded through the courtyard, along the path to the visiting area. 'I didn't catch your name, Mr—'

'Jim. Jim Price.' He seemed calmer now.

'I'm Sister Agnes,' she said, but he wasn't listening. He was turning his head from side to side, taking in the detail of the prison, the tiny barred windows, the razor wire at the top of the high walls. 'Always the same, these places,' he said. She unlocked a gate into the corridor of the wing. He stopped and ran a finger down the rough, gloss-painted brickwork. 'Make me sick, they do.'

'Here we are,' Agnes said, opening a door and ushering him into the visitors' area. 'I'll just get her. Please wait here.' She had a word with the officers overseeing the visiting session, then headed for D wing.

There was a woman drying her hair by the washbasins at the end of the landing.

'Janette?'

'She's in her cell.' The woman gestured to a door.

Agnes knocked, then unlocked the door.

'Your husband's here,' she said.

Janette was lying on her bed, her eyes open, staring at the ceiling. She turned her head and saw Agnes. 'Fuckin' bastard,' she said.

'He didn't bring his VO.'

'Stupid git.' She rolled back to face the wall.

'I had a word with Eleanor on his behalf,' Agnes added.

'Stupid bastard he is. I've had it with him.'

'He's been giving the screws merry hell.'

Janette turned back to Agnes with a flicker of interest. 'What's he been doing, then?' she asked.

'He was really abusive.'

'What'd he say to them?'

'He said they were trying to keep him from seeing you.'

'He's fuckin' right.' Janette sat up heavily, and began to comb her hair. 'Fuckin' screws.' She reached out for a lipstick.

'Threatened them with all sorts,' Agnes said.

'That's my boy.' Janette finished painting her lips, without a mirror. 'Will I do?' she asked, standing up. 'Poor love,' she said. 'And it's a cold day for waiting out by them gates.'

Agnes unlocked the gate to her wing and, escorted by an officer, she was led through the corridor and out across the yard to the visitors' wing. When she opened the door, Janette pushed through in front of her. Jim stood up. He shrugged, turning his hands out, palms upwards.

' 'Lo, doll,' he said.

'Babes,' Janette said. She lumbered towards him, into his arms, which enfolded her. They sat down at their table. Jim pushed across to her several chocolate bars which he'd bought at the counter.

Agnes nodded at the duty officers and left. Checking out at the gate, she found there was a message in her pigeon-hole from Imelda.

'Can you see Cally before you leave?' it said. 'As usual, she won't talk to me.'

Agnes reclaimed her keys from the porter and went back along the corridor, locking and unlocking doors as she went. She knocked at the door of Cally's cell, and put her head round the door.

'Cally?'

Cally was alone. Her face was stained with tears.

'I just seen Steph, didn't I? On visit.'

'What did she say?' Agnes sat down next to her.

Cally started to cry noisily. 'I never thought he'd . . . I mean, people round us, they have to look after themselves, right, but that – guns and that – different, innit?' She blew her nose.

'What did Steph say?'

'I trust her, right, she's me mate, we go back years. She said the coppers have been round me dad's place. And she said she's seen Mal, right, and he said, when they find the gun, they'll have all the evidence they need to bang him up for ever.'

Agnes looked at her. 'What did she mean?'

'Dunno, do I? That's what he said. I blame Venn.'

'Who's Venn?'

'He runs this club, right. Mal was guesting there, doing nights and DJing. Always thought it was dodgy. Right heavy types on the door, you can always tell. Mal and Marky, see, that's how they got to be mates, through their music. And then Marky got him this job, and I thought it was all goin' to be clean. But what I think is, Mal got in too deep with Venn. And now he's in real trouble.'

She clasped her hands in her lap, and swung her legs to and fro, staring at the floor. 'And the stupid thing is,' she added, suddenly, 'there were loads of people who'd want my dad out of the way. People with more reason than Mal.'

'Who?'

Agnes touched Cally's hand, but she felt Cally's fingers shrink away from hers. 'Oh, you know, loads of people.'

'Who did you have in mind?'

Cally was staring at the wall. 'I feel so helpless, stuck in here. I can't help him.' She twirled a lock of hair between her fingers. Then she looked at Agnes. 'In my dream,' she said, 'the dream I told you about, about my dad – in my dream it was my sister. It was my twin who killed my dad.'

'But Cally, that's just a dream.'

Cally's fingers circled in her hair. 'Agnes – these days my dreams are the only real things I've got.'

Chapter Five

It was a wintry morning. A thin light struggled through the still-dark sky, muffled with heavy cloud. Agnes gathered her scarf around her neck, setting her face against the wind, joining the crowds of workers hurrying to their destinations, between the scaffolding and billboards announcing new office developments and luxury apartments. She passed the back of the building site for the extension to London Bridge underground station. A sudden gust of wind made her stop in her tracks. Between the hoardings she glimpsed mud, cranes, portacabins and the old railway arches, underneath which the brand new line was being constructed. She thought of the concrete shafts being sunk in London clay, and the men tunnelling there, carving a new world out of the dark earth.

She put her hands in her pockets and felt the letter that had arrived this morning from Provence. She crumpled it between chilled fingers. In front of her she could see men in hard hats, in thin vests despite the cold, trooping into the entrance to the building site to start their day underground, scurrying down the stairways to the mud beneath.

She hunched her shoulders against the cold. She could see the spire of St Simeon's church, needle-thin between the angular glass and concrete of new buildings. She scrunched the letter in her pocket and thought about going to light a candle in the church. She wondered whether it would make her feel any better. She heard distant shouting from the building site, and an image came to mind of rows of candles laid out for these men in hard hats, these souls in purgatory, destined to tunnel away for ever in the deepest reaches of the earth.

At St Simeon's she knocked on Julius's door.

'Agnes. This is early for you. I hope you've brought croissants.' He looked up, smiling, then concerned. 'What is it?'

She took the piece of paper from her pocket and pushed it across his desk to him, then stood up, filled the kettle and switched it on. She stood silently while he read the letter.

He looked up. 'Agnes, I had no idea. You should have said.'

'There was nothing to say.'

'Is she well cared for there?'

'The best that money can buy.'

He took off his glasses and polished them. He reread the letter. 'They say that she's becoming more frail. And that you must be prepared for—'

'She's not that frail.'

'They say her mind's going.'

'She's just pretending.'

'Agnes, she can't be.'

'I saw her, Julius.'

'And she was the picture of health, was she?'

In her mind Agnes saw bleached linen, a lace collar picked out in a dazzle of sunlight; thin threads of white hair. 'Why are you cross with me, Julius?'

'Don't be silly. I'm not cross. It's just that for some reason you're avoiding—'

'No I'm not. There's nothing to avoid. She's only my mother.'

The prison corridors too seemed dark, the strip lighting defeated by the chill of the day. She unlocked the door that led to her office, picked up some messages from Imelda, and then set off for D wing. At the entrance to the wing, as the key turned in the lock, she heard shouting, and as she walked through the door Nita flew past.

'Quick, help, the showers, quick, it's Amy . . .'

Agnes ran after her, towards the noise, a mixture of abusive shouting and a strange keening sound. Agnes wondered where the officers were. She was aware of a crowd breaking up, of the shouts dying down, of women dispersing, slinking away from the bathrooms in ones and twos.

At the entrance to the showers she stopped. She could hear an odd whimpering, like a dog. She looked at Nita, then pushed open the door.

There were bloodstains on the floor. Amy cowered, her eyes staring ahead, unseeing. Her clothes were torn, and there were patches on her head where her hair had been pulled out.

Agnes looked at Nita again. 'Janette?'

Nita looked away.

Agnes took a step towards Amy, who flinched. There were footsteps outside, and then two officers appeared. They looked at each other, then went over to Amy.

'It's not over yet,' one of them said. Agnes could hear shouting outside.

'It's Cally,' Nita said. Agnes left Amy to the officers and followed Nita out on to the corridor. Janette was lounging against the wall with Tils and Barney. A group of women was forming around her.

'She didn't deserve that.' Cally stood in the group, squaring up to Janette, her fists clenched at her sides.

'We know what she's done.' Janette had a cut to the side of her mouth which was oozing red.

'And you're so whiter than white, are you?' Cally was shouting.

'She's been taking the piss—'

'She ain't done nothing to you—'

'She's trash, she is. And that's what happens to trash – we hate 'em, right?' Janette looked towards the crowd of women who were grouping on the landing. 'And anyone who goes to help her, we hate 'em too. We don't want trash like that using our showers.'

Cally took a step towards her. Janette's friends gathered, sensing more bloodshed. Far down the corridor Agnes saw Amy being carried from the shower, slumped between the two officers. From the gathered women a hooting and jeering started up, a loud cacophony that seemed to grow in volume.

Agnes looked at Cally and Cally looked at Agnes. Nita came to stand by Cally.

'You could've killed her,' Cally said.

'Shame I didn't.' Janette glanced at Agnes, then turned to her friends and grinned.

'You've got right on your side, then, have you?' Agnes moved towards Janette. 'It's Okay to batter someone who's smaller and weaker than you, is it?'

'Ain't none of your business, Sister.' Janette flashed another grin to her allies.

'It is now.'

Janette smiled at her. 'You ain't been doing your homework, have yer? There's rules, right, and you're on the wrong side of them, Sister.' Tils and Barney shifted on their feet.

Agnes looked at Janette. She looked at the piggy eyes, dulled with hostility; she thought of Amy, suffering beyond suffering, being called trash by this woman who now swaggered in front of her. 'You make me sick,' Agnes heard herself say.

Janette blinked.

'Yes,' Agnes went on, battling with the anger that rose within her, 'sick.'

In answer, Janette's mouth formed a sneer. She leaned against the wall, her hands on her hips. 'You can't talk to me like that.'

'You make me so sick I could thump you right now,' Agnes said.

'No one talks to me like that—' Janette began. A shadow of uncertainty crossed her face.

Agnes felt the words form in her throat, taking shape from her rage. 'I'm sick of seeing you pretending to rule this wing, just because violence comes so easily to you. I'm sick of hearing you call people trash, when you're the trashiest person I've ever had the misfortune to meet . . .' Agnes realised she was shouting, but found she couldn't stop. 'I've had it up to here with you, with your petty violence and your stupidity. God knows I've tried to understand you, I've tried to be compassionate, but there comes a point when you just have to say, tough shit, and this is it. I've reached that point and I've come to realise that no amount of compassion is going to change the fact that some people, and I mean you, are just plain no-good no-hopers, and they're not going to change; and no amount of social work and probation is going to make the blindest bit of difference. They just go on swimming around in the mire of their own lives, and dragging as many other people into it as they can; and you can't blame an unhappy childhood because I could show you ten people who've suffered just as much as you did as a child and I bet they're all making a go of their lives and shaking off their past and hanging on to some sense of what it might be like to be human, some sense of their own spirit – and you have none. Here you are in purgatory, and however many candles anyone in the outside world lit for you, it would make

51

no difference at all . . .' She stopped for breath.

The two officers had returned. Janette looked from her friends to the officers, and back to Agnes. A look of bewilderment passed across her face, and she stared at Agnes for a moment, incredulous. Then she turned to the screws, her hand across her injured mouth.

'Amy hurt me,' she whimpered. 'Look, I'm bleeding. Amy did it . . .' She allowed an officer to lead her away, Tils and Barney following meekly. The other officer led Cally and Nita back to their cells.

Agnes stood alone in the wing, until she heard a solitary round of applause. She turned to see Ian standing there, clapping.

'Fantastic,' he said. 'I particularly liked the bit about no social workers being able to make the slightest difference. God knows these days we're never allowed to admit it. The look on her face . . . Oh, gosh, look, I didn't mean – don't cry, really, I meant it. I really did think it was fantastic, really brave too, 'cos we won't have heard the last of it. She was amazed – no one talks to the Janettes of this world like that these days. Look, I must have a hanky somewhere. Really, there's no need to cry . . .'

Agnes took the hanky he offered her, overwhelmed by waves of sobbing.

'And it's true,' Ian went on, taking her arm and leading her gently to the door, 'some people do have terrible experiences, terrible childhoods, but they don't all turn out like Janette, do they?' He unlocked the door and ushered her through, then locked it behind them.

Agnes's sobs came in deep gasps as she tried to catch her breath. 'I'm sorry—' she tried to say.

'No, don't be sorry, really. It was high time someone spoke to her like that. This victim culture we live in . . . We'll go to

Eleanor's room. You'll be private there – she's off sick today. Really, don't waste your tears for Janette . . .'

But I'm not crying for Janette, Agnes wanted to say, allowing Ian to lead her away from the wing, out into the fresh air. I'm crying for me.

Ian unlocked Eleanor's room and she settled into a chair, while he made some sweet tea. 'For shock, you know,' he said. 'You drink this while I check out how Amy is.'

Agnes sipped on it, grateful for its warmth. She sat alone, her eyes scanning the desk, unseeing. An image came to her of the church in Provence. She remembered the candles, arranged in their rows, the Madonna and Child bathed in light, the faithful murmuring their prayers for loved ones stranded in purgatory.

She blinked, and glanced at Eleanor's desk. The pink flowers had been torn into bits, crushed and scattered on the desk.

'Amy's asleep. Sedated,' Ian said, coming back into the room. 'God knows how she'll be when she wakes up. You're looking better.'

Agnes looked up at him. 'Why was she allowed to associate with the others?' Ian pulled up a chair and sat down. 'I thought she was segregated,' Agnes went on. 'I thought that was the whole point of her being in Healthcare.'

Ian spoke quietly. 'It might look like anarchy in here, but actually there's a very tight chain of command. It's just it's not the chain of command that you see. The people who appear to have power in here sometimes have only the appearance of it.'

'But the screws must have been involved. Why was Amy out of Healthcare?'

Ian picked up a paperclip and fiddled with it.

'Why would anyone want to deliberately harm someone like Amy?'

Ian looked up at her. 'Look, you and I are ordinary human beings. But a few weeks in here is enough to skew your value systems out of all recognition. Particularly if you had none in the first place. Janette's release date is next Wednesday. She knows Amy won't press charges; she knows she can get away with it.'

'And the law thinks this is a suitable place for Amy?'

'It's best not to dwell on issues like that. It makes me too angry. For me to do my job, I just have to deal with what's in front of me. Come on, let's go. I've got some paperwork to do before I see Mal this evening.'

'This evening?'

'Yeah. He's lucky he's still out – the coppers are circling around him.'

'Would you mind if – I know it's none of my business, only – I think it might help Cally if—'

'The Sun and Stars pub. Eight thirty,' he said. 'Do you know it? It's on the corner with the High Street, just before the Croftdown estate.'

It was a cold, wet evening. Agnes hurried past the arches under London Bridge, turned off to the High Street. The pub had newly fitted plastic Georgian windows and carriage lamps that glowed warm against the rain. She pushed open the door and went in.

She could see Ian sitting in one corner, and went over to him. 'What'll you have?'

'I thought nuns didn't carry money.'

'Your round, then.' Agnes sat down.

Ian smiled and went to the bar. Agnes saw someone go over to him and greet him warmly, a tall young man in baggy black clothes emblazoned with bright symbols.

Ian brought him to join her. 'Agnes, this is Mal. Agnes is the chaplain at Silworth.'

'You the one who Cally talks to?' He sat down next to her. 'I've heard about you. Has he got you a drink?'

'Yes, thanks.'

Mal watched her take her whisky and sip from it. He picked up her glass and sniffed it. He looked at her. 'They let you out sometimes, then?'

'Yes. They do. Sometimes.'

He laughed. 'So, Ian, man, what's happening?'

'Well, Cally's waiting for her parole review. The prison is erupting in violence as usual. And as for you – you tell me.'

Mal's face clouded. 'Man, they don't let up, do they? Them pigs. They'll have me for it, man. They're round 'ere night and day.'

'You've got a lawyer?'

Mal nodded. 'He saw me right last time. But this time, this ain't no little thing. And there's me, just got work, right, signing off and everything. And now this.'

'Yes, I heard about your job.'

'Proper job, man, on the sites. Build up my muscles now.' He flexed his arm, glanced at Agnes and smiled.

'And what does your lawyer think?' Ian asked.

Mal frowned. 'It's not too good.'

'But the evidence is on your side?'

'That's not too good either.'

'Mal – if the evidence is against you—'

'What you take me for? Would I do a thing like that? Man, I'm no sooner goin' to shoot my girlfriend's dad than I am . . . than I'm goin' to join our Sister here in her convent.' He turned to her and smiled. 'Another of those?'

'Yes please. Scotch, with ice.'

'I'll get them,' Ian said, getting up.

'Thing is,' Mal went on, as Ian waited at the bar, 'Cliff wasn't what you might call a good man. You know, I'd have a pint with him same as the next guy, but man, there were people out there who knew him for what he was.'

'And what was that?'

'And he'd got above himself. Got himself a car – did you see his car?' Mal turned to Ian who was returning from the bar. 'BMW, man. Got it last month. Didn't have no time to enjoy it, did he.' Mal shook his head.

Ian handed them their drinks and sat down.

'So he had enemies?' Agnes asked.

Mal nodded. 'It's how he treated people. I've seen him with girls, right – don't know how to say this, but – no class, see. And treating them bad. It was the drinking, see. He was a different guy when he'd had a few. I didn't tell Cally, but I didn't like what I saw.'

'So—' Agnes sipped her drink. 'So, when he was shot . . .'

Mal shrugged. 'I wasn't there.'

'Not at all?'

'Nowhere near, man.'

'It's just, people are saying—' Agnes glanced at him. 'They're saying, the murder weapon, the gun . . . they're saying it implicates you.'

Mal sighed. He picked up his glass and stared at it. 'Yeah,' he said. 'Yeah. It does.'

'Why's that?'

'It's my prints'll show.'

'And only yours?'

He shrugged. 'Mine'll be enough for them.'

'Mal, why is that?' Agnes sensed him turning away from her.

He flicked her a reluctant glance.

'Mal—' Ian leaned towards him. 'We're here to help you.'

He smiled emptily. He shook his head. 'I'm beyond helping.' He drained his glass, stood up, and shook hands with both of them. 'Be seeing you. Nice meeting you, Sister.'

They watched him leave the pub. Ian turned to Agnes. 'I don't know what to make of it.'

'It does seem odd.'

'Have you eaten?'

'No.'

'Will I have to pay?'

Agnes laughed. 'No. As long as it's cheap.'

They found a pizzeria behind Tabard Street.

Agnes scanned the menu, then looked at Ian. 'Do you think he did it?'

Ian frowned. 'I don't quite get it. I'd say not, but then why doesn't he just disown this evidence, this stuff about finger-prints on the gun? If there's an explanation, why didn't he give it?'

'Shall we have some wine?'

'You're a kind of work hard, play hard kind of nun, aren't you?'

'I've struggled with it, God knows.'

Ian smiled at her. 'Red or white?'

'Red. And it seems to me . . .'

'What?'

'As far as Mal's concerned, there's something that's even more frightening than being found guilty of a crime he didn't commit.'

Chapter Six

It was after eleven when they left the pizzeria. The night air was fresh after the rain. Ian looked up to the stars and breathed in deeply. 'You could almost believe you weren't in London,' he said.

'Why should you want to do that?'

He turned to her. 'You mean, you like it here?'

'It's the nearest I've ever got to having a home.'

Ian set off towards London Bridge, walking slightly unevenly. 'A home,' he repeated.

'Why, isn't this home?' Agnes walked beside him.

'This? This sprawling, ugly, urban . . . This is where I exist.'

'So, where's home?'

'I'm from a village in Devon. Near Totnes. That's what I'd call home. Here, I have a flat, quite a nice flat, off the Walworth Road, but that doesn't mean it's home.'

'So where do you feel you belong?'

He stopped and looked at her, swaying a little. 'Good question. If I thought my life was going the way it should, I'd say, here. I suppose. But as things are . . .'

'What would you change?'

He set off walking again. 'Thing is,' he said, 'and this is probably the wine talking, I don't think living alone is what I should be doing, right? It's not natural – not for me, anyway.'

'I like it.'

'Yeah, but that's you. That's different.' They passed under

the arches of the railway. 'It's like that Imelda of yours,' Ian was saying. 'I mean, some people can live without love, and obviously she can, and that's why she couldn't cope with Amy. Because Amy is raw emotion – if you look at her, that's all you see really – and people like Imelda, who've shut that stuff away, it's all a bit much for her.'

Agnes glanced sideways at him. They had reached the river, and now paused at the wharf. Behind them towered Southwark cathedral. From somewhere came distant music, a drum beat, a voice singing, applause.

'So you don't count as someone who can live without love?' Agnes asked him.

'Who, me?' He shook his head. 'I'm talking out of turn. You shouldn't have let me finish the wine like that. I just meant that – I mean, take Amy for example . . .'

'What about her?'

'Amy kind of reaches out to me in some way.' He looked at Agnes, and then added, 'Or, I mean, someone like that, not just her, obviously . . .'

'But doesn't that make your job more difficult?'

He nodded emphatically. 'Sometimes I think I'm in the wrong job. I think I care too much.'

'So, in fact, people like me and Imelda—'

'Oh, no, I didn't mean you were like Imelda.' He stared at her. 'You mustn't think that. What I said about love, with her, it's a kind of shutting it away. Freezing it out. Whereas with you . . .'

'With me, what?'

He smiled, and shook his head. 'I was about to say the wrong thing.'

'If your flat's in Walworth. . .' Agnes said.

'I was walking you home.'

'In the opposite direction?'

'You never said where you lived.'

'You didn't ask.'

Ian let go of the railings a bit unsteadily.

'Perhaps we should share a cab,' Agnes said.

'Don't tell me,' Ian said, 'you don't carry money.'

'It'll only be a fiver.'

Agnes sat in Eleanor's office next morning, sipping a cup of tea. Eleanor stood up and went over to the window. 'I'm only sorry it happened while I wasn't here.'

Agnes sat by her desk. 'Will she be punished?'

Eleanor sighed. 'It can't go on her record, unless Amy brings charges against her.'

Agnes rubbed her forehead.

'You look tired,' Eleanor said.

'But surely, Amy must press charges.'

'It won't help her.'

'Do these things just go unpunished, then?'

Eleanor sat down again. 'There's a procedure, that's all.' She opened a large notebook and wrote something down in it.

'Won't it affect Janette's release date?'

Eleanor sighed. 'If Amy doesn't press charges, it won't be on her record. So, no, it won't.' Agnes noticed the empty vase on her desk, the flowers all cleared away as if they'd never been there. Eleanor continued to write. 'And there's your behaviour to discuss as well.'

'Mine?'

Eleanor stopped writing but didn't look up. 'Verbally abusing an inmate.' Her face was expressionless.

Agnes swallowed, hard. 'It's hardly what you'd call—' Eleanor raised her head, and Agnes saw the trace of a smile. 'I know. It's just there are rules. In fact, you're lucky. I talked to Janette's officer, Eileen, and she – let's just say, she's an understanding woman. And in any case, in the end, it's what the inmates decide that will determine whether you've got away with it.'

Agnes stared at her. 'But – all I said was the truth. I mean, it was rather an outburst, and perhaps it was a bit over the top, and maybe—'

Eleanor was smiling now. 'No one's going to argue with what you said. It's just, depending how everyone's feeling, you may have lit the blue touch paper. Unwittingly, of course.'

'So I'm not going to get sacked, then?'

Eleanor laughed. 'Not for telling a few home truths to Janette, no.'

'And are you feeling better?' Agnes asked, glad to change the subject.

Eleanor looked up. 'Me?'

'You were off sick, they said.'

'Oh, um—' She smiled awkwardly. 'Yes. Thanks. It was nothing.'

Amy was sitting in the day room in Healthcare. She sat in an armchair in front of the huge wide window, somehow too small for the room. She was leafing through a magazine. She looked up as Agnes came into the room. The sunlight gave her hair a coppery sheen. Agnes sat in the chair next to her. 'Amy, how are you?'

Amy smiled at her. 'Okay.' She seemed strangely animated, despite the bruises on her face, the scratches on her scalp where there ought to have been hair.

'It was a terrible thing,' Agnes said. Amy looked down at her magazine again.

'You should press charges.'

Amy shook her head.

'Amy, she could've killed you.'

Amy reflected for a moment. She nodded. 'S'only a matter of time before she kills someone,' she said. 'But it won't be me.' She looked up at Agnes. Her eyes now seemed bright, and her cheeks flushed a pale pink.

Agnes was surprised at the change in her. She wondered what to say.

Amy looked down at her hands, then glanced up shyly. 'Maybe you understand. You know, when the Lord speaks to you?' She paused, scanning Agnes's face for her reaction. 'I don't tell many people, but you'll understand. Maybe.'

Agnes nodded, wondering what she meant.

Amy went on, 'I wanted her to kill me, see. I thought, if I was dead . . . if Janette killed me . . .' Again she checked Agnes's reaction. 'You see, if I was dead, I'd see her again, my little girl . . . If I just let her kill me . . .' The light died from her face, and a sob welled in her throat, a cry of raw grief. She covered her face with her hands. After a moment, she took her hands away. Her eyes were dry. 'But the Lord spoke to me, and now I know the Lord don't want it to be that way. That isn't how it's going to be. She isn't dead – that's what Jesus says to me. She isn't dead, and one day I'll see her, like a miracle, He says. And it'll all be okay, then, and I can be with her again.' Again, the dry sob in her voice. 'I only wanted to save her, Agnes . . .' And then the tears came, flooding her face, shaking her body with sobs. She covered her face again. Agnes moved to touch her, but she shrank from her. 'I just want to be with her again, Agnes,' she said through her tears. 'I just want to see her again. I never meant it to be – I never – it was him, I was so frightened, I just thought I must get her out of his way, out of his reach. He said he'd take her away from me; he said he could go to the courts and show I wasn't fit to be a mother. And after he'd gone that time I just looked at her lying there. She was so beautiful, Agnes, she lay there all helpless and innocent and I thought, I must save her from him. I must make sure she's safe from him, not like me, I'll never be safe, but her, my baby, he's not having her . . . I never meant . . . Oh God, I just want to see her again, to hold her again; I just want her back . . .'

This time Agnes held her, as her cries became intense, sharp animal yelps of grief. One of the nurses appeared, but Agnes shook her head and she went out again. Amy's crying went on and on, and Agnes found herself wondering whether someone might die of grief like this. After a long time she quietened. Agnes let go of her, and she wiped her face and blew her nose. She looked away from Agnes, out of the window. A few meagre flowers still bloomed in the beds outside, and she stared at them for a while, and then smiled. She turned back to Agnes.

'You see, when Jesus talks to me, then I know it's going to be okay.' Her face was radiant again, her eyes bright. 'When He tells me about the miracle, then I know I just have to wait. It's just a matter of time, Agnes. You understand, don't you?'

Agnes glanced out of the window, at the chilled blooms of the chrysanthemums, struggling to thrive within the prison walls. She nodded.

'It's weird, isn't it, Julius?' Agnes unwrapped the sandwiches and placed one carefully on his desk in front of him. 'She's convinced it's Jesus talking to her.' She sat down opposite Julius and took a bite of sandwich. 'It might be the drugs, I suppose. They're all on so much medication there, and she's been so sedated recently . . .'

'Mmmm. Are these from the new sandwich shop?'

Agnes nodded.

'The mustard's good, isn't it?' After a moment Julius said, 'I suppose it's not an out-loud kind of voice that I hear.' Agnes stared at him. 'No,' he went on, 'I wouldn't describe it that way.'

'Julius, what are you talking about?'

'Doesn't the Lord ever talk to you?' He finished his sandwich, took off his glasses and started to polish them. 'It's a kind of awareness, a sense that someone's speaking, although I'm not sure it's actual words. When it happens to me, I mean.' He replaced his glasses on his nose, and smiled at Agnes through them. 'You know, a sense of a presence. Mind you, I'm not sure it's the Lord. I've always thought of it as feminine. The Mother of God, I suppose.'

'But Julius, this is Jesus promising her a miracle, promising to reunite her with her daughter.'

'Stranger things have happened, Agnes.'

Agnes looked at him.

'You were about to say something?'

'No.' She frowned. 'No, I just wondered if you wanted the last sandwich.'

'Not if you do.'

She walked back to the prison in the crisp, winter sunshine, but was hardly aware of it. She walked fast, her head down, staring at the pavement. But Julius, she'd wanted to say, direct contact with God? Really? You really experience the divine as a kind of real presence, an outer dialogue rather than an inner one?

And in that case, why does He refuse to speak to me? Or is it just that I'm not listening?

She reached the prison gate and showed her pass at the lodge. The gate was unlocked for her, and as she stepped through it, she saw Jim, shouting through the glass of the duty office.

'I've got my bleedin' VO now—'

Agnes turned to the officer on the gate. 'What's going on?'

'He claims he's got an appointment. But it ain't visits now, is it? And the VO's out of date.'

Agnes walked towards Jim, who was threatening to punch the duty officer. 'I've every fuckin' right to be here. That's my wife in there. She'll be waitin' for me . . .'

'I'm sorry, sir, this is out of date. This is the one you should have brought the other day.'

'I'll give you fuckin' forms. This'll be all over the papers tomorrow . . .'

'Hello,' Agnes said to him.

He turned towards her and scanned her face, screwing up his eyes. 'I know you, don't I?'

'We've met, yes. I'm one of the chaplains here.'

'Sister, innit? I remember. Sort 'em out, lady.' His tone changed instantly from belligerent to wheedling. 'I'm that sick of waiting 'ere. I found the letter, from my Janette – I found it this morning. It says today . . .' His breath made clouds in the chill air, and Agnes smelled alcohol.

Agnes looked at the form he held out to her in his shaking fingers. 'It says it expires today,' she said gently.

The prison officer had moved a step away. Jim quietened, and now stood by Agnes, blinking, his shoulders hunched.

'So I can't see her, then?'

Agnes shook her head. 'There aren't visits today.'

'Oh.' He looked at the ground. 'Oh,' he said again.

Agnes looked at his face, which was crumpled with dejection. 'I'm sorry,' she said.

'Must've got the date wrong,' he mumbled. 'I'll . . . I'll go then.'

'I expect you'll be able to visit before she's released,' Agnes said. She took his arm and led him back to the gate. The officer opened it for him, and he stepped through. 'You one of them nuns, then?' he said.

She smiled. 'Yes.'

'Got a lot of time for your kind,' he said. 'Sister.'

'Thanks.'

'My mam – my mam, God rest her soul, she was raised by your kind. Only, in those days, they wore them things.'

'Some of us still do.'

He nodded. 'Put in a good word for me missus, eh? She don't mean no harm.'

Agnes stared at him. 'But she put you in hospital for weeks.'

'She don't mean no harm,' he said again.

'But her sentence—'

'That was all wrong.'

'You must have brought charges.'

'It was them coppers. They made me – they confused me.'

'It went to court.'

He looked away, towards the street, the rumbling traffic. 'It ain't none of their business,' he said. 'What goes on between man and wife. Look at me,' he said. 'Look at me.' He drew himself up, straightened his shoulders, tapped his chest. 'D' you think I'm gonna take any nonsense from a woman? What goes on between man and wife, you see . . .' He dropped his gaze, scuffing the pavement with his toe. 'We've had our bad times, me and 'er. It's goin' to be different now. See, I got work now. My brother, he's clever, right, not like me, he lets me work for him now, security, like. He's got this music club; I work on the door. See off any undesirables.' He laughed, a deep chuckle that showed his broken teeth. 'Funny music, though, all on one note. Down by the river, it is. If you're passing, I'll get you in. They trust me, the boss's brother, right?' He puffed out his chest, and smiled at her, and his worn face seemed young for an instant. He nodded, then turned and set off heavily down the street.

* * *

Agnes locked the door behind her on Cally's wing, and then went to Cally's cell. Cally's twitchiness seemed to have subsided, and she sat morosely on her bed. She looked up as Agnes came in. 'You survived, then,' she said.

'Survived what?'

'Taking on Janette.'

'I see the word's got round.' Agnes sat down next to her.

'Always does, here. Heard all about you effing and blinding to her.'

'I was hardly effing and blinding.'

'Well, that's what Janette said you were. Said she might press charges. You know, take you to a what's-it, you know, tribunal.'

Agnes was caught between sudden anger and the urge to laugh. 'She should just try it,' she said, biting her lip.

'Nah, she won't. S'all talk with her, innit?'

'I saw Mal last night,' Agnes said.

Cally brightened. 'Did you? How was he? Was it at the club? Did he ask about me?'

'Yes,' Agnes said quickly. 'He's very concerned about you.'

'More concerned for himself, though?'

Agnes looked at her. 'Yes.'

'He didn't do nothin'. I should know. Why should he kill my dad? He didn't have nothin' against him.'

'I know. That's what he said.'

'You should talk to Steph, my mate who came here. She'll know more. Phone her up. Have you got a pen? Write down her number. Ask her. Honest, she'll know more.'

'Cally, I'm not sure it's right that I—'

'Please?'

Agnes sighed, got out a pen. Cally grabbed it and scribbled the number on a scrap of paper.

'The thing is, Cally, why should Mal's fingerprints be on a gun in the first place?'

'I told you. I blame Venn. Getting him into trouble.'

'This Venn – what does he do, then?'

'I told you. He's got a club, under the arches, by the railway. But I just know there's something dodgy going on. My sister, see, she's got in with him recently. She's always wanted to be a singer, and now she's trying to get Venn to give her a break. That's what Steph said. It's all bleedin' dodgy. I tried to warn Mal off. He should've bloody listened to me.'

Agnes folded the scrap of paper and put it in her bag. 'I'm not promising anything, Cally.'

'If you don't mind my saying so, sweetie, it's hardly any of your business, is it?' Athena was standing by her cooker stirring something in a large pot.

'But Athena—'

'Not that that's ever stopped you before.' She peered into the saucepan uncertainly.

'The thing is—'

'I mean, the father was involved in all sorts of dodgy dealings, if what that friend said was true, and then the daughter's already in prison for something else, and the boy's practically admitted it—'

'He hasn't. He's denied it.'

'But, I mean, where are you going to start? Who are you going to believe? Isn't it best left to the police, who, after all, must know more about the organised crime in that area than you do?'

'Athena, is something burning?'

Athena twitched her nose. 'Oh God, garlic bread. It said on the packet a hot oven. I knew it was a mistake.' She snatched open the oven door and a cloud of blue smoke filled the room.

Agnes opened windows and Athena flapped wildly with one hand, while with the other, wrapped in a tea towel, she drew out a baking tray on which was a blackened, sausage-shaped thing.

'Oh God—' she began, shouting above the noise of the smoke alarm on the landing which had just started to beep loudly. 'And I don't know how to turn that thing off.'

Agnes found a chair and climbed up to it and flapped fresh air around it until the beeping stopped. When she went back into the kitchen, Athena was still standing in the middle of the room holding the burnt bread on its tray.

'Athena, the saucepan—' Agnes turned off the heat underneath the saucepan. They both peered into the pot. Athena stirred it half-heartedly.

'What was it?' Agnes asked.

'The recipe said cassoulet. Look, there's a sausage. Maybe.'

'Do you think—' Agnes began.

They looked at each other. Athena said, 'Listen, you pour the G and Ts, I'll phone for the pizzas.'

By the time they sat down to eat, the kitchen had acquired a rather pleasant scent of roasted garlic.

'Cheers,' Athena said. 'To you rescuing some innocent boy from the clutches of the law.'

'You're not convinced.'

'From what you've told me about him, poppet, neither are you at the moment.'

'I don't know what to think. And I launched into one of our inmates yesterday. Practically thumped her.'

'You? Good heavens. Whatever brought that on?'

'She's probably the most dislikeable person I've ever met.'

'What did she do?'

'She'd attacked someone. A young girl. She chose the most vulnerable person on the wing. I think she's probably done her irreparable damage, mentally I mean.'

'So you thumped her in return. How Christian. An eye for an eye or something.'

'There's no need to tease, Athena. I managed not to thump her. It's just the way she behaves, as if she has a right to behave appallingly because she's suffered. She's in for GBH on her husband.'

'What's he like, then?'

'Rather like her. Belligerent. Adores her, of course. Works in security, he said, some music club down by the river. What's the matter?'

'What do you mean?'

'You're staring at me.'

'Was I? How funny. More wine?'

'What have I said?'

'Nothing, sweetie.'

'It must be something to do with this man you met.'

'Nonsense, sweetie. Oops, look, I've spilt the wine now, silly me.'

'Athena—'

'Well, it is a bit funny. You just said "music club".'

'And?'

'Greg's a musician, that's all. Jazz player. Clarinettist. Oh, look at that mess. Hang on while I find a cloth.'

Agnes watched her while she mopped up the table and poured more wine for them both. Athena sat down again, and their eyes met.

'Well?' Agnes picked up her glass.

'Well what?'

'This jazz player – Greg?'

'There's nothing to say.'

'Have you seen him again?'

'No. I mean, yes, but not properly. He comes into the gallery sometimes.'

'To see you?'

'No. I mean, yes, probably. Oh, I don't know.' She took a long swig of wine. 'Just when my life had become simple and straightforward and settled . . . it's like some voice comes into my head and tries to persuade me to wreck it.'

'Oh, not you as well.'

'What on earth do you mean?'

'All day people have been telling me they hear voices. First this girl who was attacked . . . apparently Jesus talks to her directly. I mean, it's not fair, here I am banged up in a religious order and in all these years the Lord has never once rewarded me with any direct communication, whereas this girl in prison – what's so funny?'

'Nothing. Just the way you said banged up.'

'And then there's Julius – when I tried to share it with him he owned up to some kind of divine voice which he hears, apparently. And now you – I expect now you're going to tell me that you have a regular chat with St Francis about living without possessions.'

'Nonsense, darling. It was a figure of speech. The only voice I hear is the one which says, "Go on, you need those black high heels, they'll go so fantastically well with everything else you're wearing this winter, and they're such a bargain at only a hundred and forty pounds" and when I get home I find I've already got two other pairs just the same.'

'You see, that I can understand.'

'Mind you, when I tell St Francis, he's quite nice about it, really. For a saint.'

Chapter Seven

It was still dark. Agnes followed the other nuns into the chapel, glad of the night which enfolded her in silence. She took her place in the pews, trying to clear her mind, to throw off her dreams. The ringing of her alarm clock had interrupted a thick confusion of images, something to do with searching for someone, unlocking doors only to find herself in endless corridors. She'd woken to an uneasy sense of irresolution that had persisted whilst she threw on the nearest clothes and tumbled into the community car to drive from her tiny flat to the community house.

She glanced up at the plain chapel window. The night sky was edged with soft grey, as the dawn approached and the sister leading the service stood up and began to read the first office of the day.

' "Almighty God, give us grace to cast away the works of darkness, and to put on the armour of light . . ." '

It had been dark, in the dream, Agnes remembered. There had been locked doors, and darkness. And she was searching for someone.

' "O Lord, show us the light of your countenance . . ." '

In her thoughts, Agnes echoed the words of the prayer.

Afterwards she gathered with the others in the bright kitchen, pouring out mugs of tea. Finding Sister Imelda next to her, she offered one to her.

'No thanks,' she said, and moved away.

Agnes went and sat at the large pine table. She looked out of the window at the grey drizzle of the morning.

'Saturday, eh?' Sister Madeleine joined her. 'What are you going to do today?'

'The choice is endless. Shopping in Knightsbridge. A day trip to Paris? Or maybe tea at Fortnum's. What about you?'

'I'm on the late shift at the hostel.'

'Lucky old you.'

Madeleine watched her. 'I seem to have nicked your job.'

'I don't bear grudges. Usually.'

'Julius misses you.'

'He sees me often enough.'

'But you're happy at the prison?'

Agnes sipped her tea. She nodded. 'Yes. It's hard, it's very hard . . . but there's something about it, something compelling.' Imelda slipped out of the kitchen.

'Is—' Madeleine lowered her voice. 'Is Imelda all right?'

Agnes frowned. 'I'm not sure. There have been odd things . . .'

'She made a terrible fuss about our Advent painting, apparently.'

'What painting?'

'Haven't you seen it? Sister Catherine was sent it from the order's Madrid convent. It's our turn to have it apparently. It's incredibly old and valuable. Come and see.'

Madeleine led her down the stairs to the basement. Leaning against the wall was a large, ornate frame. The painting showed the infant Jesus, asleep.

'He's lying on the cross,' Madeleine whispered.

Agnes noticed the dark angles of the wood under the sleeping child. The baby nestled contentedly, pink and radiant, semi-wrapped in velvet.

73

'It's His triumph over death,' Madeleine said. 'Look, there are angels hovering in the background. Catherine's very taken with it. She's going to hang it in the chapel during Advent. And for some reason, Imelda objected. She made a terrible fuss – not like her at all.'

'I'm not sure I like it,' Agnes said. 'It's a bit much, isn't it?'

'It's seventeenth-century.'

'It's quite powerful. I suppose I'd rather this than a nativity scene.'

They started back up the stairs. 'What's wrong with a nativity scene?' Madeleine asked.

'Oh, I don't know. All those little lambs and donkeys and things. And tinsel.'

Madeleine laughed. 'I'm not sure the tinsel's scriptural.'

'And all the usual Advent arguments about which decorations to have, and should we have a tree, and do we all give each other endless boxes of chocolates like we did last year and the year before . . .'

'And then we give them all away to deserving causes.'

'If I were a free woman I'd just go skiing instead.'

Madeleine looked at her. 'I've never heard you say that before.'

They went into the kitchen and resumed their places by the window.

'But I like skiing.'

'No, I mean, I've never heard you acknowledge that you're not a free woman.'

Agnes clapped her hand over her mouth. 'Did I say that? I must be getting old.'

Agnes left the communal car at the house and caught a bus back south towards the river. The City of London was deserted, its elegant edifices of wealth draped in the soft grey light of a

London winter. Agnes got off the bus at the river and walked across London Bridge. Halfway across the bridge she stopped. She looked back towards the City, its translucent palaces flashing silver. She looked south, towards Bermondsey. She could see scaffolding, building sites and gleaming new buildings, as the City spread its influence across the river. Further east the old wharves and warehouses stood firm, rising from the Thames as if they'd grown and taken shape from the river mud itself.

She let herself into her flat and sat at her desk. She picked up the phone, then replaced it. She took out of her bag the scrap of paper on which Cally had scribbled the number. She lifted the receiver again and dialled the number.

'Hello, I'm trying to get hold of someone called Steph.'

'That's me.'

'Hello, I'm Sister Agnes. I'm the chaplain at Silworth.'

'Oh. Yes.'

'I gather you're a friend of Cally's.'

'Yes?' The voice was uncertain.

'She – she wanted me to talk to you.'

'Yeah, well, I'm a bit busy. I'm about to go to work.'

'The thing is, she thinks Mal didn't do it.'

There was a brief silence. 'She's bound to think that, isn't she?'

Agnes tried again. 'Cally thinks you might be able to help.'

'So Cally thinks I can get Mal out of trouble? How am I goin' to do that, then? The only reason she got you to talk to me – she was hoping that I'd tell—' She clammed up suddenly.

'Tell what?'

The voice on the phone was hesitant. 'She's got some funny ideas at the moment.'

'About her sister?'

'Listen, I don't even know her sister. I met her once about

two years ago. They don't have nothin' to do with each other, and now she's going on about her killing their dad. I don't get it. Some dream she had.' The voice softened again. 'I'm sorry I can't be more helpful.'

'That's okay. I'm sorry I bothered you.'

'Listen—' Steph hesitated. 'The best place you can go, if you really want to find out what they're saying about Mal, is the club.'

'Venn's club?'

'Yeah. It's called the Pomegranate Seed. It's been there for years. No one ever used to go, but now it's livening up. Mal guests there sometimes.'

'Where is it?'

'It's under the railway arches by London Bridge, down the back of Druid Street.'

'Do I just turn up?'

'You'll probably have to queue. Depends on the night. And dress smart – they're quite picky on the door sometimes. Saturdays it's Territory, you know, garage. That's when they're all there. Friday it's SubStation – they're okay too.'

'Oh. Right.'

'Thing is, I want to help Cal, she's my mate, we've been through a lot together – but I can't start laying the blame on someone I hardly know, can I?'

'No. Of course not.'

'I'd better go.'

'Sure. Thanks for talking to me, anyway.'

'Athena, it's me. Look, I just wondered whether you were free this evening. And Nic, maybe?' Agnes tucked the phone under her chin. 'That club I mentioned – tonight it's Territory, doing house, garage and swingbeat . . . What do you mean, what am I on about? I went up the road and picked up a flyer and that's what's on tonight. They're at the Pomegranate Seed. I wondered if you wanted to come? ... Not Nic, then ... Sure. Oh, I dunno, they start about midnight these young people, don't they? Nine-ish? We can eat first. Wonderful. See you then.'

She hung up, and stared at the flyer. She placed it on her desk and smoothed it out. Next to it lay the letter from her mother's nursing home.

She'd only pretend not to recognise me, Agnes thought. She folded up the letter and put it in a drawer.

'Have you replied to the letter?' Julius greeted her after evensong at St Simeon's.

'Which letter?' Agnes stood by the door of the church, watching the straggling congregation depart into the twilight.

'I bet you put it in a drawer.'

'The letter from my mother, you mean? No, I haven't replied to it yet. There's no point promising to visit when I haven't asked permission from my provincial.'

'I just hope you're not going to allow yourself to get distracted.'

'What do you mean?'

'Agnes, I know you too well.'

'Listen, when I need you to be my conscience, I'll tell you, okay?'

'You usually do.'

'Good. That's settled.'

'You're not about to do anything stupid, then?'

'Julius, you must learn to trust me. I'm older and wiser now.'

'Hmmm.'

'What do you mean, "Hmmm"?'

'So, I'll trust you to be sensible. This evening, for example, what are you doing?'

'Oh, well, this evening. Case in point, Julius. This evening, I'm just going to a club with Athena to check out Territory in a mix of garage and swingbeat. I think.'

Julius put his hand to his head in mock alarm. 'And you wonder why I worry?'

'At least I keep you feeling young.'

'Nonsense, Agnes. Most of these white hairs I owe to you.'

'Come on, you silly old man, I'll walk you home.'

Arm in arm they walked down the drive. 'In fact, it's probably a miracle I've survived this long,' Julius said.

'Oh well, you with your divine voice, I'm sure the odd miracle doesn't pose any problem at all.' They went out of the gate and merged with the traffic of the High Street.

Agnes went home and spent two hours wondering what to wear, before, eventually, choosing black trousers and a skimpy black T-shirt.

'After all,' Athena said, when they met at an Italian restaurant near Hays Wharf for supper, 'Whatever we wear is going to be wrong. We might as well just brazen it out.' Athena was wearing black hipster jeans and a white jacket.

It was nearly eleven by the time they reached the club. There was a queue at the door, and they joined it. There were two bouncers, young and lithe and bored-looking.

They bought two tickets and went inside. They descended a narrow staircase, emerging into the club space blinking against the dim light and the smoke. A bouncer at the lower door stood back to let them in.

'Oh God,' Athena whispered, 'everyone else is half our age.'

'Think young. We'll get away with it,' Agnes whispered back. They found a table, and Athena went to the bar, returning with two glasses of white wine.

'Hideously expensive, darling,' she said, plonking them down on the sticky table surface. 'Whatever your secret agenda is, it's going to cost you an arm and a leg in booze.'

'I'll buy the next round. And there's no secret agenda.'

'Not much there isn't. You've been scanning the room ever since we set foot in here.'

Agnes turned to Athena. 'Have I?'

'Go on, tell me, it's some murderer we're looking out for, isn't it? It's always when you're on the run, these investigations. Finding a distraction against something in your life that you don't want to face.'

'A fine time to choose, Athena, to be Dr Freud. Shall we wait until we're somewhere quiet with a couch?'

Athena glanced at her friend. 'I didn't mean – I didn't seriously mean—'

'I know what you meant.'

Athena patted her arm. 'It's just sometimes real life isn't enough for you. God knows, I'm the same. Just when Nic is offering me everything I thought I wanted, here I am about to—'

Agnes picked up her glass of wine. 'About to what?'

Athena lifted her glass. 'About to do nothing at all, I hope. Cheers.'

They were both grateful for a burst of music from the decks and speakers, behind which jigged a thin young woman dressed in a tiny black dress, and two young men who looked no older than their mid-teens. Athena appeared to be saying something.

'What did you say?' Agnes shouted.

'I said, what do they call this?'

'I've no idea. Garage or something,' Agnes said. They both started to giggle. People began to crowd the dance floor. The spotlights touched their moving bodies with light.

Agnes was aware of movement behind her and she turned towards the entrance. A group of young men, four or five, were in the doorway, having an animated discussion with one of the bouncers. Behind them were two young women in big jackets and high heels, waiting with bored expressions, fiddling with their elaborate hair. Eventually some point was conceded, and the young men came into the club, the girls trailing behind them. At the back of the main aisle they paused, scanning the crowd. They stood, poised but self-conscious.

Agnes was aware that Athena had said something.

'I said,' Athena shouted, 'that if I knew how to wolf whistle I would.'

'Don't forget you look like their granny,' Agnes shouted back.

'Thanks very much. Look they're coming our way.'

Agnes turned, to find that one of the boys was standing over her.

'Mal!' she said, surprised.

'Hi,' he said. 'Can't say I thought I'd find you here.'

'No,' Agnes said. The others had gathered near by and were staring, curious.

'This is Marky,' Mal said, gesturing to his friends. 'And that's Lashaye, and that's Jex, Ant, Viv and Rock. This is Sister Agnes,' he said. 'She's helping Cally.' They nodded, vaguely. One of them gestured towards a table, and they all moved away towards it.

'See y'around,' Mal said, joining his friends.

'Well,' Athena exclaimed. 'You and your friends.'

'Don't shout.'

'And it's your round.'

Agnes fought her way to the bar, glancing back towards Mal's table. Mal didn't seem to be there. She turned back to the bar and realised he was beside her.

'You were lookin' for me?'

'Not exactly, no.'

'Curious, aren't you?'

'Yes. Yes, I am.'

'Gets you into trouble, being curious.'

'Don't I just know?'

He smiled. 'And how d'you find out about this place?'

'Steph mentioned it.'

'Steph?'

'Cally's friend.'

'Yeah, I know Steph.'

'And Cally mentioned Venn—'

'Yeah. It's his club.'

Agnes found she had been jostled right up to the bar. 'What are you drinking?' she asked Mal.

'Nah, y'all right.'

She ordered two more glasses of wine. She watched Mal get in a round for his friends.

'Cally's still determined to help you,' Agnes said.

'Yeah.' He looked suddenly young.

'Mal, what are you going to do?'

He looked at her, and his eyes were shadowed with despair. He shrugged. 'There's nothing I can do,' he said.

'But if you know—'

He shook his head. 'Y'know, like, in them stories, man. The hero on a path to hell. The land of fire waiting for him. Sheer cliff face either side of him. On them computer games, y'know? And you're on the downward slide, you're out of extra lives, and you've left your buddy on the level before, and there's nowhere to go but on, and the pit of flames staring you in the face?'

Agnes nodded.

He shrugged. 'There you are then.' He turned, balancing his tray of drinks. 'Enjoy the sound.'

* * *

Athena had taken off her jacket, revealing a bright orange crop top.

'I thought we weren't competing,' Agnes said.

'Sometimes one just has to make the effort. Anyway, I'm much too hot.'

'Shall we get some air?'

The street outside seemed muffled in comparison. They stood in the cold, watching their breath making clouds, watching the queue still filing in to hear the music. Someone was shouting on the corner of the street.

'I ain't done nothing . . .'

Agnes turned to see Jim Price. He was with another man, and he was waving his arms around, pleading with him. 'Trust me, Venn, I didn't do nothing . . .'

The other man stood silently. He was taller than Jim and looked down at him, his hands in the pockets of his long black coat. He waited for Jim to finish shouting, then spoke.

'Problem is, it's their word against yours, isn't it? And who am I to believe?'

'Your own flesh and blood, Venn, that's what.'

'I'd like to, Jim, believe me. But I've got my customers to consider. If someone says you got heavy with them on the door—'

'But you told me to, Jim, you said.'

'I told you not to anticipate trouble.' Venn turned on his heel. He was wearing expensive shoes – Italian, Agnes thought – and his coat swung like cashmere.

'One more chance,' Jim pleaded. 'I need the work, man. I've told my babe, when she gets out I'm going to look after her . . .'

Venn turned back. He looked at Jim, and then laughed.

'You'll look after her, will you? You always were a fool, Jimmy boy.'

'Please—'

Venn studied Jim, as if for amusement. A train passed overhead, flashing electric blue sparks in the darkness. Venn patted Jim's shoulder. 'One more chance. But if you drive away my business, it's out you go. Clear? Now, leave me alone. Come back on Monday, okay?'

Venn was left alone. He surveyed the street, then strolled to the corner. He watched the queue, glancing idly at Agnes and Athena, then lit a cigarette and leaned against the wall, gazing beyond the street to the railway arches which stretched into the distance.

Mal and Marky came out of the club. They saw Agnes standing with Athena.

'Too much for you, was it?' Mal smiled.

'No, not at all,' Athena said quickly. 'We'll go back in a minute.'

'We're going on,' Mal said. He hesitated. 'Well . . . see y'around.' A police car siren sounded in the distance, and he turned his head towards the noise. He turned back to Agnes and forced a smile. 'Nice to see you again. Don't they miss you in your convent?'

'I'm afraid they do.'

He smiled at her. 'Live now, eh? See you.'

The two men turned to go, and as they passed the corner of the street they saw Venn leaning there. A train hooted as it approached, and Venn looked up and saw Mal. The two men stood, outfacing each other, caught in the arcing flashes from the rails. Then, in the silent wake of the train, Mal turned and walked away, with Marky at his side.

'Sweetie, I'm cold.'

Agnes turned to Athena, who was shivering in her tiny

top. 'Shall we go back in?'

'Of course, sweetie, if you want. I just thought maybe . . .'

'Maybe we'd had enough?'

'I mean, I'm game to stay a bit longer, if you are . . .'

Agnes shook her head. 'Let's get our coats.'

They left the club and set off to London Bridge to find a taxi. Athena took Agnes's arm. 'I think my New Year's resolution is going to be to grow old gracefully.'

Chapter Eight

Agnes knelt in the prison chapel, listening to the uneven murmurings of the women's voices as they joined in the service. She looked up, trying to shake off her sleepiness. Two of the women were trying to find their places in the prayer book. Cally was staring out of the window. Amy was absorbed in the prayer, her voice sailing over the rest as she repeated the phrases with absolute conviction.

Agnes laid out the pile of candles for the intercession. With each prayer someone came forward and lit a candle. Amy lit the last candle in silence, her face softened with golden light as she leaned over the bowl, her eyes bright as she stared into the flames.

Afterwards an officer took them back to their cells. Agnes went with them, emerging from the chapel into the noise and light, blinking in the blare of radios, the shouts between cells, the slamming of doors, the turning of keys. She walked with Cally.

'I went to the Pomegranate Seed last night,' she said.

'Lucky you. Who was it?'

'Territory.'

'Even better. Was – was he there?' Cal turned to her.

'Mal? Yes, he was.'

'Did he ask after me?'

'Yes, of course.

Cally glanced at her. 'Who else was there? Was Viv there?'

'There were two girls, yes.'

'Viv and Lashaye?'

'I think so.'

'Just like her, Viv, hanging around when I'm out of it.'

'I don't think she was getting very far. Mal and Marky left on their own.'

Cally laughed. 'Good. Stupid cow.'

They reached Cally's cell, and the officer unlocked it. She walked through the door and it slammed shut behind her.

Agnes retraced her steps, passing through doors, her keys jangling at each locking. As she passed Eleanor's office, she saw the door was open. Eleanor was sitting at her desk. She was lost in thought, staring unseeing at a pile of papers in front of her. Agnes saw her drawn expression, the sadness about her eyes. She knocked at the door. Eleanor looked up, blinking, rubbing her arms as if cold.

'What are you doing here?' Agnes approached the desk.

'Shouldn't I be? 'Eleanor smiled wanly.

'It's Sunday, that's all. Do you want a coffee?'

'If you're getting one, thanks.'

Agnes went through two doors to the coffee machine. She could hear raucous laughter from D wing, loud above the blare of radios. She returned, balancing the cups to lock the doors behind her.

'Are you often here on Sundays, then?' Agnes passed a packet of sugar across, and sat down opposite Eleanor.

'Sometimes, yes.'

'I did the service today. I hope it went okay.'

'Many punters?'

'Loads. They can't all be devout.'

'There's other reasons why they go.'

Agnes nodded.

'Was Amy there?' Eleanor asked.

'Yes.'

'Did someone escort her back to Healthcare?'

'Yes, one of the nurses.'

'I feel so responsible for what happened to her.' Eleanor stirred some more sugar into her coffee. 'Sometimes it feels as if my authority here is just sort of tolerated—' The phone rang and Eleanor snatched it up. 'Yes? Oh. Hello . . . Right . . . And did they . . . ? Right. No, it's fine, thanks for letting me know.' She rang off. 'That was Ian. He's been at the police station with Mal since about five this morning. They found the gun last night. Mal's been charged with the murder.'

'Should we tell Cally?'

'I'd rather she heard it from us now than the wing in about half an hour.'

'Maybe – maybe I should talk to Ian.'

Eleanor wrote down Ian's number for her and passed it across to her. 'Could you ask Cally to come and see me?'

'Of course.' Agnes stood up. 'It's just as well you were here – I mean, to take the call.'

'Yes. My husband said he'd spare me today.' She smiled, with some effort.

In the doorway Agnes glanced back at her, but she had bent her head over the papers on her desk.

Cally paced the tiny cell. Every seven steps she reached the wall and banged her fist on it. 'He ain't fuckin' done it, Agnes. Those bastard coppers. He ain't done nothing.'

Nita was sitting on her bed, and Agnes went and sat down next to her.

'I ain't gonna sit back and watch 'im get sent down for something he never did.' Cally's voice was shrill, smothering tears.

'There's the trial—' Agnes began.

'He better get a fucking good brief.' She thumped the wall with both fists and then burst into tears. 'I don't care if they never find out who killed him. I just don't want my Mal being done for it when I know he didn't. There was enough people who wanted him dead, the stupid prat. I don't care who fucking killed him, the bastard . . .' Her words were drowned with sobs and she collapsed on the bed. Agnes went and stood over her, her hand resting on her shoulder. After a moment, she turned and let herself out of the cell. As she locked the door behind her, she could still hear Cally sobbing.

Agnes crossed the main road, dodging the traffic. If, as Cally said, there were so many people who wanted Cliff dead, where are they? she thought. She stood by the traffic lights at Bermondsey Street, waiting for them to change. Why has it been so easy for the police to implicate Mal? And there was Jim at the club last night, Jim Price. Should it be surprising that the brother he mentioned is the man who runs the club? A car screeched to a halt in front of her as the lights changed. She walked across the road, wondering whether it was worth waiting for a bus on a Sunday. She decided against it and headed towards the Embankment. She could still hear the echo of Cally's sobs, edged with sharp anger against her father.

And why was she so cross with him? For being killed? For not being there any more? Or for some other reason?

She turned off the main road and took the turning past the housing estate, the bleak rows of post-war flats. She glanced towards the end block, towards the doorway where she'd first tried to talk to the police about the murdered father, first heard the neighbour's complaining voice. Agnes hesitated, almost turning back. But what would I say? she thought. What am I going to gain by asking questions there?

She went on her way, past the council estate, leaving it

behind her as she reached the Embankment, the river a muddy brown in the distance. She thought of Mal, waiting in police custody, having run out of extra lives. Not yet, she thought. Not yet.

When she got home she dialled Ian's number. His answering machine was on. She left a message with her phone number.

' "God is light, and in Him is no darkness at all." ' Agnes listened to Sister Catherine's reading. ' "If we say that we have fellowship with him, and walk in darkness, we lie . . ." ' Agnes glanced up at the windows of the convent chapel, now darkened by the night outside. ' "But if we walk in the light, as he is in the light, we have fellowship one with another . . ." '

Agnes thought about Cally, sobbing in her cell. She remembered her words: 'I don't care who killed him, the bastard . . .' What would it feel like, not to care who'd killed one's own father? She thought about Cally's mother, and wondered who she was. All she knew was that she'd died a long time ago.

' ". . . for if our heart condemn us, God is greater than our heart, and knoweth all things." '

Agnes thought about her letter folded away in a drawer.

When she returned home, she found a rather tentative-sounding message from Ian on her machine, asking if she could meet him next day at his office at eleven thirty.

'Good heavens, Agnes—' Julius looked up from his desk next morning. 'All you do is bring me food. Anyone would think I needed looking after.'

'You do, Julius, you do.' Agnes unwrapped two bacon sandwiches.

'Nonsense.'

'Of course, I admire your disregard for your own material

requirements, but even the most saintly amongst us needs breakfast.'

'That's enough teasing, now. I'll make you some coffee.'

Agnes sat by his desk. She took from her pocket a letter that had arrived that morning from France and slit open the envelope. She read it silently and then replaced it in her pocket.

'Well?' Julius was watching her. He brought two cups of coffee to the desk, and sat down in his place.

'Well what?'

'Your letter.'

'Oh, just from France, you know.'

'From the nursing home?'

'No, not this time.'

'Well?'

Agnes sighed. 'It's from Yvette, my mother's friend – not that she has any friends.'

'And what does she say, this Yvette?'

' *"Je vous prie, Agnes . . ."* – that I should visit as a matter of urgency.'

'Agnes, if time is running out—'

'I've got a lot on.'

'Your order can spare you.'

'It's not just that. There's this boy, he was arrested yesterday, for murder, and his girlfriend says, well, you see, the victim was the father of this girl, and there's something odd about it all, the way she's angry with her father—' Agnes stopped short. She looked up and met Julius's eyes.

'Agnes—' his voice was gentle.

'Really, Julius, it's true. I'd leave it to the police only I think there's more going on than they realise. There's Cally for a start, and maybe her sister too, and Cally would die rather than tell the police anything, so you see, it's up to me.'

'Agnes, at the risk of being a bore—'

Agnes screwed up the wrapping from her sandwich and threw it in the bin. 'You can think what you like, Julius.'

'How long does this friend of your mother's give her?'

'You see, there's a particular kind of French woman. You know nothing about them, Julius. Every twinge is high drama, they think they're at death's door from their mid-fifties onwards, and then they live well into their nineties—'

'How long?'

Agnes looked up at the sharpness of his voice. She sighed. 'Weeks, not months, she said.'

'If she dies before you get there—'

Agnes stood up. 'Julius, my mother's been an invalid one way or another all the time I've known her. I think you English call it crying wolf.'

'Agnes, I'm Irish.'

'Don't change the subject.'

Julius smiled. 'It's lucky I'm so fond of you.'

'Why, in particular?'

'Because someone's going to have to pick up the pieces.'

His face was suddenly serious, and Agnes went across to him, bent over him and kissed his cheek. 'I know what I'm doing,' she said, wishing it were true.

'Agnes, sometimes wishing isn't enough.'

'And sometimes it has to do.' She picked up her coat and left.

Ian showed Agnes into his office, then vanished. Time passed. Agnes looked at his noticeboard, and at his desk which was empty of files. She picked up a newspaper and flicked through it before realising it was several days out of date. Eventually he reappeared.

'There you are. Coffee.' He handed her a tall paper cup with a lid on. She opened the lid and saw a perfect foaming head of cappuccino, sprinkled with chocolate.

Ian was smiling, triumphant, shifting from one foot to the other. 'I had to go out of the building for it.'

'Really, you shouldn't have.'

'No, I know what you're like about coffee.' He brought a chair across and sat down.

'I'm just spoilt, really.'

'Nonsense.' He sipped on his own coffee. 'By the way,' he said.

'What?'

'Um – it's just . . . the other night . . . I can't quite . . . it's not too clear in my memory . . .'

Agnes laughed. 'I drank just as much as you did.'

'Yeah, but you sisters, you can take it, you see. All those centuries of brewing up Benedictine and stuff. We ordinary mortals get sozzled instead. All I mean is, I hope I didn't say anything out of place.'

'It was a very nice evening. I'm just sorry I ended up with the taxi and you ended up walking.'

'And I ended up paying for your cab. Somehow.' Ian smiled. 'I owe you.'

'Well, this is the beginning of a long association. You've got plenty of time to pay me back. If Mal's case is anything to go by.' Ian took a file out of his briefcase and put it on his desk, unopened. 'I was with Mal from about five on Sunday morning, and I've seen him this morning too.'

'How is he?'

Ian sighed. 'Silent. I don't get it. He's been expecting this for so long, he's kind of resigned. I could see even his solicitor had doubts. But then, if you say, Mal, tell me, did you do it, he just says, no. And his friends, it's not like them to let an injustice pass. I've already had Marky in to see me, pounding the table here, insisting I do something.'

'I've met Marky.'

'Nice lad. He got him a job, just a few weeks ago. Through Marky's uncle – he's a navvy, you know, building sites. Marky's feeling really let down. They're close-knit, those teams, straight guys, you know. It reflects badly on his uncle, apparently.'

'Doesn't he have an alibi?'

'Well, Marky says Claire was with him that evening. Cally's sister.'

'Cally's sister was with Mal – that evening?'

'That's what Marky said. They were at the club together.'

Agnes sipped her coffee. 'Why do we both think he didn't do it?'

Ian looked at her. 'I don't know. Mostly 'cos he seems to have no motive at all.'

'Did you know Cliff?'

Ian shook his head. 'No.'

'So you don't know what he was like?'

Ian shrugged. 'The impression I get is that no one had much time for him. Least of all his daughters.'

'Do you think Marky would mind if I had a chat with him?'

'You can always try. He left me his phone number. I don't suppose he'd mind you having it.' Ian copied the number on to a piece of paper and handed it to her. 'It's his mobile. Don't you have work to do?'

She smiled. 'I was supposed to be back at the prison ten minutes ago.' She got up, and put the phone number in her coat pocket. 'Next time, I'll buy the coffee.'

'Don't you worry, I'm keeping a tab. When all this is over, I'll invoice your order.'

At the prison she went to find Cally, but she was over at the workshops. She went to her office, and found a phone message from Athena inviting her to call in after work. She took out the number that Ian had given her and dialled it.

'Hello, is that Marky? My name's Sister Agnes—'

The voice sounded suspicious. 'What do you want?'

'I met you at the club with Mal on Saturday.'

'Oh, yeah. I remember. You were with another woman.' The voice seemed warmer.

'That's right.'

'You know Mal – through Cally?'

'Yes.'

'They got him, you know. He's in the police cells, and he's in court tomorrow. We're all doing our best, but he'll get remanded in custody. I dunno what's going on. We've had a bit of bother over the years, him and me – it's just normal, like, but nothing like this.'

'I wondered if you'd mind . . . I wondered if we might meet. Only, Cally's very upset . . .'

'Sure. I'm working nights at the moment, but before my shift? I'm at London Bridge station. There's a café by the site on the main road . . . Tomorrow, maybe? Six o'clock?

'What's it called?'

'The café? Dunno, it's just the one we go to. It's got big red lettering and a kind of canopy. It's just by the site – you can't miss it.'

'See you then.'

At five Agnes left the prison and caught a bus to Fulham. It was already dark. By the time she rang Athena's bell it was beginning to rain. Athena let her in, shuffling up the stairs in huge furry slippers to her flat. Athena took Agnes's coat, then stood holding it for a minute.

'Um – now, what was I doing?' She put the coat down

absently on a chair. 'Eclairs, that's what it was. I've got some somewhere.'

Agnes followed her into the kitchen.

'Eclairs, I think it was. Now, where did I put them?'

'Athena – are you all right?' Agnes handed her the box of éclairs from the kitchen table.

'Me? Yes, um, fine. Scissors, to cut the ribbon . . .'

'I'll do it.' Agnes put the cakes out on a plate, put the kettle on to boil and found a tin of Darjeeling tea in Athena's cupboard. Athena watched her in a vague and distracted way.

'So, what's happened?' Agnes sat at the kitchen table.

Athena beamed at her. 'He's asked me out. Properly. On Thursday. Nic's away. It's a music gig – Greg's playing. A jazz club in Soho. It's some room above a pub in Dean Street, apparently.

'And are you going?'

'I don't know.'

'Will you tell Nic?'

'Well, sweetie, if I said to Nic, there's this new friend, he's invited us both to a jazz gig but you're away, he'd say, fine, why don't you go? That's one version. But if I said, Nic, this geezer, whenever he's within fifty yards of me I go very strange and my ears go red . . . I mean, what's he going to say? He wouldn't like it any more than I'd like it if he started seeing a woman who had that effect on him. Not the ears – it's only me that happens to. But you see what I mean.'

'Yes. I do.'

'What should I do?'

'Athena, I'm about the last person you should ask. I mean, it's like Julius.'

'What's like Julius?'

'Me telling you what you should do. Really, I've no idea. I mean, obviously, you shouldn't go. But that doesn't mean you won't, does it? It's just like Julius thinking it would be really simple for me to go and visit my mother again.'

'Your mother?'

'They keep sending me letters saying there isn't much longer, and he says I should go, but he doesn't understand . . .'

'But shouldn't you go?'

'I've already been.' Agnes went over to the window and looked down into the street below. People hurried past in the rain, splashing the puddles into yellow shards of light.

'But Agnes, shouldn't you go back?'

'I've got a lot on. Maybe when this is over . . .'

'I think I'm with Julius on this one. What do you mean, "when this is over"?'

'I really have to find out—'

'Did something happen last time? Something awful?'

'No. Course not.' Agnes fiddled with the kitchen blind.

'I mean, if she really hasn't got long . . . Is she senile or something?'

'No, just pretending.' Agnes turned away from the window and sat down again.

'Agnes, what do you mean?'

'She's a silly, spiteful old woman, and I don't see why I should give her the opportunity, yet again, to ruin my life when she's already made such a bloody good job of it once, and I've had to work so bloody hard to salvage any kind of self-esteem, any kind of sense of self. I mean, for all I complain about my order, at least it's given me a structure in which to have faith, to believe in myself, probably for the first time in my life, and if I go back into that room, to see that blank expression, that pretence that she doesn't recognise me, that spiteful, bloody self-obsessed . . .' Agnes gulped some air. 'She hates me, Athena. She always has done and I don't see why it should change just because she's on the way out. I don't see why I should put myself through it again, and if Julius knew what she was really like, he'd understand. It's just because he's so bloody compassionate and tolerant and believes the best of people. I'll never be able to make him see that there are some people who are going to be shallow and petty and selfish however much you try to believe that they're not, and there's just no point me going back into that room with those bloody nurses. It's just like when I was a child and she'd be feigning some kind of illness and I'd be ushered in by some ghastly matron and told to keep quiet and everyone would be mothering her' – Agnes suddenly burst into tears – 'and they'd all forget I was there.' She could no longer speak, sobbing, taking in great gulps of air, her hands covering her face. She felt Athena come to her, felt her arm go round her, resting on her shoulder. At last Agnes said, 'I haven't told anybody, you know.' She took her hands from her face, sniffing.

'Not even Julius?'

'Not even Julius.'

Athena went over to her drinks cupboard. She poured two whiskies, went to the fridge, clicked two large cubes of ice into the glasses, and handed one to Agnes. Agnes was dabbing at her face with a tissue.

'To surviving one's mother,' Athena said, sitting at the table.

Agnes raised her glass. She nodded, and gulped some whisky.

'All the same,' Athena said, 'you've got to go back, you know.'

'Why?'

'I was seventeen when my mother died. I'd run away from home, from our village, I was living in Athens with an unsuitable boyfriend, and finally one of my cousins tracked me down and told me. It was spring, I remember; all the blossom was out. He came and found me and said, your mother's died. It had taken him three weeks to find me. I'd missed the funeral and everything. Do you know,' – Athena took a large swig from her glass – 'I don't think I've ever forgiven myself.'

Agnes looked at Athena, at the sheen of light on her long black hair. Athena swirled her glass around, and the ice chinked against the crystal. She looked up. 'I visited her grave all the time after that. For all that year, I practically lived at the cemetery. All those old widows who were there every day, they got to know me. I was like one of them. Saying goodbye, over and over again. Just saying goodbye.' She blinked back tears. 'It passed in the end. Life took over again. For me, anyway. Those widows are probably still there, still saying goodbye.' She drained her glass, stood up and went over to the window. She drew the blind, then turned to Agnes. 'So you see, you must go.'

Agnes was about to speak, then stopped.

'Look at us both,' Athena said. 'Cast adrift. No wonder we're friends.' She sat down at the table again. 'I mean, here I am, about to make another bad decision, and there's you, and your mother no longer even recognising you, and however you feel about her, there's still a sense of loss there, isn't there?'

'Perhaps.'

'Even if it's just that you've lost the thing you're fighting against, the thing you aren't, the opposite of you that you need in order to define yourself as what you are. Does that make sense?'

'Sort of.'

'Perhaps I need another whisky.' She got up and poured two more measures. 'Cast adrift,' she said, handing Agnes her glass and sitting down again. 'And I'm just the same. If I was anchored, I wouldn't be about to say yes to this man who's asked me to his gig.'

'And are you going to say yes?'

'I dunno. What do you think I should do?'

'Athena, as I think I said once, I'm really not the person to ask.' Agnes picked up an éclair and took a large bite. She looked up to see Athena starting to laugh. She passed Athena the plate, and Athena took an éclair, and then Agnes was laughing too.

Agnes got off the bus at Southwark Bridge and walked the rest of the way to her flat. The rain had eased off, freshening the night air. As she reached her block, she saw a figure standing outside. Agnes took in the high heels, the well-cut camel coat. As she approached, the figure turned towards her.

'Are you Sister Agnes?'

Agnes nodded.

'I'm Claire. I'm Cally's sister.'

Chapter Nine

'So,' Agnes said, pouring two mugs of coffee, 'how did you find out where I live?'

Claire sat down in the armchair and crossed her legs neatly under her. She was still wearing her coat. 'I knew you were the chaplain – Mal told me – and so I found out your order. And I looked up their property lists in the library, and it has your address. I tried another one first, that house across the river, but they said you weren't there. Then I thought this place is near the prison. If you hadn't turned up, I might have just given up and never met you.' She laughed, a restrained, polite laugh.

'Sugar?'

'No thank you.' She took the mug, wrapping her hands around it.

Agnes went to the window and closed the curtains, then switched on the electric bar fire. 'I'm sorry it's so cold in here. It'll warm up.'

'I'm fine, thank you.'

Agnes sat in her chair by the window. She wondered what to say. She looked at the fine weave of the coat, at the blonde highlights in the expensively cut hair. 'So, you and Cally are twins.'

'Yes.' She sipped her coffee.

'Why did you want to see me?'

Claire looked up, her clear blue eyes meeting Agnes's.

'Because – because I kind of heard that you were . . . interested in this business with my dad.' Her voice was clear, with clipped, neat vowels.

'And who did you hear that from?'

Claire looked at the floor. She twisted her fingers together, and in the neat chin, the morose, drooping posture, Agnes saw the image of Cally.

'From Mal?' Agnes persisted.

Claire lifted her head. She nodded.

'And how come Mal hasn't mentioned you to me?'

Claire shrugged. 'Dunno.'

'I thought you and Cally didn't get on.'

'We don't.' A brief smile crossed Claire's features, and again, Agnes saw Cally in her face.

'And does Cally know that you see Mal?'

'I've been hanging around the club a bit these days. Venn's going to let me try out some singing there. She must know.' She crossed and recrossed her legs. 'And whether I see him or not, it doesn't make much difference – she hates me anyway.'

'Why?'

'It's a long story.'

'I see.' Agnes was beginning to feel irritated, by her poise, her manners, her polite accent that betrayed nothing at all. 'So it's not a story you've come here to tell me?'

'I've come because I think Cally might be spreading rumours about me and my dad, and I wanted to check with you, and also Mal said—' She stopped, looked at the floor, twisted her fingers again.

'Mal said what?'

'Has she been saying things, Cally? About me?'

Agnes hesitated, unsure how much to give away to this young woman in front of her, so shockingly similar to Cally, so surprisingly different.

'She's very upset about your father's death.'

'Aren't we all?' Claire's calm remained unaltered.

'Were you close to him?'

Claire looked at Agnes sharply. 'What's she said?'

Agnes sighed. 'She seems to think it might have been you who killed him?'

'Why?' Claire stood up, agitated. 'What reason did she give? Stupid bleedin' cow, shoutin' her mouth off to all and sundry about stuff she doesn't know the first bleedin' thing about—'

'She didn't give a reason. When I asked, she said she didn't know why you'd have done it; she just thought, for some reason, you might have done.' Agnes watched Claire collect herself, then added, 'People get funny ideas in prison.'

Claire breathed again, sat down, crossed her legs neatly. 'Yes. I'm sure people do.' The clipped accent was restored.

'So, we're all none the wiser,' Agnes said.

Claire faced her, with her direct, blue gaze. She nodded.

'And did Mal suggest you see me?' Agnes asked.

Claire shook her head. 'No, it was my idea. I was with him the night my dad was shot. And he thinks I can give him an alibi. But the thing is, I wasn't with him at the moment of the shooting. I wasn't there. I can't vouch for him. Do you understand?'

'But he wants you to?'

She shrugged. 'I think he was hoping I would.'

'And who do you think did it?'

Claire sighed. 'I think it was him. What can I do? We've all been questioned by the police, and in the end, it's his fingerprints on the gun. I didn't see my dad shot, so how can I say anything?'

'What did you see, then?'

Claire met her gaze. 'I got to my dad's place . . . afterwards.

Soon after. It was horrible. I'd rather not talk about it. I've told the police all I know.'

Agnes studied her briefly. 'Is Mal hoping you'll be an alibi?'

She shrugged. 'Don't think so. Not really.'

Agnes glanced at her clock. It was not yet eleven, but it felt later. 'What motive would Mal have to kill Cliff?'

Claire frowned. 'I don't know.'

'Was Cliff involved with this Venn person, the guy who runs the club?'

Claire flicked a nervous glance at her. She shook her head.

'But other people might have wanted Cliff dead?'

Claire shifted in her chair, then shrugged. 'Dunno.'

'You still think it was Mal?'

Claire nodded.

'Shall I tell Cally you've come to see me?'

Claire's expression seemed to shut down. 'If you want.'

'Does Mal care about her, do you think?'

Claire looked at her. 'I think he did once. I think if she wasn't inside he might still . . . but that lot, they're . . . I dunno, they're a bit, you know. Whatever's happening now, that's what they're into, then they all move on . . . I see them at the club, when I'm with Venn, but I don't go around with them any more.' She looked away, towards the window, and Agnes saw tension in her face that seemed to age her. She gathered her coat around her. 'I only saw Mal recently because . . . because we were brought together by my dad's death. That's why I've seen him since. We're not close.' Claire stood up to go. She put her mug neatly on Agnes's desk. It was still half full of coffee.

'Can I contact you?' Agnes asked her.

Claire shook her head. 'It's a bit difficult. I'll phone you, okay? Next week?'

'Fine. Do you need my phone number, or did you find that out too?'

Claire smiled, and for a moment she looked vulnerable, childlike. She shook her head. Agnes scribbled it down for her and handed it to her.

At the door, Claire held out her hand. 'Thanks,' she said.

Agnes took her hand, which was thin and chilled.

'I'll phone you,' Claire said. The door closed behind her, and Agnes heard the click of her heels on the concrete stairs.

Agnes took the mugs into her kitchen. She ran some water to wash them. None of it made sense. She was with Mal on the night Cliff died, but not at the actual moment. She wouldn't say why she and Cally weren't close. She was well dressed, with a poise and assurance totally lacking in her twin, but with the same hard edge. Agnes found herself wondering how Claire could afford to dress like that. And she'd cultivated a whole new accent, and didn't go around with Cally's friends any more . . . And she wasn't happy when Cliff was mentioned.

Agnes lit her candle and knelt in preparation for her prayers. She looked up at her postcard of the Madonna and Child. Most of all, Agnes thought, she seems to be able to talk about her father's death without a shred of emotion.

Agnes settled her breathing, collected her thoughts, allowed her mind to focus on her night prayers, addressing Our Lady, Mary, Mother of God . . . Mother of God, Agnes murmured, seeing in her mind Athena, aged seventeen, clinging to the gravestone of her mother in the hot Greek sunshine. 'Holy Mary, Mother of God, pray for us, now and at the hour of our death,' Agnes murmured, blinking back tears.

Agnes unlocked one door, locked it behind her, and went through the corridor to the chapel. She went to put her key in the lock, but found the door was already slightly ajar. She was about to call to Imelda, wondering why she was there so early in the morning, when she saw, through the crack in the door, a figure standing by the altar. She pushed at the door and it opened, noiselessly. It was a woman, smartly dressed, and as Agnes took a step towards her, she realised it was Eleanor.

Eleanor was unaware that she was being watched. She seemed to be holding something, and Agnes realised it was a single white flower. Eleanor walked up to the altar, which was arranged very simply with a cross and candles. In front of the altar was a vase of flowers which Imelda had placed there yesterday, and Agnes saw Eleanor take her single bloom and add it carefully to the arrangement. As she turned towards the light, Agnes could see her cheeks were wet with tears.

Agnes withdrew from the doorway, and slipped silently away along the corridor.

In the corridor she met Eileen, one of the officers from Janette's wing. 'Sister, there's a woman come to talk about Janette, and I can't find Eleanor anywhere. She's out by the gate at the moment. Said she had an appointment – she's got a letter and everything. And I'm supposed to be there, under this new system, not that there's much I can say . . .'

Agnes had forgotten all about the case meeting for Janette. 'Thank you, Eileen. I'm supposed to be there too. I think Eleanor's just on her way back to her office. I'll go out and see to it, shall I?'

Agnes unlocked the last door, locked it behind her, and found herself outside. The air was sharp against her face. The tarmac of the forecourt was still sugared with frost.

In the lodge at the main gate, a woman sat on the leather benches. She was round-faced, and was knitting something that looked like a baby cardigan in bright yellow wool. She looked up placidly as Agnes came in.

The security officer was on the phone. 'Yes, Mrs Jeffries. Sure. I'll give her a pass, then?' He nodded, and hung up. 'That was the governor. I tracked her down. You're okay, love.' He wrote out a pass and handed it to her.

The woman stood up, and followed Agnes out across the tarmac to the main gate.

Eleanor was sitting in her office. She was clear-eyed and brisk as she stood up to welcome her visitor. Agnes wondered if she'd imagined the scene in the chapel.

'Ah, yes, Miss Langdon, do come in. Take a seat. I'll just get Eileen to join us.' Eleanor picked up her phone and dialled a number. The woman stood, uncertainly, glancing about her at the chairs.

'Miss Langdon—' Agnes began, gesturing to a chair.

'Myra,' she said, sitting down. 'You see, with her being released tomorrow, and no one to look after her, apart from her old man, that is, I'm the nearest she's got to family...'

Eileen appeared, came in nervously, and sat down.

Eleanor smiled at her, then turned to Myra. 'She's going back to her former home.'

Eileen made a snorting noise. 'If he'll have her.'

Myra picked up her knitting again. 'Oh, he will.'

'That girl should've pressed charges,' Eileen said. 'Then she'd have got more time.'

'I thought your lot would be glad to see the back of her,' Myra said, her needles calmly clicking.

'There is that, yes.' Eileen sat back in her chair. 'It's just the injustice – I don't like seeing folk get away with it, that's all.'

'She'll always get away with it, Janette will. Always has done. It's always someone else's fault with her, isn't it?' Myra finished a row and swapped her needles into the other hand.

Eleanor pulled out some forms for Myra to sign. 'This is the address, is it?' Myra looked at the form and nodded.

'Can't see her and Jim lasting either,' Eileen said.

Eleanor looked up at Eileen. 'She'll have a probation order, obviously, for the next few months. We'll see how she goes.' She stood up. 'It's true, she should have served more time for her behaviour here, but Amy won't press charges, and anyway' – she glanced at Agnes – 'we all agree that for someone like Amy to go through a tribunal process, it would simply add to her trauma . . . I think we should just wish Janette well and hope that D wing is calmer in her absence.'

'Until she comes back.' Eileen stood up too. 'May I go now? I'm on workshop duty.'

Eleanor nodded, and Eileen left the room. Myra gathered up her knitting.

Agnes followed her out into the corridor. 'Are you a relative, then?'

'Oh, no. But my godmother is Janette's sort-of-aunt, well, Jim's aunt, really – it's all a bit complicated. She asked me to keep an eye on her and Jim. She doesn't live in London, you see. I've done my bit, although . . .' she waited while Agnes unlocked a door. 'There's not much you can do for someone like Janette,' she said, as they passed through the door into the corridor. 'It just seems to be in her nature. And Jim, too, I'm afraid. That's what Glenys, Jim's aunt, was worried about, I think, when she asked me to keep an eye out for them. But she's always said there's not much you can do when folks won't help themselves.' Agnes unlocked the last door. 'I'll give this pass back at the lodge, shall I?' Myra asked, as she went out into reception.

Agnes went back to her office. Imelda was sitting at her desk, eating a sandwich. Agnes sat at her place, and flicked through the rota for the week.

'It's the start of Advent on Thursday,' Agnes said, checking the date.

Imelda took a bite of sandwich.

'It won't make much different to us, as we're here,' Agnes said, trying to cover the silence, which she sensed had become uneasy. 'Do we – does the prison do anything special for Christmas?'

Imelda turned to her, reluctantly. 'The usual Christmas things,' she said. 'There's a tree, and carol singing. It's pretty miserable, because no one feels like celebrating. And why should they?' She turned back to her sandwich.

'The birth of Our Lord . . .' Agnes began.

'That's for families,' Imelda said suddenly. 'Christmas is for people who live in families. It doesn't have to be imposed on the rest of us, those of us who've chosen to live in other ways . . .'

'A family's a community like any other, surely?'

Imelda dabbed at her thin lips with a tissue. 'In the old days, when I became a novice, we were taught that we'd left our families behind us; we'd become followers of Christ instead.'

'But surely, in community—'

Imelda shook her head. 'We have no family.' She picked up a pencil from her desk and turned it over in her fingers. 'In my first order, I worked in the laundry for my first winter there. I spent that Christmas Day up to my elbows in freezing cold water, because we heated the water only for the washing, not for the rinsing. I wasn't that well, but there was no point complaining – we were taught not to. It was a lesson. I learned through that not to ask for anything for myself. If I'd said I was ill, then another nun would have had to do my work, and that was wrong. As our novice mistress said, why should I demand special treatment for myself? So I carried on, even though I had flu. And I began to see that we are alone, that there's no point relying on our mere fellow human beings, that we can only rely on God. At some point in our lives we must acknowledge that we are on our own. We're born into this life alone, and we leave it on our own too. As religious, we're privileged in being able to live that truth.'

Imelda gazed into the distance, as if she was talking more to herself than to Agnes.

Agnes spoke quietly. 'Did you get over the flu?'

Imelda blinked, and looked at her. 'I ended up with pneumonia. Novices weren't expected to change their duties.' Her mouth lifted in an attempt at a smile, and Agnes saw how grey and tired she looked. 'What were we discussing?' Imelda asked. 'Oh, yes, Christmas. It comes round every year, doesn't it?' She stood up, and smoothed down her skirt. 'Must get on.' She straightened up, nodded at Agnes, and left the office.

Agnes thought about the painting at the convent, the baby Jesus asleep in the shadow of the cross. She thought about Imelda's uncharacteristic outburst at the decision to hang it in the chapel. She wondered about Imelda's life, so different from her own.

Agnes left the prison at a quarter to six, joining the crowds on the streets as people hurried to get home. The evening had brought an icy chill with it, and people hunched their shoulders against the cold. Agnes turned on to the main street, passing the building site, the towering cranes eerie in their floodlights. She could see the café Marky had mentioned, its window misted with warmth.

As she walked through the door, she was aware of a pause in the conversation's hum. Several faces turned towards her, all men, scanning her with a vague curiosity dulled by habit. Then the conversations resumed, the heads turned away from her. She ordered a mug of tea and took a seat by the window. She rubbed her gloved hand against the condensation. Across the road she could see the entrance to the building site. 'Jubilee Line extension, London Bridge,' was written on the hoardings in large letters. Outside a group of men stood smoking, their cigarettes glowing in the cold night.

'Another of those?'

Agnes turned to see Marky pointing at her cup, smiling.

'I'm fine, thanks.'

He went to the counter. The men greeted him, with a wave here and there, a call of 'All right, Marky?' 'How's Big Harry?' someone asked. Then he returned with his mug of tea and sat down opposite her.

'They're about to start too, same shift as me,' he said, jerking his head towards the others. 'I hate this time of the day. It's okay once you're down there – then you just get into it. But before you go on shift . . .' He shook his head, then stirred a large spoonful of sugar into his mug. 'What did you want to see me about?'

'Mal.'

Marky looked at her, then looked down at his mug, stirring it slowly. 'I was with him when they got him. That night, after we saw you at the club, we went to another club down at Elephant; then we went back to Mal's place, only they were outside, waiting for him.'

'What happened?'

Marky shrugged. 'Nothing. It was a bit weird. When he said it wasn't him, at first, I believed him, but, it's like, when they came for him, he kind of expected it. Like all the evidence pointed at him. Now I don't know what to think.'

'Do you know Cally?'

'Yeah, nice kid. Bad crowd, though. Her sister always said—'

'You know Claire too?'

He sipped his tea. 'A bit. She got out of that crowd, though

– I didn't see her for a while. Don't blame her. Cally was caught shoplifting, see, but it was her mate Viv that got most of the stuff. In court, Viv had no previous, she walked.'

'Why don't Cally and Claire get on?'

'It's something about their family. It goes back to when their mum died – they were only little kids. Something went wrong then between them. That's what they say. But they each blame the other, so no one really knows.'

'What does Claire do? I mean, for a living?'

'Dunno. I think she works for an agency. Like, you know, recruitment. Secretaries, that kind of thing. She's quite high up, I think.' He finished his tea. 'I don't know her that well.' He looked at his watch. Around them the other men were beginning to get up, gathering up coats.

Agnes looked at him. 'One other thing. Outside the club, on Saturday – that man, Venn?'

Marky nodded.

'What was going on between him and Mal?'

Marky met her gaze. 'If I knew that . . .' He sighed. 'Mal's been working there, on and off, DJing for him. He's good, Mal is. I helped him out a bit. It's great, the music. But something's gone wrong between them.'

'Since Cliff died?'

'Before that, man. You see, Venn gets people working for him. Like Doc, the heavy guy on the door. And Rosanna, his girlfriend. They become part of Venn's circle. He's got a brother, as well – he's working for him now. They sit around him, in the club, when he's there. Not Jim, he just does the door; everyone laughs at him. But Mal was kind of getting drawn in: Venn was talking to him a lot, Mal was sitting at his table. I kept my distance then, man, working here. It wasn't easy to be around there the whole time. And then it went wrong, and I don't know what about, and Mal wouldn't say.

And then Cliff got shot, but it was going wrong before that.'

'Drugs, do you think?' Through the window Agnes could see men grouping by the site entrance.

Marky shrugged. 'I'm a country boy, me. What these people here get up to . . .' He looked at her. 'Yeah. Drugs. Have you seen the car Venn drives?'

'What does he drive?'

Marky stood up. 'Depends which day. Monday it's the BMW, Tuesday it's the Merc, Wednesday he's got some four-wheel drive thing . . .' He laughed. 'Gotta go.'

'Marky, if I need to talk to you again . . .'

'You've got my number, haven't you? Not that I've got anything useful to add,' he said. He got up and put on his jacket.

They went out into the street. 'Thing is,' Marky said, as they crossed the road to the site, 'I don't care what Venn does. It's up to him. I only wish . . . I just wish he hadn't brought Mal in on it. Then he wouldn't have ended up shooting someone.'

'But why Cliff?'

Marky looked at her. He shrugged. 'I don't know, man.'

At the site entrance, men emerged from the end of their shift, laughing, jostling, their eyes bright in the grime of their faces.

'Come here,' Marky said. 'I'll show you something.' They walked to the edge of the hoarding. Marky glanced round, then led Agnes through a narrow gap. They were standing in a floodlit site. Cranes rose up around them. At one side there was a half-built concrete structure, gaping with rough twists of steel. Marky led her across the site, and Agnes picked her way through the mud behind him. He stopped at a fence. He pointed. 'Look down there.'

Agnes peered through the fence, and found she was looking

right down a shaft into the site itself. She could see scaffolding, criss-crossing in an endless downward structure, and a series of long concrete pillars, their height broken at intervals by crosswise beams of light. At every level men were working, climbing, driving JCBs, moving around their subterranean city in their hard hats as if they'd always lived there, like some alien race.

Marky turned to her. 'Bet you've never seen that before. Come on.' He led her back to the street, and went to the Portakabin at the entrance to clock on. 'Be seeing you,' he said.

Agnes was left alone. She turned away from the site and headed back to Borough High Street, strangely reassured to find that life on the surface of the city streets was just the same: grimy, anonymous and familiar.

Chapter Ten

It was odd, Agnes thought as the last door was unlocked, this change of status. One minute Janette was a prisoner; the next, a free woman. Janette was strangely subdued as they went through the door into the prison reception. The reception officer was there, and she handed Janette some papers to sign. Janette handed them back, her eyes lowered, all bravado gone. Eileen handed her a bag of her possessions and a travel warrant, and then the door was opened for her, and she walked out into the cold morning.

Agnes watched her as she took a few steps across the courtyard, her feet leaving imprints in the frost. She stopped, and appeared to sniff the air. She lifted her head, and her shoulders straightened, scenting her freedom in the chill of the air, the fumes of the traffic.

At the other side of the courtyard stood a figure, waiting. Janette saw him, and quickened her pace, and he took a few steps towards her.

'Jim,' Janette yelled, breaking into a run, and then they were in each other's arms, gripped in a huge, clumsy embrace. Arm in arm they walked through the gate and vanished out of sight.

'Humph,' Eileen snorted at Agnes's side. 'The only question is which one gets to top the other one first.' She turned and went back into the prison.

Agnes followed, and went straight to see Cally. Cally looked up as she came into the cell and put her hands over her ears. 'I don't wanna know,' she said.

'I thought you ought to—'

'I don't want to hear. Mal's been in court and got refused bail, innit?'

Agnes nodded.

'Bastards.'

'He pleaded guilty.'

Cally took her hands away from her ears and looked at Agnes. 'Guilty? Who said?'

'Ian phoned me this morning. He was with him.'

Cally stared at Agnes. Then she punched the wall by her bed. 'Bastards.'

'Cally, if you've got any information that might help him, isn't it time you told it to someone?'

Cally was rubbing her knuckles. 'I told you who I thought it was.'

'On what evidence?'

'On what I know.'

'And what's that?'

'It's just a hunch.'

'A hunch isn't good enough. If you think Claire really did it—'

'There's a difference between thinkin' something and knowing it, ain't there?'

'Cally – why do you and Claire hate each other so much?'

'It's her bleedin' fault.'

'How old were you when your mother died?'

'We were eight.'

'How did she die?'

Cally sighed, still rubbing her hand. 'She got ill. Turned out it were cancer, but she didn't find out till it were too late. She was only thirty-six.' She smiled. 'S'funny, when I think about my future I always think I've only got till I'm thirty-six too.'

'And how did Cliff respond?'

Cally's smile died. She stared at the floor. 'He weren't that good with kids. Not really. He tried, I suppose.'

'What happened?'

'He just went to pieces. We were happy, see, the four of us. He loved our mum. But after she died . . . he just couldn't cope. He started drinking. It was the booze, really – that's what did it.'

'But you still lived with him?'

'For a while. But I was angry, see. I was angry about my mum, and about the booze, and then I got angry with him . . . I got taken into care in the end.'

'With Claire?'

Cally shook her head. 'No, only me. I was eleven. Claire coped better at home. They split us up. She was in care for a bit, but she went home and dad allowed her back. He wouldn't have me. It was me or the bottle, and the bottle won.' She bit her lip, and Agnes saw her eyes water. She put on a smile. 'It was my own fault. I was wild, really. Out of control.'

'Didn't you live at home again?'

'I left care when I was sixteen, lived in a hostel. When I got thrown out of there I went to Dad's – there weren't nowhere else they could send me. It was okay, then. For a while.'

'And what was it about Claire, then, that makes you think she'd want to kill Cliff?'

Cally ignored the question. 'Claire was always the favourite. It's like she always got her own way. There was a teddy bear. It was mine, but she nicked it. I ain't never seen it again. My mum gave it to me, not long before she died. It was our birthday, and she gave us one each. But mine was nicer than Claire's. It was bigger than hers, real cuddly . . . And after

Mum died, and we got split up, she ended up with my bear. Typical of her. She just bleedin' gets what she wants, she just goes for it without thinkin' about anyone else . . .' She glanced up at Agnes. 'I still miss that bear, you know.'

'Saying that Claire did it – people might say you're just trying to find someone else to pin it on to save Mal.'

'People can say what they fuckin' well like.' Cally wrapped her fingers around each other.

'Marky said Venn might have tried to involve Mal in something dodgy.'

Cally shrugged.

'I just thought it might give us someone else with a motive.'

'What's Venn got to do with my dad?'

'I've no idea. I just meant, it might be why Mal's so reluctant to explain where he was that night.'

'Maybe.'

Agnes got up. 'We've got some time until his trial. He could change his plea in the meantime. If anything new comes up.'

In the doorway she looked back. Cally was sitting on her bed, twisting her fingers together.

At five, Agnes left the prison and went back to her flat. She picked up her post, and noticed an envelope with a French stamp addressed in even handwriting.

She opened it. It was from Yvette again, her mother's friend. '*Chère Agnes*,' it began. It went on to say that she hoped she would soon have the pleasure of a visit from Agnes. In the meantime, she said, I enclose some photographs that your mother wished you to have.

Agnes took the photos from the envelope. She held them by the edges, as if reluctant to touch them. She looked at them by the light of her anglepoise lamp. There were five, all black and white. One was a studio photograph of a woman in a long bridal costume. The dress was beautiful, Agnes conceded. The chiffon hung in tailored folds. The tones of the photograph were dulled by age, but the embroidery showed up in sharp relief. The woman's face was that of her mother. She clutched a bouquet of flowers, and allowed a slight smile to touch her face, just enough to offset the elegance of the pose, the flow of the dress. Agnes knew how deliberate that smile was.

She picked up the next photograph. Again, it was carefully posed, and it showed her mother with the infant Agnes. The baby wore a christening robe. This time the smile expressed radiant motherhood.

There were two more, both informal snaps taken at the house in Provence. Agnes was surprised how smart and well cared for the house appeared. She remembered it as peeling and faded. One of the two was of her parents. Her mother was looking at her father, and he was looking out of the frame to the left, as if momentarily distracted. The other was of her mother and her grandmother, both sitting on the verandah. Her grandmother was asleep.

The fifth was of nowhere that Agnes recognised. It was the outside of a tumbledown cottage, barely two rooms in size, in a row with about six others, all the same. In the background there was some kind of industrial structure, like a winding tower or a crane. Standing in front of the cottage was a thin, ragged girl of about nine or ten. Agnes looked at it, frowned, wondered how it had got in with the ones from her mother.

The intercom buzzer rang, and Agnes discarded the photos on her desk, and ran to answer it.

'Sweetie, you're there, how wonderful. Can I come up?'

Agnes pressed the buzzer, and a few moments later heard Athena's heels clicking up the stairway.

'Poppet, I am so glad to see you,' Athena said, throwing her coat on to Agnes's sofa bed, flinging herself into the armchair, almost immediately jumping up again and handing Agnes a patisserie box tied with paper ribbon. 'Cakes,' she said. 'Cream things. Have you got a plate?'

Agnes went into the kitchen and put on the kettle.

'You see, sweetie, I knew it would happen,' Athena said from the sofa.

'And what has happened?' Agnes put out a pastry on each plate, and handed one to Athena.

'We went out for lunch. Yesterday. He popped into the gallery, on the off chance. Simon was there, so he said I could go.'

'And?'

Athena leaned back in her chair. 'It was bliss, poppet.'

'Bliss?' Agnes was struggling with a large mouthful of cake.

'It's just fantastic. He says I'm beautiful – do you know, he saw me through the window of the gallery and noticed me at once, and he just had to come in? And he doesn't even like modern sculpture, and he thinks about me all the time, and he knows I'm in a relationship, and that's okay, he respects my needs, and he doesn't want to do anything to destabilise my life—'

'He can count on you to do that all by yourself.'

Athena laughed. 'And it's just electric, darling. Do you know, we've barely touched each other, and it's like . . . the air just crackles around us. Simon noticed – you'd have to be brain dead not to. When he said I could take a lunch break he gave me such a wink, naughty man – he probably fancied Greg too . . .' She burst into peals of laughter.

'And what's in it for Greg, then?'

'What do you mean?'

'I can't see what he gets out of this apart from someone he can admire through a gallery window.'

'He adores me.'

'How does he know he adores you?'

'Sweetie, don't be silly. It's obvious, when two people just, you know, just click. He spotted it at once.'

'Hmmm, as Julius would say.'

'Well, obviously, it's years since it's happened to you. Perhaps you've forgotten.'

'Thank goodness I have.'

'How tiresome of you, to come over all old and wise just when I need a friend. Anyway,' Athena went on, 'the point is, this jazz gig, when he's playing, you're to come too. Tomorrow. You're free, aren't you?'

'Why me?'

'It's the only way to explain it to Nic.'

'It's the only way to explain it to yourself, more like.'

'Oh ho ho, Dr Freud. You'll be there, won't you?'

Agnes sighed. 'Okay.'

'Good, that's settled, then.' Athena got up and wandered over to the window. She picked up a photograph and turned it over. 'What's this? This old Victorian slum thing?'

'Oh, that. It got in by mistake, I think. My mother's sent me some old photos. She's trying to blackmail me to visit by showing me a past that never was.' Agnes handed Athena the four other photographs.

'Gosh, she's beautiful in this wedding one, isn't she?'

Agnes went to the table and began to clear away the wrapping from the cakes.

'Blackmail's rather a strong word, isn't it?' Athena picked up another photo.

'That one with me as a baby . . .' Agnes shook her head. 'It's all posed, and she knows it.'

'I thought you said she was senile.'

'That's a pose too.'

Athena put the photos down. 'I still think you might regret it. Not visiting, I mean.'

'Athena, we're all capable of doing things we might regret.'

Athena looked at Agnes. 'Oh, sweetie, how right you are.'

Catherine had hung the painting perfectly. It was just to one side of the altar, and she'd placed a lamp above it, so that, in the chill of the December morning, the infant Jesus seemed to be illumined from within.

' "Behold, I am coming soon, says the Lord . . ." ' The sisters' voices filled the chapel.

Agnes looked across to Imelda. Her face was rigid, her eyes fixed on the painting.

' "I am the Alpha and the Omega, the first and the last, the beginning and the end . . ." '

The birth and the death, Agnes thought, looking at the painting.

' "I, Jesus, have sent my angel to you . . . I am the bright morning star . . ." '

Imelda stood up noisily. She walked down the aisle of the chapel, her shoes clumping on the polished wood of the floor. The singing faltered just for a moment while the door closed behind her, then continued: ' "Glory be to the Father, and to the Son, and to the Holy Spirit . . ." '

After the Advent service, Agnes caught the bus to the prison. There was no sign of Imelda, although according to the rota, she was supposed to cover for Agnes that afternoon. There was a note from Eleanor, saying that Amy had had a bad night and could she visit her?

Agnes found the duty nurse, who unlocked Amy's room for her. Amy was lying on her bed, curled towards the wall.

'Amy?' She didn't move. 'Amy, it's Agnes.'

Slowly, Amy turned to look at her. Her blue eyes seemed faded and distant. She was obviously heavily sedated.

The nurse stood at Agnes's shoulder. 'She was very upset in the night, screaming an' that. She's had some pills and she's better now.'

Agnes sat on the bed. 'Amy?'

Amy shook her head, and smiled crookedly.

'What was it?'

Amy put her thumb in her mouth.

'She was trying to open the window,' the nurse said. 'She was going on about the stars, like she was seeing things. Craning her neck upwards, she was, like having a fit.'

Amy had her eyes fixed on the nurse, and her face was set in an expression of hostility.

'Perhaps you could leave us alone,' Agnes said. When the nurse had gone, she turned to Amy. 'What was it about stars?' she asked her gently. Amy shook her head. 'Did you want to see the stars?'

Amy turned to Agnes, and her eyes filled with tears. 'They followed a star, to see baby Jesus.' Her speech was slurred.

It took Agnes a moment to catch up. 'The three wise men?'

Amy nodded. 'In the Bible. They followed a star, and they saw the baby. And they brought him them things, that incense stuff, for when someone dies, only he never died, did he, Jesus? He never died.'

Amy was clutching Agnes's hand. 'No, Jesus didn't die,' Agnes said. 'Or rather, he did, but he overcame death.'

'And the wise men, they was wishing on the star, weren't they, and they saw the baby, and the baby didn't die. And Jesus told me, he'd save my baby for me, he told me . . . And all you have to do is wish. Wish on a star. Only, in here, I can't see the stars.' A single tear rolled down her cheek. 'All I wanted to do was look at the stars . . . but – but they wouldn't let me. I was fighting them off – they wouldn't let me explain. And then they made me go to sleep.'

Agnes held the hand that clutched at hers. She wondered what to say.

Amy turned her heavy eyes to her. 'Soon I'll see the stars, won't I?'

'Yes,' Agnes said. 'Soon.'

Amy smiled, and let go of her hand, and curled back up on her bed. The nurse came and let Agnes out.

Back in the office, Imelda was sitting at her desk as if nothing had happened. She handed Agnes a small envelope. 'This was left for you at the gate.'

It was a scruffy envelope, addressed to Agnes in large, uneven writing. Inside was an even scruffier note.

'Please get in touch. I need to talk to you.' A phone number was scrawled on the paper. Underneath, it said, 'Janette.'

Chapter Eleven

The phone rang and rang. Agnes was about to hang up when a female voice answered.

'Janette?'

'*Hóla?*' The voice was hoarse and unfamiliar.

'I'm trying to find Janette Price.'

'*Que?*'

'Janette?'

'No. No here.'

'Do you know her?'

'*Que?*'

'Do you know Janette?'

'No, madame. Not know. Bye-bye.'

The line went dead. Agnes opened Janette's file on her desk and made a note of the address in it. She glanced across at Imelda, then left the office.

Cally was unimpressed. 'Janette? Wants to talk to you? Silly cow.'

'Typical,' Nita chipped in. 'It ain't like her to keep her bleedin' mouth shut, is it?' They both laughed.

'She's just missing the attention,' Cally said. 'It's like with you, right, she met her match. She's missing you.'

'Hope not.'

'Yeah, really,' Nita said, 'that must be it. She must have been hangin' around the lodge, waiting to drop off that note for you. In here, right, she were Queen Bee, weren't she? Three years of it, she had. Out there, she's lonely.'

'Apart from her old man.' Again they both laughed.

'That's what it'll be,' Cally said, nodding.

Walking back home at lunchtime, Agnes wondered what to make of it. The girls' view was the most likely one, she thought. But then, perhaps she should track down Janette, just to make sure. Even though, she thought, going up the stairs to her flat, she'd quite happily never see Janette again in her life.

She let herself in, and saw the light flash on her answering machine. She pressed Play.

'Sweetie, it's me,' Athena's voice trilled from the machine. 'Just checking you're on for tonight. Maybe meet me at the gallery, eight-ish? Hope you get this message.'

Agnes sighed. She'd forgotten that she'd agreed to be embroiled in Athena's schemes. Also, she was exhausted.

She sat down and dialled the gallery. 'Hi, it's me. Yes, I'll meet you there. At eight . . . Yes, I'm busy too, see you.'

She hung up, then picked up the receiver and dialled Ian's office.

'Ian, is that you?'

'Agnes, is that you?'

'I wondered if you'd be free to meet me this afternoon at some point. It's supposed to be my afternoon off, but I'm worried about Amy.'

'Amy? What – what's happened?'

She was surprised by the tone of urgency in his voice. 'Nothing specific, but I saw her this morning. She'd had a bad night, and she was drugged up to her eyeballs. It can't be doing her any good.'

'No. It can't. Agnes, I can't tell you how much of a failure Amy's case makes me feel.'

'It's not your failure.'

'I'm her probation officer. And there's nothing I can do, even though the hell she's created for herself is made a hundred times worse by her being in Silworth. What time were you thinking of? I can meet you for a coffee about four.'

'That'd be great. See you then.'

She hung up, then dialled Marky's mobile number. He answered, sleepily.

'Could we meet again?' Agnes asked.

He sounded reluctant. 'I'm on a different shift now. Days, I come out at six thirty. You can find me at the site then, if you want. But like I said, I can't be any more help.'

Ian stirred his cappuccino. Agnes poured herself Darjeeling from a white teapot.

'I thought you were a coffee person,' Ian said.

'I'm not that easily labelled,' Agnes said, and was glad when he smiled. She poured some milk, then said, 'Amy's case has really got to you, hasn't it?'

He nodded. 'I know the law is the law, and I know she's committed a serious crime, and I can see that society has to have some kind of punishment when people have killed, but—' He reached for his cigarettes. 'I mean, if prison worked as a system I'd be happier about it. If the hospital at Silworth was really somewhere she could get care, and therapy, instead of just drugs . . .' He pulled out a cigarette and lit it. 'For some time, I've been wondering why I do this job. Occasionally, very occasionally, I manage to keep someone out of prison and get them on to a training scheme, something that just sets them off on a different path . . . but most of the time, I'm watching my clients circulate between petty crime and jail, with no sense that I can break the cycle. And Amy . . .' He took a pull of his cigarette, blew out the smoke, and studied the cigarette as if seeing it for the first time. 'Did I light this?'

Agnes laughed.

'It's not funny,' he said, smiling too. 'It would be all right if it were mere hedonism, but this has become a compulsion. Listen,' he said, serious again, 'I've got to see a client right near Silworth tomorrow evening. Why don't we both go and visit Amy after that? About eight – is that okay for you?'

'That would be fine,' Agnes said.

'Great help you are,' he said, as Agnes reached across and helped herself to one of his cigarettes.

'God, isn't the clarinet a sexy instrument?' Athena whispered to Agnes.

Agnes kept her eyes on the stage, where Greg and his band were absorbed in their music. 'Perhaps it depends who's playing it,' she whispered back, and Athena giggled.

The room was smoky and crowded. The stage was shrouded in black drapes, with single white spotlights on the band. The audience sat around tables, but despite the informal setting the music commanded their attention.

Greg played the clarinet as if it were an extension of himself, as if its voice was his voice. He wore a black shirt and black trousers, and his straight dark hair flopped across his face as he moved with the rhythm, occasionally glancing across to the bass player. Agnes wondered when she'd last heard live jazz, and realised it was probably in Paris, with Hugo, her ex-husband, when she was about nineteen and he was still being nice to her. She shivered, and wondered whether it was the music, which was evocative and lyrical, or the memory, or some convergence of the two.

They finished the set, to restrained but appreciative applause. Greg took a brief bow, peering through the bright lights to find Athena. When he saw her, he smiled at her, then joined the rest of the band and left the stage. Agnes looked at her friend, who seemed to be in a trance.

'Athena?'

Athena was having some difficulty speaking. 'Isn't he gorgeous?'

'Well, um . . .'

'His body, for example . . .'

'It's not for me to say—'

'I told you he was gorgeous.'

'I'll get you a drink.'

'I don't think you need bother, sweetie.' Athena looked up as Greg joined them at their table with a bottle of champagne and three glasses.

'Did you enjoy it?' He was softly spoken, clean-shaven, with even features and dark eyes.

'It was fantastic,' Athena said.

'Considering we don't know anything about jazz,' Agnes added.

Athena scowled at her. 'Take no notice of her – she's just a philistine. Nuns, you see, they don't get out much.'

'Yours must be an Ignatian order,' he said.

'That's right,' Agnes replied, surprised.

'I studied theology at university,' he said. 'I did an essay on monasticism.'

'You'll know more about it than me, then,' Agnes said, and he smiled at her.

'Not that I'm religious, particularly,' he went on. 'But things to do with spirituality interest me, I suppose.'

'Well, with your music,' Athena said, leaning in to the conversation.

'Yes,' he said. He touched her fingers with his, still turned towards Agnes. 'Was it really a vocation with you?'

Agnes smiled. 'I think there's a very long answer to that question.'

'Maybe you'll tell me some time.' He got up, resting his hand briefly on Athena's shoulder. 'I'll just check if the others need me any more. We could maybe go and eat?' He went back up to the stage where people were clearing the stage.

'There's no need to look at me like that,' Agnes said. 'It's not my fault he turns out to have studied theology.'

'I don't know what you mean,' Athena said. Then she saw Greg approach their table again and put on her best smile.

The three of them left the club. Greg took Athena's arm as they crossed the road. When they reached the other side, he was still holding on to her. He said something to her, and she giggled.

Agnes yawned. 'Actually,' she said, 'I'm going to go home. I'm very tired.'

'Are you sure?' Greg said, 'There's a really nice bistroish place in the next street—'

'Really, thanks all the same—'

'Nuns have to get up very early,' Athena said. Agnes looked at her hard.

'Can I get you a cab?' Greg asked.

'I'll get a bus,' Agnes said.

'Well, if you're sure . . .'

They said their goodbyes. Athena kissed Agnes on both cheeks. 'Don't say anything,' she whispered, giggling.

'I wasn't going to,' Agnes whispered back, laughing too. Then she turned and joined the jostling crowds on Old Compton Street. She walked to Trafalgar Square, turned down Villiers Street, and decided to cross the river at Hungerford Bridge. The tide was high and a fog was settling over the water. She paused by the railings, watching the waves slap blackly against the pillars beneath. A train rattled past behind her.

Something was very wrong, she felt. A vague, uneasy sense of things not being right. A sense of responsibility, perhaps, about leaving Athena to go laughing into the night with a new man. Although Athena had always done what she wanted and their friendship had always survived.

A river barge glided by, its chugging muffled by the night. Agnes watched it go, its heavy shape shrouded in darkness. At the helm a lamp swung from side to side, and Agnes could see in the shifting light a figure stooped over the motor, his thick coat, the peak of his flat cap. In the wake of the barge the waves broke more noisily against the columns of the bridge.

No, it wasn't Athena, this feeling. It was Janette. Agnes stared into the churning depths of the Thames and realised that their paths had to cross again. She felt a sense of dread. She left the railings and set off quickly across the bridge, heading for Waterloo station.

The fog persisted over the Thames the next day. Returning on the bus from early mass at the community house, Agnes stared out of the steamed-up windows, and an image came to her: something to do with drowning. She remembered a dream from the night before, of waters meeting over her head.

She went straight to the prison. Imelda was sitting at her desk in their office, and she looked up nervously when Agnes came into the room. 'You look tired,' she said to Agnes.

'I'm okay.'

'Did they miss me at mass?'

'No one asked, if that's what you mean.'

'I overslept.' Imelda said abruptly.

Agnes looked at her, a question forming in her mind. But something about Imelda's straight back and pinched lips made it impossible to ask her anything at all.

'Eleanor wants to see you,' Imelda said.

* * *

Agnes knocked on Eleanor's door and then put her head round the door. Eleanor was standing by the window, gazing out. She turned, distracted.

'Oh, Agnes.'

'You asked for me.'

'Yes. Ian, Amy's probation officer – I've had him on the phone this morning. He's adamant that we must limit her medication. He said you'd know about this too.'

'Well – only that she seems to be constantly sedated.'

'This is a prison, Agnes.'

Agnes was surprised by Eleanor's irritation. 'I know it's a prison. But—'

'The measures available to us are somewhat limited.'

'Yes. I know.'

'Still, I've asked that they move her out of the cell and on to the ward. She might be happier there.'

'Thank you.'

Eleanor left the window and came to sit down. Agnes noticed that she winced as she lowered herself into her chair.

'I was going to ask you something,' Agnes said.

'What was that?'

'I just wondered if you'd have a phone number for Myra, that woman who came to the meeting for Janette.'

'Anna will have it in the office. I'll ask her to get it for you.'

'Thanks.' Agnes stood up.

'Agnes—'

Agnes waited. 'Yes?'

Eleanor opened her mouth as if to speak, then closed it again. She looked up at Agnes.

'What is it?' Agnes asked.

Eleanor managed a brisk, tense smile. 'Perhaps you could

write a brief report on Amy,' she said. 'Just your suggestions. It might help her.'

'Of course. I'll do it now. I've nothing else to do this morning.'

And what were you really going to say? Agnes thought as she left the room, closing the door softly behind her.

She set off along the corridor. Nothing else to do, she thought. When in fact there was Mal remanded in custody, Cliff shot dead, Cally in distress . . . There was the mysterious Claire. There was Athena hurtling towards self-destruction. There was Janette. And there was her own mother. Agnes jangled her keys as she unlocked the door to the next corridor, then the next, each lock somehow more difficult than the last, the keys heavier, her fingers more clumsy. My own mother, she thought, coming out into the central courtyard of the prison, breathing the damp air and trying to erase from her mind an image that had returned to her, of dark muddy waters closing over her head.

Six thirty, Marky had said. Agnes waited by the site entrance, her scarf around her face, pressed against the hoardings by the tide of passing commuters headed for home. There was noise behind her, and she turned to see the day shift emerging, grimy and noisy. She heard someone shouting.

'Marky, boy, you goin' to take all day or what?' And then a man emerged, two men, and Marky with them. He saw Agnes as she stepped forward.

'Well?' He glanced at her, then at his two companions.

'Hello.'

'Hi,' he said.

'Who's your lady friend?' someone said.

'It's um – she's a – she knows Mal,' he mumbled.

'Oh, him, eh?'

'You comin' or what?' A younger man passed them.

'Where to?'

'Down the King's, where else?'

'Your friend can join us, Marky,' the older man said. 'We're going to the King's Arms, just on the corner there.'

Marky glanced at Agnes and nodded, his reluctance showing in his eyes.

Agnes's glass of white wine looked odd on the circular mahogany table, surrounded by pint glasses of bitter. She tried to think of something to say to Marky, but was interrupted by the older man.

'So, you know Mal?'

'I know his girlfriend, Cally. I work in the prison as a chaplain. I'm a nun.'

'Oh, aye. What's she in for?'

'Nothing serious.' Agnes smiled at him. He had a round face and black hair which stood up in tufts.

'We got him this job, di'n't we, Marky?' Marky nodded. 'Good mates, weren't you, boy?'

'Harry here, he's my uncle,' Marky said. 'From Wales.'

'We're all from Wales,' Harry said, then laughed as if he'd made a joke. 'Still,' he went on, 'it weren't your fault, were it? You weren't to know, boy.'

Agnes felt the ranks closing against Mal, felt the group reshaping to close the gap where Mal had been.

'What'll you have?' Harry gestured to her empty glass.

'Um, it was white wine, thanks.'

'And Emlyn, here?'

'He'll have a pint of stout and a whisky chaser,' someone said, and then roared with laughter.

Emlyn sat unsmiling. 'Same again, please, Harry.'

Harry went to the bar. Agnes glanced at Emlyn. He was a

thick-set man, his face still grimy from his shift.

'Em don't drink, do you?' Marky said. Emlyn looked at him briefly and nodded. 'Any news on Mal?' Marky asked Agnes.

Agnes shook her head. 'It's all much the same.'

Emlyn stared at the table in front of him. 'We gave him a chance, di'n't we?' Agnes glanced at him, but he seemed lost in thought. Harry reappeared with the drinks. Marky took his pint of beer and downed it. He put the glass back on the table, aware that Emlyn was watching him, a tall glass of fizzy lemonade in front of him, which he now picked up and drank from.

'I get thirsty, this job,' Marky said, almost apologetically.

Emlyn shook his head. 'You're all right, lad. You can either take it or you can't.'

Behind them there were shouts, and two men were squaring up to each other. Emlyn swivelled round to watch, then turned back to his glass. 'See what I mean?' he said. Voices were raised as one of the men went to attack the other. Emlyn nodded. 'In the blood, see?' He glanced up at Agnes, then looked away.

'He won't touch a drop,' Marky said. The landlord had intervened behind them, and one of the aggressors was now leaving, issuing dire and incoherent threats from the door before being hustled away by his friends. Agnes looked at her watch. 'Marky, before I go,' she said, lowering her voice.

'Yes?'

'Did Venn know Cliff?'

'A bit, yeah.'

'And Cally knows Venn.'

'Yeah, but that's through Mal, through his music at the club. And anyway, Rosanna knows Cally too.'

'Who's Rosanna?'

'Venn's girlfriend. She's a singer.'

'At the club?'

'Sort of. See, Venn started that club as a jazz club, some time ago now. It was all for Rosanna – said he'd make her name. But it never took off – wrong place, wrong time. Then the club scene got going, and he's no fool, Venn; he saw his chance then, turned the club round, he did, and then when he brought Mal in, Mal really got it goin' for him. So it's left Rosanna a bit, you know . . .' He shrugged. 'Venn still does a jazz night there on Sundays. She sings then.'

'Was Cliff brought into Venn's circle by Cally, then?'

'Doubt it. You see, Cally and Cliff – they didn't have much to do with each other these days. It was more likely Claire. She's quite in with Venn now.'

'But why would Mal have shot him?'

Marky raised his eyes to Agnes. 'Who knows, eh?'

Agnes gathered up her coat and bag. 'I've got to go. Thanks for the drinks.'

She left the warmth of the pub and found herself out in the street. She felt the door of the pub close behind her, felt the ranks closing against Mal. She glanced back to the pub, and saw them all through the window, in the warmth. She thought of Mal, in a prison cell somewhere, alone and cold.

The bright lights of the prison shone out against the night, and the corridors reverberated with noise, with radios and shouting and music, and occasional shrieks and banging on the walls. Ian met Agnes in her office and they went over to Healthcare. Amy was sitting on her bed, humming to herself. She looked up at them and smiled, and patted the bed beside her. She looked awake and her eyes were clear and bright. Agnes sat next to her, and Ian pulled up a chair.

Amy smiled at Ian. 'When's it to be, then?'

'When's what?' Ian looked flustered.

'My release, of course.'

'These things take time,' Ian said.

'Have you come here to tell me that, then?'

'We came to see how you are.'

She looked at him, her face uncertain, framed by long wisps of blonde hair. She looked down at the cheap bedspread and pulled at a thread on it. 'And how am I?' she said.

Ian reached out as if to touch her. His hand was left briefly in mid-air before he withdrew it again. She turned to face Agnes. 'He still talks to me, you know. If it weren't for Him, I'd have done myself in by now.' She turned back to Ian. 'The Lord Jesus,' she said. 'He tells me not to give up.' Ian glanced at Agnes. 'Although He should know,' Amy went on, her voice suddenly sharp. 'He should bleedin' know how difficult it is. Day after day, missing my baby, missing her like – like every bone in my body is crushed by wanting her . . .' Her voice choked, and her eyes filled with tears. 'You can't know,' she said, hiding behind her hair. 'It's like all I am is the pain. It takes me over, it's what I become. I just want her back . . .' her voice dissolved into sobs. Ian reached out and this time his hand touched hers, and she grasped his fingers, her tears falling on the bedspread as she wept.

'It'll be all right,' Ian said, and Agnes saw there were tears in his eyes too.

'What can we do?' They strode back to Agnes's office, and Ian's voice echoed in the corridors, louder even than the noise from the cells. 'What the hell can we do? How long is Jesus going to keep her from hanging herself with her sheets – no disrespect, of course,' he added hastily, glancing at Agnes.

'How much longer is it likely to take?' Agnes asked, as they reached her door and she unlocked it.

'Weeks rather than days.' Ian walked into Agnes's office and flung himself into a chair. 'She needs help, for God's sake. There she is, waiting for her baby to come back from the dead, and what do we do? Lock her up. That's hardly going to help her. If that girl dies, I'll feel it's because of . . .' He shook his head. 'There's only one answer.'

'And what's that?'

'We must get her out. Do a jump, you know. Disguise her as someone and walk out of the gates with her.'

'And what would that do to your career?' Agnes smiled at him, but he seemed serious.

'Blow my career. No, really, I'm serious. Maybe not about her breaking out, but I mean, look, does me pushing paper around and filling in forms and sitting in court really matter more than – than her' – he sighed, then carried on – 'that young woman, sitting on that bed, needing . . . needing . . . ?' He looked up at Agnes. 'She needs love, Agnes. That's all she's ever needed. Like any of the rest of us. She's just a nice, normal girl who's had a vicious, abnormal life. She needs to be healed.' He looked down to hide the tears that welled in his eyes. He picked up his briefcase, opened it, then closed it again.

'So what are you going to do?'

'I'll think of something.' He took a deep breath, and looked up, then smiled. 'I'll run into the nearest phone box and put my pants on over my jeans.'

'Sorry?'

'You know. Superman.' He looked at her blank face. He started to laugh. 'You really are a foreigner, aren't you? Superman's a cultural icon.' He stood up. 'Let's go. I'll buy you a drink if it's not too late.'

'And Superman wears pants on the outside?' Agnes was frowning. 'Actually, I do vaguely remember . . . even in France, we couldn't avoid American cultural icons. I know, first phone box we see, you go in and do your thing with pants, and then I'll know for future reference.'

'In that case you're paying for the drinks.'

'But I live in poverty.' Agnes was laughing.

'And anyway, he normally wears a cape too. And a mask.'

'I'm sure he does.' They were both giggling as they came out into the lodge, and Agnes went to hand in her keys.

Eileen was on the desk. 'I thought I might see you,' she said, taking the keys. 'Funny piece of news reached us here about an hour ago.'

'Oh yes?' Agnes and Ian exchanged glances, still amused.

'That Janette, you know? Well, her husband Jim, he was found dead this morning. Copper told us – that nice detective sergeant comes in here with the escorts, he told us.'

'Dead – Jim?' Agnes felt suddenly dizzy.

'Yeah, Jim Price. He was drowned in the river, fished out this morning. Down by Rotherhithe. They think he only died last night. Someone tried to strangle him, then threw him in the Thames. Mind you, copper said, he were pickled in alcohol anyway.'

'Perhaps he just fell in,' Ian said.

'Nah, strangled he were, then thrown in. Died from drowning, though – still alive when he went in. Might have stayed down there days in this weather, if it weren't for the reeds. Course, we all know who did it, don't we?' Eileen pursed her lips. 'Told you it was a matter of time, didn't I, Sister?'

'Um – yes. Yes, you did.'

The three stood for a moment, as if somehow respects had to be paid. Then Ian said, 'I think we really need that drink now.'

Chapter Twelve

The pub was warm and crowded, but Agnes and Ian both shivered as they found a seat in the corner.

'I can't take it in,' Ian said. 'She's let out, and then this—'

'My second bout of drinking this evening,' Agnes said. She swirled her whisky around in her glass. 'I was over at the King's Arms earlier on.'

'I wonder where Janette is.'

'And he seemed so glad to have her back.' Agnes took a swig of her drink.

'Mutual and destructive dependency, those two.' Ian sighed.

Agnes breathed out slowly. 'It's funny, I had it in mind to get in touch with her. And now this.'

'You? Why?'

'She left me a note.'

'What about?'

'She asked me to phone her. When I tried, no one seemed to have heard of her. I've got her address, and the number of that Myra woman, Jim's aunt.'

Ian drained his glass. 'Well, you don't need to look for her any more.'

'Why not?'

'Don't you think—'

'That she did it?'

'It seems most likely. After all, she did it before. He just happened to survive last time.'

Agnes allowed him to help her on with her coat. 'We'll see. I'm in the office tomorrow. Give me a ring.'

Ian left her at the junction of Borough High Street, loping away without a backward glance. She walked north towards the embankment, then turned off and took a route home through the housing estates to avoid the river. She let herself into her flat, undressed and went to bed. She lay in the darkness, watching the shadows made by the streetlights on her ceiling, feeling not unpleasantly dizzy from the whisky. She tried to fend off sleep, wary of being dragged back into dreams of drowning, but in fact fell almost instantly into deep, dreamless sleep.

'I've brought you some breakfast,' Agnes announced, walking into Eleanor's office. 'From outside – that new espresso place.'

Eleanor looked up. Her face was set in a serious expression. 'Thank you.' She took the lid from her cup and savoured the scent of the coffee. Her face relaxed into a brief smile, and Agnes realised how rare it was to see Eleanor looking happy. She really needs to be looked after, Agnes thought.

'And croissants,' Agnes said, handing her one on a paper serviette.

'It's true, I do forget to eat.' Eleanor took her croissant and gazed at it. 'My husband has to tell me off about it sometimes.' She broke off a piece of croissant and put it in her mouth. 'Just sometimes,' she added; then, as if to change the subject, she said, 'Janette.'

'Yes. I heard.'

'I knew she'd be back.'

'Will she come here?'

'Almost certainly, she'll be remanded here.'

'Do you think she did it?'

Eleanor shrugged. 'Who knows? But the police have already been on to me about her.'

Agnes sipped her coffee. 'I was thinking of seeing her myself.'

'She might have gone, of course. Run away somewhere. Although I doubt she's clever enough for that.'

Anna, Eleanor's secretary, buzzed through to say someone was waiting to see her. Agnes gathered up her things to go. As she stood up, Eleanor said, 'Agnes?'

'Yes?'

'What – what I said just then about my husband . . .'

'Yes?'

'He's not a bad man really.'

'You didn't imply that he was.'

Eleanor seemed relieved. 'Oh. Good.'

Agnes went over to the door.

'Thanks for breakfast,' Eleanor said. Her croissant lay untouched in front of her.

' "The Lord sets the prisoners free; The Lord opens the eyes of the blind; the Lord lifts up those who are bowed down . . ." '

Julius read the words of the Psalm as if they had never been spoken before, as if they were new to the world. ' "The Lord shall reign for ever . . . Alleluia." '

Agnes bowed her head, aware of her breathing, aware of a calm descending upon her.

After the mass she waited for him by the church door.

'I'm glad you're still here,' he said, hurrying out to join her. 'There's a letter for you, from France. It came to the convent. Sister Madeleine passed it to me.'

Agnes took the letter, glanced at the unfamiliar, spidery handwriting, and put it in her pocket.

'Aren't you going to open it?'

'Eventually.'

'Agnes—'

'I can't go to France. Not just yet.'

'But—'

'I'll go when it's time.'

'And when will that be?'

'Julius—'

'I mean it. There isn't going to be a right time, is there? If you carry on like this.'

'I'm needed.'

'The order can spare you.'

'But the prison—'

'They can manage without you, surely?'

'But you see, Janette's husband was found dead, in the Thames, and I think I ought to see her, and Mal's been charged with a murder for which he seems to have no motive . . . And there's Amy – no one else can help her . . .'

'And who else can help your mother?' Julius was gazing at her, his eyes intense with feeling. Agnes traced the square stone flagstones of the church porch with her toe.

'She's beyond my help,' Agnes said, but she knew it sounded weak.

Julius shook his head. 'If she dies—'

'That's what Athena said.'

'Then Athena and I are in agreement. It must be an all-time first.'

Agnes smiled at him. He locked the church and they walked down the drive to the main road.

Back at her office she got out Myra's phone number and dialled it.

'Hello, it's Sister Agnes, from the prison . . . Yes, I thought you'd have heard . . . I just wondered . . . You're going to the

142

flat? . . . okay, yes. Four o'clock . . . Yes, I've got the address. See you then.'

She hung up and almost immediately the phone rang. It was Ian.

'I just thought you'd like to know Janette's vanished. I heard from the office this morning.'

'Oh. I was going to visit her flat this afternoon. With Myra.'

'Why?'

'Because . . . because I feel I should.'

'Oh. All right then. She won't be there.'

'She might come back.'

'She'll be arrested if she does.'

'I'm going anyway.'

'Fine. See you soon. Maybe—'

'Yes?'

'Meet you for coffee? Next week sometime?'

'Sure. Tuesday?'

'Um, yes, sure. Tuesday morning. We could – we could visit Amy again.'

'Okay. See you then.'

Alone in the office, Agnes felt in her pocket and brought out the letter from France. The handwriting on the envelope was uneven, blotched with ink. The address was simply the name of her order, followed by the London postal area. It was lucky it had arrived at all. Slowly, Agnes slit the envelope open. She knew who it was from.

'*Ma chère Agnes*,' it said. There followed a few lines of writing, which Agnes read. The gist of it was that 'they' were keeping the truth from Agnes, which was that time was running out. 'You are my only child,' the letter said. Then it said, '*J'ai peur* . . .' I'm frightened. It was signed, '*Maman*.'

Maman. Agnes stared at the word. *Maman*. The word

shocked her, so familiar, so intimate. And yet Agnes knew, as she trawled her memory for evidence, that she had hardly ever addressed her mother as '*Maman*'. All she could remember were countless times when the word had died on her lips, occasions when she'd found herself alone in the house and wanted to call for her mother, or social events, where she hadn't known how to address her mother because there were other ladies present and '*Maman*' might have been wrong. All she could remember was her own awkwardness about the word; her own silence.

She looked at the word again. The shape of the letters was blurred by her tears. Now, at last, the silence had been broken. The word had been given back to her. And now it was too late.

She screwed up the letter and threw it in the bin. She walked over to the window of her office and looked out, through the bars, seeing the high wall of the prison grounds, seeing the other wings, other windows, other bars. She went over to the bin, picked out the letter and stuffed it in her jeans pocket. She put on her coat and left the prison.

The address she'd been given for Janette was on a low-rise estate near Southwark Park in Bermondsey. She saw the figure of Myra, waiting stolidly outside in her blue furry hat with the wind blowing around her.

'It's Number 17,' she said, as Agnes approached. 'I've got a key.'

The lift was broken, and they walked up foul-smelling concrete stairs to the second floor. They passed barred windows and boarded-up doors to Number 17, and Myra knocked on the door. There was no answer. She knocked again, then tried the key in the lock. The door opened.

The hallway was dark and smelt damp. On the left was a door, which Agnes gingerly opened, letting in dim light. The room was entirely empty of furniture. There was an old, dusty rug on the bare concrete floor. They went to the end of the hall and opened another door. Inside they saw a mattress on the floor, a blanket flung over it. A cardboard box served as a table, on which stood two dirty mugs and a candle in a holder.

Myra spoke first. 'I never came here. I – I should've come. Seen how she was, you know. I'm all she's got, when it comes down to it.' The floor was bare concrete, apart from a mat, which was faded pink and stained. The room smelt sour and stale. 'I should have known. I didn't hear from her yesterday – I thought it was odd. The first day she was on to me, needing this and that, bedding, cigarettes, you know what she's like . . .'

'It's not your fault,' Agnes said. She went into the kitchen. There was no cooker, a dirty sink in one corner and a fold-up table which wobbled if you put any weight on it. There was a black dustbin bag full of cartons from takeaway food. Agnes opened a window.

'Best not to,' Myra said. 'Security, you know.'

'What can anyone nick?' Agnes said.

'They wreck the place, though.'

Agnes closed the window again. In the corner of the kitchen was a brand-new broom, its price tag still on it. On the floor next to it was a little heap of dust and bits, carefully swept up.

'That's what she asked me for,' Myra said. ' "I want to sweep up," she said. Money for a broom, that's what she asked me for. I gave it to her. Thought she'd drink it.' She stared at the swept-up dirt for a moment.

They left the flat. 'Where now?' Agnes asked as they gathered on the landing and Myra locked the door. They heard bolts being drawn back, and the door of Number 18 opened. A woman came out and stared at them, then went back in, leaving her door open.

'There's more, Roy,' they heard her say inside. 'More snoopin' around out there.'

'Leave 'em alone, Bren,' a male voice said.

'First the coppers, and now there's more.'

'Ain't none of our business,' the man said.

'Told you one of them's dead,' the woman said. 'Told you it would happen.'

'Yeah, and I told you to keep your bleedin' nose out, didn't I?'

The woman reappeared. She stared at them, then said to Agnes, 'One of them's dead, i'n't they?'

Agnes glanced at Myra.

'We've 'ad coppers round all day, and now you lot. Did she kill him in the end?'

Agnes said quietly, 'Jim's dead.'

The woman nodded. 'I knew it. I knew she'd do it, if he didn't get her first. Thought they'd come through the bleedin' wall the other night. Nearly got the law on 'em, though my Roy said not to. But he can say that, can't he? Measles when he was twelve, lost his hearing in one ear. 'S'all right for him, innit?'

They trooped back down the stairs and out to the street. Myra smoothed her hat over her ears. 'I should've gone to see them,' she said.

'Do you really think anyone can help her?' Agnes asked.

Myra frowned. 'Glenys, in the village, you see, she asked me to keep an eye on them both.'

'Glenys?'

'Jim's aunt. She's my godmother, my guardian, more like. Not legally, but she got me through a bad time when I ran away. Years ago. I was sixteen. It was here in London. She was a friend of my mother's, you see. She was living in London, then. She married a man here, but it didn't work out, so she moved back to the Valleys. And she's related to Jim, and so

146

when he came to London, she asked me to keep an eye. It was for her, really, that I got involved.'

Agnes wrapped her scarf around her neck. 'When did Jim come to London?'

'Oh, it was years ago now. He met Janette here. They married here.'

'There's Venn, of course,' Agnes said.

'Venn?'

'Jim's brother.'

'I expect he's been told.'

'What shall we do now?'

Myra fiddled with a button on her coat. 'There is one place she might be. Are you in a car?'

'We'll get a cab.'

They walked out on to the main road, and eventually saw a cab for hire. Myra gave the driver directions. Agnes sat back in her seat, watching the urban landscape pass by, the grey concrete giving way to Victorian brick as they reached the river, and then the floodlit grandeur of Tower Bridge as they crossed towards Aldgate, the gleaming towers of the city in the distance. The driver followed Myra's directions down Commercial Road, turning off eventually to the docks. He stopped where Myra asked him to, on the main road.

'Shall I wait, love?'

'Yes, please,' Agnes said, wondering where they were.

They got out of the car. It was nearly dark, and a light rain was falling. Myra walked a few steps away from the taxi. Set back from the street, dwarfed by derelict warehouses, stood a tiny chapel. Someone was sitting on the steps. As they approached, the figure stirred, gathered her coat around her, and got clumsily to her feet. Agnes saw it was Janette.

'Is he dead?' she asked, her voice thin, her hands shaking as she reached them out to Myra.

Myra nodded.

Janette looked at Agnes, then back to Myra. 'You been followed?'

'No, dear,' Myra said. 'We came in a taxi. It's all right.'

Janette eyed Agnes again, with a look that was blank with defeat but still beady with malice. 'She'll have brought them coppers with her,' she said to Myra.

'How might I have done that?' Agnes tried to keep her voice neutral.

'Stickin' yer bleedin' nose in again,' Janette went on. 'What's it to you, eh? And them coppers after me. What use is it to me, you coming here all teary-eyed to tell me 'e's gone, eh?'

'But you left me a note,' Agnes said.

'It's too bloody late now, innit?'

'What did you want to tell me?'

'I said, it's too late now.'

'I tried to phone you.'

'I was there.'

'No one there had heard of you.'

'You could've checked it. I might have wrote it down wrong.'

'I'm getting back in the cab.' Agnes turned to go. Behind her she heard Janette whimper, 'I'm frightened.' Agnes turned back and saw her wipe a tear from her eye.

'Janette – what did happen?' Myra said.

Janette shook her head. 'We was on the river bank, right. It was his fault – he'd drunk too much. We went down the social, got our giro, and then he fuckin' drank the money, an' then he turned on me, the bastard . . . I know we had a bit of a to-do, but I didn't mean 'im no harm. I left him by the river. I went back to that shit-hole flat on me own . . . He's such a stupid bastard – if he hadn't drunk the fuckin' money none of this would've happened . . .' She dissolved into noisy sobs.

'What will you do?' Myra tried.

'Dunno.' Her voice found its strength again. 'Nowhere to fuckin' go now – the coppers watchin' me house. When he didn't come back, I thought, that's it. They'll be after me, I thought. No point stickin' around to fight my corner – I'm off. When he didn't come back . . .' She suddenly burst into renewed sobbing. 'He was the only man I ever loved, as God's my witness. I know we had our ups and downs, but he was all I had, and I loved him.' The sobbing continued, and she leaned against the wall to steady herself, her hands over her face. Her raincoat flapped around her, revealing laddered tights and a worn cardigan of uncertain colour. She sniffed loudly, wiped her nose on her sleeve, and glanced up. Agnes saw her shifting expression, her careful calculation of the effect she was having.

Agnes thought of the warmth of the taxi waiting for them. 'Perhaps we'd better go,' she whispered.

Janette gathered her coat around her. 'Nowhere for me to go now,' she said. Her tears had dried. Her raincoat was unevenly buttoned. She looked at Myra. 'Haven't eaten since yesterday,' she said. Myra fished in her pocket and handed Janette some small change. Janette looked down at the coins in her hand, then pocketed them. She glanced at Agnes, then turned away and began to walk away from them, away from the church, towards Limehouse. On the main road lorries thundered past within inches of her, and she seemed to sway in their wake as she faded into the distance, blurred by the rain which was now falling quite heavily.

'Do you think we were followed?' Agnes asked, as they got back into the taxi.

'Makes no difference, does it?' Myra placed her hat neatly on her head. 'The poor thing can't spend the rest of her life on the run, can she?'

'She implied she didn't do it,' Agnes said.

Myra shrugged. 'She's an old hand, she is.'

'He's quite some weight to finish off, though.'

Myra considered this. 'He was drunk, though. And maybe he'd have killed her if she hadn't . . . if she hadn't done whatever she did. That's how it was the first time – he'd have got her if she hadn't got him.'

Agnes watched the windscreen wipers against the driver's window. 'How did you know she'd be there?'

Myra smiled. 'They were married there, her and Jim. It's the Welsh chapel. She's done it before, run away there. I just knew it was the first place to look.'

Agnes dropped Myra back to her street, then took the cab home, emptying her pockets of every last bit of change to pay the driver. She let herself in, and switched on all the lights, and the electric fire. She thought about Janette still walking the streets, probably drunk by now on whatever Myra had given her. She lit her candles and knelt in prayer.

'As evening falls, Lord, you renew your promise, to reveal among us the light of your presence. May your word be a lantern to our feet . . .' An image came to her of Janette's raincoat, crookedly fastened, swaying unsteadily into the rainswept distance. 'Strengthen us in our stumbling weakness, O Lord . . .' Agnes allowed the image to recede, keeping it at bay. 'Give us grace to cast away the works of darkness and to put on the armour of light . . .' Again she saw in her mind the laddered tights, the mottled legs. She pushed the image away. 'For God alone my soul in silence waits; from him comes my salvation . . .' Agnes opened her eyes, and her gaze fell on the postcard of the Madonna which she'd pinned to her wall.

'Glory be to the Father, and to the Son, . . .' Janette's destiny is separate from mine, she told herself. '. . . world without end, Amen.'

Chapter Thirteen

Agnes woke late, having slept so heavily that even now she emerged from sleep with difficulty. Her dreams still clutched at her like tiny fingers: the river, with yellow lights shimmering on its surface ... someone in a shabby raincoat, laddered tights ... spidery inky handwriting. Janette saying, I'm frightened. Only for some reason she said it in French.

Agnes yawned. She felt her dreams fading from her, as she turned towards the window and saw her curtains dappled with sunlight. She lay there, relishing the sensation of a Sunday to herself, of having nothing in particular to do until midday mass at the community house.

She had a shower, wrapped herself in her dressing gown, made some coffee, and sat by the window drinking it slowly, looking out at the sunlit day, at the passing people in their bright winter coats. She went to get dressed, picking up the jeans she wore yesterday, deciding they should go in the wash. She went through the pockets, and her hand closed around a crumpled piece of paper. She pulled it out, trying not to look at the handwriting, and put it in her desk drawer. She found clean jeans and a warm jumper, and settled at her desk. She got out her notebook and stared at an empty page, before picking up a pen and writing the name 'Jim'. Then she wrote 'Mal'. She wondered what it was that Mal had got involved in, then thought about Venn being Jim's brother. She wrote 'Venn'. She stared at the name, then got up, put on her coat and left the flat.

* * *

'Didn't think you was working today.' Cally looked up lethargically from her magazine. 'Thought you were too busy talking to Him up there.' She giggled, glancing at Nita, who ignored her.

'I'm not working. I just wanted to talk to you.'

'What is it this time?'

'It's about Mal and Venn.'

Cally turned a page of her magazine. 'What about them?'

'Were they friends?'

'No one's friends with Venn. Either he thinks you're useful, or he doesn't.'

'And he thought Mal was useful?'

'Yeah. He'd turned the club round for him, with his music. Brought in the punters. And—'

'And what?' Agnes asked.

Nita looked up too.

Cally shrugged. 'Dunno. They were quite – you know. They talked a lot.'

'What about?'

Cally shrugged again.

'And Cliff was friendly with Venn too?'

'Who said?'

'Marky.'

'Oh. Well, maybe he was.'

'And Rosanna?'

Cally blinked at the name. 'What about her?'

'You know her?'

'I got to know her a bit. When Mal was doing the turntables and Venn was busy, we'd sit together.'

'What's she like?'

'Nice. Yeah, I liked her. She's kind. She let me come and watch her sing on a Sunday.'

'Does she sing there much?'

'Yeah. Every week there. She'd sing more, for other clubs, if Venn would let her. It's her life, singing. Venn said he'd make her career. He started the club for her. You should see them together – pair of bleedin' lovebirds. Rather her than me, though. I don't trust him. You going already?'

Agnes had got up. 'I'd better. I'm not supposed to be here.'

'It's nice having visitors. We're locked in till lunchtime today. Enough to send you mad.' She giggled, and this time Nita joined in.

Back home she found a message on her answering machine.

'Poppet, for heaven's sake, where are you? I've been trying to get you for days. You're never in. So much to talk about. Phone me.'

She dialled Athena's number.

'Sweetie, how lovely to hear from you.' Athena sounded breathless and giggly.

'The thing is,' Agnes said, 'I was wondering if you fancied hearing some jazz this evening?'

'What, just on the off chance? Gorgeous clarinettists aren't two a penny, you know. I'm not sure you find them just lying around.'

'Don't be silly—'

'Particularly ones who use words like Ignatius or whatever it was.'

'Athena—'

'I could see you were impressed—'

'Do stop it.'

'How can I? I'm in love, sweetie. It's fantastic. God, you can't imagine, or maybe you can, but anyway, I'm just wondering how I've survived for so long without this. And I've been dying to talk to you, and you're never in, and I couldn't leave a message, and – oh God, it's wonderful, and he's so lovely, and I'm seeing him again tomorrow...'

'Anyway. This jazz – it's at the same club we went to before. The one under the arches.'

'Oh. Yes.'

'I'll go on my own if you want.'

'No, I'm not doing anything tonight. Nic's so busy at the moment – he's got an all-day workshop thing today. What time?'

'Thing is, I'm not sure yet when it starts. Come and have supper here, and by then I'll know the details.'

'Sure. Can't wait.'

Agnes walked down to London Bridge station, and skirted the arches until she reached Venn's club. She noticed a painted sign above the door, which said 'The Pomegranate Seed', and wondered why she hadn't noticed it before. The shutters were open, and she pushed at the door. It opened, revealing the staircase leading down. She descended into the darkness, and came out into the dim light of the club room. It seemed dark, lit only by a skylight. People on the surface made passing shadows with their footprints.

'Hello?' Agnes peered around the room. The stage was empty, with only a couple of microphones, some speakers. It seemed hardly the sort of place where careers were made.

Agnes heard movement on the stage and a switch being flicked, and a dull yellow light came on.

'Can I help you?' A woman appeared. She had a stately bearing and a graceful demeanour. She had thick black hair tied back in a bright scarf, and now she studied Agnes with eyes that were so dark they seemed devoid of feeling.

'I was wondering ... I was hoping to come here this evening.'

'Nine o'clock it starts.' The woman moved her head just enough to indicate the door, and stood, waiting.

Agnes moved towards the door. 'It was open,' she said, apologetically.

'You can close it behind you, then,' the woman said.

Agnes was slightly late for mass, and took her place at the back of the chapel. She scanned the pews, and was surprised to see Imelda kneeling in her customary place. When it was time to go up to the altar, Agnes waited in the line. Imelda was one of the first to receive communion, and as she passed back down the line, Agnes saw that her face was wet with tears.

Afterwards, Agnes went into the kitchen. Madeleine was working that day, and the other sisters dispersed quickly to their tasks. Agnes sat on her own at the table with a mug of tea. She looked up as someone came into the kitchen. Imelda went to the kettle and poured herself some tea. She was just about to go out again, clutching her mug, when Agnes said, 'Imelda.' Imelda turned to her. She looked weary, her face tense.

'Imelda – is it the painting?'

Imelda looked away, then looked back at Agnes. 'It was thoughtless of her, very thoughtless.'

'Of Catherine?'

'To hang it like that, right where I can't avoid . . .'

'But perhaps she didn't realise it would offend you.'

Imelda met Agnes's eyes. 'How can she know?'

'Then surely, you can't be angry with her, if she didn't know—'

'No one knows.' Her fingers were long and pale as she twisted them together. 'There's nothing to know.'

'Imelda – surely you can't go on like this?' It wasn't quite what Agnes had intended to say.

'I've managed all these years so far.' Imelda looked at Agnes, and her face was hollow with anguish. It was as if she'd said too much, and she turned and fled from the kitchen.

Agnes sat for a while, reflecting on what it was about Amy that seemed to have brought on this crisis in Imelda. Then she washed up her mug and left the house.

Agnes put a bowl of salad down on the table. She went to get French bread, butter, cheese, a bottle of red wine and a bottle opener. She sat down with the wine and opened it, poured two glasses and said, 'So?'

'Sweetie, where do I start?' Athena took the glass she passed her and sipped from it.

'Last Thursday, I imagine.'

'Right, well, after you left us, eventually—'

'What do you mean, eventually? I scuttled off as soon as I could. I was a model of tact and discretion. Even though it was obvious he really wanted to engage me in a lengthy conversation about the difference between Benedictine and Ignatian orders . . .'

'Just as well I distracted him, then.'

'Did you even get to a restaurant?'

Athena looked at Agnes and shook her head, laughing.

'You're terrible,' Agnes said, laughing too.

'We went straight back to his place.'

'And?'

'What do you think? And it's funny, because although it took me completely by surprise, I'd still remembered to wear that new underwear I told you about—'

'What underwear?'

'Darling, I must have told you about it – I bought it last week. Black, of course, pure silk, kind of lacy, but not overdone, just perfect . . .'

'And by sheer coincidence you were wearing it.'

Athena shrugged. 'Funny, isn't it?'

Agnes helped herself to some salad. 'And?'

Athena sighed. 'You can tell, of course, by the way he plays music . . . he's just . . . oh God, really, I can't tell you, it's like some kind of miracle that a man like that can just walk off the street and into my life . . .'

Agnes went into the kitchen to get salad dressing. 'So what's going to happen?'

Athena looked blank. 'In what way?'

'Well, I mean, there's Nic—'

Athena piled salad onto her plate. 'For goodness' sake, sweetie, it's early days yet.'

'Right.' Agnes sat down again.

'And there's no need to say "right" like that.'

'Like what?'

'In that judgemental way, as if I've done the wrong thing—'

'I wasn't being judgemental.'

'Good. Because I'm happier than I've been for ages, and that must be a good thing, mustn't it?'

'Yes. It must.'

Athena ate an olive. 'I mean, even your God must want people to be happy, else what on earth is the point of him?'

'Yes. Quite.'

'So that's settled, then. And who's this singer we're going to see?'

'She's called Rosanna Legrand. I found a notice up outside the club. Nine o'clock, it starts. It might be her I saw in the room downstairs, in which case she's quite a presence.'

'I can't stay up too late. I'm seeing Greg tomorrow.'

'Lucky old you.'

'I don't suppose the musicians will be anything as good as him.'

'I don't suppose they will. At least you'll be able to concentrate on the music.'

Agnes and Athena walked down the stairs to the club, and found some seats by a table at the far side of the room. Even with the small crowd, there was a buzz about the atmosphere that Agnes hadn't expected. The stage was bathed in soft light, and flooded at the centre with bright white spotlamps, and the audience waited in anticipation. The bar was doing brisk business.

Agnes went to the bar and came back with two glasses of wine. There was sudden activity from the stage, and the band came on, and immediately went into their first number. There was a keyboard player, drums and bass, and the music seemed to be a loose rendering of something familiar. Agnes tried to remember what it was called. Then the spotlights focused on centre stage, and Agnes saw the woman she'd met that day. There was warm applause from the audience. Rosanna was wearing a full-length black sleeveless dress, and her hair hung in heavy tresses, through which were threaded glittery ribbons which sparkled in the pool of light. She took up the song with words of love and loss, and her voice gave each word its meaning, each phrase its shape. She moved effortlessly on to the next song, and the next, and with each number her voice seemed to change its tone, singing with soft warmth to tell of her love, or edged with harsh discord to sing of betrayal. She stood beside the keyboard player, and her body rippled with the rhythm. Agnes watched her, amazed that such waves of feeling could erupt from a place of such stillness.

When she'd finished her set there was a slight silence, before the audience exploded in applause.

'Wow,' Athena whispered.

Agnes was still watching Rosanna. She had stepped to the

front of the stage, and now bowed low, smiling broadly, sparkling in the lights, her gaze travelling right to the back of the room. Agnes turned round and saw Venn, standing alone to one side of the bar, his hands raised to join in the applause.

Then Rosanna left the stage with the band, and some houselights faded up, and people left their seats, mingled around, went to the bar.

'I had no idea,' Athena said.

'Neither did I,' Agnes replied.

'Two fantastic gigs in one week,' Athena said. 'Shall I get us a drink?'

'No, it's all right, I will,' Agnes said.

At the bar she stood in the queue. She glanced across to Venn, who was still standing there, his hands in the pockets of his long black coat. A young woman appeared at his side, and he turned and greeted her. Agnes saw that it was Claire. Claire talked with Venn for a moment, while Agnes found herself at the front of the queue and ordered two more glasses of wine. She looked back to Claire and in that moment Claire looked in her direction and recognised her. Then Agnes saw her say a few words to Venn, who glanced towards her too.

Agnes carried the drinks over to Athena.

'What is it?' Athena took her glass of wine.

'Don't know. I think I might have made a mistake coming here.'

'But she's fantastic.'

'No, I meant . . .'

'Oh, don't tell me, sweetie, there's some subtext about murderers again. I might have known.' Athena sighed theatrically and took a large gulp of wine.

A moment later, Agnes was aware of someone standing at her elbow. She looked up. 'Hello, Claire.'

Claire stood, looking down at her. 'Who's your friend?' She seemed tense.

'This is Athena. Athena, this is Claire, she's someone I know from . . . oh, just around, you know. Why don't you join us?'

Claire pulled up a chair and sat down nervously. 'Venn said he recognised you from coming here the other night. Both of you.'

'He must have a good memory for faces,' Agnes said.

'He needs it.'

Agnes looked beyond Claire, through the crowds at the bar, and saw Venn standing in the same place. He was watching their table, and for a moment their eyes met.

Agnes turned back to Claire. 'You didn't phone me.'

'I had nothing more to say.'

Agnes studied her for a moment. 'Cally said Venn knew your dad.'

Claire stared at her. She shifted her glance towards Venn, then said, 'Yeah. Maybe. Why shouldn't he?'

'Just wondered.'

'What's Cally been saying? She'll say anything to save Mal, won't she? I bet that's why she's—' She froze as her eyes met Venn's. He'd approached their table and now stood over her.

'Perhaps you'll introduce me to your friends,' he said. He had a deep bass voice. He pulled up a chair and sat down. He had short, very black hair, and his skin was pale. His features were set in stern lines. He still wore his coat, and Agnes could see the collar of an expensive white shirt showing at his neck.

'This is – um—' Claire began.

'Sister Agnes,' Agnes said, holding out her hand. He looked at her hand, then took it in his.

'Sister?' he said. He had very dark eyes, and his expression was veiled as he met her gaze.

'I'm a nun. I work at Silworth, in the chaplaincy . . .' Venn was still holding her hand.

'She knows Cally,' Claire said.

Venn let go of her hand. 'Your job must be very interesting,' he said. 'Perhaps we'll talk more, after the second set.' He looked towards the stage, where the band had reappeared. He gestured to Claire, and they retreated back to the bar.

Athena leaned towards Agnes. 'What was that about?'

'I'm not quite sure.'

'He's quite . . . he seems rather . . .'

'What?'

'If I didn't have Greg to compare him with, I'd say he was rather a tasty geezer.'

'If I wasn't filled with misgivings about him, I might agree with you.'

'That's never stopped you before.'

Then Rosanna appeared, and commanded their attention again. This time she was if anything more powerful, more poised. Agnes was aware of her seeking out Venn in the audience from time to time, as if somehow his presence was part of her performance. Towards the end, the keyboard player picked up a saxophone. Rosanna stepped forward to the edge of the stage. 'This song's called "Gilded Cage". Some of you may know it.'

The regulars in the audience clapped. Rosanna started the song unaccompanied, her singing the only sound in the room. 'You built me a cage, a gilded cage and lined it with pearl . . .' Then the sax joined in, and the two voices wove in and out of each other. Agnes glanced at Venn. He was staring at the floor. Then he looked up, in Agnes's direction, and once again their eyes met. He looked away, shifted on his feet and turned his attention to Rosanna again.

The last number was upbeat and funky, and people started

to dance. Even when Rosanna had finished, and taken her applause, and left the stage, the band stayed, playing on, and people danced.

Venn came over to Agnes's table and sat down. 'You weren't thinking of leaving yet, were you?'

'Not particularly.'

'We have a late licence here,' he said. He turned to the bar and signalled something, and a few moments later a man appeared with a bottle of champagne and three glasses.

'Where's Claire?' Agnes asked.

'Oh, she had to go.' Venn poured the champagne. 'So, you know her sister?'

'Yes. At the prison.' He nodded. 'It's a shame about their father,' Agnes said.

Venn kept his eyes locked with hers. 'A great shame,' he said. 'No doubt Cally has her views about it.'

'Yes, she has. After all, it's her boyfriend they've charged.' Agnes watched him carefully.

'It must be tough for her.'

'She thinks he didn't do it.'

'Well, everyone's entitled to their opinion,' he said, and his gaze didn't falter.

The crowd was thinning out. Some people had left. The band were still on the stage, and a small group of people were still dancing.

Athena yawned, loudly.

'Your friend's tired,' Venn said. He signalled to someone. 'I'll get you a cab.'

Athena flashed a glance at Agnes, and Agnes was about to say something, when Rosanna appeared at their table. She ignored Agnes and Athena and looked straight at Venn. 'No glass for me, honey?'

Almost immediately, someone appeared with a fourth

glass and a second bottle of champagne. She sat down, still looking only at Venn as he poured her a drink. She waited for him to put the bottle down, then picked it up, and, not taking her eyes from his, topped her glass up to the brim. It was only when she'd drunk the whole glass that she looked at Agnes.

'You were the one who came in this morning.'

'That's right.'

She turned to Venn. 'You know her?'

'I met her this evening.'

She eyed Agnes.

'She's a nun,' Venn said.

Rosanna continued to stare at her. A smile started at the corners of her mouth, and spread across her face. 'A nun?'

'Yes,' Agnes said, 'a nun.'

'What is it, Doc?' Venn addressed a man who hovered at his elbow.

'The cab's here.' Doc smoothed the sleeves of his leather jacket.

Athena looked at Agnes. 'Um – are we – are we going?'

Rosanna put her hand on Agnes's. 'I ain't never had a nun come to hear me sing. I ain't going to let her disappear into the night so soon.'

'You go,' Agnes said.

Athena shrugged, kissed her briefly, gathered up her coat. 'Thanks for the drinks,' she said to Venn. She turned to Rosanna, blushing, and said, 'You were – you were fantastic.' Rosanna smiled at her, and inclined her head, restrained and gracious. Then Athena turned and followed Doc up the stairs to the street.

'How was I really?' Rosanna said to Venn.

'Great. Really great. Babe, you know how you were.'

Rosanna nodded. 'It went okay. That number in the first

set, "Autumn Leaves", I got out of line with the bass, but we worked it out.'

'You were great,' Venn said.

Rosanna skewed round to the bar. 'There's Paul,' she said. 'He said he'd be in tonight. I've got to talk to him.' She refilled her glass, downed it in one, then stood up and went over to the bar.

'He plays sessions with them sometimes,' Venn said, his eyes following Rosanna for a moment, before turning back to Agnes. 'Did you bring your friend for moral support?'

'Do I need moral support to listen to some music?'

'Then, because you were frightened to come back here on your own, maybe.' He held her gaze.

'I don't scare easily,' Agnes said.

He looked at her and smiled, and the warmth in his eyes seemed to soften the angles of his face.

Venn looked towards the band, who were still playing, then turned back to Agnes. 'Do you dance?'

'Well – I—'

'Properly, I mean?'

'I did once.'

'It's easy. Just follow me.'

He led her to the space by the stage. The keyboard player glanced at him as he approached, and the band went into a Latin rhythm. Agnes felt the music, felt Venn's hand on her back, as they began to move across the floor. 'I'm not used to—'

'Just follow,' he said.

A memory flashed through her mind, of a shabby church hall in France, of a strict and oddly shaped woman of indeterminate age shouting out orders to a bunch of awkward teenagers. 'I was made to learn to dance,' she said.

'Unlearn it, then.' Venn moved effortlessly, and although

she had no idea what she was supposed to do, it was easy to keep up with him. He stopped, took off his coat and flung it over a chair. His shirt was loosely fitted in fine white cotton. Agnes was glad she'd worn her low heels.

'See?' he said after a while. The rhythm changed again, and Agnes was aware that they'd become a spectacle, and that the few people left were watching them, and suddenly she didn't care, and the drumbeat and the rhythm were enough, and she abandoned herself to the feeling of the dance.

Venn said something in her ear.

'What did you say?'

'I said, you sought me out here, didn't you?'

'Yes,' she said. 'Yes, I did.'

'Why?'

They were still dancing, and she was breathless as she raised her eyes to his. 'Do I have to tell you?'

'I'll find out,' he said.

'Jim,' she said.

His step never faltered, but his eyes seemed to darken, and Agnes sensed his grief. 'He was my brother,' he said.

'I know.'

'I've known dark nights since I heard he was dead. I'm used to the dark, but not like this.' He was speaking softly, and his voice almost gave up. 'Jim made his own destiny,' he went on. 'In the end, I always come back to that. He made his own destiny.'

The music finished. Venn let go of Agnes. 'Thank you for the dance.' He held her gaze for a long moment. 'Another drink?'

She followed him back to their table and sat down. He poured more champagne.

'And me, honey.' Rosanna came and joined them and passed him her glass. 'Or have you forgotten all about me?' Venn poured her a drink. 'Mind you, a nun,' Rosanna went on. 'It's enough to turn a man's head.' She fixed Agnes with a hard look. 'A nun who can dance.'

'Oh, not me.' Agnes smiled at her. 'I can't dance.'

'No, I mean it. It's rare in an English woman.'

'I'm not English.'

'How come that always happens – you talk to an English person, and they always say, but I'm not English? Are there any English people left? I mean, Venn, here, he's not English, are you, honey?'

Venn looked at the table, uncomfortable.

'See,' Rosanna went on, 'look at him. Brooding Celt, he is. Look at those dark curls, those eyes – black, they are, not brown. And his anger, honey – you should see it. Inbred it is, years of fighting off invasions and taking to the hills . . . It leaves its mark, I can tell you, Sister.'

Venn was shaking his head, trying to smile. 'Rosanna, girl, you don't see me taking to the hills—'

'And gypsy's curses, you ask his family: any ill befalls them, it goes back to some—'

'That's enough.' Venn's voice was sharp, and people turned to look in his direction. Rosanna met his eyes. For a moment the couple seemed locked in some kind of silent combat. Then Rosanna smiled, and turned to Agnes. 'So, honey, if you're not English, what are you?'

Agnes glanced at Venn, then said, her voice light, 'I'm half-French. What are you?'

'I'm a Londoner,' Rosanna said, and laughed, a warm, deliberate laugh.

'She's a mongrel,' Venn said.

'Well, isn't that a nice way of putting it?' Rosanna looked at Venn levelly, then rested her hand on his. 'A citizen of the world, that's what I am. I had one Jewish grandmother, on my mother's side. My other grandmother was African. Yoruba, she was. Both my grandfathers were no-good boys, born to itinerants. One of them was Irish, I think. It's great for the music. I can sing to you about exile, and every cell in my body will take up the harmony.'

The band were still on the stage, laughing, doodling on their instruments. The keyboard player started to play a tango. Rosanna touched Venn's hand. 'Come on, kid, let's show these people how it's done.' She stood up. Venn sat still. Rosanna waited. Venn took a sip from his glass, a silent move in the game. Rosanna stood, cool and composed, her hand resting lightly on the back of his chair. Then, wordlessly, he stood up, took her hand and led her to the dance floor.

Agnes watched them, watched them take up the rhythm with their bodies, watched the perfect shifting of their balance, their eyes locked together, Rosanna held by Venn in a grip that was both fixed and fluid. Rosanna abandoned herself to the music, and half-closed her eyes, her head flung back, still moving with loose-limbed precision. Venn didn't take his eyes from Rosanna's face, his expression chiselled like marble in the beam of light.

I should have asked more about Cliff, Agnes thought. I should have seen what he had to say. But instead I mentioned Jim.

She looked at him, his partner in his arms, their bodies brushing against each other with a seemingly careless sensuality. And yet, when their eyes met, there was a flash of white heat, as if each move in the dance was a challenge, a declaration of battle.

I know why it was, she thought. I wanted to see if a man like that could grieve.

She picked up her bag, glancing at the dance floor. Venn's face was half-shadowed by the spotlight as he moved within its beam.

A man like that, she thought. She got up quietly, gathered up her coat and went to the door. She ascended the stairs, relieved to find herself out in the cold night air. It was very late, and the streets were deserted. From Borough market she could hear shouts, and an odd kind of drunken bellowing. She skirted the edge of the market. In the High Street she hailed a cab, as her shoes were hurting her feet and she didn't feel like walking any more.

Chapter Fourteen

'Course she did it, didn't she?'

'But to throw him in the Thames—' Agnes sat next to Nita on her bed.

'She was there, with him, by the river. She went for him.' Cally sat on her bed, dragging a comb through her hair.

'How do you know that?'

'That's what I heard, anyway. This bloody comb's knackered, Nita, can I lend yours?'

Nita passed a comb across. 'Maria in the cell opposite, she has a friend who works in the pub where Jim used to drink, and this mate said that Janette came to get him, from the pub, that night, and she practically went for him right there. And that was the night he drowned.'

'But he was strangled, she didn't do that last time.'

'They can do what they want with the fuckin' evidence, can't they?' Cally's voice was sharp. 'It's like my Mal, innit? All points to 'im, don't it? Whether he done it or not. This comb's rubbish too, Nita.' She threw the comb across to Nita, who caught it and giggled.

The window of the lady chapel at St Simeon's rippled with thin sunlight. Agnes sat alone in the front pew, her head bowed in the silence. She heard Julius approach, heard him go to the altar to prepare for that evening's mass. She knelt in prayer for a while, her thoughts returning to Janette, to Cally. To Venn.

She heard in her mind the words of Rosanna's song. 'You built me a cage, a gilded cage . . .'

Hearing Julius go down the steps to his little office, she went to join him there.

'What did your letter say?' he asked her. He went over to the kettle and switched it on.

'Oh, you know . . .' Agnes sat down on one of the shabby red velvet chairs.

'I know, do I?'

'It was from my mother.'

'I thought she couldn't speak.'

'She can't. But she can write. Sort of. It was rather incoherent, actually.' She stood up, and took off her raincoat, then sat down again.

'But sufficiently coherent to have affected you.'

Agnes shrugged.

'Look at you, Agnes. You look exhausted.'

Agnes glanced up at him. His gaze was serious, filled with compassion. It made her feel like crying.

'Agnes, what is it?'

She shook her head.

'Tell me.' He sat down next to her.

'Julius, did you like your mother?'

'Like her?'

'Yes. As a person, I mean.'

'She was my mother. I loved her.'

'Was it that simple?'

Julius frowned, then nodded. 'Yes. I suppose it was.'

'That's the problem, you see. You just can't know what it's like, not to be able . . . not to feel . . . I must be abnormal.'

'No, not abnormal,' Julius said.

'But you just said—'

'Perhaps I was just lucky.'

Agnes stood up and put her coat on. 'Perhaps you were.'

'Won't you stay for coffee?'

'I'd better get back.' At the door, Agnes hesitated. 'The thing is, Julius—'

'What?'

'How can you tell me what I should do, if you don't know – if you have no idea, absolutely no idea, what it's like . . .' She felt her eyes well with tears.

'All I know, Agnes, is that you should be there. Particularly if she's asking for you. If there's any resolution possible, if there's any chance that you might feel better about . . . about her, about your own past, your childhood . . . then you must take it. It's weighing you down, all this, and maybe the Lord wants you to be able to move on from this, to be freer, to lighten your spirit.' He absently took off his glasses and polished them. 'And all this insistence that the wrong people have been arrested for things, and that they all need you, when the fact is they've all got lawyers who know the truth of it all better than you do, maybe that's part of you being weighed down. And maybe if you go and visit your mother, you'll be able to see more clearly afterwards. You see, we can't know what the Lord intends for us. We can't see what good might come of things.' He looked up at her, and in his soft blue gaze she saw his stillness and his love. She started to cry.

'Oh, Agnes, I didn't want . . . I didn't mean . . .' He went to her and helped her into a chair. He stood there, his hand on her shoulder. She reached up and took his hand in hers. Eventually she said, through her tears, 'You're right. I'll go.'

Back in the prison she went through the corridors, unlocking and locking doors, until she reached her office, glad to find that Imelda wasn't there. She flung herself into a chair, and stared at the rota list on the wall. She picked up the phone, put it down, picked up the list of visits that Imelda had left for her and stared at that for a while. She left the office, locking it behind her, and set off down the corridor.

Two hours later she walked into the staff room, made herself a cup of tea, and sat down, exhausted.

'I've listened to every possible account of every possible human misery, I think,' she said to the person standing by the kettle next to her, who, she realised, was Sarah, the Anglican chaplain.

'Same here,' Sarah said. 'There's no doubt it's worse when it's women. Don't you think, Eleanor?' she added, as Eleanor came into the kitchen. 'When a mother's sent down, she's doing two sentences. Tragic, I call it.'

'Sometimes,' Eleanor said. 'Sometimes I'd call it tragic. It depends.' She went to the coffee machine.

Sarah turned to Agnes. 'Are you all right? You look tired.'

'It's just – my mother's ill.'

'I'm sorry to hear that. You should go and see her.'

'Yes. Yes, um – I will.'

Sarah patted her shoulder, and left the kitchen.

'Well,' Eleanor said, 'I've had a lovely morning. Janette's arrived. On remand, charged with Jim's murder.' Agnes looked at Eleanor. 'I could do without it,' Eleanor said. 'She'll make everything worse. It's Christmas, you see – terrible time here. All it needs is one outburst from Janette and we'll have serious trouble on our hands.'

'Shall I go and see her?'

'Do you want to?'

'I'm not sure.'

'She's worse this time. She's swearing blind she didn't do it. But she admits she went for him, she admits he was drunk. Given her previous record, what does she expect? The best she'll get is manslaughter, given that he was so drunk he might have drowned anyway without her help.'

'But if she says she didn't do it—'

Eleanor gave a hollow laugh. 'As far as that woman's concerned, life has been a conspiracy against her from the moment she was born. It makes me so angry, when some of us have to work so hard with what life gives us, and we're still expected to put on a brave face and cope, and keep our troubles to ourselves, and there she is parading her sorrows for all to see when she herself is the cause of them . . .' Eleanor took a deep breath and looked across at Agnes. Her cheeks were flushed. She collected herself. 'I'm sorry. It's not like me . . . and there you were talking about your mother. I'm sorry to hear she's unwell. I hope it's not serious.'

'Well, it is really. That's why I may go and visit.'

'I suppose your order wouldn't allow you the time away otherwise.'

'I wouldn't be going otherwise.'

Eleanor looked at her oddly. As she stood up and put her cup away, Agnes had the impression they'd both traded confidences.

She found Cally on association.

'Did you see her, then? Janette?' Cally was sitting at a distance from the others.

'No, not yet.'

'She tried to get me on her side earlier on. I saw her at canteen. She tried to talk to me about it. I didn't listen. I don't care no more; I don't care about her nor no one else. I don't even care about Mal. If he says he did it, then I can't help him, can I?'

'But you've always said—'

'I know what I've said, and I still stand by that. But listen, Agnes, when I first come in here, he wrote to me every day.

He promised me it was going to be all right, he said he'd stand by me; when I came out he was goin' to look after me – and then the letters weren't so often, and now they've stopped.'

'Cally – he's got a lot to think about.'

'Yeah, but you'd think he'd need me on his side. It's like he don't care no more. So I don't care neither.' Her hair looked rougher than usual, and her skin was in poor condition.

'Cally – I saw Claire last night. She was at the jazz night, at the club, and Rosanna was there, and so was Venn.'

'Yeah?' Cally's expression was veiled.

'Does that surprise you?'

'She can do what she fuckin' well likes.'

'I just thought it might shed some light on Mal's relationship with Venn, and I thought Venn must have had something to do with Cliff, because Mal isn't talking, is he? I mean, he's frightened of something, isn't he?'

'And?' Cally examined her nails, picking at the chipped pink varnish.

'I thought maybe he was frightened of Venn.'

Cally shrugged. 'I don't see why Venn should scare him. Venn's been good to him – given him a break. I mean, sure, Venn's a bit of an operator, but then Mal can look after himself, you know.'

'Claire seems to be quite good friends with Venn.'

'Listen, I don't trust that bitch an inch, but whatever it is she's doing, she don't need Venn. However bad she is, he's worse.'

But Cally, Agnes wanted to say, Claire arrived at your father's home the night he died, maybe within hours of it, if she's telling the truth. She seems to be quite closely involved with Venn. And he's someone who appears to wield some kind of power over people, and Mal is refusing to talk to anyone. Agnes looked at Cally, at her bleached-out hair and sallow skin which gave her the appearance of somehow fading from view. 'What was he like, your dad?' Agnes said.

Cally looked up, as if the question had taken her by surprise. 'Like?' She frowned. 'Don't know, really.'

'What did he do, for a living?'

Cally pulled at the ends of her hair. 'Not much. On the dole mostly. Bits of work, market stalls – never came to much.'

'And when your mother was alive?'

'Can't remember that much.'

'You said it all went wrong after your mother died.'

Cally shrugged. 'But even then, I might have got it wrong. You see, when I think about the time we lived at home, with Mum there too, I think of it as a happy time. But then I think my memory's playing tricks.'

'Why?'

' 'Cos nothing's that perfect, is it?' Her expression hardened.

'They weren't happy?'

'Dunno. I remember good times. And I remember bad times, rows, shouting an' that. But then, again,' Cally went on, 'he always said he loved her. And she said she loved him. I dunno. My memory, see, playing tricks. I remember later, I remember seeing her in hospital: she looked like a ghost and I just cried and cried. Claire didn't: she never shed a tear, she kept it all bottled up. We're like that. After she died . . .' Cally twirled a lock of hair round and round. 'When it all started going wrong, that was the first time I tried to run away. But one of Dad's mates saw me, on the end of our street, and he told my dad, and Dad came and got me back.'

'And what happened?'

'You see, I ran away lots, so it's all mixed together in my mind.'

'When you say it all started going wrong . . .'

'It was the drinking, mostly. He'd never touched a drop in his life, but he couldn't cope when Mum was gone. And he was left with us two. I think he was scared. That's what made him so strict.'

'Were you frightened of him?'

Cally's fingers froze in her hair. She looked at Agnes. She nodded. 'I'd run away, and I'd try and hide, but someone always told him where I was. But maybe it was 'cos he cared about me, I dunno.'

Agnes thought, briefly, of her husband. It had been part of her life, his violence, a huge and simple fact so obvious that she couldn't step far enough away from it to say, yes, he's a violent man.

'He always favoured Claire, anyway,' Cally said suddenly. 'It was always me who got the worst of it.'

'Cally, no one seems to have a good word to say for him.'

Cally disentangled her fingers from a twist of hair. 'He made enemies. In these last few years. It was the drinking. He was always feeling sorry for himself. He was raised by his mum, and he had a stepfather who he hated. He always said we were lucky to have a dad who really cared about us. But these last few years, he'd screw up. You know, business things and that. And then he'd be accusing people of letting him down.'

'And was he still drinking?'

Cally nodded.

'But when you were little?'

Cally sighed. 'When I was little, it was all different. He was a good dad. He was a laugh. I have good memories. And then, towards the end, it was like having him back.'

'Towards the end?'

'The last few weeks. He was his old self. Trust me to get banged up and miss it.'

'You mean, he was nice again?'

'Yeah. There was this friend of his . . . this bloke he met. He was like – you know, a good influence. He seemed to care about him.'

'Who was he?'

'Dunno. He was a new friend. I only met him once, down the pub, before I was banged up. He seemed really nice, though. It was like he really cared about my dad. That one time I met him, down the pub, I saw him just take away the whisky from in front of my dad and put a glass of water there instead. And my dad, he took it from him. He just laughed, and drank the water. It was like I said, like having my dad back, like the old days. And the one time he came to see me in here, before he . . . he was sober, you know? And he – he tried to say sorry. He said he'd worked it out, and he was staying off the booze, and everything was going to be different, when I got out, and I could come and live with him again . . . and he – he said he was sorry . . .' Her eyes welled with tears.

'Do you think Claire met this guy? This new friend?'

'Claire?' Cally's eyes were suddenly dry. 'I don't care if she did.'

'But Cally – if your dad was getting his act together, and if he was so nice to Claire, why do you think she killed him?'

Cally met her eyes, her distant gaze suddenly sharply focused. ''Cos she always said she would.'

'Why? Why did she say that?'

Cally shrugged. 'Dunno. She just always did.'

'Up until he died?'

'It was more when we were kids, after Mum died. When we still lived there. But then, I'd see her cuddling up with him, and I'd think it's typical of her, to twist him round her finger like that. So maybe she never meant it anyway. Maybe it was

a way of keeping me out of the relationship she had with him.'
Cally smiled a thin smile.

And who else? Agnes wanted to ask. Who else might have
wanted Cliff dead? And why should Mal have shot him? And
surely—

Julius's words came into her mind, quite unbidden, as if he
was standing next to her. Maybe all this insistence that
everyone needs you is just part of being weighed down.

She looked at Cally and said, 'Well, you know her better
than I do.' She touched Cally's arm. 'Take care of yourself.'
She left her sitting in the association room, and let herself out
of the wing.

Agnes walked slowly along the corridor. Perhaps Julius is
right, she thought. Perhaps I could leave all this behind me
and it would make no difference to anyone. Perhaps my
presence in these people's lives has absolutely no influence
over the eventual outcome of those lives. She found herself at
the entrance to Janette's wing, and unlocked the door. She
hesitated by Janette's cell. She knocked, then opened the door.

Janette was lying on her bed. She turned her puffy face
slowly towards Agnes, blinking at her with her heavy-lidded
eyes. Seeing who it was, she lifted herself clumsily on to one
elbow and began to gabble at her. 'You can tell them – they'll
listen to you, won't they? You can tell them I didn't do it.
I never did it, right. I know I left him in a bit of state, but he
had marks on his neck when they found him – I never did
them, honest.' She heaved herself upright, making grabbing
movements towards Agnes's clothes. 'You're the only one
they'll believe, you are. Tell them . . .'

Agnes stepped back instinctively. 'The evidence doesn't
help you,' she said.

'I weren't there, though, was I?

'I'd heard you were.'

'I left him on the riverbank. We left the pub together. I keep goin' through it in my mind: we'd had a few, and then we was messin' about a bit on the river, and he wouldn't listen to reason, so I got really angry. I admit I did – I know what I'm like. And then I walked off. I thought he was behind me. I got home on me own, and then I didn't know it was so late. I'd had a few to drink by then too, so it weren't till the morning that I got worried. And them stupid coppers, they wouldn't believe me neither. I tried to report him missing, and they just laughed.' She sank back on her bed, drained by her own indignation. 'And you,' she suddenly went on, 'you never rang me neither.'

'I tried. What was it about?'

'Too late now, innit?' She seemed to sink into the mattress, heavy with self-pity.

'It was about Jim?'

' 'Course it bleedin' was. I thought he was in danger. He was all nervy, goin' on about some job. I thought you could keep an eye.'

'What job was he talking about?'

'Something to do with his brother. He's no good, that one. I've never liked him. Wouldn't have asked him to the wedding, only my Jim insisted.'

'What was he nervous about?'

'I think they wanted him to do a job for them – you know, courier job. Venn's involved in all sorts. You go round for tea at his place and there's his bird clearing the guns off the kitchen table to lay the plates.'

'And do you think Jim refused?'

'Sure he did. He's not like that, my Jim. He wouldn't get into trouble like that. Bit of security, but nothin' else. He's a fair man, my Jim. Except he's not here no more.' She began to snuffle noisily, and heaved herself up on one arm to reach for a tissue.

Agnes was still standing, her back to the door. 'There's not much I can do now, is there?' she heard herself say.

'Tell them I didn't do it.'

'You've got a lawyer for that.'

'You've got the Lord on your side.' Janette's features softened as she stared trustingly at Agnes.

Agnes looked at her. 'Haven't you?' She knew it was a weak response.

'What's the Lord got to do with the likes of me?' Janette spread her hands out.

Agnes took in the blotchy face, the shapeless grey mass of cardigan. 'You're always welcome at mass.'

'What good's that goin' to do? I can go in that chapel and say all the prayers I can remember, and it still won't bring him back, will it?'

'I don't think there's much else I can do.'

'Story of my bleedin' life, innit? There's men who kill their wives: they stand up in court and plead all sorts in their defence – You see, Your Honour, she nagged me, I couldn't bear it no longer, Your Honour – and the judge feels sorry for them, and they walk, they do. And here's me, pleading not guilty, and they bang me up anyway. All my life it's been like that, the odds stacked against me.' She flopped heavily back on to her pillow. 'Bastard,' she said. 'Typical of him, to bugger off just when I need him. If he was here he'd vouch for me, wouldn't he? Bastard. If he came back now I'd kill him, I would.' She rolled over to face the wall, breathless, and closed her eyes.

Agnes looked at her. It was almost funny, she thought. Funny. And tragic. She left, trying to lock the door quietly behind her, cradling her keys in her hand to prevent them jangling so loudly.

* * *

She walked home through a damp, misty twilight, the sky seared with pink behind the western reaches of the river. She let herself into her flat and sat at her desk, the lamp unlit, allowing the last light of the daylight to seep away. She opened the drawer and took out the letter from her mother and stared at it. The writing made inky shapes in the gathering dark. She got up, went to her kitchen, poured herself a glass of chilled white wine and returned to her desk.

She switched on her lamp, picked up her phone and dialled the number for the central office of her order, which responded with an answering machine. Agnes left a message for her provincial saying that she'd phone the next day, then hung up.

She sipped her wine. Her eye fell on the clock that, technically at least, belonged to her mother. It had stopped some time last year and she had never wound it up. She knew that if she did its four brass spheres would start to spin again, perfect in their precision and their timing: a promise of order in the chaos of universe. She went to it and picked it up, her fingers on the key in the base. A false promise, she thought, tears welling in her eyes. She replaced it on her mantelpiece. She went to her fridge, looked at the bottle of white wine, then put it down and went to her phone. She dialled a number.

'It's Agnes.'

'Sweetie, where are you?'

'At home. I didn't think you'd be there.'

There was a silence.

'Athena, are you all right?'

'Not really, no. Are you?'

'No. Not really, either!'

'That's brilliant. Have you eaten?'

'I was going to ask you the same thing.'

'There's a fab new tapas bar at the end of my road, just off Fulham Broadway – you can't miss it.'

'I feel better already.'

'Half an hour?'

'Make it three quarters. I'll have to get the bus.'

Athena was sitting near the window, an open bottle of Rioja in front of her.

'Thank God for women friends,' she said, pouring a glass for Agnes as she sat down opposite her. 'That's a great lipstick. Is it new?'

'New? Me? I'm a nun, Athena. It's the one I bought about five years ago with you.'

Athena tutted and shook her head. 'It's not much of a life, is it, being a nun?'

For the first time in hours, Agnes felt like laughing.

'And that shirt,' Athena went on, 'that's just right. Neutral. Not too ageing. There's no point us competing with the Young People.'

'Thanks very much.'

'Sweetie, it's just a fact. We're not twenty any more.' She surveyed the room. 'These young women, we could be their mothers.'

'Great. And to think I nearly wore my lime green Lycra disco top.'

'Sweetie, don't be silly. You're a nun.'

'And what's put you in this mid-life mood, then?'

'What do you think?'

'The path of true love not running smooth, maybe?'

'Didn't I tell you I was supposed to be seeing him this evening?'

'Yes, I remember.'

'He cancelled. This morning. On the phone, not even in

person. Barely apologised. Said he'd see me later in the week. Can you imagine?'

'How terrible.'

'No, you don't understand, sweetie. I mean, I've slept with him, it was absolutely fantastic, and now here he is behaving as if the greatest intimacy we've ever shared was taking back an overdue library book.'

'There's that idea people talk about at the moment, isn't there? Men are from Mars—'

'Mars? Mars? Mars is just down the bloody road. If you ask me, men are from some universe so many million light years away they haven't even evolved the power of speech at all, and they're still wallowing in mud and grunting at each other.'

'It would explain the attraction of football.'

'You're not taking this very seriously.'

'Look, you took a chance. If it was me—'

'You'd have done exactly the same.'

Agnes picked up the menu. 'What are patatas bravas?'

'You know I'm right. And I wish that waitress wouldn't treat us as invisible.'

'Menopausal women, Athena, she can't even see us. It's a classic example.'

'Now hold on, I never meant that old. Heaven forbid.' She gestured to the room around her. 'It's all about maturity, isn't it? This lot are just callow youth, when you look closely. Blank pages waiting to be written on. Whereas we're—'

'In our prime?'

Athena raised her glass. 'Absolutely, sweetie. And see, the waitress isn't ignoring us at all.'

They gave their order to a smooth-skinned black-clad young woman.

'Anyway,' Athena went on, refilling their glasses, 'what happened after I left last night?'

184

Agnes ran her hands through her hair. 'Well, Rosanna befriended me in a guarded kind of way, and then Venn asked me to dance, which was kind of weird, and then she danced with him. And then I left.'

'I couldn't make them out at all.'

'No. They danced so well together, it was compelling to watch. They seemed kind of locked together.'

'What I thought was, she loves him, and he's keeping his options open. In other words, just like men and women all around the world.'

'This is new, this cynicism. And what about you and Nic, then?'

'What about us?'

'Well, last time we spoke about him, he was suggesting you buy a house together.'

'He still is.'

'That's hardly keeping one's options open.'

Athena broke off a piece of bread.

'Is it?' Agnes persisted.

Athena sighed. 'The more he senses me drifting away from him, the more he goes on about this living together idea. I can't bear it. When I met him, I wanted us to live together, but whenever I suggested it, he'd say, let's just keep things as they are, and I was really disappointed, wasn't I? You remember. And I thought maybe he didn't love me as much as I loved him. But I kind of got used to it, and now, after lots of hard emotional work, I've grown to like it. I like us living apart.' She sipped her wine. 'And now here he is, trying to change it all again, and I only accepted that we should live apart because *he* wanted it, and it's been so hard won, this acceptance of things as he bloody wanted them. I've had to really work on my feelings, just because of what *he* wanted . . . It makes me so angry. I'm tired of it, Agnes, I really am.'

'Tell him you want to keep things as they are, then. If it's suited him for all these years—'

'It makes me so angry, these chaps. It's always in their favour, isn't it? I mean, like the pill, for example. There's an invention, you'd say, entirely of benefit to women. And what happens? Thirty years on, there's women who want children not having them, and men happily shagging away without a thought for the consequences.'

'Good heavens, Athena, I never thought you'd make such a good Catholic.'

'How do men do it? Like Greg. The odds are entirely in his favour, aren't they? Just because I care more than him.' She was interrupted by the arrival of their food.

'Maybe he cares just as much.' Agnes tasted her chilli sauce with the prongs of her fork.

'Do you think so?' Athena looked up, her face bright with hope.

'But even if he does, that doesn't resolve anything, does it? There's still Nic making plans, and you being angry with him.'

'Yes. Angry. I suppose I am.'

'Would you have slept with Greg if you weren't?'

Athena sighed. She refilled their glasses, then looked at Agnes. 'It's all so confusing. Really, you're lucky, being out of it all. What's so funny?'

'If only I was.'

'But men, sweetie – you nuns are free to leave them on Mars or wherever it is they're supposed to lurk, and get on with your lives.'

'We just have other challenges.'

'Yes. Like pinching other women's men and dancing with them in nightclubs. And you were wearing that skirt of yours. I've always thought you look fantastic in that. No wonder she grabbed him for the next dance.'

* * *

They left the restaurant late. Agnes walked with Athena towards her mansion block. The night was cold and there was an icy wind. Looking up, Agnes could see the stars in the clear night sky. 'It's all about loss, isn't it?' she said.

'What is?' Athena teetered unsteadily on her heels.

'Life. That's what Julius meant, about me having to give up thinking that I'm important to all these people – Cally and Mal and Janette and everyone. Julius thinks that it weighs me down, the way I insist on being needed by everyone, and he was saying that if I went to France, and removed myself from all this, I could concentrate on the important things . . . It made much more sense the way he said it.'

'He hadn't drunk half a bottle of Rioja.'

'But he's right. If I go to France, if I remove myself from all this – you see, Julius says that if I go away, nothing would change for Mal and everyone; their destinies would be the same without me interfering in them.'

'Sweetie, isn't that obvious?'

Agnes sighed. 'Not to me.'

'We all want to be needed, though. It's only human.'

'It's a failing, Athena. It's like whatever Mal's story is, and Janette's, I have to have a part in it. It's a kind of compulsion.'

'There are other stories, though, aren't there? Like the story of you and your mother. Perhaps you should become part of that instead.'

'But that's just it.'

'So, you mean all this other stuff is to give you an excuse not to go away.'

'Pathetic, isn't it? The idea of removing myself from all this, even if it's just for a few days, because that's all the order will give me – it still gives me a huge sense of loss. Almost unbearable.'

187

'Maybe you have to work with that, then.'

Agnes met her eyes. 'That's just what Julius said. Really, Athena, life's going to become very tiresome if you and Julius start agreeing about everything.'

Athena laughed. They'd reached her door, and now she leaned against the lamp-post outside, serious again. 'Will you go to France?'

Agnes looked up. She saw the milky constellations through the yellow haze. She thought of Amy, wishing on stars. She sighed. 'I have to, Athena. I know I have to. It's just a question of how long I can put it off.'

Chapter Fifteen

'I've worked it out, you see.' Ian raised his voice slightly above the hubbub of the café. 'I went to this meditation session last night, and there was a teaching, all about the idea of self. It all makes sense, you see.'

Agnes looked across at him. His face seemed suffused with energy in the light from the terracotta wall lamp above them.

'It's a paradox at the heart of things, you see,' he went on. 'We're constantly running away from ourselves, and yet, if we simply stop and experience the self, experience the self within the moment, then what we're really experiencing is non-self.'

Agnes sprinkled some sugar on her cappuccino.

'And so, it's all about relinquishment, about letting go of all the things that prevent us just being in that moment. And that means the self. Or rather, what we experience as self. I thought you didn't take sugar?'

Agnes looked up and smiled. 'I just felt like it.'

'Anyway – where was I? Oh, yes, about giving up the self to live fully in the moment.'

Agnes stirred her coffee. 'I think you have to watch it, though, that one. I think there's a hair's breadth between experiencing the moment and grasping at it. If you try to grab hold of the moment, then you lose it.'

'I didn't know you were a Buddhist.'

'No. It's the same for us, though. Only I'd call it experiencing God's love, rather than the moment. But that stillness, that sense of oneness – we're all after that, aren't we?'

'And here I was thinking I'd found some great wisdom to share with you.'

'There's no need to sulk. Just because I know the theory doesn't mean I'm any good at it in practice.'

He laughed. 'Last one to reach enlightenment's a cissy. And if we're going to see Amy before lunch, we'd better get going.'

'I didn't expect any more visitors.' Amy was lying on her bed. She sat up slowly, but the effort seemed to tire her.

'Any more visitors?' Ian repeated.

'What with Sister Imelda coming here last night. I thought that was my lot for a while.' She smiled weakly.

'Imelda?' Agnes couldn't conceal her surprise.

'Yes, she came to see me last night.'

'Last night?' Agnes echoed.

'Yes.'

Agnes felt suddenly anxious. 'What did she want?'

'I'm not sure. I think she wanted me to help her, but I'm not sure I did.'

'You? Help her?' Agnes glanced across at Ian, who was staring at Amy.

'She asked me lots of questions about my baby.'

No wonder Amy looked tired. Agnes wished she'd been there to protect her.

'I was frightened when I saw her,' Amy was saying. 'I thought she was just coming to be horrible to me again, but she was quite nice, really. She asked about my baby, and how did I know she was coming back, and I told her about what the Lord has been saying to me, and she listened, then. She even asked me to pray with her, although when I looked at her I could see that she'd closed her mind to the Lord, and there wasn't much point, but I didn't say so. And she talked about bleeding too.'

'Bleeding?' Agnes was so bewildered, she could barely take in what Amy was saying.

Amy fiddled with her bedcover. She glanced at Ian, then said, 'You know. Monthly bleeding. Do nuns get that like other women?'

Agnes smiled. Ian was looking out of the window through the bars. 'Yes,' Agnes said 'Yes we do. All at the same time, if we're living in community.'

Amy nodded. 'Like here. Anyway, Imelda says hers has stopped and so that's it for her. I think she meant something about not having a baby any more, but she didn't say it like that.' Agnes stared at Amy. 'But it's funny,' Amy went on, 'because she wouldn't cry about it. I asked her why not, and she said if she started to cry about it now her tears would become a river, a flood, like – um – something, something melting, she said – what was it, like an iceberg? No, I know, a glacier, she said, and it would wash away everything she'd made of her life, and maybe even drown her too. And then I realised that was why she couldn't listen to the Lord when we prayed, because she's locked herself away for so many years, locked in the tears. I felt sorry for her then, even though she's said such horrible things to me.'

'When?' Ian was watching her. 'When has she said these things to you?'

'She used to come in the night, sometimes, when I was first here, before you started coming instead.'

'What did she say? What sort of things?' Ian's gaze was intense, focused on Amy like light through a magnifying glass.

'She said I'd never see my baby again because my baby was pure and innocent and had gone to heaven, and I'd go straight to hell because of . . .' Amy faltered, and the radiance of her face grew dim. 'Because of what I'd done.'

Ian reached out and took both her hands. 'Oh my poor . . .' He checked himself. 'It's preposterous. I'll talk to someone. It's quite out of the question that anyone here should be able to behave like that. I'll have words with the authorities—'

Agnes touched his arm. 'Shhh. Go on, Amy.'

'That's all really. Then you took over from her.' Amy lifted her face towards Agnes. 'And then she didn't come no more. So I was quite surprised to see her last night.'

'When you prayed with her—' Agnes began. 'It must have been difficult. After what she'd said.'

Amy shook her head. 'When I saw it was her I was a bit upset. But when I looked at her, and I saw what the Lord Jesus must see when he looks at her, I just felt sorry for her . . . because, you see, it's been years for her, hasn't it, not knowing if she'll see her baby again? But for me, Jesus says I won't have to wait much longer.' She smiled, and Ian smiled too.

'What did she mean, about her baby?' Agnes asked.

'She didn't talk about a baby.'

'But you just said – about seeing her baby . . . ?'

'Oh, no, it was nothing she said. She didn't say anything. I just knew.'

Ian looked down at his hands, which were still holding Amy's. He stared at them as if surprised.

'I knew because—' Amy hesitated. 'Because of how she looked when I showed her my baby. I don't show many people but she seemed so upset.'

'Y-your baby?' Ian looked up and let go of Amy's hands.

Amy glanced around, then put her hand under her pillow and withdrew a colour photograph. She cradled it against her, then kissed it, and only then allowed Ian and Agnes to look at it. The photo showed a pretty, smiling baby, in a lacy white dress, lying on a pink cushion.

Amy was biting back tears. 'That was when she looked like she was going to cry, you see. When I showed her.'

'I'm not surprised,' Ian murmured, blinking hard.

Amy gave the photo another kiss, then tucked it away again.

Ian looked at his watch, as if it reminded him of another, parallel world. He glanced at Agnes. 'We should go,' he said, reluctantly.

Agnes nodded.

Ian stood up slowly, still drawn to Amy, to her peculiar, illuminated calm. She dabbed the tears from her eyes with a tissue, and still managed to smile at them as they left.

'You should have a word with Imelda's superiors, about her behaviour.' Ian was striding forcefully along the corridor. 'It's quite out of the question that Imelda should behave that way.'

'Yes.'

'Don't you think?'

'Mmm.'

They paused by a door, which Agnes unlocked. 'You're very quiet,' Ian said.

'Am I?'

'If you won't talk to your convent, I will.' They came out of the Healthcare wing into the main prison building. 'I'll just say it's quite inappropriate to place someone like her in a job like this, don't you think? Agnes, what is it? You're not listening.'

'Sorry? I was thinking about that photo. The way Amy – the the way she . . . loves it. Like a mother.'

'It's hardly surprising—'

'It's that expression, isn't it? To love someone like your own child.'

Ian looked at her sideways, slowing his pace. 'And?'

Agnes shrugged. She picked up her keys to let them pass through a door. 'I don't know. It's funny to think we were all babies once. Perhaps when we're babies, we all have . . . a mother's love.' She locked the door behind them. 'Whatever happens afterwards.'

Ian noticed the crack in her voice. They walked in silence to the main entrance, and paused by the door.

'But you will talk to someone, will you?' He looked out at the metallic sky. 'About Imelda?'

'Me?'

'She must be moved.'

'Ian – it's not that easy.'

'But as employers—'

'Employers?' Agnes almost laughed.

'Have I made a joke?'

'Ian, it's a religious order.'

'I don't understand.'

'You certainly don't. If our superiors don't know anything of Imelda's past, it would be breaking confidences to tell them. Particularly as I don't actually know what's caused her to behave like this. And if they do know, the last thing they'll want is to be reminded of it.'

'It's so archaic . . .'

'Ian, our order is our life, our home, the repository of all our hopes and aspirations. It's our new beginning, a new life to which we submit, totally. It feeds us, shelters us, and in turn we owe it everything. We've handed over our past, our memories, our future. Whatever happened to Imelda, and God knows, we have no idea what that actually was, she's handed it over. She's made some kind of pact, either with the order's knowledge or without it. It's none of my business.'

Ian turned away from the outside world and looked at her.

'But you, Agnes – have you given your order all your memories, your past, your future?'

Agnes reached up and ran her fingers down one of the bars on the door. 'I'm not a good example,' she said. They opened the door and both of them walked out of the prison, out into the courtyard, through the main gate into the London traffic.

At home there was a message on her answering machine. Her provincial had tried to get hold of her: could she please phone?

She dialled the number straight away and spoke to Sister Christiane's secretary. Sister Christiane was unavailable; could she take a message?

'Yes, um, yes, please. It's Sister Agnes ... It's just – my mother's state of health has worsened – yes, in France, that's right – and I wanted to ask permission to visit her again. I know I've been once, but she's much worse, and um – she's asking for me herself. If you could let her know ... thanks. Yes, okay. Goodbye.'

She replaced the phone. She wondered if she'd changed. The old Agnes would have just bought a ticket and gone, by now, and sorted out the permission afterwards. But no, she realised, she hadn't changed at all. Asking permission was simply a symptom of her reluctance to go.

She looked out of the window. The geometric lines of the tower blocks were etched in flinty grey against the sky. She thought about Imelda's faith, her stoic discipline, her unquestioning obedience to the order. And yet Amy had described her as locked away from the Lord. Agnes shivered, and switched on her bar fire. She thought about the warmth of Amy's faith, her generosity of spirit. She thought about Imelda's feelings, kept on ice so as not to melt. Perhaps there was always a high price to pay.

She picked up the phone directory and looked up Travel

Agents. She wrote down a local address, rehearsing in her mind, Hello, I want to book a flight to Nice. She put away the phone book, and folded the telephone numbers into her notebook. Tomorrow, maybe.

' "Arise, shine; for thy light is come, and the glory of the Lord is risen upon thee . . ." ' Madeleine read the lesson for evening prayer.

Agnes was surprised to see Imelda sitting in her usual place, straight-backed and composed.

' "Lift up thine eyes round about, and see: they gather themselves together, they come to thee; thy sons shall come from far, and thy daughters shall be nursed at thy side." '

Imelda bent her head. Her hands went to her cheeks, her fingers digging into her face until her nails left red marks. She began to murmur, 'nursed at thy side', repeating the words in an odd monotone.

Madeleine finished the reading, and went back to her place. As the silence filled the chapel, Imelda looked up in surprise, blinking around her as if awakening from a dream. She placed her hands slowly in her lap, gripping her fingers together, and straightened her back again, stone-faced.

Photographs, Agnes thought, waking the next morning. I dreamed of photographs. Pink cushions, and wedding gowns, and little babies, and white frilly dresses, all shuffled like a pack of cards.

On her mantelpiece her mother's clock sat, its very stillness a reproach.

The travel agent's is on the way to the prison, Agnes thought.

She dressed in her jeans and sweater, and made herself a pot of tea, her mood as heavy as the day. Outside, the morning struggled to break through the wintry sky, and the urban skyline seemed flat in the dull light. Photographs, Agnes thought, finishing her tea and putting on her coat.

She walked past the travel agent's and went straight to the prison.

Cally doesn't need me, she repeated to herself, walking straight past Cally's cell. Imelda doesn't need me, she said, letting herself into her office, finding it empty. Janette – Janette needs everyone, so one person less won't make any difference. All the same, Agnes thought, locking her office door again, I might as well say goodbye.

'It's all right for you, innit?' Janette was sitting on her bed, exuding hostility. 'Coming in here and saying you're buggering off somewhere. South of France, I'll bet.'

'Actually, um, well, it's only that she happens to live there—'

'Makes me bloody sick, all you do-gooders, saying you understand our problems, us inmates, and then you all go back to your homes, and we're still stuck here. And you nuns are the worst of all: you don't even have to live in this world, do you? You can just shut yourself away when you've had enough.'

Agnes opened her mouth to speak. But isn't that just what you—she was about to say, but then Janette interrupted again.

'See, people like me, ordinary people, right, we have to live whatever life the good Lord sends us, right? We have to try and make it work. We can't just escape into our little world whenever it goes wrong. It's like me and my Jim, right – we had our ups and downs, but we tried, God knows we tried . . .' A huge tear welled up in one eye and trickled down her mottled cheek.

'My mother's dying—' Agnes heard herself blurt out the words, words she hadn't meant to say.

Janette nodded. 'Mine died five years ago. Almost to the day,' she added. 'I still miss her. Not a day goes by when I don't pray to the Lord to keep her in His care. Is she very ill, your mother? Lord, how mine suffered in her last years. That's my regret, you know: how I didn't see as much of her as I should've done in those last years. We had a bit of a difficult relationship when I was a kid, I s'pose, but still, she was my old mum when all's said and done, weren't she?' Again, another tear rolled down her cheek, following the weathered crevices of her face. She picked up her comb and fiddled with it, then looked up at Agnes. 'She used to beat me, my mum. Bet you didn't know that, did you?'

It was like a challenge, and Agnes wasn't sure what to say.

'Regular as clockwork. I'd always know when one was coming. I can remember now. I'd be about eight. I came in from school and she'd put out a drink for me – that orange stuff you used to have in them days, orange squash, and a biscuit maybe. And I sat on my own and drank the drink and ate the biscuit, and I used to eat it real slowly 'cos I thought, this is the time when I'm a normal little girl; all the time I'm sitting here on my own eating and drinking these things what she's put out for me, this is what normal people's lives are like. I used to think about the other girls in my class, and I used to think of them having a drink and a biscuit after school, just like me. And as soon as I finished I knew, regular as clockwork, she'd come out of her bedroom and I'd be for it . . .' Janette grew suddenly angry. 'What do you know about that? Eh? You in your convent? Shut away from all that? Eh?' Her face reddened, and her gaze, which had been unfocused, suddenly fixed itself on Agnes.

'More than you know,' Agnes managed to say, but Janette wasn't listening any more.

'Mind you,' Janette went on, lost in her own reverie again, 'I was a right difficult kid. I was asking for it half the time.'

Agnes stood up, and unlocked the cell door. She glanced back at Janette, who was staring at the bedspread, chewing over her jumbled memories.

One person less won't make any difference at all, Agnes thought, locking the cell behind her again.

She went back to her office, phoned her provincial and got put straight through to Sister Christiane. They had a few amicable words, and Sister Christiane wished her well. Agnes put on her coat, vaguely wondering where Imelda was, locked the office behind her, and walked straight to the travel agent's.

'Hello,' she said to the girl behind the counter, who had bright blue eyeshadow and thick mascara, 'I'd like to buy an air ticket to Nice. Return.'

Chapter Sixteen

Agnes was aware that her phone had been ringing for some time. Eventually she stirred herself from her bed and picked it up.

'Yes?'

'Ah, you are there, then.'

'Oh, Julius.'

'Only, the order assured me you were back from France, and you haven't been answering the phone, and I was beginning to worry . . .'

'Yes, I'm back.'

'From the sound of it . . . perhaps I'm intruding. Phone me, maybe, at some point . . . when you're ready.'

'Julius?' He'd gone. Agnes replaced the phone, and flopped back on to her pillows. Then she got up, switched on her answering machine and got back into bed.

Some time later the phone rang again. Agnes heard her machine pick up the message.

'Agnes, it's Eleanor. I thought maybe I'd see you today. It's just we knew you were back and . . . anyway, maybe you could ring me at the prison as soon as possible. Thank you.'

Agnes pulled the covers around her ears. She fell into a confused and dozing sleep, and woke to hear Athena's voice on her answering machine.

'Oh, you poor sweetie, bet it was terrible in France. Loads to talk about. Phone me. Byeee.'

Agnes smiled. She stared at the ceiling. The afternoon sunlight flickered through her curtains, and she thought about the flight back to London yesterday. Closer to God, she'd wondered, hurtling through the heavens above the clouds. Unfettered, like Julius had said. Lightening the spirit. Certainly, Agnes thought, getting out of bed and switching on her bar fire, she'd felt her spirit lighten as they'd reached London.

She showered, made some tea and phoned Athena.

'Yes, it was terrible. Are you free this evening?'

'I certainly am, sweetie. Tapas bar again?'

'Fine. Eight-ish?'

'See you then.'

'And how's Greg?' Agnes looked at Athena, who was wearing a new maroon silk shirt and matching lipstick. 'You look great, by the way.'

Athena smiled smugly. 'Greg's fine, actually.'

'All right for some.'

'Poor sweetie. Did you have a rough time?'

'You could put it like that.'

'Despite it being what, twenty-five degrees? Sunshine every day, beautiful beach, wonderful food . . . ?'

'It almost compensated,' Agnes laughed. 'And so Greg's made up for his thoughtless phone manner?'

'It's a boy thing, isn't it, being hopeless on the phone? It turned out he was desperately sorry. I saw him while you were away. We went out for dinner and afterwards . . .'

'Yes?'

Athena leaned back in her chair. 'Mmmmm.'

'So the path of true love is back on course again?'

Athena beamed. 'Absolutely. Although, sweetie, on course for what? At least Nic's stopped going on about this house business. In fact, he's leaving me in peace, thank goodness. Anyway, enough about me, what about you? How was she, your mother?'

Agnes poured herself another glass of wine and drank half of it.

'That bad?' Athena waited.

Eventually Agnes said, 'She's much worse, physically. She can't speak at all. I thought at first she was pretending, but she isn't. She doesn't speak to anyone. And' – Agnes drank more wine – 'she didn't seem to recognise me. I showed her the note she'd written – Yvette, her friend suggested it – but it didn't seem to mean anything to her. I sat beside her, and talked to her, although I couldn't think of anything to say. Yvette had to fill in most of the conversation. She responds to her because she sees her all the time. The first time I visited, I gave her back that clock, the one that was hers, and she started singing some children's song about a clock, and kind of chuckling. I left the clock there, but it clearly doesn't register with her.'

'Did you see her much?'

'Once a day, and I was there three days. The second day was much the same, except . . . when I was leaving . . . it was strange . . .'

'What?'

'She kind of focused on me, just when I was thinking there was no point staying any longer, and she stared at me, and tried to speak. And then she – it was weird: she had this piece of bread she'd saved, from breakfast or something – she'd obviously saved it very carefully, and she grabbed my hand, and placed this bread in my hand, like that, closing my fingers round it, and she was looking at me as if she knew exactly who I was—' Agnes gulped some wine.

'How odd.' Athena frowned. 'Saving food – it's a kind of

instinct, isn't it? Some of the old people in my village, the ones who lost everything in the war, they used to do that – fill their pockets with leftovers, just in case.'

'And she was really staring at me, as if she saw me properly. And – and she was crying . . .'

Athena reached across and patted her hand. 'You did the right thing, to visit.'

'Except it's too late. The next day, the last day, I could have been anyone; she ignored me, mostly. I'd brought the photos with me – Yvette's idea again – she's a really nice woman – and there's a young woman there, a nurse, Celine, who does a lot of the caring. At least she's in good hands . . . where was I?'

'The photos?'

''Oh, yes, well, I brought them, you know, the wedding one, and me as a baby . . .

'Did she look at them?'

'She gave them all a cursory glance, as if they were toys she'd lost interest in.'

'Even the baby one?'

Agnes nodded. 'Even that one.'

'That must have been hard for you.'

'Yes. It was. Except it's my own fault, not visiting till now. But there was one odd thing.'

'What was that?'

'Remember that photo we thought didn't belong, the one with that tower in the background, and that row of cottages, and that little girl standing there?'

'Yes?'

'I was getting ready to leave, as there was no point me staying, and I was gathering my stuff, and packing the photos away in my bag, and my mother was lying very quiet. And we realised, Yvette and I, that she'd got hold of a photograph. And she was staring at it, gripping it with both hands. And it was that photo. And she was calm, then. Just looking at it. She'd ignored all the others, and that one was the only one she wanted to look at.'

'Did she recognise something about it?'

'That's what I thought. But Yvette thought not. She said sometimes she's behaved as if all sorts of things meant something, when they turned out not to.'

'Did you leave the photo for her?'

'I did then. But when I came to say goodbye, before I caught my flight back, she was asleep, and Yvette gave it back to me. She said it had upset her.'

'So are you glad you went?'

Agnes nodded. 'Yes. It gave me a kind of view of things . . . On the plane back, I started to think about her life: all that wealth and privilege and a husband who neglected her, and a baby that she didn't want—'

'You don't know that.'

'I went back to the old house. There's some family friend living there now, rattling around on her own in all those rooms. I walked through the village, up the drive. I haven't been back there since . . . not for years. I must have visited with Hugo a couple of times. Not since then.'

'Did you go in?'

Agnes shook her head. 'I couldn't face old Mme Grillon. Horrible old woman. She'd like nothing better than to show me round my own house. And also, Yvette said it might upset me – it's been rather neglected. Mind you, it was never that well looked after when we were there.'

'How did you feel?'

'I don't know. It's been so long. It was nice to see it there. It's a beautiful place.'

'Will you inherit it?'

'Heavens, Athena, I hadn't thought.' Agnes stared at her. 'I really hadn't thought. When my mother dies . . . although, it'll probably turn out that there's all sorts of debts to be settled . . . And if I do get it, the order will get their hands on it.'

'They're terrible, aren't they?'

Agnes smiled. 'It was good to go and see it. I think my past has held such terrors for me, and somehow, with my mother fading from view as she is, the terrors are lessening. On the plane, I had lots of weird thoughts. I thought about the first hours of our lives, all of us. We come into the world, and our mother is what we know. And we may be instantly loved, or not. And then we become people, with memories, and what we know of being mothered comes from much later in our lives . . . but we can't know what it was like, our first moments, our sense of being wanted or not. It's like Amy, at the prison: she really loved her baby, even though she killed her—'

'What did you say?' Athena's glass was half way to her lips.

'Oh, it's just a girl at the prison—'

'She – she killed her?'

'It sounds mad, now I hear you say it. Prison's so topsy-turvy. There she is, a murderess, and she seems to know more about faith than I do. Her faith is simple and generous, and she's just lit up by it, and she loves that baby so much—'

'But you just said she—'

'She loved her baby so much she had to kill her. It's just an extreme form of love, that's all.'

'I'm not sure the courts would agree with you.'

'No. I'm sure they won't.' Agnes shrugged. 'Perhaps I'm wrong. Prison skews your view of things.'

'Have you been back yet?'

'No. I'll go in tomorrow.'

'We'd better go. Early nights all round. I'm seeing Greg again tomorrow.' Athena grinned.

They left the bar and went out into the street. Athena shivered in her short coat as they walked to Agnes's bus stop. 'I know, come to supper, next week some time – Monday?'

'Sure. That would be nice. Maybe I'll be less serious by then.'

'Maybe it's time we were grown up. One of us, anyway.'

'Does it have to be me?' Agnes laughed.

'Well, don't look at me, sweetie. Here's your bus.'

As the bus pulled away from the stop, Agnes saw through the steamed-up window Athena still standing there, waving, wobbling on her ridiculous heels.

Agnes knocked on Eleanor's door and then opened it. Eleanor looked up.

'Ah, it's you. I was rather hoping you'd come in today. Your order was expecting you yesterday—'

'Yes. I had to, um, recover.'

'Of course. How's your mother?'

Agnes sighed. 'What does one say? As well as can be expected. In other words, old, frail, ill . . .' Agnes sat down opposite Eleanor. 'How are things here?'

'Tense, to be honest. That's why I'm doing overtime. It's this time of year. Everyone's more upset than usual, and Amy seems to have become a focus for general hostility. We can't let her out into the general wings at all, and we can't really keep her in Healthcare much longer, but I don't want to segregate her . . . And Janette's got a new friend on her wing, a trouble-maker, and between them they seem to be able to brew up all sorts of bad behaviour . . . I thought Janette was bad last time, but this continuous whining about her innocence is driving lots of women mad . . .'

'How long was I away? It feels like ages.'

'Five days? Not long.'

'How's Cally?'

Eleanor grimaced. 'I'd be more sympathetic to her if she'd help herself. She's retreated into a drugged stupor. God knows where they get the stuff. She's only tested positive once but I know for a fact she's using all the time. And she's self-harming again. I personally removed anything remotely resembling a sharp edge from her cell, and she managed to cut herself with a biro that she nicked from education and split in two . . .'

'She's supposed to be out of here before Christmas, isn't she?'

'She'll get more time if she tests positive again. It's this Mal business – it hasn't helped her at all. Ian was asking when you were back. He's in his office today. He wants to talk to you.'

'I'll phone him.' Agnes stood up to leave.

'The chaplaincy's been a bit unreliable in your absence,' Eleanor said. Her eyes were lowered, and she moved a file across her desk.

'Yes. I know.'

'I trust your order is aware of Imelda's problems.'

'I'm sure they are.'

'Only we do rely on our chaplaincy services . . .' Eleanor looked up. Her expression was neutral, her face set.

'Of course. I'll do what I can.'

'Thank you.'

At the door Agnes hesitated. 'Imelda's not usually like this.'

'No. I know.'

Agnes had her hand on the door handle. 'I suppose sometimes life throws something at us that we're not prepared for. I mean, we think we can go on as we are for ever, and then something happens that turns everything upside-down . . . Anyway, I'd better get to work.'

As she closed the door, Agnes caught sight of Eleanor. She was staring after her, her face flushed with feeling. Agnes had the impression that she'd said too much.

'Hello, Ian, it's Sister Agnes.' Agnes tucked the phone receiver under her chin.

'I've missed you.'

'Thank you. It's nice to be back.'

'How was your mother?'

'Pretty bad.'

'I went to a teaching the other night, and they said that we have to remember that our parents are just gateways into this world, and we mustn't attach too closely to family love.'

'How very helpful.'

'Don't be like that.'

'I suppose even Christ said, leave your mother and your father and follow me . . .'

'There you are, then.'

'Anyway, leaving the important things for a moment to concentrate on merely worldly ones, what news?'

'Lots. Have you time for a coffee?'

'Lunch, even.'

'Lunch, then. Usual place – one-ish?'

'See you then.'

Agnes hung up. She checked through various papers that had accumulated in her pigeon-hole. Imelda's desk seemed not to have been touched, but according to the rota she had been in most days. Agnes worked through some paperwork, signing forms, writing letters. She thought of going to see Cally, or Janette, or any of the others, but decided to leave it until later.

* * *

The café was crowded. She ordered a smoked salmon sandwich and a cappuccino, and sat down opposite Ian, who'd saved her a place in the lunchtime rush.

'So?'

Ian smiled at her. 'So?'

'How's Mal?'

'Not brilliant. Won't say a word about anything. He wants to plead guilty and get it over with, he said. He can't face a trial. His lawyer can't decide whether it's because he did do it, or because he didn't.'

'He had no motive.'

'Don't know about that. It seems from what the police are saying that Venn runs quite a complicated and lucrative business. His club is part of it, but he also provides the door staff for other clubs. And if you control the security, then you control the dealing. Venn's a rich man, you see.'

'That still doesn't explain what Cliff had to do with anything.'

'Cliff was a loser. He lived on the dole. Recently he'd been driving a flashy car, and showing off a lot.'

'And he was connected to Venn?'

'Mal said so, yes. They'd met recently, through Claire. Mal's lawyer, Chris, he thinks there was some kind of job going on, through Venn, that Mal and Cliff were both involved with.'

'And there was Jim, too. Janette said Jim had been talking about doing some job for Venn.'

'Doesn't surprise me.'

'But have they checked out Venn?'

'Sure, they're very keen to lay something on Venn. They searched his place, a nice detached house in Kent, pretty village, you know. Found various weaponry. He's got licences

209

for them all, though. They can't touch him at the moment, but I expect they're biding their time.'

'Cally's release date is soon, you know.'

'I gather she's not in a brilliant state.'

Agnes shook her head. 'Not really, no.'

'I think I'm going to give up this job.'

'We all have times when—'

'No, seriously. I've been thinking about it. I can't bear what the system does to people. I've realised that if I really care about people, then this isn't the way to help them. Like Amy . . .'

'Have you seen her?'

'Yes.' He concentrated on cutting his remaining sandwich into two neat halves.

'And?'

'There was a teaching at the centre last weekend, about feelings, about how they're illusions.' He subdivided one half of sandwich. 'You see, we can set ourselves free.'

'What, from our feelings?'

'Yes.'

'Why should we?'

Ian looked up at her. 'Because – well, you see, this monk said, they get in the way.'

'But what if they're true?'

'But we convince ourselves they're true, because we're so attached to the idea of self, and that we're the person feeling whatever the feeling is.'

'But love is a feeling.' Agnes watched Ian divide the other half-sandwich. 'Surely,' Agnes went on, 'love is – love is what we are, when we're being true to ourselves.'

'I think even that isn't quite . . . I mean, if I say I love someone, it can still be . . . it can still be an illusion.'

'Your religion sounds no fun at all.'

Ian smiled at her. 'Perhaps it's not supposed to be fun.'

'My tradition—' Agnes began. 'My tradition is passionate. It has Christ's passion at the very centre. Jesus shared our humanity, so if we love Christ, we're loving God as a human. We're allowed to feel, to suffer, to love, to feel joy. And surely your Buddha – aren't you supposed to devote yourself to him?'

'We haven't done much about the Buddha yet.'

Agnes shook her head. 'It's easy to take a religion away from its culture and call it pure, and then anyone who follows it can make of it what they like.'

'Whereas your tradition has always been utterly united, with no disputes over doctrine, no wars, no unspeakable treatments of heretics . . .'

Agnes looked up at him. She smiled. 'Okay, okay.'

Ian met her gaze. His face reddened. 'I didn't want us to fall out over . . . I mean, I'm only just learning about this stuff. It's just quite disturbing; it's kind of feeding into areas of my life and making me question everything. I didn't mean to criticise your way of life. And I ought to get back to the office.'

At the counter, Agnes produced a crisp ten-pound note and insisted on paying.

'I'm surprised I deserve it,' he said, as they went out into the street.

'It does me good, to have my beliefs questioned from time to time.'

'It strikes me you do a pretty good job of that yourself.' Ian smiled at her.

Agnes laughed.

'Perhaps you're right,' Ian said, as they set off along the street. 'About feelings. It's like Amy,' he said, wrapping his scarf around his neck against the icy wind. 'The way I feel, you know, when I'm with her . . . She's – she's like no one I've ever met before. It's crazy, but just sitting in the same room as her, that awful hospital cell, I feel . . . kind of . . . it just makes me feel better. Don't you go that way at these lights?'

Agnes glanced at him. His cheeks were pink, perhaps from the cold. 'Yes,' she said.

They stopped to say their goodbyes. Ian shifted from foot to foot. 'It's all a bit—'

'A bit what?'

'Just rather a lot to think about at the moment.' He left her at the traffic lights and loped away down the road towards his office.

She went to Julius's church for evening mass. She sat in the lady chapel, looking up at the darkened windows, which were dotted with light from the flickering candles.

Afterwards Julius made them tea in his office. 'It was nice to hear your voice on the phone,' he said. 'I wasn't sure when you were coming back.'

'Well, I'm back now,' Agnes said.

He poured boiling water on to tea leaves. 'How was it?'

'Oh, you know. Okay.'

'Agnes—' His tone was reproachful.

'I've said all there is to say about it,' she said. 'She's old and ill and I know if I'd visited earlier at least she'd have recognised me . . . but if I'm honest with myself I'm relieved to have left it till now.' He was shaking his head. 'I'm just telling you the truth, Julius,' Agnes said. 'And anyway, at lunchtime I was talking to Ian, you know, the probation officer, and he was saying all this Buddhist stuff about feelings being illusory, and how you just have to see your parents as gateways and not attach to them too much. I did argue with him, about love and everything, I felt it was my duty as a good nun – there's no need to smirk like that – but I've been thinking about it all afternoon, and I thought, it is rather liberating, isn't it?'

'Agnes, I never smirk.' He handed her a mug of tea. 'And with all due respect, I'm not sure your friend has quite got the point. Surely it's about seeing feelings for what they are? That's not the same as denying them. Sitting quietly with one's feelings is one thing; watching them, letting them go, that's one thing. Trying to push them away in the belief that they're illusions is altogether different. I mean,' he went on, settling down in a chair opposite her, 'it's like with your mother. If you weren't feeling a sense of loss about her, it would be odd. More than odd: it would be less than human. I believe God wishes us to feel, in fact, I know he does, but the point is not to get bogged down in it, not to allow it to weigh you down. Not to allow it to obscure your own dialogue with God's love. Increasingly I find,' Julius went on, 'that it's all about just accepting God's love, this huge, compassionate presence that's all around us – and all human suffering is simply our resistance to God's love. It's easier to ignore it than to accept it, a lot of the time, and that's where our troubles start. Why are you staring at me like that?'

'Was I?' She smiled at him. 'I was just wondering why you're always right.'

He laughed, and shook his head.

'No, really,' Agnes said. 'You are. You were right about me going to France. I went back to work today, and nothing had changed – well, hardly anything, certainly nothing I could have influenced in any way at all. There was no point me thinking I was so important to those people's lives. I saw Janette in passing this afternoon and she hadn't even missed me. So now I'm just going to concentrate on my own story, not everyone else's; I'm just going to get on with being a good nun . . . Julius, that was definitely a smirk.'

'Nonsense, an affectionate smile, that's all.'

'Hmmm. As you would say.'

She let herself into her flat with a sense of relief. She switched on all the lights, allowing the warmth and light of her surroundings to soothe her. She filled a saucepan with water, and opened a cupboard to look for pasta, when her intercom buzzed.

She stared at it. Athena? Claire? She picked up the receiver. 'Who is it?'

'Is that Sister Agnes?' It was a gruff, male voice.

'Who's that?'

'You don't know me. I'm called Des. It's about Mal, and Cliff. Cliff Fisher . . .'

Agnes pressed the buzzer, heard the door open, heard heavy footsteps on the staircase. A man appeared in her doorway, tall, thick-set, wearing an old-fashioned heavy overcoat in navy wool. He had grizzled hair, and a stubbly grey beard. He put out his hand. 'Des Ambler,' he said, shaking her hand. His fingers felt warm and large. 'I'm sorry to bother you, but I didn't know what else to do. You see, Mal didn't kill Cliff.'

'Why are you so sure?' Agnes pulled out her armchair for him to sit down.

'Because I know who did.'

Chapter Seventeen

Agnes poured two glasses of whisky and handed one to Des. He sat down, shifting uncomfortably in the chair. He looked at the glass as he held it in his hand.

'So,' Agnes said, sitting down opposite him, 'who did kill Cliff?'

He raised his glass, then drained its contents in one go and put the empty glass down on her desk. He wiped his mouth on the back of his hand. 'I had to talk to someone, see,' he said, his voice rough with the whisky.

Agnes waited, sipping her drink.

'And I couldn't go to the police, obviously,' he went on. He was still wearing his coat, and now he began slowly to unbutton it.

'Why not?'

He looked at her, surprised. 'Because these guys, they have too many friends.'

Agnes nodded.

'I thought of coming to see you because I met Claire the other day – one of the twins, you know? I don't usually have much to do with her, but she came by the stall, and we were talking about Cliff and that. She said that you were helping Cally. She told me where you lived. I hope that's okay.'

This seemed odd. Agnes tried again. 'So – who did kill Cliff?'

Des sighed, as if the word weighed heavily on him. 'Venn.'

'How do you know it was Venn?'

'Because that night, I saw Cliff. I was down the pub, and he came in, as usual, but he was in a right old state. And he was saying he was going to get someone. He was often doing that – he always asked too much of people and then got angry when they let him down. And I said, who, Cliff? But he wouldn't say. He just kept saying, this time it's for real – words to that effect, you know. And then he opened his jacket, and I saw he had a gun there. And I got scared then. I ain't never seen him with a gun before.'

Agnes got up and refilled his glass. He took a mouthful of whisky, then went on, 'I asked him where he got the gun, and he said he'd been working for someone, and he needed it for his work. And I thought it must be Venn, then – he's the only guy round our way who dishes out guns like that. And then Cliff said, I'm going to shoot him with his own gun, and that way the police wouldn't know it was him. Well, I tried to reason with him, you can imagine. I said, the coppers ain't stupid. But he was that angry. I've seen Cliff angry before but it weren't nothing like this. And I said, why, Cliff, what's he done? But he wouldn't say. And then he left the pub, still going on about it. I left with him, but he said not to follow him. I didn't know what to do.'

'What did you do?'

'I walked him home. We were mates, me and Cliff, go back a long way, and he trusts me . . . he trusted me.' He cleared his throat, then went on, 'I managed to get him home. Made him promise to stay there and sleep on it. I left him then . . . but—' Des sighed, a heavy breath that lifted his wide shoulders. 'Something must have happened, 'cos he was shot that night.'

'In his own home.'

'Yes.'

216

'So you don't know it was Venn.'

'Yeah, I do, 'cos Claire said – she said she saw him later on. He'd gone out again – he came for Venn.'

'Claire said this? When?'

'When I heard he died, I went round, the next day – afternoon it must have been. Claire was there. She was in a terrible state, sitting on her own in her dad's flat. She said she'd been in the club with Venn, and Cliff had come in, much the worse for drink, and had threatened Venn. And Venn had refused to go outside with him, and Cliff had gone. But later, right, Venn said he was going to find Cliff. And he left the club, and no one saw him again that night.'

'And Claire was there?'

'Yeah. And she told me her dad had found something out. Something to do with Venn. He was really angry.'

'That still doesn't explain—'

'And there's another thing. Cliff was in love with Rosanna. He told me himself.'

'Cliff and—'

'He said they'd had a thing together, said she really wanted him, but couldn't cut loose from Venn. He gets a hold over people, he does.'

'When? When did this thing happen?'

'Not long ago, he said. A few months, I think.'

'The police think that Mal and Cliff were both involved in some kind of drug dealing.'

Des scratched his forehead. 'Doesn't surprise me. Venn's got his finger in all sorts.'

'They'd be working for Venn?'

'Reckon so.' He drained his glass.

'We only have Claire's word about these events on the night he died,' Agnes said.

'I think she was telling the truth. She was that upset.'

'And then she suggested you see me.'

'Yeah. I thought it was a bit odd.'

'If it was true that Cliff was after Venn, then Venn could plead self-defence.'

'Venn's not going to let himself get banged up, even for that.'

'So he'd really sacrifice Mal?'

Des looked at her. 'You don't know Venn, do you?'

'But why should Mal agree to all this?'

''Cos if he doesn't, he's dead.' Des stood up, pulling himself out of the chair. He seemed huge in the tiny room. 'Don't want anyone to know I've been here. Okay?'

'Of course.' She stood up to let him out. 'Why did you want to come today?'

He looked at her. 'I loved Cliff. He was like a brother to me. We were doing market stalls, years ago now – we were kids really. There was a girl I was in love with, Gemmie. She was the love of my life. But she was doing stuff, a junkie, you know. In the end she died of an overdose. It did me in. I fell apart, lost my business, ended up living on the streets. It was Cliff who stood by me. Helped me out of it. Got me started in work again, saved my life. He was with Alma then. The girls were only babies. See, for all they'll tell you about Cliff, he had a heart of gold, that man. If it wasn't for the juice, he'd have survived, I reckon.' He buttoned his coat up carefully. 'Happier times, eh? Thanks for the drink.'

Agnes opened the door for him. 'But – but knowing what you know, isn't there anything we can do?'

'Who's going to listen? No witnesses.'

'Claire—'

'She's not going to stand up in court and say any of this, is she?'

Agnes was silent at the truth of this.

'I just wanted someone to know, I suppose.' He went out on to the landing, then hesitantly offered her his hand.

'Where can I find you?' Agnes asked, as they shook hands.

'Bermondsey market. I've got a china stall there. Need any seconds, I'm your man. Perfect nick, Denby, Wedgwood, Doulton – wouldn't know the difference. Pay a quarter of what it's worth.' For the first time he smiled. 'Thanks for the drink,' he said again, then turned and lumbered away along the landing.

Agnes bolted the door behind him. She went and sat down again, and rested her head on her hand. She got up and stared out of the window for a while, then drew the curtains, undressed and went to bed.

'She ain't comin' today.'

Agnes turned away from her preparations at the altar, reluctantly. Janette was smiling at her. 'Amy. She ain't allowed to associate with us now. Good bleedin' riddance.'

Janette was with her new friend, a thin-faced woman with hair that was cut so short it revealed a scar across her skull. The woman grinned too.

'It's only temporary,' Agnes said, trying to keep her voice level. 'She'll be back on Tuesday. Would you like to find a seat?'

Agnes turned back to the altar, arranging a bowl of lilies, lighting the last candle. There were squawks and giggles as more women arrived and found places to sit. She found the readings for the service. Janette was slouching on a chair. As the noise subsided Agnes began the service.

' "O Lord our God, make us watchful and keep us faithful, as we await the coming of your Son our Lord . . ." ' Agnes saw Janette fidgeting, nudging her neighbour. She saw Cally and Nita whispering together at the back.

' "Who can ascend the hill of the Lord, and who can stand in his holy place? Those who have clean hands and a pure heart . . ." '

Janette's new friend suddenly let out a shriek of abuse at the woman sitting next to her. 'Ow, she kicked me, she did. You fuckin' did, bitch . . .' Two prison officers stepped forward, nervously.

' "God will feed his flock like a shepherd, and gather the lambs in his arms . . ." ' What was the point? Agnes wondered. She scanned the pews. There were about fifteen women there, some sitting mute and dull, some whispering, like Cally and Nita. Those who have clean hands and a pure heart, Agnes thought, preparing to distribute the host.

Afterwards Agnes began to tidy things away and became aware of Janette at her side. 'Sister,' she began, hovering awkwardly.

'What is it?'

'When you talk to the Lord, right—'

Agnes sighed. 'Yes?'

'Can you ask him about my Jim?'

'And what would you like me to ask, Janette?'

'He's got to send me a message.'

'Who, Jim?'

'Yeah. Get my Jim to communicate a message to me from the other side.'

'And I have to ask God this?'

'He'll listen to you, won't he?'

'Janette, it may not be that simple.'

'Yeah, but you and God, you're on the same side, aren't you? And Lise, you know, the new woman on my wing, she said she'd visited one of them women, you know, when you get sent messages from the other side, and she's got this sister who died, right, and her sister spoke to her. And I thought that might help me, if Jim could talk to me from the other side. Only if he sends me a message about who done him in, right, then I can get out of here, can't I?'

Agnes looked at her. She sighed. 'Yes, Janette. If he does, then you can. I'll see what I can do.'

Janette didn't move. 'And there's something else.'

'And what's that?'

'Them tranquillisers. They've forgotten to give me the right ones. Can you go down Healthcare and ask for another lot for me, can you? They'll listen to you, they will.'

'So it's both God and Healthcare who respect my word, is it?'

Janette nodded, her face blank, waiting for Agnes's response.

'I think I'll have more luck with God. You'd better ask one of the screws about your drugs.' Agnes turned to leave.

'But they don't believe me,' Janette whined, hovering at Agnes's side as they went to the door.

'Really? I can't think why.' Agnes locked the door behind her, and was relieved when a waiting officer escorted Janette away from her, down the corridor to her wing.

The idea of asking God for a message for Janette . . . Agnes let herself into her office. It was typical of this world, where just that kind of thing was perfectly possible.

There was a message on her answering machine from Ian, giving his home number. She dialled it straight away.

'I'm sorry to bother you on a Sunday.'

'That's okay.'

'I figured you religious types must work on Sunday.'

'Thanks very much.'

'I wondered if you wanted to see Mal? He's leaving his dispersal prison and being moved out of London.'

'Why's he being moved?'

'It's just administrative. His trial won't come up for months. I can arrange a visit in the next day or two.'

'I'd love to see him. I got a visit last night from someone who knew Cliff from way back. He says it wasn't Mal who did it.'

'How dramatic.'

'A guy called Des. Do you know him?'

'No.'

'He says it was Venn.'

'Has he got proof?'

'I think it's called circumstantial evidence. In other words, no. Only that the night he died, Cliff had a gun and claimed he was going to kill Venn.'

'Blimey. Listen, I'm due to see Chris, Mal's solicitor. Do you want to meet him too? I'll let you know a time when I've arranged one, if you like.'

'Thanks.'

' "Out of the depths have I called to you, O Lord . . ." ' Kneeling in the chapel for the evening office, Agnes was aware of Imelda's voice rising up above the others in a cracked and uneven pitch. ' "Lord hear my voice, let your ears consider well the voice of my supplication . . ." '

Agnes had been welcomed back, and everyone had asked her about her mother. She'd wanted to have a quiet word with Sister Catherine about Imelda, but there'd been no time before chapel.

' "If you, Lord, were to note what is done amiss, O Lord, who could stand . . ." ' Imelda was practically shouting, and the sisters were exchanging glances. Agnes felt that it was no longer her responsibility to alert them to Imelda's state of mind.

She settled her breathing and concentrated on the service.

' "I wait for the Lord; my soul waits for him, in his word is my hope." ' In her mind she saw the winding tower in the old photograph, its dark angles slashed across the charcoal sky. She pushed the image away. ' "My soul waits for the Lord, more than the night-watch for the morning . . ." ' She thought of Mal, languishing in prison, waiting for his trial. She thought of Des, risking his safety to come and see her, to tell her about Cliff and Venn. 'More than the night-watch for the morning . . .' Another image, this time of Rosanna, glittering on stage. 'Lord, hear my voice . . .' 'Out of the depths have I called to you, O Lord.' Agnes heard the distant bells of the City chiming in waves. Eight o'clock. There was still time.

She dressed carefully, in black silk trousers and high heels. She got out of the cab and walked the few yards along the street to the Pomegranate Seed, enjoying the click of her heels on the pavement. The night was damp and misty, which made it feel later than it was. She bought her ticket, went down the steps and found a table near the back. It was emptier than last time, with most of the audience grouped at the front. There was an air of anticipation.

She was about to get a drink when the young woman from behind the bar approached her table. She was carrying a glass of white wine, which she placed in front of Agnes with an ill grace, and said, 'Compliments of the house.'

'Oh. From whom?'

The young woman gestured with her head towards a table at the other side. Agnes could see Rosanna sitting there, with two or three men.

'And she says would you like to join her?'

'Thank you, I would.' Agnes took her glass and went over to Rosanna's table. As she approached, the men slipped away, and Rosanna was left alone.

'Nice to have a fan,' Rosanna said. A brief smile lifted her features. 'But I'm afraid Venn ain't here tonight.'

'It was you I came to see,' Agnes said.

'Well, isn't that nice?' She was heavily made up, and her eyes were bright as she looked at Agnes.

'I heard a rumour, you see,' Agnes began, taking the seat next to her.

'Oh yeah?'

'I heard that Mal didn't kill Cliff.'

Rosanna smiled, slowly. 'Yeah, well, haven't we all?'

'I heard that Venn—'

'Don't even go there,' Rosanna said, holding up her hand.

'But—'

'We all have our prisons, Sister.' Rosanna was looking at her, and Agnes saw the weariness in the depth of her gaze. 'Mal's got his. I've got mine. And I'm sure as hell you've got yours. But thing is, Sister, whatever your prison is, at least you're alive. Try and keep it that way, don't you think?'

Agnes was silent for a moment, taking in the implication of what Rosanna said. When she next spoke, she chose her words carefully. 'It must be hard to love such a man.'

Rosanna closed her eyes, then opened them. 'What do you know of love?'

'More than you think.'

'I've never seen a nun dance the way you do.' A smile flicked across Rosanna's face and then was gone.

'It depends how I'm partnered.'

'And you ask me how I can love such a man?' Her eyes darkened as she held Agnes's gaze.

'Dancing's one thing. It's when you find you're clearing his guns off your kitchen table . . .'

Rosanna eyed her levelly. 'It's like I said, Sister. Every one of us has our own special prison cell. Tailormade.'

The man with the leather jacket was suddenly at Agnes's elbow, and she realised he must have been watching them. 'Is this woman bothering you?' he asked Rosanna.

Rosanna smiled and shook her head. 'This woman is the nearest I've got to a friend in the world,' she said. She laid her hand on Agnes's. 'What'll you drink?'

Agnes glanced at the empty glass in front of Rosanna. 'Whatever that was.'

'Two more whiskies, Doc.' Rosanna stroked his arm and smiled up into his face. 'I'm on in a minute. That'll just top me up nicely.'

'You heard what Venn said about your boozing,' Doc began, but she laughed.

'Venn cares so very very much about me, doesn't he, baby? While he's not here you can do as I say. Off you go now, you naughty boy.' She turned back towards Agnes and held her hands out. 'Welcome to my prison, Sister. Or shall I call you by your name? What was your name?'

'Agnes.'

'Agnes. Of course. Look, they're waving at me. I'll be there in five.' She put her hand up, palm outwards, gesturing to someone at the side of the stage. 'Where's that boy with the drinks?' She leaned suddenly towards Agnes. 'We were talking of love, weren't we?'

Doc arrived and placed two glasses of whisky and ice in front of them, then vanished into the shadows.

'Yes,' Agnes said. 'Love.'

'The path of true love—'

'Never runs smooth,' Agnes said. 'I'd heard that Cliff and you—'

Rosanna leaned forward and touched Agnes's lips with her fingertip. She held Agnes's gaze. 'As I value my life, Sister,' – she was almost whispering – 'I can never speak that name again.' She leaned back in her chair. 'Tell me,' she said, speaking normally again, 'how did you learn to dance like that, the way you were dancing the other night?'

'You really want to know?'

'I really do.'

'Same way as you.'

Rosanna threw her head back and laughed. 'But you're a nun.'

'When I was eighteen I married a man—'

'You were married?'

'– who was beautiful.'

Rosanna looked at her. 'They always are.'

'And who treated me very badly.'

Rosanna touched her hand again. 'Like I said, we all have our prisons. Only you got out of yours.'

'Or maybe just swapped.'

Rosanna smiled at her. 'But you still know how to dance.'

There was an edge of steel in her smile. She drained her glass, rose from the table in one graceful move and walked down the side of the tables, out through a side door, ready for the start of her set. A few minutes later the band came on stage to a ripple of applause. Then Rosanna appeared. She walked into the white circle of the spotlight, her eyes shining, her hair glittering. She had the same air of stillness about her, and her face was radiant as she turned outwards to the audience. As she started her first number, her eyes seemed to Agnes to be fixed only on her.

Agnes woke next morning aware of bright sunshine, a slight headache and a fragment of music circling in her mind. She got out of bed and put on the kettle, wondering whether the headache would go away by itself, parting the curtains slightly, touching with her finger the beads of condensation on the window. She shivered, and pulled on a dressing gown. The music was wistful, haunting, and she realised it had been part of her dreams, a single female voice with a saxophone accompaniment, singing of loss and betrayal and love.

And I told Rosanna about Hugo, she thought. But then she did ask. And it was the truth.

The kettle boiled and she made some tea, and felt her headache begin to lift. It was only a couple of whiskies, after all, she thought.

She'd left before the end of Rosanna's set, partly because she was tired, and partly because Doc spent the set standing uncomfortably near to her table. When she'd got up to go, she found he was already holding her coat. He'd handed it to her and waited while she'd put it on. Even out in the street, waiting for a cab, she'd had the impression he was lurking, just making sure she'd really gone.

She showered and dressed, thinking about what Des had said, wondering who on earth would verify his version of events, when Venn had such a tight grip on the people around him. She thought about Claire, and wished she had a phone number for her. She drank a second cup of tea, then left for the prison.

Cally seemed unusually cheerful and there was a shine about her eyes that didn't seem quite natural.

'I had one of my dreams, you see, Sister.'

'Oh yes?' Agnes pulled up the solitary chair and sat down.

'It's goin' to be okay.'

'Is it?'

She nodded, smiling.

'The thing is, Cally, you're due out of here in about two weeks.'

'That's why it's goin' to be okay.' She giggled.

'And what will you do?'

'I'll live, that's what I'll do. I'm going to go shopping, and I'm going to get some of those boots, you know, black ones, with the soles and the chunky heel, up to about here, not too high, and I'm going to get a Walkman and a stack of tapes, and I'm going to be happy. 'In't I, Nita?'

Nita looked up briefly from her book and nodded in a vague sort of way.

'And what will you use for money?'

Cally laughed. 'That's a stupid question.'

'Actually, it's about the most sensible question anyone could ask you at the moment. Because unless you clean up your act you're going to be out on the streets when you get out of here.'

'Mal'll take care of me.'

'And how's he going to do that?'

'I told you, in my dream, it was all okay.'

'Did Mal get acquitted in your dream?' Cally looked doubtful. 'Cally – I need you to think about all this.'

Cally looked across to Nita, who turned a page of her book and continued reading.

'It's just,' Agnes went on, 'I've heard this rumour that Mal's been framed. By Venn.'

Cally shrugged.

'Cally – in two weeks I want you out of here. I want you out and free, and I want you to get a hostel place, which means you have to clean up. And I want you signing on, and not nicking stuff, and doing some kind of training, and sorting out your life. And sitting here dreaming isn't going to help you one bit.'

'Who's the one who's dreaming?' Cally spoke sharply. 'A hostel place and training and a new life and a new me? That's dreaming, man. Innit, Nita?' Nita didn't even look up. Cally went on, 'Face it, Sister. When I get out of here, nothing's goin' to have changed. Except Mal's inside. So it's worse than it was. An' even if Venn is behind it, what can I do? I've told you who I think did it, and if Venn's protecting her, what can I do? I can kill her for putting my Mal inside, an' I might just do that, but nothin's changed. You leave me to my dreams, and I'll leave you to yours, Sister.'

The strange brightness had left her face. She looked tired, her eyes hollow, her skin papery. She picked up a comb and began to drag it through her hair. Nita continued to read.

Agnes left, locking the door behind her. She made her way to her office, unlocked the door, and sank into a chair. At least I belonged, she thought. She thought about the house in Provence. She thought about herself as a child, opening the shutters, with their old paintwork that you could peel off in flakes with your nails. She remembered how the shutters would swing open and let in the sun. She remembered what it was like to go into the kitchen, barefoot, the stone floor cool against her feet. She'd pull herself up on to a stool and sit at the wide oak table and contemplate the day. The housekeeper would pour her a bowl of hot chocolate, and she'd look at the steam rising and wonder whether to ride her pony or investigate the woods or watch the gardener. The day belonged only to her. Most days, anyway, unless yet another governess appeared, with instructions to educate the child. They would attempt to instil some order into the chaos, invariably giving up within the month. Or unless her mother decided the child needed guidance, and then she'd have to stay with her and do needlework or play the piano, sitting upright and awkward and waiting for her mother to get bored so that she could resume her normal life.

But at least I belonged, Agnes thought. Whereas Cally – Cally hates her sister, she doesn't seem to mind that her father's dead, she trusts no one, and she thinks she might as well destroy herself because she sees no alternative. She has nowhere to go. I . . . I simply had the misfortune to be born into a marriage that should never have happened. My father, vaguely affectionate but constantly preoccupied, and my mother . . . my mother . . . Agnes felt her eyes fill with tears and she leaned her head on her hand. My mother was . . . my mother was very unhappy.

The phone rang loud and sudden. Agnes picked it up.

'Hello?' It was Ian's voice.

'Oh.'

'Agnes, is that you?'

'Yes.'

'You all right?'

'Um, yes.'

'I've fixed up a meeting with Mal for this evening. With Chris, his lawyer. Can you make it? Six-ish, for about an hour? I'll meet you at Silworth, and then we can go in my car.'

'Yes, that's fine. Thanks.'

'Are you sure you're all right?'

'Really, yes.'

'See you later, then.'

Agnes hung up. She stared out of the window, through the bars. My mother was very unhappy. We all have our prisons, Rosanna said.

She heard the door open and Imelda came in. She sat heavily at her desk, and stared unseeing at the paperwork that had accumulated there.

'Imelda?'

Imelda blinked, and turned slowly towards Agnes, screwing up her eyes against the light from the window. She didn't speak.

'How are you?' Agnes tried.

'I'm – I'm . . .' She shrugged.

'Imelda, hadn't you better—'

'Hadn't I better what?'

'Seek help.' The words came out as almost a whisper.

Imelda stared at her blankly for a moment, then shook her head. She stood up, then put one hand in her pocket and pulled out an envelope, which she handed to Agnes. 'This came for you. Catherine said to give it to you. I nearly forgot.' She stumbled to the door and left as abruptly as she'd arrived.

The letter was from France. Agnes sliced it open with a paperknife. It was from Yvette.

'*Chère Agnes*,' it began. 'Your mother seems to be insisting that I send you the enclosed photo. She sent Celine to get it from the old house. She drew her a plan to find it. She knew exactly where it would be. As you know, her old friend Henriette is living there now.

'You will be pleased to hear that your mother is in good spirits, although she has no power of speech at all. Otherwise, of course, she is much as you saw her. I hope it's not too long before we see you here again.'

Agnes was aware of the emotion held in restraint by the polite French words. She pulled out the photograph.

It showed a young woman, probably not yet twenty, standing outside a stone cottage, small and shabby, roughly built, laid out on a hillside with several similar cottages near by. Agnes realised, with a tightening of her breath, that it was the same row of cottages that appeared in the first photograph. In the background was the same skeletal tower. The cottages were shadowed by a black hill that rose up behind them, and which seemed, as Agnes peered closer at it, to be made of coal. She turned it over in her hands. On the back she saw the words, written in faint ink, '*Dernières semaines à Rieulay*.' Last weeks at Rieulay . . .

Agnes stared at the image of the woman in the picture. She though she heard the footsteps of someone coming into the room, but when she looked up, there was no one there.

Chapter Eighteen

It was strange, Agnes thought, being in a prison without hearing piercing screams and squeals. Instead there was gruff shouting, loud abuse, male voices raised in anger. Agnes and Ian took their places in the visitors' area, waiting for Mal. Young men came in jostling; the older men had a gait that Agnes recognised from Silworth, the shuffle of the long-term inmate, eyes with the light gone out of them. Mal appeared at the doorway. He was upright, his head held high, pausing just for a moment before walking through the large room to their table.

He smiled at Agnes, and nodded, then sat down. Close up he seemed thinner than before.

'How are you?' Ian said.

He shrugged. 'You got anything for me?'

Agnes pushed across some bars of chocolate. He snatched one up and unwrapped it.

'How're you feeling about the move?' Ian asked him.

'Pretty crap,' he said, through a mouthful of chocolate. 'Fuckin' Lincolnshire. Bloody miles away. Thought they didn't shift remand people around?'

'The overstretched prison service . . . ' Ian began.

'You're telling me. Four of us in one room? Fuckin' nightmare, man. Thought my brief was going to be here?'

'He's been delayed. He'll be here shortly. Agnes wants to talk to you, though.'

He turned to her, quietening, attentive.

'Mal – someone came to see me . . . about Venn.'

'Who?'

'I can't say.'

'Someone who knows Venn's ways, then.'

'They said they know you didn't do it, because they know that Venn did.'

Mal broke off a piece of chocolate and put it in his mouth.

'They said Venn deliberately implicated you.'

Mal looked at her hard. He blinked. Very slowly, he unwrapped the next bar of chocolate, staring at it in his fingers. 'Was it Claire,' he asked her, 'who came to you?'

'No,' Agnes said. 'Not Claire.'

Mal looked up at her, then took a bite of chocolate. He shook his head. 'Ain't no good to me.'

'He said that Cliff went after Venn because he'd found out something, and—'

'Your man wants to stay anonymous?' Mal said suddenly.

Agnes nodded.

'Don't say no more. I don't want to hear no more.'

Agnes glanced at Ian.

Mal looked at them both. 'I ain't been inside before,' he said. 'Things I've done, I coulda been, but luck was on my side. Things I've learnt in here, man. I'm an old man now. Old and wise. You people . . .' He shook his head again. 'You people don't know nothin'. You think the outside stops right at that gate, right? The outside is here, now, inside. Venn's people are out there – and they're in here too, man. You say any more, I'm dead, your man is dead and you, Sister, you're on the way to Venn having a little chat with you. Believe me, that's not a thing you want. Y'know what I'm saying?'

'Mal, you could get life.' Agnes watched the last piece of chocolate disappear into Mal's mouth.

'Then I'm still alive, man.'

'Surely I could tell your lawyer?' she said.

'And all your witnesses end up dead meat? Trust me, Sister, there ain't no way out.'

'I could go to the police.'

Mal laughed, his brown eyes holding Agnes's gaze. She wanted to shake him. 'Cally's out in a month,' she said. 'Who's going to look after her?'

The smile died on Mal's lips. He put his hand up to his face, rubbing his jaw. 'She's a good kid,' he said at last. 'Look after her.'

'Mal—'

His eyes flashed anger. 'Listen, Sister, it's shit here. I've been more scared in here than I've been in my life. Where I'm goin' next, it'll be worse shit. You find me a way out that doesn't involve my brains bein' blown out, I'll take it. You find me a way to live happy ever after, and I'll shake you by the hand. But I don't want no false hope, so don't come here givin' me none. And now here's my brief, and I'd like to hear what he has to say.'

A tall man with neat dark hair, in an elegant suit and tortoiseshell spectacles, approached them. 'Hi, Ian,' he said.

'And Sister Agnes,' Ian said.

Chris nodded at Agnes.

'We were just going,' Agnes said.

Outside Ian hugged himself against the icy wind. 'Fancy a pizza?' he said. 'But nowhere with smoking. I've really given up now. I mean it.'

'I'd love to, but I'm due to see a friend this evening.'

'Can I give you a lift?'

'She lives in Fulham.'

'I'll at least take you part of the way, if you like.'

They walked to Ian's car. 'That didn't go too well,' Ian said.

'How can we fight for him if he won't fight for himself?'

'And why is everyone so scared of this Venn person?'

'You'd know if you met him.' Agnes gathered her scarf around her face.

'You mean, even you're scared of him?'

They'd reached Ian's car and Agnes stood by the passenger door. 'I don't know,' she said. 'I hadn't really thought about it.'

'You're asking me if I think he's frightening? But sweetie, you always fancy dangerous men.' Athena put a bottle of Côtes du Rhône and a corkscrew down on the table in front of Agnes. 'I'm hopeless at those things. You have a go.' She went into the kitchen, then emerged with a large steaming hot saucepan which she placed carefully on a table mat.

'Why are you grinning like that, Athena?'

'It's foolproof, this one. It's bound to be edible. God bless modern food technology. Fresh tortellini, with ready-made mushroom cream sauce. You just put them together.' She ladled out two helpings on to elegant white plates.

'But there's dangerous and dangerous, Athena. I mean, this one is drugs and guns dangerous, not just—'

'Not just what?'

'Whatever the usual kind of dangerous is.'

'Did we think he was gorgeous?'

Agnes smiled. 'We agreed that we might think he was, if I weren't a nun, of course, and you weren't otherwise occupied.'

'Well, then, that makes him the usual kind of dangerous too. Hang on, there's salad.' Athena fetched a bowl of mixed leaves and a bottle of salad dressing. 'Balsamic vinegar and sun-dried tomato. I bought it specially. And grated Parmesan. And look, paper napkins. Disney ones – they've got

Dalmatians all over them. They were in the children's party section – I couldn't resist them. You know, sweetie, this really is my era. I was born for a time of twenty-four-hour supermarkets. Did you open that wine?'

Agnes poured them both a glass. 'I'm not sure he is gorgeous, actually.'

'Make your mind up.' Athena tasted her wine.

'I think it's more than that. He has a kind of power. People seem to do what he says.'

'Stay away, poppet.'

'I wish I could. What's so funny?'

'Because you always have reasons not to stay away. All the time I've known you.'

'And you and Greg?'

Athena ate a forkful of pasta. 'You're right. I suppose I'm not staying away either. Although . . .'

'What?'

'I'm not sure what it's all for.'

'What what's all for?'

'You see, when I'm with him it's just fantastic, and he's so wonderful and he makes me feel alive and young and . . . and he's so different, and special, and the time we have together is so precious and . . .' She sighed. 'And then days pass when I don't see him and I settle back into things with Nic and then I can't quite remember what the Greg thing is for. And then maybe he doesn't phone when he said he would, so I'm yearning for him all over again, and then when he does phone I'm in such a state that it all starts again . . . It can't last, sweetie.'

'And Nic?'

She shrugged. 'We're okay.'

'As in not okay?'

'As in leading separate lives and not talking about anything important.'

'Does he still want to live with you?'

'He seems to have lost interest.'

'Maybe he suspects.'

'About Greg?' Athena shook her head. 'I don't think it would ever occur to him.' She sighed. 'Oh, life is so easy for you celibate people.'

'If only, Athena.'

Athena looked at her. 'So, this dangerous man, is that what's preoccupying you?'

'Am I preoccupied?'

'You've hardly touched your plate. And even worse, your wine.'

Agnes smiled. 'I don't think it's him.'

'It's your mother, isn't it?'

'Between you and Julius, my thoughts are not my own.'

'We just care about you, sweetie. What's happened?'

'I got this in the post today. Look.' Agnes got up and went to her bag. 'Yvette sent me another photo. My mother, apparently, wanted me to have it.' She came back to the table and passed the photo to Athena, who wiped her hands carefully on a Dalmatian serviette and then took it. Agnes handed her another photograph. 'And this is the first one, the one I showed you before.'

Athena looked at both, one in each hand. 'Is this the child grown up, then?' she said, after a moment.

'I think so.'

'The grown-up one looks like you.' Athena eyed Agnes. 'A lot like you.'

'It's hardly surprising.'

'Why?'

'It's my mother.'

Athena stared at the photo. Then she stared at Agnes. Then she stared at the photo again. 'But – what's she – why this place?'

'God knows. But whatever she's trying to tell me, sending me these photos, it's too late. She's lost her speech, and she's so frail, and – and it's too late.'

'I'd say perhaps it's all a mistake, only – this woman here . . .'

Agnes nodded. 'She looks just like me.'

'But your grandmother, her mother, living in the big old house in Provence, and your pony, and the orchards . . .'

Agnes shook her head. 'I don't know what to think. It's as if she's trying to make up for something.'

'Isn't there someone you can ask, someone who'd know?'

'There's Henriette – Henriette Grillon. She's living in the house now. She's very old and amazingly rude – at least she was when she used to visit us. If anyone knows, she will.'

'Write to her.'

'I would. Except . . .' Agnes picked up the two photos again and stared at them. 'Except I'm not sure I want to know.' She picked up her glass of wine, drained it and held it out to Athena to replenish it. 'What was that you said about forgetting to drink?'

Much later, Agnes lit her candles in the quiet of her flat and knelt in prayer.

'Hail Mary, full of grace,' she began. 'Holy Mary, Mother of God . . .' She stopped. Mother of God. What was it Imelda had said, once, about not searching in vain for a replacement family? Religious life is simply an acknowledgement of our solitary state, she'd said.

Poor Imelda, Agnes thought. The edifice of all her certainties now cracking around the fault lines of her past.

'Holy Mary, Mother of God, pray for us now . . .'

When we join an order, we give up all family, all memories, all our past.

Agnes opened her eyes. But I have a mother, she thought. I have a mother. Just.

She got up from her cushion and went to her desk. She grabbed a piece of notepaper, sat down and wrote her own address at the top. Then she wrote, 'Mme Henriette Grillon. Les Sablons,' and the rest of the address. Then she wrote, '*Madame*.' She put down her pen, picked up the photograph of the young woman standing by a miner's cottage and stared at it. She picked up her pen. '*Madame*. I have to know. Please tell me.'

Bright sunlight streamed through the windows of the prison chapel, drowning out the solitary candle flame. Agnes placed a pile of unlit candles next to the bowl and returned to her place in the circle.

'If anyone wishes to light a candle as a mark of prayer, please feel welcome to do so,' she said.

There was a shuffling silence, then a woman got up. She went to the bowl, knelt in front of it, took an unlit candle to the flame and, when it was lit, placed it in the sand. 'For my little girl,' she said, barely audibly. 'She's just turned eleven today and I wasn't there to see it. God bless her and keep her . . . and tell her I'd light eleven candles for her if I could.' She went back to her place and covered her face with her hands.

A thin and unsteady young woman went into the middle of the circle, lit a candle and knelt for a moment in silence, then returned to her place, her face wet with tears. She was followed by an older, grey-haired woman, who lit her candle and then spoke in a clear voice. 'My sister, God rest her soul, died a year ago today. She was the best friend anyone could have. If she'd lived another year, I'd never have ended up like this.'

There was a scrape of chairs as Janette got up from her

place. Agnes saw her brush roughly past Amy as she came to the bowl. 'This is for my Jim,' she said loudly, digging her candle into the sand. 'He was a light in my life like this light 'ere. And now he's gone. And Jim, if you can hear me, my love, I'm still here, Jim. I'm still here for you. And you might have left me on my own, but I know you didn't mean to, and I know you was brutally murdered, and when I find out who did it, they'll be dead, Jim, I'll see to it, my love, as God's my witness, won't I, love? And try and talk to me, love, maybe in a dream or something. You spirits can do that, can't you, love . . . ?'

Agnes stood up and went to Janette. 'I think maybe that's enough,' she said, quietly, taking her arm.

Janette got up from her knees, then shook Agnes's grip from her elbow. 'Who are you to say that's enough? This ain't your bleedin' chapel. You don't fuckin' own it, do you?'

'Perhaps you'd like to sit down now,' Agnes said.

'Why ain't I allowed to talk to my Jim in a holy place, eh?'

'Janette, shut it, gel,' someone said.

She whirled round. 'And you can shut yer mouth too, Melanie.'

Two of the screws stood up. 'Right. Out. Now,' one of them said. Two more stood by the door, preparing to marshal people out of the chapel. There were murmurs of indignation. Women started to object, clustering towards the altar, murmuring angrily.

'I know what you lot fuckin' think,' Janette was shouting. 'You're all wrong, you ugly bitches. Look, we've got a bleedin' child killer here, sitting there like she owns the bleedin' place, just 'cos she's getting all the best treatment. It ain't fair, is it girls—'

Agnes moved fast to stand by Amy, who was still in her place, staring around bewildered. Two officers grabbed hold of Janette, who began to shriek. 'You keep your hands off of me. It's her you should be moving out of here. She has no right to be here . . .' Her friend Lise was shrieking too, kicking out at the officers who restrained her. An alarm started to ring, and more officers arrived, running, seizing hold of the women and moving them towards the door. The women were defiant, shouting abuse, shrieking above the noise of the alarm, as they were manhandled out of the chapel and down the corridor.

The alarm stopped. A silence filled the chapel. The chairs were scattered, some overturned. A vase of flowers had been pushed over and lay in a pool of water on the carpet. The sun had deserted the windows. In the dim room the bowl of candles now burned brightly. One person was still there, kneeling by the bowl. It was Amy. She was lighting candle after candle, digging them into the sand, and singing quietly to herself. She had placed her photograph behind the bowl, and its image was illumined by the flames. Amy continued to sing, and when she'd lit all the candles she leaned across the bowl and stroked the face of the baby in the photo.

Agnes knelt beside her. 'Amy?'

Amy didn't move, her fingers still touching the photo. Agnes saw the skin on her arm turn red where she reached over the candle flames. 'Amy, you're burning yourself.'

Amy continued to hum to her baby. Gently, Agnes took her hand and removed it from the photo. The skin of her forearm was already blistering. Amy made a yelping noise, snatched the photo away with her other hand and tucked it under her T-shirt. She cowered from Agnes. 'Not my baby,' she whimpered. 'Don't take my baby . . .'

'I won't take your baby,' Agnes said quietly, helping Amy to her feet. 'Your baby's safe, Amy. No one can take your baby.' Amy stood, hunched but docile. She allowed Agnes to lead her to the chapel door, placing one foot in front of the other as if she had to think about each step.

Agnes got home at about five. She was exhausted. She let herself into her flat, put on the kettle and collapsed into a chair. Almost immediately, there was a buzz from the intercom.

'Who is it?'

'It's Claire. Can I come up?'

Agnes buzzed the door open and stood, waiting. Claire appeared on the landing, beautifully dressed as before, breathing fast.

'Tea?' Agnes showed her in and shut the door.

'Only if you are.'

'I certainly am.'

Claire took off her coat, slung it across Agnes's divan, then sat down by the window and crossed her legs. Agnes went into the kitchen, wanting to ask Claire about Des but realising that she had to protect Des even from Claire. She made a pot of tea and brought it into her room on a tray with two cups and saucers and a jug of milk.

'Des came to see you, didn't he?' Claire said.

Agnes stirred the tea in the pot. 'Do you take sugar?' she said.

'Two please. He did, didn't he? I bet he told you not to say anything an' all.'

Agnes went to find the sugar bowl.

'My dad's oldest friend, he was. Oldest and best.'

Agnes poured two cups of tea.

'So anything he said, you can tell me. He was like an uncle to me, Des was.'

Agnes handed her a cup in one hand, and the sugar bowl in another. 'You'll need a teaspoon,' she said, going back into her kitchen.

'He told you who killed my dad, didn't he?' There was a nervous edge to her voice.

Agnes gave her the spoon, picked up her cup of tea and sat down opposite Claire. 'I thought you knew who killed your dad,' she said at last.

Claire crossed and uncrossed her legs. 'Yeah. Well. Maybe.'

'I thought you knew it was Mal because you weren't with him when the shooting happened.'

Claire put down her cup. She stared at her hands in her lap.

'Surely you weren't making that up, were you, Claire?'

Claire looked up, and her eyes were hard like flint.

'The thing is, Claire, I can't really trust you with any confidences if you won't even begin to tell me the truth. Can I? If this Des, whoever he is, is like an uncle to you, perhaps you should go and talk to him.'

Claire met her gaze, and now the blue of her eyes was softened with tears. She stood up, went over to the bed and picked up her coat. She put it on, then went to the door.

'I thought you'd help me,' she said in a small voice. She hesitated, stooped and miserable.

'Claire – how can I help you?'

Claire shook her head, then opened the door and went out. The door closed behind her.

Chapter Nineteen

Agnes was left alone. She paced her room, trying to shake off the feeling that she'd done the wrong thing. By the time she'd realised that Claire's tears weren't just a performance, the girl had gone.

We all have our prisons, Rosanna had said. And Claire's was certainly weighing heavily on her.

It's quite clear, Agnes thought, that Claire knows that Mal didn't do it. She's known all along, but for reasons of her own, she's stuck to her story. And now she's about to change her story, and she comes to me, and I manage to be so unsympathetic that she goes away again. Leaving no phone number, no address. Damn.

She must have given Des my address deliberately. In the hope he'd come here and say something. And then she could find out from me what it was.

Agnes went to her kitchen and opened a new bottle of whisky. She poured herself a glass and cracked an ice cube into it. She went over to her window. It was dark; a clear, cold night. She swirled the ice around in her drink, watching the condensation form on the glass.

And yet when I wouldn't tell her anything, she was clearly upset. Really, truly upset, rather than a pretence. So did she come here for herself, or on someone else's behalf? Mal's, even? But then Mal knows what Des said, about it being Venn who killed Cliff. And even then, in the prison, perhaps I said too much.

She switched on her anglepoise lamp, and sat down. She sipped her whisky.

And who can I ask about Claire? she wondered. Not Rosanna. Not Venn. Not even her own sister. There was Des, she thought, but then, if a trap's been laid for him, I don't want to be the one to spring it by going back to see him. And there's Marky.

She yawned, drained her glass, stood up and put on her coat. She wished the prospect of an evening in the pub on a cold December night was more appealing.

The King's Arms was warm and crowded. At first Agnes couldn't see anyone familiar, as she blinked against the cigarette smoke and wondered whether Marky was on a different shift this week. Then in the corner she saw Harry and Emlyn sitting over their drinks.

Harry looked up as she approached, then nodded. 'Marky's friend, aren't you?'

'That's right.'

'He's just by the bar, there. Better get your order in.'

Agnes stood at Marky's elbow. He turned and saw her.

'Oh. Hi.'

'I'll get these,' Agnes said.

'No, you're all right. What'll you have?'

'I'd better stick to whisky, I think.'

Marky gave her an odd look, and ordered a whisky.

'The thing is, Claire came to see me,' Agnes said.

'Claire?' He was suddenly animated.

'Yes. Earlier today.'

'What did she want?' He turned to face her.

'Well, that's just it. I'm not too sure. Help, I think.'

'What did she say?'

The barman interrupted. 'I haven't got all day, son. I said, that'll be three fifty-nine please.'

Marky fished for the money and gathered up the drinks. Agnes took her whisky and a tall glass of lemonade. They made their way to the others and Agnes handed the glass to Emlyn, who acknowledged her presence with a very brief nod. Marky sat with Agnes, slightly at a distance. 'What did she say?'

'Very little. It's all a bit complicated, but I think she knows Mal didn't do it. She was quite tearful.'

'She's trapped, that's what it is.'

Agnes looked at him. 'How well do you know her?'

Marky glanced away, picked up his glass and drank from it. 'Not very well,' he said at last.

'How did you meet her?'

'Through Mal. Some months ago. Mal knew her before. She used to hang out with his crowd. She had this idea about being a singer, and I was going around with them more in them days. Then when Cally appeared, Claire kind of went off them. They don't get on, those two. Then when Cally and Mal were going out together, Claire stopped seeing us altogether. And then Mal and I were working together, and then it all went bad, and some of the crowd got into trouble, and then Cally and Viv were caught out shopping, and Cally got sent down. And then there was her dad being killed, and you know the rest.'

'Did you see Claire during that time?'

'Once Cally got sent down, Claire took up with Venn again. And this singing thing took hold, and she started hanging out more at the club again. She's good mates with Rosanna now.'

'Do you like Claire?'

He looked up from his drink. He nodded. 'We get on. She's got class, she has. Not in a – you know, not like that. We get on like mates. I don't have that with many girls. Only – something happened . . .'

'What?'

Marky drank slowly from his glass. When he spoke it was almost in a whisper. 'I saw her once in town. Before Mal got arrested and everything. Earlier this year, after she stopped goin' around with us. I was up the West End with some mates. We were looking for a club up there. And we went into a bar first, and I saw Claire. And she was looking fantastic, man, sitting on her own, really cool, y'know? And I went up to her, and she was like, really nice to me, really pleased to see me. But she was nervous, and kept looking towards the stairs, and in the end this bloke came up the stairs, from the phones or something, and sat down, and she just froze me out.'

'Did you know him?'

Marky shook his head. 'I went then, went back to my mates. And after that I didn't see her for ages, not till – not till just before all this happened with her dad. It was that Sunday, the night he died. It was my day off, and I was having a drink – there's a pub near where I live, I'm often in there on my days off with a couple of mates – and Claire came in.'

'Did she know you'd be there?'

'Yeah, I'm known there. She was looking for me. I bought her a drink. She was looking kind of rough, you know, and she seemed upset. I asked her what it was, and she wouldn't say. I said, is it your dad, 'cos we all knew she'd been seeing him again, and we knew he could be a bit difficult. And she kind of shook her head, but then she started to cry. And I said, is it your dad, and she said, yes. And she said she was really worried about him; she thought he was going to do something stupid, just when everything was going better for him, she said.'

'What did she mean?'

'Dunno. I asked her about it. See, it was funny, 'cos Emlyn was mates with him.'

'Emlyn?'

'Yeah. They'd got quite pally. Em was trying to sort out some work for him. And Claire said he'd been much better, her dad. Not drinking, you know.'

'Emlyn?' Agnes repeated, more to herself than to Marky. She looked up at Marky. 'So why was Claire upset?'

'She said she was frightened about what he might do. She said it was like she'd got her dad back, and she didn't want it to go wrong now.'

'Having her dad back – that's what Cally said.'

'Yeah, like in the old days, when it was good with him.'

'And Emlyn . . .' Agnes sipped her drink, frowning. 'So what else did she say?'

'Not much else. Just that she thought he was heading for trouble. I bought her another drink or two, and she cheered up a bit, and she went to the loo and came out with all her make-up on – you know how girls do.' He blushed, and took another swig of beer. 'And then she said not to take no notice of what she'd said. And then she went off.'

'Where did she go?'

'She said she was going to the club – you know, the Pomegranate.'

'And that night Cliff was shot?'

Marky nodded. 'I didn't mention it before, 'cos when they got Mal for it . . . and 'cos she said not to. But I've been thinking about it a bit. There was something else—'

One of the men interrupted them. 'Another drink, you two?'

'Not for me, thanks,' Agnes said.

'Same again, please,' Marky said.

'What was the something else?' Agnes asked him.

'They came to the club once, not long before Cliff – before

he died. Em and Cliff.' Marky glanced across to Emlyn where he sat, and lowered his voice. 'And Venn – it was weird, see, 'cos Venn, it was like he couldn't bear the sight of him. But then, there was something going on between Cliff and Rosanna, so it might have been that. But I ain't never seen Venn so put out before – white he was, white as a sheet. They left after a while. Em talked to Rosanna a bit.'

'Em—?' Agnes was whispering.

Marky nodded. 'Don't know what it was about.'

'Marky—' Agnes hesitated, wondering how the question would sound. 'Marky – you're not related to Venn, are you?'

Marky laughed. 'You mean, both Welsh boyos?'

'And Jim,' Agnes added.

'Lot of us about,' Marky said, and smiled. 'But no, we're not related. I'm a Roberts, and this lot are Morgans.'

'So the Prices—' Agnes persisted.

'Emlyn's a Price.' Marky glanced at Emlyn where he sat at the next table.

Agnes looked at Emlyn. He looked up and met her eyes. 'I was just asking,' she said, 'whether you were related to Venn and Jim. Price,' she added.

Emlyn's gaze bore into her. He shook his head. 'Who are they?' he asked her.

'You know,' Marky said. 'That club you went to once, with Claire's dad.'

Emlyn blinked. 'Yes . . .' he began. 'That club. With Cliff. I remember.'

'Venn is in charge there,' Agnes said. 'Venn Price.'

Emlyn shrugged. 'We went to see someone there. A woman. Cliff wanted me to meet her. Don't remember any Welshman there.' He shook his head and turned back to his glass of lemonade.

'Of course, all true Welshman are related,' Harry said,

leaning towards them, red-faced and jovial. 'Scratch a Welshman and you find . . .' his lips moved, as he struggled for the words.

'What do you find, Harry?' The others were laughing at him from the other side of the table.

'A son of Glyndwr.' Harry laughed.

'A different line you see.' Emlyn's deep voice cut through the jollity. He was staring at Marky. 'That's why you can drink.' He sat heavily at the table, unmoved by the laughter. He turned away, scowling at his hands as they gripped the table's edge.

Agnes was aware silence had fallen around him. 'What do you mean?' she asked.

He turned to her with reluctance, and his dark eyes, sunk deep under his heavy brow, barely met her own. 'My cousin, Abbie, Marky's her boy.' He turned back as if to end the conversation.

'It's the old gypsy curse,' Harry chipped in, cheerfully, ignoring Emlyn's mood. 'At least, that's Emlyn's view.'

'Don't need no curse.' Emlyn's voice was raised, his accent thick. 'I've had it with that curse.'

Agnes stared at him. Gypsy's curse, she thought.

'It's the male line,' Harry went on. 'We're all cousins, see, only me and Marky here, we're from the female line. There's some tale of the male line being cursed by a gypsy some way back. My great-granddaddy brought a curse down upon him, so the tale goes, but I've never got it straight. It depends which of us you talk to about it. You go back to the Valleys, you'll get the story ten times over, all different. The women'll say it's because he wronged a gypsy woman, and she cursed his son and his son's sons, but I've never got it straight.'

'Don't need no bloody curse—' Emlyn's deep bass voice was almost a growl.

But Emlyn denied it. Agnes's mind was racing. He denied being related to Venn. Even though . . . Even though he knew Cliff and he'd been to the club.

'There weren't no gypsies,' another man said. 'Cornish, we were, way back. When the tin mines went, we moved to Wales – miners, see. Chapel we are. That's why our mam always told us not to drink.'

Emlyn stumbled to his feet. 'That's it, Huw. Chapel, see,' he echoed. 'My mam always said not to drink.' He was shaking his head, leaning on the table, breathing hard.

A man was standing by the door, swaying from side to side. A boy of about ten was next to him, trying to get hold of his arm. 'Dad, come on,' he was saying, 'let's get you home now.' The man aimed for the door handle, missed, staggered heavily. The boy leaned against him with all his weight to steady him. 'Come on, Dad,' he was saying, but the man turned to him, shouting, red-faced and abusive, then grabbed at the door and stumbled out, the boy close behind.

'There, see?' Emlyn looked round him at them all. 'Drink. There's the evil.' He straightened up, then walked heavily to the door, and left. Harry exchanged glances with Huw, and they both shook their heads.

Agnes finished her whisky. Questions tumbled in her mind, as the men resumed their conversation. She turned to Marky.

'Are you sure – you and Venn—'

'What about us?'

'You're not related?'

He laughed. 'Honest, we're not.'

'How well does Claire know Rosanna?'

'Quite well, I think.'

'And Cally?'

'Rosanna's friendly with both girls. Claire's closer, I'd say, because of her singing.'

'Marky—' Agnes was frowning. 'Who do you think killed Cliff?'

'I think – I think it must have been Mal. I'm sorry, I know it would be nice to think it was someone else, but . . . I don't trust Venn. And I think Mal was an idiot to get involved with him.' Marky circled a beer mat under his glass.

The conversation behind them dissolved into loud laughter. Marky, still sober, turned to Agnes. 'Will you see Claire again?'

'I don't know. She turns up when she feels like it.'

'I hope she comes back.'

Agnes touched his arm. 'She will,' she said.

She walked away from the pub, along the main road, then turned off to Borough High Street, the night air sharp against her face.

Marky really cares about Claire, she thought.

Cally must be wrong to think Claire could kill her own father. No one else thinks so.

Unless Marky's covering for her.

And Emlyn's surname is the same as Venn's. And he's never heard of him. But he knew Cliff.

It's much more likely to be Venn who killed Cliff. What Des said rings true. That Cliff went for Venn and came off worst.

Because he'd found something out about Venn.

Or because he was in love with Rosanna.

Or both.

The street lamp outside her block wasn't working, leaving the courtyard in darkness. She fumbled for her key with numb fingers, glancing up at the windows. Beyond the shadowed angles of the building she could see the stars, beads of light in the clear sky. She let herself in and hurried up to her flat, switching on lights, the bar fire, the kettle. She sat by the fire, still in her coat.

In Provence, Agnes had sometimes slipped out of the house at night and run to the orchard. She'd sit on the gate, enjoying the warm darkness and the sharp scent of the trees. Agnes stared into the bar fire and remembered the shivery fear of watching the trees in the dark, of wondering if she'd be found out – of knowing, deep down, that no one would even miss her. She could stay there all night, she told herself, trying to make it a game.

And then she'd gaze up at the stars, and wonder what it was like to live in a house where people cared about what you did. Sometimes she'd see a shooting star and think about a wish, but she never wished. She knew what she'd wish for, and she knew it was simply impossible. You can't change grown-ups, she'd tell herself, knowing it was true.

Eventually she'd wander back into the house, up the stairs, back to bed, trying to tell herself she'd had a lovely adventure. And it had been nice to see the stars.

Agnes stood up and took off her coat. She hung it on its hook and went into the kitchen. The kettle had boiled, and she looked at it, picked it up, put it down again. In the distance a church clock chimed midnight. She lit her candles and knelt in prayer.

Restore us, O Lord God of Hosts. Show the light of your countenance and we shall be saved . . .

What had Cliff found out? The question circled in her mind.

Let your ways be known upon Earth, your saving help among the nations.

What connection was there, between Cliff and Venn, that could have such fatal consequences? Or between Cliff and Emlyn?

Agnes stood up and blew out her candles. And who was there to ask? she wondered.

The alarm clock shattered her dreams. She woke reluctantly, still wrapped in the warmth of sleep. She showered and dressed, her mind fogged with thoughts of Claire; of Des, and Venn, and Cliff. On the way to the prison she bought a double espresso from the new coffee place on Borough High Street.

At eleven Imelda crept into the Catholic chaplaincy office and found Agnes sitting at her desk staring into space.

'Message for you,' Imelda said, making her jump. Agnes took the piece of paper that Imelda handed her. It was from Ian, asking her to meet him that evening to discuss Amy.

'It's about . . .' Imelda was still staring at the paper that Agnes held in her hand. 'It's about that girl . . .' Then she stumbled to her desk and sat down. 'I was that age,' she said suddenly. 'Look.' She got up and pulled open the filing cabinet, and took out Amy's file. 'Look.' She put the file on Agnes's desk, pointing at the first page, where it said 'Date of Birth'. '18 July. That's my birthday too. She's seventeen, isn't she? And I was too.' She stood at Agnes's elbow, breathing hard.

'Imelda—' Agnes looked up at her. 'What happened?'

Imelda shook her head. 'I didn't know anything. These young girls now, they know everything, things that only married women should know. Me, I didn't know anything, just that I loved him, that's all. I was going to marry him. I didn't know we'd done anything wrong until . . .' Her words died away and she stood there, breathing.

'There was a child?'

Imelda's face went chalk white. She chewed at her lip. 'No,' she said. 'There was no child. Never any child.' She walked to the door with an oddly regal gait, opened it and walked out. Agnes waited a while, then went out to join the women on association.

'The problem with her sort, right,' – Janette jabbed her finger about an inch away from Agnes's face – 'is that she don't know nothing about real life.' Janette turned to her friend Lise, who was sitting next to her, then turned back to Agnes. 'Do yer? Shut away in your religious life, you don't have to have nothin' to do with real people.'

Here we go again, Agnes thought. She noticed the other women, some glancing up to see if the scene was worth watching, most bored, watching the television, reading magazines, talking to each other in small groups. Tils and Barney sat at a distance, eyeing Lise with a certain hostility. Somewhere an alarm bell went off. There was the distant slamming of doors. Agnes looked at the officers, who shifted nervously but didn't move.

'You fuckin' listening to me?'

'Yes, Janette, I always pay attention to general abuse.'

'No, I mean it. If you knew something about real life, you'd understand better. You'd know how difficult it is to live in the world, instead of just in your—'

'Cell?'

'Yeah.' Janette nodded vigorously. 'I've been married, right. I know about love, and what a man's like, and I've had tough times, and I've survived . . .'

'My husband nearly killed me,' Agnes said. 'Ex-husband, of course, now.'

Janette blinked.

'Yes,' Agnes went on. 'My fault, of course, for marrying someone who turned out to be violent. You'd understand, wouldn't you, Janette?'

'But—' Janette was staring at her, her mouth open.

'Life's full of surprises.' Agnes turned to go. She felt Janette's grip on her arm.

'Thing is, Sister . . .' the voice was lower, now, softer, 'they've screwed up my prescription again, and I wondered if you could—'

'The answer's no, Janette. And anyway, haven't you got a visitor this afternoon?'

'Yes. Myra.' Janette brightened, suddenly wide-eyed in anticipation. It seemed pathetic that such a small thing should make such a difference, and Agnes felt a brief tug of pity for her.

Janette let go of her arm. 'I hope she brings me more than she brought last time.'

' "O God, who set before us the great hope that your Kingdom shall come on earth . . ." ' Julius read the collect in his calm and even tones.

Perhaps it's true, Agnes thought, staring up at the altar window in the lady chapel at St Simeon's. Perhaps it's true that it's easier to retreat to a convent cell than stay in the world.

' "Give us grace to discern the signs of its dawning, and to work for the perfect day when the whole world shall reflect your glory . . ." '

'Amen,' Agnes echoed, joining her voices to the handful of parishioners gathered for lunchtime mass.

'Perhaps it is just an escape, Julius.' Agnes scuffed her feet in the gravel of the drive as she waited for him to lock the church door.

'What is?'

'Janette said that we nuns are just escaping from life.'

'And is that what you think?'

'Well, my first order, the enclosed one. That was an escape. From Hugo.'

'That's different.'

'And now—'

'Is it an escape, now?'

Agnes shook her head. 'No. It's very difficult.'

'I don't think anyone who knew about it would say that religious life is an escape.'

'Even in the most enclosed, silent order?'

'I would have thought that's the hardest of all.'

'For Imelda—' Agnes began, then stopped. 'Sister Imelda. She seems to have known nothing but suffering. Something in her past . . .' Agnes looked up at Julius. 'We can't run away, can we? From what we are?'

Julius shook his head. 'We have to make peace with our past, I think. If we can.'

'My mother sent me a photo. Of a different past, I mean. Not the one I knew. Except she can't tell me what it's about. And now it's too late.'

'If she's trying to make peace . . .' Julius's voice was gentle. 'It's not too late. It's just that sometimes it's very difficult. Depending on what happened, if it involves forgiveness, maybe, or coming to terms with something . . . we all carry our stories with us, but some are heavier to bear than others.'

'And me?'

'Oh, you, Agnes – you carry your story so lightly you're determined to carry everyone else's as well.'

Chapter Twenty

Agnes caught up with Myra outside the visitors' wing.

'Oh, hello, Sister, I was just leaving.' She fished in her carrier bag and brought out her blue hat.

'How did Janette seem?' Agnes asked her.

'Much the same.'

Agnes nodded.

'I mean, if she didn't do it, who on earth did?' Myra pulled on her hat. 'You know what I'm beginning to think? I think she needed to come back here. I think she attacked him so that she could come back. I don't think she meant to kill him. I think she just wanted everything to be as it was. It was easier to love Jim when she couldn't see much of him, and then he became her ideal man. As soon as she was out in the world she had to face up to the man she'd married, and she couldn't bear it. She can't cope with real life, you see; after all this time inside, she'd much rather be shut away safely in a cell.'

Agnes smiled.

'Did I say something funny?'

'Janette accused me of just that this afternoon, of needing to be shut away in my cell.'

'You? Oh, it's different with you people. Isn't it?' Myra buttoned her coat neatly. 'I must be off now.'

'Is it different with us people?' Agnes sat down opposite Ian.

The coffee bar was warm and busy, and Ian wrinkled his nose against the smoke.

'Is what different with you people?'

'Me and Janette. We're both shut away in cells and able to ignore the real world.'

Ian laughed. 'Says who?'

'Janette says it of me, Myra says it of Janette. But she said it was different for me.'

'Of course it's different for you. God, it's so smoky.'

'How's the giving up?'

'Two days now. And don't give me all your hedonistic rubbish – it's not what I need to hear.'

Agnes laughed.

'And anyway,' Ian said, 'what do you people know about it, shut away in your cloistered existence?'

'Quite. Perhaps I should enter an enclosed order and have done with it.'

'Perhaps we all should.' Ian tipped two large spoonfuls of sugar into his coffee.

'There's no point replacing one dependency with another,' Agnes said, watching his cup.

'There certainly is. Otherwise I'd go under altogether.'

'That bad?'

He nodded. 'Everything seems to be conspiring to make it as difficult as possible to actually do the job I'm supposed to do. The job I want to do. I'm supposed to be caring for clients, visiting them, setting up support systems for them . . . instead of which I'm filling in forms, and forms about forms . . . and even if I do visit a client, I have to justify it in impossible terms, like what progress they have made in relation to the performance targets I've been set . . . It's crazy, Agnes, it really is. I keep thinking there must be a better way for me to do this kind of work, through the voluntary sector or something.'

'It must be the worst time to give up smoking.'

'Don't you start.'

They both laughed.

'It's like this Amy stuff. I've got loads of forms for you to fill in, about her being a good Catholic girl and you being able to find accommodation for her . . . But in my heart I know it's not going to work. They have to give her a custodial sentence, even though it'll destroy her . . .' He paused, swallowed hard, took a sip of coffee. 'And I'm contributing to it, even though Amy's the most . . . the most extraordinary person I've ever met.' His face was flushed, and he glanced up nervously at Agnes. 'She has that radiance, despite what she's gone through, that light about her . . . I think about her all the time, you know?'

Agnes poured herself some more tea.

'I think –' Ian went on, 'I think it's because she represents something . . .' He was talking rather fast. 'She represents everything I can't bear about my job. I think that must be what it is. It's like here I am, having to play some kind of game with the courts in apportioning blame to her, when what I should be doing is rescuing her.' His eyes were dark with feeling.

Agnes spoke carefully. 'She isn't what you'd call sane, is she?'

Ian looked up. 'I think she is. She's just doing what she needs to do to protect herself.'

'But claiming that Jesus talks to her – it's crazy.'

'No it isn't.' Ian started to laugh. 'This is the wrong way round. You should think it's perfectly sane to hear divine voices, and I should be saying it's mad. You're the one who believes in Jesus, after all.'

Agnes laughed. 'A test of my faith,' she said.

Ian stirred his coffee, serious again. 'I mean it, though. I'm going to give up this job.'

'What will you do instead?'

He shrugged. 'I've no idea. Nursing, maybe, in mental health. Live on the dole and busk with my flute. I don't know.'

'And all because of Amy?'

'No, not because of Amy. I've been thinking all this for some time.'

'But you love her?' Agnes heard herself say.

Ian looked at her. He passed his hand across his forehead. 'If that's what love is, then, yes. Yes, I do.'

Agnes walked home through drizzle, let herself in, flung her coat over a chair and sat at her desk. She got up, made tea, poured herself a cup and sat at her desk again.

A thought surfaced, and she realised it had been at the edges of her mind all day. This gypsy's curse, she thought. The only thing that connects Venn Price with Emlyn Price is a gypsy's curse.

I don't believe in things like that, Agnes thought. Any more than I believe that Jesus will rescue Amy with a miracle.

Agnes got up and walked to the window. Jim had come to join his brother, to get work. And this woman that Myra knew had asked her to keep an eye on him. Her godmother, or guardian or someone, from the Valleys. Jim's aunt. Venn's aunt too, presumably. And Marky knows Venn, and he's never said he's related to him. And when I asked, they just thought I was joking . . . And Marky knew Cliff too – but then, that was only through the girls. No one else knew Cliff. Apart from Venn. And Emlyn. Emlyn, who'd befriended him, who'd tried to help him start a new life.

Agnes went to her kitchen. She unwrapped a fresh loaf of bread and placed it on the bread board. She stood, the knife poised over the loaf. The Welsh chapel, Agnes thought, her mind racing, remembering Janette sitting, drunk, on the steps of the chapel, drawn there by the memories of her wedding day.

Perhaps I should talk to Myra . . . She put down the knife, and went and sat at her desk again. She picked up the phone, found Myra's number in her notebook, and dialled the first two digits. She hesitated, then hung up.

Here I go again, she thought. Just because a man I hardly know behaves very oddly in a pub, and just because he's Welsh, and just because I can't stand Janette, and just because my mother's dying and I'd rather not think about it, and just because all God really wants of me is to keep my mind on my own story rather than trying to be part of everybody else's . . .

She got up, and made herself a tuna sandwich and a fresh pot of tea. She ate the sandwich slowly. Making peace with my past, she thought. Making peace with my own story. She thought about Imelda, wondering what the order would do to help her. She thought about the hierarchies of priests and confessors and spiritual directors, and wondered where Imelda might start if she wished to confide in someone. If it were me, Agnes thought, I wouldn't tell them anything at all.

At eight thirty next morning, Agnes was startled by the sound of a letter landing on her doormat. She went and picked it up, knowing what it was. She took the letter to her desk and slit it open. It was long, several thin pages, written in Mme Grillon's frail, delicate handwriting.

'*Chère Agnes*,' it began, followed by polite words of gratitude for her letter. Then the tone changed, with apologies for what she was about to say, and regret that there was no way to lessen its impact.

'Yes,' Henriette Grillon said, 'your mother was born and grew up in the mining regions of northern France, near Marchiennes. Rieulay was the name of the village. Her father was a miner's son, and her mother a local woman too. There were two girls, your mother was the elder of the two. The younger one, Catherine, died young. There was terrible poverty, as is all too apparent from the photograph.

'When your mother was eighteen, soon after that photo was taken, she fled. She disappeared altogether. No one in the village heard from her, not even her parents. When she next made contact, she was a wealthy woman, married to your father and living between this house and the flat in Paris. Her father had died by then, and she arranged for your grandmother to join her here.

'The only reason I know of her past is that my dear husband, God keep him, was their solicitor. We were both sworn to secrecy. You see, the intervening years between her flight from Marchiennes and her appearance here were far from happy. She was reluctant to reveal any of it, but for various legal reasons much of the truth had to come out. Much of it your father didn't know, and I think that explains their unhappiness, if you will forgive me for commenting on such a personal aspect of their life together.

'She was a determined young woman. Ruthless, some might say. She ran away to Paris, penniless. By the time your father met her, some years later, she had money, a business, an establishment. To put it as gently as possible, it was not a respectable establishment, only of course he didn't know that. She had long ago realised that her only asset was her body. I am sorry to say this to her own daughter.

'She hid all details of her business from your father, and told him instead that her family had a country estate. Your father, being English, didn't think to question what she said, and anyway he was besotted. He too was quite wealthy from his business affairs, which was just as well for her. She organised a quick and secret wedding, claiming that her father wouldn't approve of her marrying an Englishman. She was now a wealthy bride, and with your father she looked for property here, eventually finding this house. It had been empty for some time, and they bought it. By this time your mother had completely reinvented her life. She made sure to tell everyone in the village that the house had come to her from some family legacy.

'Of course, the old families here always knew your family were imposters, and there was a certain amount of debate in the village about Madame's northern accent, not to mention your grandmother's. The true story came only to me and my husband, and even then in fragments, which often contradicted themselves.

'When she sent Celine to collect the photograph, you can imagine the state of my feelings. I wasn't sure what to do for the best. I visited her before writing this letter, and I asked if this was what she wanted. She didn't appear to be listening, but when I'd finished she tried to speak. Yvette fetched some paper and she wrote on it. I'm afraid it wasn't very coherent, but in any case I enclose the note with this letter. I hope that it bears out the truth of the story as I have told it.

'Please accept my profound regrets at having to convey to you these facts. I gather you have visited recently. Please, *chère Agnes*, when you are next here, do not hesitate to call at the old house.'

The letter was signed, 'Henriette Grillon'.

Profound regrets. Agnes wondered how much she'd enjoyed informing little Agnes, the spoilt child from the big house, of her true lowly origins. On the other hand, the letter was sympathetic, and, to her credit, Mme Grillon had sat on this information for years and managed to keep it to herself. Perhaps her habitual rudeness was cover for a warm heart after all.

Agnes picked up a scrap of paper that had fallen out of the letter. On it, in a painstaking scrawl, was written, '*C'est l'histoire. Pardonne.*'

Agnes stared at the clumsy words. *C'est l'histoire*. It's the story. Or, it's history. And *pardonne*. Forgive. As in *pardonnes-moi*. Forgive me. Or, just, sorry.

Sorry. A whole lifetime. A whole childhood of loneliness and confusion, born of her father's bitterness and her mother's disappointment. A legacy of a reinvented past, falsehoods laid down in layers, in strata like sandstone, accumulating over years, forming fault lines for the future.

My grandparents were impoverished miners. And I had an aunt who died in childhood. And my mother lied.

Agnes flung on her coat and went out. She walked, fast, crossing Bermondsey Street, past the excavation site at London Bridge, then skirting Southwark Cathedral to the embankment. Agnes felt the thin rain on her cheeks, and lifted her face towards it.

She reached the river. She stopped by some old stone steps. They led down to the water, but the tide was out, leaving wide stretches of mud. She went down the steps, and set off eastwards along the mud, stumbling over stones, the rain now heavy, soaking through her coat, drenching her hair.

What did she hope to gain? And my father, fool enough to believe her, until the truth gradually revealed itself through the cracks. Agnes remembered how it felt, the way he kept his distance; it was as if you had to shout at him across an invisible divide, and even then he'd pretend not to hear.

And me, with my sense of family, trying to belong in spite of everything, putting down roots in what appeared to be ancient soil, and which now turns out to have been quicksand.

Agnes paused, breathless. The river churned slowly, flinging waves like spittle against the mud as the tide began to turn.

Agnes flicked wet hair from her face.

C'est l'histoire. Histories. Stories. All false. Like a gypsy's curse, a semi-truth lost in the time before memory, but still somehow to blame, still used as an explanation for . . .

Agnes put her hand across her mouth, unsure whether she'd spoken out loud. A gypsy's curse. An explanation. She looked down at her feet, where the waves licked at the mud, brown and laddered with weeds. Agnes thought of laddered stockings, and mottled blue legs, and the steps of the chapel. She remembered Rosanna teasing Venn, about being a Celt. A true Celt, complete with gypsy's curse . . .

But I don't believe in gypsy's curses.

She began to walk again, hurrying to the nearest set of steps, ascending them just as the water began to lap at the old stone. She came out on to Bermondsey Wall, and went to find a bus. On Jamaica Road, the new Bermondsey underground station rose up behind its hoardings, a brave new world of glass and light against the drab estates.

'When did Jim come from Wales?'

Janette looked up from her bed, surprised out of her habitual sulk by Agnes's sudden appearance in her cell. 'Where the bleedin' hell have you been? Look at you. Eh, look, Lise, look at our Sister 'ere. Been mud-wrestling, 'ave you?'

'When?' Only now did Agnes become aware that she was wet through, her hair spiked with rain, her shoes more mud than leather.

'When what?'

'When did he come here from Wales?'

'I told you, didn't I?'

'And whereabouts in Wales?'

'I dunno, do I? Some village. He never took me there, never went back, as far as I know, like his brother – he's just the same. Myra'll know. She knows his aunt.'

Agnes locked the door, strode through the corridors to her office, let herself in and dialled Myra's number. There was no answer. Agnes heard the phone ring, heard her heart beating in her ears, heard it ring and ring and ring.

She hung up, put on her filthy coat and went out of the prison. On the way home she went into a newsagent's and bought a map of Wales.

At home she flung herself into a chair and dialled Myra again. This time she answered.

'It's Sister Agnes.'

'Hello, dear.'

'I was wondering . . . this village, where your godmother lives . . .'

'Draenllwyn.'

'Where is it?'

'Near Merthyr. Very near – you can practically walk it out of Merthyr. It's one of the old iron villages, all gone now, of course.'

'And that's where Jim came from?'

'That's right. And his no-good brother.'

'Do you know Harry? And Emlyn?' Agnes tucked the phone under her chin and unfolded her new map.

'Harry who?'

'Harry Morgan. They work at London Bridge, on the site there. Used to be miners in Wales. They're a group of cousins.' Agnes scanned the map, following roads and rivers with a finger.

'No, dear, I don't. Glenys has never mentioned them.'

'They're Welsh.'

'There's quite a lot of Wales, isn't there?'

'Yes. Yes, there is. Ah, here it is. Merthyr Tydfil, is that what you mean?'

'That's right, dear.'

'Would Glenys mind . . . ? Do you think I might . . . ? You see, I was thinking of visiting Drine . . . Drineclo—'

'Draenllwyn.'

'That's right. Would Glenys mind if I went to see her?'

'Whatever for?'

'It was just something that Emlyn said. Have you heard anything about a gypsy's curse?'

There was a brief pause while Myra wondered what Agnes was talking about. 'Should I have?'

'I meant, from Glenys?'

Again, a doubtful pause. 'No, dear. Not that I can think of.'

'You see, I was wondering . . .' Agnes could sense Myra's uncertainty. 'I mean, I thought Glenys might be able to . . .' Agnes stopped. The truth was, she wanted to go to Wales because . . . Why? Why was she going? 'I just thought I'd get away, actually,' Agnes heard herself say in a small voice.

'It's pretty there. Nice hills. Have you got a pen? I'll give you Glenys's number. Glenys Allen, it is. She's a kind woman. Mention me. I'm sure she'll be pleased to see you.'

Agnes copied the phone number into her notebook, her hand still on the phone. She picked up the receiver again and dialled Athena.

'Oh, Agnes, it's you.'

'Yes, it's me.'

'And?'

'Um, it's just – I might be going away.'

'Um . . . right . . . Sorry?'

'Is everything all right? You sound distracted.'

'No, it's fine. Um, yes, it's fine. Nic's here.'

'I said I might be going away. To Wales.'

'Wales? What on earth has given you that idea? Have you ever been there?'

'No, never.'

'Really, sweetie, not Wales, surely?'

'It's quite pretty, apparently.'

'I suppose it is, if you don't mind seeing it all through windscreen wipers.'

'It's just, I've had an odd note, from my mother's friend—'

'About the photo?'

'Yes. And – are you listening?'

'Sorry? Nic was saying something. It's not a good time, sweetie.'

'And I think this village is something to do with how Venn is now, and Emlyn said something which made me think there's more to it than just Jim and Janette and everything, and so I thought – Athena, are you there?'

'Pardon? Oh, sweetie, I'm sorry. Listen, if you're a bit upset, go somewhere other than Wales, don't you think? Somewhere it doesn't rain the whole time, maybe with a beach, and a bit of sun. Or a health club? I'll come with you if you like.'

'Athena, really, I know what I'm doing.'

'Well, as long as you're sure . . .'

Agnes could hear someone talking in the background. 'I'd better go. I'll phone you when I'm back.'

'Yes. Yes, sure. I'll be, um, more able to talk then. Bye, sweetie. Take a raincoat. Take several, in fact.'

Agnes got up and looked at herself in the mirror. Her hair stood up in tufts, and her face was smeared with grime. Her jeans were caked with mud around the ankles. She got undressed, piled up her clothes for the launderette, put her coat on one side for the dry cleaner's, and went into the shower. She watched the foamy bubbles of shower gel on her skin. I know what I'm doing, she thought. If only I did.

She dried herself, put on clean jeans and her Aran sweater, took her raincoat down from its hanger in the wardrobe and laid it across her bed. She sat at her desk and reread the letter from Henriette, and then looked at her mother's note and turned it over and over between her fingers. She picked up the phone and dialled Julius.

'Hello?'

'Oh, thank goodness you're there.'

'Agnes, what is it?'

'I'm going away. Now.'

'Now? Where?'

'To Wales. It's a long story.'

'No doubt, several long stories. None of them yours, I expect.'

'Julius—'

'And you haven't asked permission, and you want me to phone Sister Christiane or someone in the morning and explain your absence . . .'

'It's a lot to ask, I know.'

'It certainly is.' They sat for a moment, listening to each other's silence. Then Julius said, 'Couldn't you do it properly, for once? Wait a few days, ask permission, reflect on whether it's necessary, that kind of thing?'

'I would, only . . . you see, I have to go now.'

'Why?'

'Because I can't face spending a night here, in my flat, knowing what I know now. I won't be able to sleep; it'll be awful. There's nothing I can do about it, you see, nothing I can do to change it back. It was all so long ago . . .' Her words came to a halt.

'Agnes, what's happened? What is it you've found out?'

'I've had a letter about my mother. She lived a total lie, she told me nothing truthful about anything, she was a hollow

270

person, a shadow, with no past, no roots – it explains everything, you see . . .'

'And Wales will help?'

'I have to get away.'

Julius was quiet. Eventually he said, 'I'll phone Christiane for you. And the prison. Anyone else?'

'I don't know what I'd do without you.'

Julius was about to say something, but then he heard that she was crying. 'Goodbye, then,' he said.

'It's only a day or two.'

'Right. Bye, then.'

Her goodbye was drowned in tears.

Agnes hung up, put her face down on her arms and wept. After a while she dried her tears, checked her watch and went out into the High Street. She went into a bank, and stood at the enquiries desk for ages while a brisk young man made efforts on her behalf to transfer money from a deposit account in France. Eventually he produced a wad of notes, which he handed to her with a certain triumph.

She left the bank, went back home, phoned British Rail, wrote down some train times, packed a small case, put on her raincoat, locked up her flat and went down into the street where she hailed a cab to Paddington station. It was nearly four o'clock, and already beginning to get dark, when she boarded a train for Cardiff.

Chapter Twenty-One

The train pulled away from the city, the urban landscape indigo in the twilight, the suburbs drab and endless.

Agnes leaned back in her seat and looked out of the window at the fading daylight. Quicksand, she thought. All my sense of self, built on shifting sand, on falsehood. We have to make peace with our past, Julius had said. But how can you, Agnes thought, if your past is veiled by deceit?

Perhaps it is all illusory, like Ian said. Perhaps I should just ditch the whole lot, just let it fade away, like shadows, like a dream.

And then who would I be?

Night was falling. The train slowed as it approached Reading. Agnes rolled up her raincoat and leaned against it, and closed her eyes.

She woke with a start. The guard's announcement informed all passengers that they were now approaching Cardiff. She gathered up her things, put on her coat and joined the line of people waiting to get off the train.

She stood, sleepy and shivering, on the platform. People jostled past her, hurrying with purpose. It was raining. She heard a station announcement that mentioned Merthyr Tydfil, platform six. She picked up her bag and went to find the platform.

She sat on a bench on platform six, waiting for the Merthyr train. Other people were waiting, groups of young people, a mother with two children, a few solitary commuters at the end of their working day. She listened to the conversations around her and realised that all this time she'd heard Harry, and Emlyn, and Venn, without placing their accent. She realised now that even Marky had that slight sing-song tone mixed in with his guttural London.

It's what comes of being foreign, she thought. Even now.

A two-coach train chugged into the platform. 'Does this train go to Merthyr Tydfil?' Agnes asked a young woman who was leaning against the wall.

The girl looked at her through a fringe of dyed black hair. 'Yes,' she said, as if waiting to be contradicted.

Agnes got on the train. The girl got on too with her friends, and Agnes watched them as they piled into one corner of the carriage and started to swig from cans of fizzy drinks. They discarded the sticky cans one by one, leaving them to roll around in the aisles with the movement of the train.

The train stopped at frequent intervals. Agnes peered out into the darkness. Occasionally the floodlights of an industrial estate would break up the night, but as the train went further into the valleys and fewer people boarded it, Agnes had a sense of venturing into the unknown, into territory where she knew no one and no one knew her; and where no one could have any expectations about her. She felt a strange excitement, glad it was dark, glad it was raining, glad that she had no idea where she was going to sleep that night.

The train stopped at Pontypridd. A group of young people got on and began to eat chips out of paper bags. Agnes realised she was hungry. The train set off again, moving further up the valley. Two or three more stations, and then the train pulled into Merthyr. Agnes got out, and followed the straggling crowd of passengers out of the station. It was still raining. She pulled her scarf around her neck, standing on the platform, her bag at her feet. People passed her, walking purposefully, all with destinations, she thought, warm and dry destinations, homes and families.

She thought with a jolt of her mother arriving in Paris. Agnes touched her pocket, where her wallet was safely tucked away. My mother had nothing, she thought. She had only her decision, her willpower, her determination to flee, to get away, to escape from everything she'd been and start again.

It's too early in this process, Agnes thought, shivering in the rain, to decide I'm like my mother.

Or too late.

She wandered up to the main street. It was deserted, the shops all closed. A few young people hung around the entrance to the shopping centre. Chain stores she recognised stood side by side with 'Closing Down Sale' and 'Everything a Pound' printed on desperate strips of paper stuck across the window, and draped with tinsel in an attempt to be festive.

The high street opened out to an empty car park, lit with a few bleak streetlights. She walked across the tarmac towards a pub which described itself as the George Inn. In the window there was a handwritten sign in fat black letters saying 'Rooms'.

Agnes approached the door, then went inside. People sat in small groups, and she was aware of a lowering of voices as she went up to the bar.

'Excuse me—' The barman was young, with bad skin. 'Do you have any rooms to let?'

He stared at her with pale blue eyes. 'Um – I'll just get someone.' He went out of a door and she heard him call, 'Mum?' and then a middle-aged woman with tight black curls and a stained apron appeared. 'I gather you want a room,' she said, as if the request was unusual.

'Yes.'

'For how long?'

'Um, a night or two.'

The woman was appraising her. The conversation in the bar behind her was hushed, as if the scene being played out before them, of a stranger asking to stay in Merthyr on a cold, wet night in December, was far more interesting and odd than anything they could find to talk about.

'We have a room,' the woman said. 'I'll get the key.'

She showed Agnes upstairs to a room which had bright floral curtains and bedspread, and an angular wallpaper design in contrasting colours. 'It's thirteen pounds a night,' she said, placing a clean towel by the wash basin. 'We can do you a breakfast downstairs, if you like.'

'Yes, please,' Agnes said, reminded once again of her hunger.

'Eight thirty suit you? I'll leave you this registration card – just a formality. Do knock on the door at the foot of the stairs if you need anything.' The woman was still guarded, but friendlier.

Left alone, Agnes went to the window. The room overlooked the car park. A group of young people clustered under one of the streetlights, lounging, drinking from cans, the boys wrestling with each other, the girls dressed in thin jackets and strappy shoes despite the cold.

Agnes thought about food. She thought about her mother, who must have known hunger as a constant presence in her early life. She closed the curtains and sat on the bed.

No one knows where I am, she thought. Anything could be happening in London, and no one would be able to find me. This is freedom, she thought. This is true freedom. Not Ian's freedom, freedom from illusion, and not the freedom of handing everything over to an order, but this: being in a strange town, where no one knows me and no one knows where I am.

She unpacked her things and took out a candle, placed it on the shelf above the mantelpiece and lit it. She knelt in prayer, summoning up the familiar words, settling her breathing. Even God's presence seemed dimmed, as if this new-found liberation had dispensed with everything she'd known before.

She woke to sunshine and the smell of bacon frying. She washed and dressed and went downstairs, reflecting that it was ages since she'd felt this hungry, a sharp, desperate hunger. There was something exhilarating about it.

She sat down to breakfast, and handed the registration card to the landlady. Agnes was aware of her hesitation as she scanned the card.

'Bourdillon,' she said. 'Is that a foreign name?'

'Yes,' Agnes said. 'French.'

'I'll bring you a pot of tea.'

Bourdillon, Agnes thought, buttering toast, wondering why she was still burdened with her husband's surname when it meant so little to her. Perhaps I could revert to my maiden name. My father's name, tricked out of him by my mother. That doesn't seem much better, really. Perhaps, she thought, slicing a rasher of bacon, all names tie us down in some way. Perhaps in my new liberated state I should have no name at all.

The landlady reappeared with her tea, and Agnes turned to her. 'Do you have a phone, Mrs – um—'

'Thomas. Yes we do, just outside the bar there.'

Agnes finished her breakfast, and found Glenys's phone number in her notebook.

'Is that Mrs Allen?'

'Yes?'

Agnes wondered what to say. 'I – er – I got your number from Myra, your goddaughter.'

'Oh, Myra, yes.'

'I'm visiting Merthyr, you see, and she said maybe I could look you up, if it's not inconvenient, of course . . . my name's – um—' Agnes hesitated. 'Agnes. Sister Agnes. I'm – I'm a nun.'

'And you know Myra?'

'Yes. Well, you see, I work at the prison where Janette is, you know, who was married to Jim—'

'Oh, yes, our Jim.' Glenys sounded uncertain. 'Well, you're very welcome to call in. Later today, perhaps? Teatime? Come about three. There's a bus from town, the number nine. Or you could take a taxi – people sometimes do.'

Agnes thanked her and rang off. She must be wondering why I want to see her, she thought. And I don't know what to tell her, because I don't know myself.

She went out, wandering aimlessly around the town, which in daylight was bustling and crowded with shoppers. She set off along the main street. Beyond the town she could see the hills, their peaks capped with snow which sparkled white in the sunshine. Agnes kept walking, leaving the town centre behind her, following a half-built ring road, picking her way between traffic cones. New office blocks in clean red brick rose up from redeveloped sites, windswept and isolated. Beyond them she could see stranded terraces of houses. Across the valley there was an old pumping station, a Victorian building in yellow stone, beautifully restored. A sign pointing towards it said 'Heritage Centre'. Next to it she could see the derelict remnants of an ironworks: a few pillars and arches clustered together, empty and desolate.

I wonder if the village where my mother grew up looks the

same, Agnes thought. Rieulay, she thought, allowing the name to settle in her mind. The sun was disappearing behind cloud, and a sleety rain began to fall. Agnes turned back towards the town.

At three o'clock Agnes got out of the taxi. She found herself standing in front of a row of cottages, built in a line to follow the slope of the hillside, their slate roofs forming a gentle staircase. She looked at the neat symmetry of the doors and windows. Beyond the cottages rose up the stark wintry slopes of the hills, dark grey in the chill of the afternoon, like the black slag heap in her mother's photograph. She knocked at the door of Number 4.

An elderly, motherly looking woman answered the door. She was small and round, dressed in a Paisley-print dress.

'Sister Agnes? Do come in.' She led Agnes through to a front room, which looked out over the valley. 'Tea?' She studied Agnes. 'And I've made some Welsh cakes,' she added shyly. 'Have you ever tried them before?'

'No, I haven't.' Agnes smiled, glad of the warm welcome, aware that it was some hours since she'd heard the sound of her own voice.

Glenys went out to the kitchen. Agnes stood by the window. She could see the thin metallic strip of the river, the faceless sheds of the industrial estate.

Glenys reappeared with a tray, and Agnes settled down in a chintz armchair.

'So,' she said, 'how's Myra?' She sat opposite Agnes, and waited for the tea to brew.

'Oh, fine. I – I, um, don't know her that well. It's just, I'm the prison chaplain where Janette is, um, staying, and I met Myra when she visited her.'

'She's a nice person, Myra. I've been trying to persuade

her to move up this way. I don't think London's the place for someone like her. Her mother was from there – Dulwich, it was. That's when I met her. I did some of my war service in London, and I stayed on afterwards. Her mother, Sylvia, one of my closest friends, she was. Then I came back here. My father needed me in his last illness. But we kept in touch, even after Sylvia passed away. Myra's been very good.'

'And Jim—'

Glenys's face clouded. She leaned over and stirred the tea, then poured two cups. 'Terrible business. They say it was Janette.' Her tone was interrogative.

'Yes,' Agnes said. 'They do.'

'My brother's boy, Jim. Lewis, my brother, he had the two boys, Venn and Jim.' She passed Agnes a cup of tea.

'Are you a close family?'

Glenys nodded. 'There's me, I'm the eldest. Then Lewie. Then Rhys . . .' She broke off. 'Sugar?'

'No thanks.'

'And then our kid sister Bronwen. She married Davey Morgan, and moved away. They live over Rhondda way.'

Morgan, Agnes thought.

'Those cakes will have cooled by now.' Glenys got up and went out to the kitchen. Agnes surveyed the room. There were two china dogs on the mantelpiece, and an ornate teapot. On each side of the teapot were some photographs. Agnes went over to have a look at them. They were mostly black and white, and they showed various people, all short, dark-haired. There was a wedding photograph, with bride and groom, the bride looking just like Glenys, only with dark curls instead of grey.

'That's – that's in London, that is.' Glenys came back into the room. 'Streatham. Where I got married. It – um – it didn't work out. Put it all behind me now. Try one of these.'

Agnes sat down again and took the Welsh cake that Glenys passed her. She looked up and said, 'Morgan. Your sister.'

'Yes?'

'I met some other people, from Wales. Harry Morgan. And Marky. Marky Roberts.'

'You do know us well.' Glenys was frowning, her gaze fixed on Agnes, still holding the plate of Welsh cakes.

'It's rather odd—' Agnes felt her cheeks growing hot. 'They – um – they work on the underground. Tunnelling.'

'Yes. That's right.' Glenys was still eyeing her. She put down the plate of cakes. 'Harry's my sister's boy. And Marky's his nephew, on his sister's side.'

'And Emlyn.'

Glenys sat down. She stared at the floor for a moment, then looked up at Agnes. She nodded. 'Emlyn,' she said.

'He denied being related. To Venn, I mean. They all did.'

'Harry wouldn't know. Nor Marky. Neither of them know that other side of the family.'

'But – but they're first cousins.'

'My sister moved away a long time ago. Raised her family separately. After . . . She wouldn't mention Lewie's boys, wouldn't hear their names.' Glenys sighed. 'Harry's a lot younger, and Marky, well, he's a boy, isn't he?'

'After what?'

'And Emlyn knows very well.' Glenys ignored the question. 'He knows Venn. And Jim. Might not have seen them for years, but he knows who they are.'

'So why did he deny it?'

Glenys looked directly at Agnes. 'What did you want to see me for?'

Agnes held her gaze. 'You see, Jim's death . . . Janette's been charged, but she says she wasn't there when it happened. She'd left him by the river, he was drunk . . .'

Glenys nodded. 'Drink,' she said.

'And – and someone who Venn knows, he was killed too, and I think it's something to do with Venn, and . . .' Her words sounded weak. 'And then, when Emlyn denied it, I thought . . . I thought . . .' She stopped.

'What's he like, now, Venn?' Glenys's tone was light, but her gaze was fixed on Agnes.

Agnes spoke carefully. 'He – he's, um, very successful.'

'A villain?'

Agnes nodded. 'I think so.'

'But charming? A cross between a devil and an angel?'

Agnes smiled. 'Yes.'

'He hasn't changed, then. I always had a soft spot for our Venn. Lovely boy, always was, from the day he was born, beautiful boy. Mischievous. And sharp. Always one step ahead of his teachers.' She smiled. 'You knew he was up to no good, but you didn't have the heart to challenge him, see. He had a kind of grace about him. Even the way he moved – it was like a dance.'

'He hasn't changed at all,' Agnes said.

'Whereas Jim . . .' She shook her head. 'Lewis, you see, their da, he was an unhappy soul. Dead now – his lungs, it was. But life wasn't easy for him. There he was, with one son who'd come from the angels, flew through life with such ease. And then his next boy was just like his dad. Same gingery hair, same bad luck. Well, Lewis always said it was bad luck, but I think you make your own luck in this life.' A shadow passed across her face.

'They – they talk about a gypsy's curse.'

Glenys took another cake. 'They do, I know.' She was silent for a moment, staring at her teacup. 'But curse or no curse . . .' She stopped, her gaze fixed ahead of her.

'What – what happened?'

Glenys picked up the plate of cakes and offered it to Agnes. 'There was an accident, see. You might as well know, although no one will thank me for telling you. But it's in the past, now. Finished with.' She took a deep breath, then went on, 'Mining accident. Tragic, it was. Our Rhys. The trucks, see, go at a terrible rate they do. He was in the way . . . Our Lewis was there, tried to save him, but . . .' She shook her head. 'We were called to the mine, me and mam. We got there first. Our mam never got over it.'

'How old was he?'

'A young man, still. Not yet forty. And Emlyn still a boy, and our Joan, Rhys's wife, having to manage as best she could, raising the lad on her own. It had a bad effect on Emlyn; he were never the same. Went off to London as soon as he could. Broke her heart it did. Never came back, see – no word, nothing. It was like he wanted nothing more to do with this family, no more a part of it.' She pursed her lips, frowning. 'That'll be why he denied knowing us.'

'And Venn and Jim, they wouldn't know Emlyn?'

'See, it got Lewis bad, after Rhys . . . after it happened. Em was the first to go to London. When Venn went, it was years later, see? Venn would have had no reason to look for Emlyn.' She fiddled with her teacup in its saucer. 'Our mam never recovered, really. Went on about how she'd married bad blood. The old women of the village had warned her, she said. Our grandad, he'd come from somewhere else, the West Country, and he'd done some wrong against a gypsy woman, and she'd cursed his male line, that's how the story goes. Only our ma had never mentioned it, until the accident . . . and then she got upset about it all, wouldn't stop talking about it. Blamed our dad for some reason.' She picked up the plate of cakes, put it down again. 'It's not to my way of thinking, see. A curse, it doesn't explain things, does it? For instance, this business with Jim, you don't need no gypsy's curse to explain that, do you?'

'No. No, I suppose not.'

'Just the drinking, see. Jim was always a weak lad, like his dad. The bottle got the better of them both.'

'Emlyn doesn't drink.'

'What's he like, now, our Emlyn?'

Agnes took another cake. 'He works hard. They all do. They're tunnelling, for the tube. You know, London Underground, railway lines. It's very hard work.'

Glenys leaned back in her chair. 'So it was Em who got Harry the job?'

'I think so, yes. And Marky, and there's a couple of others – someone called Huw.'

Glenys smiled. 'Harry's cousins, they'll be, on the other side. They'll be used to hard work. It's in our blood, here. The ironworks, and the colliery. It's them that don't have the work I worry for. The young ones, you can see them – don't know what to do with themselves.'

'So – so Marky really didn't know that he and Venn were related?'

'No reason why he should. You see, Abbie, my niece, she'd never have mentioned it.'

'Just because . . . just because of this accident?'

'You can't know what it did to us. Our family fell apart. Terrible scars, you see. Our Bronwen, our kid sister . . . afterwards, I was the only one she'd see. And her children, Abbie and Harry, they were only babies when it happened.' She stood up and went over to the window. The last of the sun had broken through the clouds, tinging the sky with pink.

'Glenys—' Agnes hesitated. 'You don't know someone called Cliff, do you? Cliff Fisher?'

Glenys turned back to her. She shook her head. 'No. From

round here, is he?' She sat back down in her chair.

'No, he's from London. It's just he was working for Venn, and he's the one I mentioned, who's also been killed, and I just thought . . .'

'I don't know any one of that name,' she said. 'But people come and go from here, these days. It didn't used to be like that. When the ironworks was still going, you knew everyone, ironworkers and miners, you know. The coal fed the mill and everyone had work. Now the young people go, to Cardiff, or to London even. And the older ones, those that have the skills, they go too. They go to where there's redevelopment, they get work on the sites. Some do, anyway. It's no good for a family, is it? And there's still coal in the ground up there. And then there's those with no work: they just live, day by day, getting poorer and poorer. You can see it in those kids that hang around in Merthyr now. No work, no prospects, nothing . . .' She took a deep breath. 'Not even the chapel, see. No one's interested any more. When I was young we had work, and church, and our family, we knew who we were. It's all changed now. I don't suppose you know very much about mining, coming from London, do you?'

'My grandfather was a miner,' Agnes said. 'In northern France. My mother's father.' The words hung in the air, clear and sharp like ice. Agnes felt she could watch them, see their shape, see how the truth appeared now it was out in the world. 'You're the first person I've told,' she said. She looked at Glenys, at her round, sympathetic face. 'You see, my mother's dying, and she'd never told me before, but I got this letter, just before I came away, which explained it all. I'm half-French, you see, and I always thought we came from Provence, but my mother – my mother reinvented herself and didn't tell me. And then I was thinking about Jim and Cliff, and Emlyn . . . and I needed to get away, and Myra said I could give you a ring . . .' Agnes paused for breath. 'I think perhaps . . . I think I just needed to be free.'

Glenys smiled at her and nodded. 'We all need that sometimes.' She refilled Agnes's cup. 'You could go up to the hills,' Glenys said, 'behind here. Up to the cairns. There's a circle up there; it's a peaceful place. I often go up there. Past the graveyard. After our Rhys died . . . I spent a lot of time up there. Take the path to Aberdare out of the village. Tomorrow, maybe; it's getting dark now. When are you back to London?'

'Um, a day or two. Probably. I'm not sure.'

'Nice to be able to get away, isn't it? People come here now, on holiday. There's a heritage centre, see. People come and see how it was. It's funny, isn't it, to find your own life in a museum, like history? Some of the miners, they go and work as volunteers, in the pit, up at the centre. They go back, to show how it was. Only difference is, they don't get paid. And they don't produce coal. So it's not really how it was at all.' She laughed, briefly. She turned towards the window and looked across the valley, seeing the ghosts of the chimneys in the dying light, hearing the silent echo of the ironworks. 'If you're walking this way tomorrow, do pop in again, won't you? I'm always here, teatime. You're more than welcome.'

A drizzle was falling when Agnes left. She set off on the road back towards town, then stopped, suddenly unable to face a solitary evening in her room in the pub. She turned round and took the little path away from the village that Glenys had indicated. She passed the graveyard as Glenys had said. She opened the little gate and went in, passing silently amongst the gravestones, their lettering sharpened by the dusk. She paused by one or two, reading the names, the rollcall of the dead. Some were children, some were soldiers, or women who'd died in childbirth, or victims of accidents or cholera.

Nearly all were Prices or Morgans, with a few Joneses and Pritchards. Agnes walked amongst their shadows. It's funny, Glenys had said, to find your life's become history. History. Like the word in her mother's note.

Rhys Price, she saw, the words cut squarely in the stone. Died 30th April 1967, aged thirty-eight. Blessed are the pure in heart.

Next to his grave was a David Price, born 1883. His father, perhaps. Beyond that one was Lewis Price, born 1927. That must have been his brother, who was with him when he died.

Agnes sat down on a grave that was so thickly covered with moss and lichen it had become anonymous, its very identity returned to the earth, no longer named. She listened to the soft silence of the rain, to the shadows in the darkness. She could almost hear the ivy growing, reaching out its tendrils to the stones.

I could become a hermit, Agnes thought. I could stay here and never go back. I could change my name to some Celtic saint's name, and become a holy woman, and never speak again, and a holy well would spring from here, and people would flock to listen to my silence. I'd vanish from London, and no one would know where I'd gone. Well, she thought, maybe I'd tell Julius. He'll be so surprised. Who'd have thought, he'll say, you of all people, a Celtic saint, holy wells and everything . . . Yes, I'll tell him. Just to see the look on his face. And Athena, she'll have to know. She can bring me secret supplies of Chardonnay, and ciabatta bread, and those nice olives you get in that delicatessen near her street, those ones they do with coriander.

She thought about the ivy, twisting and winding. She thought about it taking root amongst the soil, growing out of memories, weaving its stems out of other people's lives, clinging to their epitaphs. Agnes looked up at the sky. The blackness was softened by cloud, obscuring the stars. Across the valley dwellings twinkled in clusters.

She thought about her mother all those years ago, looking out across a similar landscape. For me, now, Agnes thought, this is my freedom. For her, it was her prison. Until she got away.

Her hand touched something wet. She looked down, straining to see in the darkness. A slug nudged her finger, before moving away to find a leaf. And under this ground, Agnes thought, lie the dead. The underworld, like Hades, like the mines, she thought, where all these Prices and Morgans worked, where Rhys Price met his death. And after he died, Emlyn, his son, ran away to London. And works as a miner, digging not coal, but railways.

Perhaps it's in the blood, Agnes mused. Perhaps that's what I'm missing.

A gentle wind stirred the trees, scattering drops of rain. Agnes stood up, her legs stiff from cold. At first she couldn't see the path at all. She felt her way to the gate, then set off down the track in the darkness, following the direction of the lights in the valley.

Maybe I'll be an underground saint, she thought. That's the answer. I'll acknowledge my mining heritage. I'll live inside the holy well, and shout out words of wisdom to the waiting crowds above.

It took over an hour to walk back to Merthyr. The pub now seemed warm and welcoming, and the landlady greeted her as if she was family. She sat in the bar and had a whisky, and no one even gave her a second glance.

Chapter Twenty-Two

'I hope you don't mind,' Glenys said, showing her into her front room the next afternoon, 'I've a neighbour here, Mavis. She lives down the road. Just dropped in.'

'I don't mind at all,' Agnes said.

'Did you go for a walk? Mavis, this is Sister Agnes, she's a nun, she knows our Emlyn, and Harry, and Marky-boy.'

'Really? Do you?' Mavis had wide blue eyes, and tight grey curls. She offered Agnes a delicate hand, which Agnes shook carefully.

'I don't know them that well,' Agnes said. 'I met them because of . . . well, I met Jim first.'

Mavis shook her head. 'Poor Jim. We heard, didn't we, Glen? Myra phoned you, didn't she? And then the police, of course, came to talk to us. You don't like to point the finger, do you, but in that case . . .'

'Sister Agnes visits Janette in the prison, don't you?' Glenys poured a third cup of tea and handed it to Agnes.

'Yes.'

'She came to see me yesterday, we talked about our family.'

Agnes took a Welsh cake that was offered her.

'And did you go for a walk?'

'Yes. I went up to the graveyard. And then, this morning, I went to the museum.'

'Oh, the museum. In the big house.'

'The family collected some wonderful paintings over

the years, didn't they?' Agnes said.

Both women nodded, dutifully.

'Her grandfather was a miner,' Glenys said to Mavis. 'In France, though.'

'Oh. That must have been nice.'

There was a silence. Mavis sipped her tea, then said, 'Our Davey went off to Singapore. Last year. Tunnelling. He was only twenty. Like your Bronwen's Marky, he's only young.' She sipped her tea again. 'Only London's nearer,' she said.

'Not that we see much of Marky,' Glenys said.

'Do you think it's nice in Singapore?' Mavis turned to Agnes.

'I'm afraid . . . I've never really—'

'Breaks up families, doesn't it?' Mavis said. 'The way the work is these days. It can't be right, can it? Merthyr used to be just a tiny village. It says in that museum – you'll have seen it, won't you? Then there was the iron, and water power and steam power and coal and mills . . . and a whole town. And then it all goes away, and we're all just left here.' She stopped, pink with the effort.

'Agnes knows our Venn, too.' Glenys refilled their cups.

'Venn, eh?' Mavis smiled. 'He was always a sharp one, wasn't he? Is he still?'

Agnes nodded.

'I thought so. Rich, I bet?'

'Yes,' Agnes said. 'Yes, he is.'

'Agnes said someone else got killed, not just our Jim.'

'Really?' Mavis's eyes widened.

'Oh, it was just . . . he was working with Venn. He was shot.'

'There's London for you, eh?' Mavis was shaking her head. 'Maybe Singapore is better after all.'

'And there's a singer,' Agnes said, 'called Rosanna. Have you heard of her?'

The women looked blankly at each other, then shook their heads. 'Is she – is she Venn's . . . ?' Glenys blushed. 'You know . . .'

'They seem to be a couple, yes.'

'Not married, then?' Mavis bit into her cake. 'I didn't see him ever getting married.'

There was another silence. The rain had cleared during the morning. The snow-capped hills were brushed with brilliant white as the sun broke through.

'Cliff, he was called. The boy who was killed,' Glenys said suddenly.

'He wasn't a boy,' Agnes said. 'A man.'

'She wanted to know if I'd heard of him. But he's not from round here.'

'Cliff Fisher,' Agnes said.

Mavis shook her head. 'No Fishers round here. Oh, I meant to tell you,' Mavis said to Glenys, 'old Mrs Pritchard escaped from her nursing home. Yvonne came back from the shops to find her sitting in the chair by the fire, same as always. She'd got hold of a key and let herself in, sitting there in her nightie, talking to her ghosts just like old times.'

'What did she do, Yvonne?'

'Well, she doesn't know what to do. Mrs P. says she'll do it again if they take her back. So they've got a social worker. Nice young woman, she is, but I can't see she's a match for Mrs P.' Mavis stood up. 'I must be going. Got to catch the bread shop.' She turned to Agnes, as Glenys went to get her coat. 'Nice to meet you.' She picked up her handbag. 'Do you know, now I think of it, there was a Fisher. Denise, she was. She was in my class at school. She lived with her ma and da, down Pentrebach way. Odd girl. Not there very long. You remember, don't you?'

Glenys stood in the doorway, frowning.

'She was in my class,' Mavis prompted.

'I was the year behind you, mind.'

'No need to rub it in.' Mavis's laugh seemed thin from lack of use. 'Yes, I remember her now. She ran away, before our exams. Missed them all. And then her mam left her husband, and took up with that man from the butchers – you remember, the one with the finger on his left hand that went like that, all crooked – you remember, and she had four more children.'

'I didn't know she was a Fisher.'

'They went to Bridgend, or somewhere. Oh, look at the time! They'll be closed if I don't get a move on.' She hurried out to the hall, followed by Glenys.

Agnes was left alone. She looked out of the window. She wondered whether it was because of the landscape that time seemed to have slowed here, the valley enclosing its own past, trapping it like mist between the hills. All these memories, Agnes thought. All these stories. And none of them mine.

'Will you be going back to London, soon?' Glenys asked, coming back into the room.

'Yes,' Agnes said, making a decision. 'Tomorrow.'

That evening she phoned Julius from a coin box in the pub.

'Hello, Agnes,' he said, answering the phone.

'How did you know it was me?'

'It's nine o'clock on a Saturday night.'

'You sound tired.'

'No, I'm fine.'

'Don't you want to know where I am?'

'Wales, I imagine. That's where I've told your order you are. Not that such information in any way appeased them.'

'I'm coming home tomorrow.'

'Good.'

'Um – right, then.'

'Right.' There was a silence. 'Was there anything else?' Julius asked.

'No. Not particularly.'

'Right, then. See you soon, I expect.'

'Yes. Bye, Julius.'

He'd hung up.

Silly old Julius, choosing this moment to decide to be cross, Agnes thought. Just when I've decided to come home. I've made a good decision. I've realised that I've got to commit myself to my life, and not distract myself with everybody else's. I've got to leave this valley, these misty, whispering memories, and go back to the city.

In the city, I shall see clearly, she thought.

That night she set a candle on the windowsill of her room in the pub and knelt in prayer. As she murmured the liturgy, she felt a peace descend upon her, a sense of calm and joy. It was like a release, as if Janette and Jim and Cliff and Venn and Amy and Claire had been with her all this time, reaching out their tendrils, tugging at her. Now they were dying back, fading away into their own stories, their own pasts and futures.

This is what it is to be free, Agnes thought.

She blew out the candle, got into bed and fell almost immediately into a deep, dreamless sleep.

She woke to bright sunshine and the sound of church bells.

She felt summoned by them, and then remembered they were almost certain to be Protestant bells.

She smiled, got out of bed, washed and dressed, and went down to the bar.

Mrs Thomas's breakfasts had got larger each day, and today she set before Agnes a huge and generous plateful.

'It's a shame you're leaving us, on such a nice morning,' she said.

'It is a shame,' Agnes agreed. The sunlight spilled through the low windows, streaking the mahogany tables with purple.

'There's a Cardiff train at ten thirty,' Mrs Thomas said.

The morning continued bright and cold. Agnes packed her bag, settled her bill with warm farewells from the Thomases, and went to the station. She sat on a solitary bench waiting for the train to come in, looking out beyond the town at the hills, still dusted with snow. She wondered when she'd last felt this kind of happiness.

She glanced back towards the town. The shopping mall cut a grey concrete line across the older slopes of the high street. Dominating the view was the Temperance Hall, and Agnes smiled, as the train came in, thinking that it was the first thing you saw when you arrived in Merthyr, and the last thing you saw when you left.

She got on to the train, and settled herself down in a seat. Two teenage girls got on too, and immediately started trying on each other's jackets.

The train left, and Agnes looked out of the window at the view that she'd only seen before in pitch darkness. It was beautiful scenery. She wondered whether the mining areas of northern France were as beautiful. The train chugged on its way, through Quakers Yard and Pontypridd. Agnes glanced out of the window from time to time. They passed a cemetery, and she thought about the graveyard at Draenllwyn. She wondered where her mining ancestors were buried. She leaned back in her seat and closed her eyes, wondering whether Marchiennes had a temperance hall.

Temperance hall. Agnes opened her eyes. Why hadn't she thought to ask? The most obvious, stupidly obvious question. I'm a fool, she thought, willing the train to hurry, suddenly desperate to get to Cardiff, to a phone, rummaging in her bag to find her notebook with Glenys's number. At Radyr a large group of women with children got on, with prams and pushchairs, and Agnes felt almost sick with impatience. At Cardiff Agnes was waiting by the door, bags in her hand.

She got off the train, and raced to a phone box, checking the departures screen for the London train. She had twenty minutes.

'Hello, Glenys.' Thank God she was there.

'Hello, dear. I thought you'd left.'

'I have. Um, I'm in Cardiff now. It's just, there was something I forgot to ask you.' Agnes was out of breath.

'And what was that?'

'Why doesn't Emlyn drink?'

'Well, we're all chapel, you know.'

'But Harry does – I mean, not a lot, just moderately. And Marky.'

'Emlyn's mother, Joan, she wouldn't have it in the house. She instilled it into him.'

'Is that the only reason? He's so adamant—'

'And then, when Rhys died . . .' Her voice grew faint over the phone line.

'What?'

'Well, they'd been drinking, you see.' Agnes heard the hesitation in her voice. 'That was part of it, see. Not so much Rhys, but Lewis – he'd had a lot to drink that night. Contributing factor, the coroner said. No one knew why. It was against the rules. You could get sacked just for one drink. He'd never done it before, our Lewie. So you see, when the coroner said it was accidental death, there was some doubt . . . because of the drink. People started to talk, asking why Lewis had gone down there drunk. They started to say that Lewis could have prevented it if he'd been quicker off the mark. Those trucks roll past all the time; it's not that difficult to stop them if you've got your wits about you. That's what people said, anyway. The women, mostly, not the men. The men kept quiet – they knew better what it was like down there. They'd all known accidents. But my sister, see, it was enough for her . . .' Her voice tailed off.

Agnes stuffed more coins into the phone box. 'There must have been witnesses.'

'Yes, at the inquest, all the boys came forward. It was terrible for us all. And Joan was so upset, see, so angry about the drinking. She was temperance, see.'

'So that's why—'

'She wouldn't let Emlyn touch a drop. From that day. And our ma, she was the same. Our da drank, and our ma hated it, hated it with a vengeance. And when she heard that Lewie had been drunk, it made her worse. And so she started to blame our dad, and that's when all this gypsy's curse story came out. And I think that's what the curse was, see: not a gypsy's curse at all, but just the drink. Does that answer your question, dear? Are you there?'

'Um, yes, sorry . . .' Agnes caught at a thought that had drifted past her mind. 'Yes, I am here. Thank you, yes it does answer my question. I'm sorry to bother you. You must think my interest in your family is rather odd.'

'Not at all, dear. It's nice to talk about it from time to time. Even the sad bits – you have to think about them sometimes, don't you? Old Mrs Pritchard, she lost two sons in a mining accident. She talks to them as if they're still with her. Sometimes I think she's saner than the rest of us. Maybe without our memories we'd all lose track of ourselves.' She laughed. 'Do visit again, won't you, dear? Bring Myra with you.'

'I will,' Agnes promised, as they said their goodbyes.

She hung up, retrieved some coins, and went to find

the platform for the London train.

She sat on a bench on platform two. The sky had clouded over, and a damp, chilly breeze gusted through the station.

I didn't listen, Agnes thought. I sat in the graveyard, and voices reached me from the underworld, telling their stories of betrayal and revenge, beseeching me to listen, tugging at my sleeves with their ivy fingers, whispering through the leaves. And I was so busy deciding to be a saint that I didn't even hear.

Julius is wrong, Agnes thought, as the Intercity train screeched into the station and people bound for London began to cluster round its doors. There's no single story that belongs to each one of us. There is no story that we can call our own. All our stories are intertwined, interdependent, stretching back into the past and forward into the future.

She got on to the train and found a seat by the window.

That's why my mother was wrong, Agnes thought, as the train slid slowly out of the station. Because she tried to cut off one thread of the story and start again. Only to find the whole thing had unravelled.

Agnes thought suddenly of Imelda, unravelling too.

Agnes took off her raincoat and rolled it up, and leaned against it. In two hours I'll be in London, she thought. In two hours I'll be home.

Chapter Twenty-Three

'You look exhausted, sweetie.' Athena opened the door of her flat and let Agnes in. 'I was so glad when you phoned. I thought I'd never see you again.'

'Surely you never believed I'd stay in Wales?'

Athena pursed her lips while she considered this. 'No, sweetie, you're right. Are you hungry?'

'I certainly am. I only got back about an hour ago. I haven't refilled my fridge yet.'

'Tea? Wine?'

'Tea, I think. It's still the afternoon.'

'I bet you didn't get sunshine like this in Wales.'

'We did. Some of the time. It was rather pretty, actually.'

Athena made tea and cucumber sandwiches, laid out on a pretty blue plate. They carried everything through to the living room and Agnes settled in an armchair in the corner by the window. She looked out over the streets, listening to the traffic, watching the late sun glancing off the distant office blocks in flashes of pink.

'It's such a relief to be back,' she said.

'Sweetie, I know. Milk?'

'Yes please.'

'It feels like ages since I've seen you. There's been so much to talk about, and no one to tell.' She handed Agnes a cup. Agnes noticed, now, how tired she looked. Her black hair hung in untidy tresses against her pale skin.

'What's happened? When I left,' Agnes said, recalling her last conversation with Athena, 'Nic was here and you couldn't talk.'

'It was showdown time.'

'Athena, I'm so sorry.'

'Sorry? What for?'

'I've been so wrapped up in my version of events, I've completely neglected you. I could at least have phoned you from Merthyr . . .'

'I'd only have sobbed on the phone and used up all your money.'

'That bad?'

'Nic challenged me.'

'About Greg?'

'Oh, silly old Greg, no, not him. About what I wanted.'

'What did you say?'

'I had to be honest. I said I didn't know. I said there was no point him and me pretending to play happy families in some new house somewhere if we couldn't even communicate as we were, and he said we'd communicate better if we lived together, and then I got really cross—'

'Was this when I phoned?'

'Yes, we were in the early stages then. It ended with me getting really angry with him, screaming and crying, and then he walked out.'

'Why were you angry?'

'Because . . . because . . .' Athena took a sandwich and held it between her fingers. 'You know why I was angry with him. But then he goes and points this out to me in his therapy-workshop way – does all that "I hear what you're saying" number . . . Well, can you imagine, if that's not guaranteed to make you burst into flames of pure rage – which I did, of course. I threw something at him. I haven't done that for years. It made me feel young again.'

'What did you throw?'

Athena looked sheepish. 'My jacket.'

'A jacket? That's no good, that's soft.'

'Leather jacket.'

'Hmm. Better, maybe.'

'It has hard buttons. And I rolled it up, like that. It was the first thing that came to hand.'

They both started to giggle. 'Athena, if we're going to feel young again, it's at least got to be crockery.'

'Pathetic, isn't it?'

'And then what happened?'

'He left. And he didn't phone. I sat here all evening. And then Greg came round. We'd sort of half-arranged it and I'd forgotten.'

'And how was that?'

'Well, I was still upset about Nic, and I tried to talk to him about it; not in great detail, obviously, but I thought if I was considering my future he had a right to know. And he went all quiet, like they do, you know. It was quite clear he'd just come for a shag.'

'Isn't that what affairs are for?'

'Oh, sweetie, it's all so straightforward with you nuns. For us mere mortals, it's much more complicated.' She sighed. 'Greg was sitting there, on the sofa . . . and I was sitting where you are, and he is so gorgeous, it's true, so bloody sexy, and I looked across at him and thought, I can't make sense of any of it. Maybe this'll do. This'll do for now. And I found I was over there, undoing his shirt, like I just couldn't help it. And then we made love, and it was all lovely, and we talked about silly things, and then he went.'

'And what was wrong with that?'

'Because, sweetie, as soon as he'd gone, I started to cry,

and I didn't stop for about two hours, and then I found I'd finished half a bottle of whisky, and I cried about that for a while.'

'I can see that would be upsetting – ow,' Agnes said, as a cushion hit the side of her head.

'You're lucky it wasn't an item of clothing.' Athena ate a sandwich, then grew serious again. 'The point is, sweetie, that that night I realised this huge truth. It's taken me all these years, but that night I grasped this enormous truth . . . well, it seemed enormous, what with the whisky; it might just seem obvious now. But I realised men are simple. And I was partly crying because I realised I loved Nic and I was partly crying because I realised Greg wasn't worth it, but mostly I was crying because of all the bloody years I've wasted on men believing that they're more complicated than they really are, believing that they think like we do, feel like we do. You know, all this time I've expected them to have normal human feelings. But of course, they don't. They're just too simple. And finally I realised we can't expect them to have the imagination to even begin, even for one tiny second, to ask themselves how someone else might feel. They can't even begin to imagine the way their behaviour might affect someone else. I watched Greg go out of the door that night, and I thought, all these weeks, these days, these hours, that I've been thinking about him – and what's he been thinking about? Him. And there I was thinking that my life had changed, irrevocably, because of him. And what was he thinking? That he fancied a shag. And what made me really cry was the number of times I've allowed that to happen. Not just with him, 'cos he's quite nice really, but with really stupid, prattish, boorish, boring, unattractive pillocks. And after a while I was so angry I forgot to cry. And then I forgot to feel angry.'

'Was this after the whisky was finished?'

'It took the rest of the whisky, yes. Oh, stop laughing, you.'

'I hope you bought some more.'

'Course I did. But listen, see, I realised, though maybe I wasn't thinking very clearly, that Nic at least had tried. In my new enlightened state, I could see that within the limited expectations that we should have of men, he'd done rather well. So I phoned him—'

'What time was it?'

'God knows, sweetie. One or two, maybe.'

'And you were drunk?'

'Yes, but perfectly coherent. And I told him I loved him. And he said—' Athena stopped suddenly, her smile gone.

'What did he say?'

Athena was drained, ashen-faced. 'He said, you're having an affair, aren't you? And he put the phone down.' Her eyes filled with tears. 'I'm such a bloody fool, Agnes.'

She picked up the empty sandwich plate and stomped through to the kitchen. There was a loud smash. Agnes ran to the kitchen. Athena was standing, staring at the floor, where the plate lay in pieces. 'I could have thrown it at someone,' she said. 'Instead of just dropping it by accident because I was crying too much to see where I was going.' Agnes knelt and began to gather up the fragments. 'At least it would been therapeutic,' Athena was saying, 'to aim it at someone, someone I was really angry with. I might have felt better then.' She sniffed, loudly, and sat on a stool.

Agnes found a brush and swept up the remains. 'And who would you have thrown it at?'

'Dunno.' She sniffed again. 'Me.'

Agnes wrapped the broken china in newspaper and threw it away. Then she started opening kitchen cupboards.

'The whisky's in that one,' Athena said, pointing.

Agnes poured them two large measures, and sat down opposite Athena.

'Cheers,' Athena said, dabbing at her eyes with a tissue. 'To making a God-awful mess of my life.'

'Perhaps that's what life's for.'

Athena shook her head. 'I dunno. I've blown it altogether this time. And just in time for Christmas.'

'Does that make it worse?'

'Yes. No. And you're just as bad, running off like that. Why did you go to Wales?'

'Partly because I needed to find out about Jim and Venn and everyone, and partly – mostly – because it turns out my mother lied about everything and I wasn't thinking straight. I had to get away.'

'Your mother?'

'Yes. That photo, the old one with the coal mines – it's her, just before she ran away. She went to Paris, earned a living by dubious means, selling her body, the only thing she possessed, met my father, persuaded him she was some kind of heiress, married him and rewrote the whole story of her life.'

'Wow.'

'Except she couldn't really paper the cracks.'

'Still, eh, good for her.'

Agnes stared at her.

'That's where you get it from,' Athena went on. 'All that spirit, that questing energy. I've often wondered.'

Agnes was still staring at her.

Athena poured them both some more whisky. 'It must have taken such courage – working on the streets, in Paris. To have survived that too, and ended up with that lovely house, and her little daughter . . . what a story! Good for her.'

Agnes found her voice at last. 'But – but Athena – she lied.'

Athena looked up from her glass. 'And?'

'But, surely you can see – I've only just found out. I'm not who I thought I was.'

'So?'

Agnes looked at her, incredulous.

'Listen,' Athena said, 'which would you rather be? The woman you are, having had a childhood of orchards and ponies—'

'And loneliness and neglect.'

'And loneliness and neglect? Or the woman you'd have been if she'd stayed put, with a childhood of toil, and filth, and not enough to eat – and loneliness and neglect? For Christ's sake, sweetie, she rescued you. And you're blaming her. She had a vision of how it might be, she found a life, she found money and comfort and she raised you in money and comfort.'

'But she lied.'

'So, when was she going to tell you the truth? When was it ever going to be a good time, to say, actually, this is how it was? I sold my body in Paris, and I conned your father into marrying me, and that's why things aren't so good between us, but it's still sure as hell better than it might have been.'

Agnes was silent. After a while she said, 'She had a sister, who died. When she was young.'

'No wonder she had to get away.'

'I suppose I shouldn't blame her.'

Athena topped up their glasses.

'It's just—' Agnes hesitated. 'It's just suddenly finding out. It really threw me. When you suddenly find out who you are, if it's not what you think.'

'Sure, sweetie.' She raised her glass. 'To the whole darn mess, sweetie. And to surviving it.'

Agnes clinked her glass with Athena's. 'To not breaking any more crockery. Except on purpose.'

* * *

Agnes woke next morning thinking, Athena's right. I don't have to blame my mother. Then she thought, how much whisky did we drink? It must have been more than I thought for my head to feel like this.

She went to the kettle, made some tea, wondered about taking a headache tablet.

Monday morning, she thought. I ought to go the prison. I ought to phone Sister Catherine, tell her I'm back, face the music with Christiane. I wonder how Imelda is. Maybe I should talk to her, see if I can help. I ought to phone Ian and see how Amy is. And Cally, if she can emerge from her doped stupor long enough to talk to me. I ought to find Marky and Harry and Emlyn. And Venn.

She poured her tea, wrapping her dressing gown tighter around her against the frosty chill of the morning. She carried her cup to her desk. She opened a drawer and pulled out the two photographs, one of the little girl outside the miner's cottage, the other some years later of the same cottage, the same, grown-up girl.

I don't have to blame my mother, she thought. It's just finding out you're not who you thought – it was a shock, that's all. It made me behave in an extreme way.

Like Cliff, she mused. He'd found something out. That was what Claire had told Des. He'd gone to find Venn at the club, in a bit of a state.

Agnes put down her cup, staring straight ahead of her.

Cliff Fisher didn't drink.

Cliff Fisher didn't drink. Until his wife died.

Agnes thought about the temperance hall at Merthyr.

Lots of people don't drink, Agnes thought, going into the shower.

Denise Fisher ran away from Draenllwyn.

304

Denise Fisher was her maiden name, Agnes thought, finding a clean towel and drying herself. It doesn't mean anything.

The phone rang, and she heard the answering machine pick up the message.

'Hello, it's Sister Catherine here, on Monday morning. We, um, we were just wondering—' Agnes reached the machine and turned the volume down.

I'll listen to it later, she thought, pulling on clean clothes. This is too important.

How many china stalls are there in Bermondsey Market, Agnes wondered, wandering amongst the wares, looking at bric-a-brac, CDs, cheap jewellery – new china. She looked up from some white teacups spread out on the stall and found she was staring at Des.

'I hoped I'd never see you again,' he said.

'Thanks very much.'

'Nothing personal.' He almost smiled.

'Of course not.'

'If I knew what I was risking by coming to see you,' he said.

'What happened?'

'Venn's mates decided to warn me off. Look—' he rolled up his sleeve, and she saw his arm was covered with bruises.

'They said it's my business next. I hope you wasn't followed.'

'I'm sure I wasn't. I'll be gone in a minute. I just wanted to ask you—'

'Anything in particular you're after, madam? Denby, maybe? Lovely stuff they do these days. Last you for years, it will.'

'How long did you know Cliff?'

'Wedgwood, then, perhaps. Can't do better than Wedgwood for quality.'

'Des – please?'

Des looked at her sullenly, then said, 'Since he was about sixteen.'

'Where did he come from?'

'Here. London.'

'Before that?'

'He was born here.'

'And his mum and dad?'

'He never had no dad.'

'Why didn't he drink?'

'He said his mum had always told him never to touch the stuff.'

'Why?'

'I've no idea.'

'She's not still around, is she?'

'Nah. She died some years ago.'

'Where was she from?'

'What is this? Mastermind or something?'

'It's important. I think someone else might get killed.'

'Yeah, and I know who it'll be if you carry on hanging around here.'

'Des, please?'

He sighed. 'Cliff's mum? No idea.'

'Where's her grave?'

'I remember now. She was a Londoner too. Kilburn, that's where the funeral was. She's buried round there somewhere.'

'You see, what Cliff had found out, the night he died—'

'I told you all I know about that.'

'I think there's more to it.'

Des raised his voice suddenly. 'Look at that casserole, madam. Lovely, that is. You won't find better quality than that if you tried. Or perhaps you'd like something more in the teapot line of things?'

'Actually, there is something I'm looking for. A plate. A large, wide plate. Blue, preferably.'

Des eyed her suspiciously.

'I'm serious.'

'How about this? These go for twelve quid in the shops. I'll sell it to you for four.'

'Done.' Agnes fished in her purse and handed over four coins. 'And I promise not to come back.'

His face broke into a wide, warm smile. 'Nah, y'all right, lady. You're a customer now.'

She walked slowly back towards her flat, her plate wrapped in tissue paper tucked under her arm. Kilburn, she thought. It's not going to tell me much. Another graveyard, she thought, another session consulting the underworld. I might as well ask Janette to contact the other side on my behalf.

No, she thought, arriving back home. There are quicker ways into the underworld. It's just a question of what I'm going to find when I get there.

Her machine flashed five messages. Sister Catherine, asking her to get in touch. Eleanor, wondering where she was. She sounded strained, and Agnes sensed from her voice that things weren't going too smoothly at the prison. Ian, saying that things were happening on Amy's case and he needed her help with some official forms. Also, he was worried about Amy because she seemed to have stopped eating. The fourth one was a hesitant, elderly voice. It spoke in French. Yvette, Agnes realised. The message simply said there wasn't much time. They would welcome a response from Agnes as soon as possible. The fifth message was just a click as a phone hung up.

Agnes dialled 1471, and the voice gave her a London number. Agnes noted it down. Then she pulled out notepaper and a pen and started to write, in French. It felt odd, this language that she'd spoken for her first words, her first definition of her world, the naming of things – but now used so rarely. She thanked Henriette for her letter, reassured her that she was grateful to know the story in its full version. Asked her to tell Yvette that she'd visit very soon. And my mother, she added. Please tell my mother that I'll be there very soon.

She signed the letter 'Agnes', folded it and sealed it.

Soon, she thought. Soon I'll be ready.

She picked up the phone and dialled the number she'd noted down. A young female voice said, 'Yeah?'

'Someone there phoned me.'

'You what?'

Agnes made a quick guess. 'Is Claire there? Claire Fisher.'

There was a moment's hesitation, then the girl said, 'I'll see.'

A few moments later, Claire came on the line.

'It's Agnes. You phoned me.'

'Oh.'

'What was it?'

'Can't speak now.'

'Where are you?'

'At – um – at work.'

'What did you phone me about?'

'Nothing.'

'But—'

'Just wanted to know you're around.'

'How nice.'

'There was one thing.' Claire lowered her voice.

'What?'

'Marky said that guy he works with, his cousin or something, he's gone crazy.'

'What's happened?'

'He's gone into hiding down the tunnels. Won't come out.'

'Emlyn?'

'That's it, yeah. Thing is, that was the guy who helped my dad. The one me and Marky saw at the club. Emlyn. Cliff said he owed him everything. He said his life was going to change. You know, when he gave up the booze? He said it was all thanks to him. And he was right, you know. Those last few weeks before he died, he was a changed man. It was like the old days, before Mum died. That friendship between them, it seemed to keep him out of trouble. Until . . . until the end. I s'pose no one could help him then. But now it's the same guy in the tunnel. Weird or what?'

Agnes was silent for a moment. 'Weird,' she said.

'Listen, I've gotta go.'

'Will you be at the club, later?'

'If you are.'

'I'll see you then.'

'Okay.' She hung up.

Agnes dialled Eleanor's number.

'It's Agnes,' she said.

'Where have you been?'

'I'm sorry.'

'It's not good enough, really. I've had Janette running amok. That new friend of hers, Lise, she's a terrible influence. We've separated them, but that's just made it worse. And as for Imelda, we hardly see her.' Her voice was edged with weariness.

'Eleanor, I'll be there soon. I promise. Things are a bit difficult.'

'You're telling me. Things are difficult for everyone. It must be Christmas. They say the strain always shows more then.'

'Eleanor – are you all right?'

'No. Not really.' Eleanor tried to sound bright. 'I'll be lucky to get through the next fortnight here without a riot.'

'I'll be there soon, I promise.'

Eleanor had hung up.

The next number Agnes dialled was Julius's.

'Where are you now?' he asked.

'London. Home.'

'Ah, well, that's something.'

'Are you still cross with me?'

'Agnes, I'm never cross.'

'No, of course not.'

'And will normal life resume now, or have you found something else to get in its way?'

'The thing is, Julius . . .'

'Don't tell me. This murder investigation—'

'Julius, I worked it out. In Wales. You're wrong about me following my story. We don't own our stories. All that happens to us, all that we are, all that we become, is interlinked with everyone else. With all God's creation. We don't choose our stories.'

'I never said we did. I just said that within the Lord's plan for us, we should still strive to listen to his voice.'

'Julius, I have. I have listened. I know what I have to do.'

'Well, then, that's fine.'

'I told you you were cross.'

'No, not cross. Just slightly impatient. Assuming, of course, that the next question is, can I tell your order not to expect to see you for another – how long? Week? Month? Year? Does this investigation take in other countries, perhaps?'

'Father Julius does his world-famous impression of someone not being cross.'

Julius's tone changed. 'Agnes, I fear for you, that's all.

Being in danger. Can't you see? You've always been self-destructive. Whenever you get like this, you end up putting yourself in danger, deliberately. You seem to seek out some downward path into dark places and then you follow it. And each time, you check with me before you go. What else am I going to say, except, don't? Don't go. I want you to be safe, Agnes.'

Agnes's eyes filled with tears.

After a moment, Julius said, 'Each time, I say don't go. And each time I know you will.' There was another silence. Then Julius said, 'But if it's the Lord's voice who calls you, then who am I to argue?'

'You're Julius. That's who.' She heard him smile. 'Julius?'

'What?'

'Nothing.'

'I know,' Julius said. 'Same here.'

Chapter Twenty-Four

Agnes walked into the King's Arms at six o'clock that evening.
It was barely half full, and there was no one there she knew.
She got herself a mineral water and sat at the table by the
window.

At six twenty, she saw Harry arrive in a large crowd of
men, with Marky and Huw and the rest of their gang. They
clustered by the bar. Marky saw her, and waved. There was no
sign of Emlyn.

'What you doing here, then?' Marky came and sat next to
her.

'I've been to your village,' she said. 'Draenllwyn.'

'Hear that, boys?' Harry said. 'And she can almost
pronounce it, too.' There was laughter. 'Draen,' Harry said,
leaning towards her.

'Drine,' Agnes tried.

'Llwyn,' Harry said.

'Cluw . . .' Agnes gave up, to great merriment.

'What did you do there?' Harry asked.

'I met Glenys,' Agnes said.

Harry blinked in surprise. 'Glenys?'

'Your aunt.'

'My aunt.' He eyed Agnes uncertainly.

'She gave me Welsh cakes,' Agnes said.

'Aunt Glenys's Welsh cakes,' Harry sighed. 'Seems you've
been to heaven, Sister.'

'While we're stuck in hell,' someone said, to more laughter.

'I heard about Emlyn,' Agnes said. The laughter stopped abruptly. Harry looked down at his drink.

'Terrible,' someone murmured.

'What happened?' Agnes addressed Harry.

Harry looked up. 'Two days he's been down there now. They're saying they'll get him out by force. They send down all those managers, doctors and psychiatrists, all sorts, but half the time they can't even find him. He knows those tunnels better than anyone.'

'What made him decide to stay there?'

'He was having a bad time, weren't he?' People nodded in support. Harry went on, 'He were drinking. Never seen a drop touch his lips before, but these last days, him and the whisky, never apart they were. Worried me, I can tell you, but a man's free to drink if he wants. Not much I could do, see. And then, when was it, day before yesterday, on the late shift, we hadn't seen much of him, and then, when we come out, like, no sign of him. And the duty officer's calling me, and then later, the site manager's on to me. Wakes me up at home, did I know where he was . . . and by the next shift we realised what was happening. I went to talk to him down there, yesterday, didn't I, Marky boy?'

Marky nodded. 'We brought him some food. He's – he's not himself.' He fiddled with a beer mat, staring at the table in front of him. 'He – it was like he didn't know us. He was saying things, odd things . . .'

'That curse again. Going on about it.'

'He said, he couldn't come out because of what he might do.'

Agnes turned to Harry. 'His father died, didn't he? In the mines?'

Harry nodded. 'Never talked about, it wasn't, not in our

313

family. My da's from the next valley, see. My ma moved away when she married. It upset my Nan, it did. She never recovered.'

'And Emlyn's mother?'

'We didn't see much of them. Em came to London years ago. I only got to know him when I joined him here.'

'And you had another uncle,' Agnes said.

Harry circled his pint on its beer mat. He nodded.

'Glenys told me. She said your mother wouldn't see him.'

Harry looked at her. 'I had cousins on that side too. Glenys told me once. Don't know them.'

'Yes,' Agnes said. 'Two cousins, both boys. Lewis's sons.' Agnes turned to Harry. 'Venn and Jim. Only Jim's dead.'

Harry looked at her. 'That's what he said, wasn't it, Marky? "Jim's dead." That's what he was saying. Only I didn't know what he meant. So . . . this Jim—' Harry shook his head. 'Whatever it is, it's driven him down there.' Harry sighed. 'And now he's roaming round those tunnels, ventilation shafts, service areas – he knows them all. He could stay down there rest of his life if he wants. No one could catch him.'

Agnes put her empty glass down on the table. 'I know what he meant. About being frightened of what he'll do. I know exactly what he meant.'

'Can you talk to him?' Harry leaned towards her.

'I – I can try.'

'Marky – you go with her,' Harry said.

'I'm going to the club first,' Agnes said. 'I said I'd meet Claire there.'

'I'll find you there,' Marky said. 'Give me an hour.'

Agnes got up, and said her goodbyes, and was made to say the name of the village again a few times.

She walked out of the pub, leaving the laughter behind her. The cold night hit her face like a slap. She went to find a cab.

* * *

A solitary bouncer stood outside the club, trying not to look cold. There was no queue. A train passed overhead on the railway bridge. The wind tossed litter in and out of the shadows of the arches like a game. Agnes went to the door and bought a ticket, watched by the bouncer. She descended the stairs, blinking in the darkness.

On the stage a DJ moved amongst his decks and speakers. The club was almost empty. Someone touched her elbow, and Agnes was aware that Venn was standing next to her.

'May I take your coat?' he said. His eyes danced with cold irony.

'I might keep it on,' Agnes said. 'It seems a bit chilly in here.'

'It'll warm up,' Venn said. His hand was still on her arm, and now he led her to a table and sat her down. 'A drink, maybe?'

'Mineral water, please,' Agnes said.

He was gone for a second, and then reappeared with her drink. He sat next to her. 'I was hoping to see you,' he said.

'How nice.'

'I thought maybe you'd been asking about me, see,' he said.

'Did you?'

'And I thought, if there was something you needed to know, perhaps you should ask me, directly.'

'And then you'd tell me?'

He smiled, a broad, charming smile. 'Of course, Sister. I'd have no secrets from a woman of God.'

She smiled too. 'I've been called many things in my time, but never that.'

Someone brought him a drink, a clear spirit with ice. He raised his glass. 'There's always a first time,' he said. He clinked her glass with his.

'It's just, you see – Emlyn . . .' Agnes watched him closely. 'Emlyn Price. I believe you know him. He's taken refuge in the tunnels he's been building. He won't come out.' Agnes saw Venn's expression freeze. 'He's been drinking. For days,' she added.

Venn attempted a smile. 'The booze,' he said, trying to keep his voice light. 'It'll get us all in the end.' He raised his glass to her, but his eyes were blank as steel.

'Well, if it isn't Sister Agnes?' The warm voice came from behind them, and Rosanna joined them at their table. 'How are you, girl?'

'I'm fine, thank you,' Agnes said. 'I've been trying to tell Venn something very important, but he won't listen.'

'And what was that, honey?' Rosanna threw Venn a glance that was sharp as a blade.

'I was talking to him about Emlyn. His cousin,' she added, aware of Venn beside her.

Rosanna smiled warmly and patted her hand. 'Oh, family, Sister. Nothing but trouble. You and me, Sister, we're the better for having ditched all that.'

'Don't you have family?' Agnes smiled at her.

'Not me, kid. Me, I belong to the world. Oh, look—' Her eyes shifted, and Agnes felt Venn's nervousness as he looked towards the door. 'Here's our sweet Claire,' Rosanna said, and Agnes felt Venn breathe again. Claire kissed Rosanna on her cheek, and then came and sat next to Agnes. She looked drawn and tense. Rosanna said something to Doc, and he looked at Venn, then went to the bar and came back with a bottle of champagne and some glasses.

'Save a glass for Marky,' Agnes said. 'He said he'd be here tonight.'

'What are we celebrating?' Claire turned to the others with a nervous giggle.

'Family,' Rosanna said, her eyes fixed on Venn.

'Talking of family,' Agnes said, turning to Venn, 'I've been to Wales. I met your aunt, Glenys.'

Venn stared at her, his bewilderment showing in his face. 'What did she tell—' he began to say.

'She said you were always a charming child,' Agnes said.

Rosanna laughed. 'Oh, can't you imagine . . . ? Little angel, I bet you were, with your black curls and your dark eyes.' She put out a hand to ruffle his hair, but he jerked his head away. 'What else did she say?' Rosanna said.

'She said,' Agnes went on, 'you'd always know he was up to no good, but you never had the heart to challenge him.'

'Well, isn't that funny?' Rosanna said, her gaze holding Agnes's. ''Cos nothing's changed, has it?'

'That's just what I thought.' They both laughed.

'You see,' Agnes continued to address Rosanna, 'Venn's cousin, Emlyn, he's hiding in the Underground. He's cracked up, apparently. Marky and I are going to try to talk to him.'

'Now, why's he doing a thing like that?'

'What makes anyone hide themselves away?' Agnes kept her voice level. 'Guilt, maybe. Fear. Or both, perhaps.' She was aware of Venn next to her, so close she could hear him breathing.

'And what's he got to be afraid of?' Rosanna glanced at Venn.

'His past. He was friends with Cliff, you see. As you know,' Agnes added. Rosanna's expression hardened, like a curtain coming down. 'And maybe his future.' Agnes held Rosanna's gaze for a moment, then looked towards the door as Marky appeared. Claire jumped up to greet him, and brought him over to their table. Marky accepted the drink that was offered him and downed it, fast. He turned to Agnes.

'Shall we go?'

Agnes shrugged. 'Okay.'

Claire touched Agnes's sleeve. 'I'm coming too. I want to know . . . about my dad . . . He must know . . .'

Agnes looked at her. 'I'm not sure . . .' She turned to Marky. 'Is he – will it be—'

Marky shrugged. 'Don't ask me. I'm scared as it is. He's off his rocker, man. I reckon Claire'll help calm him down.'

Claire was still holding Agnes's sleeve, still pleading. 'Anything that will give me some clue, any tiny detail . . . I need to know, Agnes. Do you think he knows?'

Again, Agnes felt Venn's tension. 'Yes,' she said quietly. 'Yes, I do.' She got up to go.

Rosanna looked up at her. 'You take care now,' she said. Her voice was warm, but her eyes were veiled.

The three of them went to the door, and up the stairs, leaving Venn sipping his drink, Rosanna at his side.

'What was all that about?' Marky wrapped his arms about him against the cold outside.

Agnes watched her breath making clouds in the frozen air. 'Whatever it was, we're about to find out,' she said. 'Which way do we go?'

Marky led them away from the club, under the arches of the railway, picking their way across the rough tarmac in the silence of the night. They came out on to the main road, skirting the hoardings of the building site. Marky stopped short. There was a gate, a Portakabin at the entrance to the site. In the bright light they could see a sleepy security guard sitting at the desk. Marky led them on, past the entrance, still keeping close to the hoardings. The surface of the silence rippled with the muffled hum of machinery, the distant rumble of traffic. Then there was a gap in the fence, and Marky slipped inside, Claire and Agnes following, stumbling through mud and clay and rubble under the railway arches, sloshing through puddles of oily water.

'Here,' Marky said.

There was a rough wooden fence. Behind it Agnes could see the top rungs of a ladder, leading downwards into blackness. Suddenly a car screeched towards them, shredding the silence, gleaming white in the darkness. It lurched to a halt and Venn jumped out, with Rosanna behind him.

'I told you it was up to him,' Agnes said quietly.

Venn ran across the tarmac towards them, Rosanna hurrying behind him. She looked different, Agnes realised, her face pinched with cold. And fear, real fear. Rosanna came up to her and grabbed her arm, her eyes huge, her voice urgent.

'Tell him not to go down there, Sister. Just tell him.'

Venn was already at the fence. He turned to Marky. 'Here?'

Marky glanced at Agnes, then nodded at Venn.

Agnes felt Rosanna's grip tighten on her arm. 'I'm afraid of what he'll do,' she said.

Agnes looked at her. 'Isn't it a bit late for that?'

Rosanna bit her lip, but didn't answer.

Venn shouted something to Marky. Marky joined him by the fence, followed by Claire, Agnes and Rosanna.

'Baby—' Rosanna appealed to Venn.

Venn ignored her. Silently Marky squeezed through the fence and climbed on to the ladder, Venn close behind him, then Claire, and finally Agnes and Rosanna.

Agnes climbed downwards, one foot after the other, one hand after the other, the rungs narrow and smelling of metal. She was aware of Marky beneath her, slowing his pace to hers, climbing with an ease born of years of practice. In the blood, Agnes thought. I should be good at this. The shaft was dark, lit from time to time with a pale light that threw long shadows on to the curved rough concrete of the walls.

'We're there,' Marky whispered. Agnes felt her feet hit solid ground.

'Where are we?' Agnes asked.

'In the tunnel. Between London Bridge and Bermondsey.'

'I thought it would be mud,' Agnes said, looking at the concrete at her feet, the brand new rails lying in neat lines, the bundles of electric cable hanging from the half-clad concrete walls.

Marky shook his head. 'It was. Not now.'

'I thought you were miners.'

'Cladders, our gang. Steel work, that's us.'

'Where is he?' Venn looked hollow-eyed and fearful in the thin light.

'He won't be far,' Marky said. His fear seemed to have left him.

There was a rumble, the noise of a train approaching. Rosanna froze. Venn's eyes widened with terror, and Agnes looked at Marky.

'Works train,' Marky said. 'It's in the other tunnel. Just sounds like it's coming this way.' He even smiled.

'But the electricity—'

'Diesel, they are, the works trains,' Marky said. 'Juice isn't on yet. Not in this tunnel anyway. It's live through there, where the next site starts.' He pointed behind them.

'Where is he?' Venn said again.

Marky shrugged. He seemed to have relaxed, at ease in the familiar surroundings. 'That's just the trouble. Could be anywhere.'

'Find him,' Venn said, his mouth a hard line in the pallor of his face.

Marky looked at him. 'I'll try,' he said, evenly.

From the far reaches of the tunnel came a noise, a brief scuffling. Then silence. They all looked at each other, then turned to the direction of the sound. A single bulb hung from the ceiling at the end of the tunnel, and now it started to sway slightly.

'Call him,' hissed Venn.

'If he's in the shaft, he won't hear.'

'I said, call him.'

Agnes intervened. 'Maybe it's best if he hears Claire's voice first. We don't want to frighten him.'

'I don't care what—'

'He might be armed,' Agnes said.

Venn held her gaze for an instant, then looked towards the tunnel. 'Sure,' he said. 'Claire, then.'

Marky took Claire's arm. 'Just yell. Just yell "Emlyn".'

Claire's soft voice echoed through the tunnel, calling Emlyn's name. The lightbulb swung dimly in the darkness, shifting the shadows. Again there was a noise. By silent consensus, the little group set off towards it, Claire still calling out from time to time. They walked unevenly between the rails, eastwards, away from London Bridge. The tunnel darkened as it stretched away from them. Agnes thought about the outside world above them. Oh Julius, she thought. She saw Venn, leading the way, silhouetted in the darkness. They passed a light, roughly fixed into the ceiling, then darkness again. There was a notice on the wall. 'DANGER: Permanent cables are being energised. Treat all cables as live.'

The tunnel widened out into a space, and then they were climbing steps, and found themselves on a concrete station platform. 'Welcome to Bermondsey,' Marky whispered. 'Try calling him again.'

'Emlyn,' Claire called. 'It's me. Claire.'

A door slammed overhead, and everyone jumped. Venn's hand went to his inside pocket. There were footsteps, then silence. 'It's the service tunnel,' Marky whispered. 'Try again, Claire.'

'It's me,' Claire shouted. 'I'm Cliff's daughter.'

Above them, someone coughed. The sound seemed to come from the ceiling, and they all looked up. Then there were more footsteps, descending, then silence.

'Please—' Claire began.

'Cliff's – Cliff's daughter?' The voice was rough and seemed to float in the air. Agnes saw Venn looking round desperately for its source. She began to feel afraid.

'Did we meet?' the voice said. 'Which daughter?'

'There's two of us,' Claire said. 'We're twins.'

'Twins. Of course. He told me.' There was a fit of coughing, then the voice said, 'Why have you come?'

'Because – because – um—' Claire looked at Marky.

'We want to help,' Marky said.

'You here too? Have you brought food?'

Damn, Agnes thought. He'll be hungry. I should have thought.

'No,' Marky replied, lamely.

'No use to me, then,' Emlyn said. His voice was still disembodied. A sudden draught came from the far end of the platform, and everyone looked towards it. Venn took a few steps in that direction.

'Who else is there?' Emlyn said.

Agnes spoke. 'I think maybe you should come out and see.'

There was a silence. 'I'm not going back,' Emlyn said suddenly. 'You can't make me. There's no going back.' He appeared at the end of the platform. A lightbulb swung directly above him, hiding his face in shadow. There was a pause while he took in the scene, then he saw Venn. 'You—' He took a step towards him.

'Me.' Venn stood still.

'Bastard.'

'Tell me,' Venn said to him. 'Tell me about Jim.'

The lightbulb swayed behind Emlyn. 'He's dead,' Emlyn said at last.

'My brother,' Venn said.

'Brothers? I know all about brothers,' Emlyn replied. His voice grew harsh. 'Your da, and my da. Brothers.'

'Jim,' Venn said again. 'Tell me.'

Emlyn seemed to shiver in the flickering shadows. 'Drowned,' he said. His voice faded, and he coughed, violently. Venn stayed still. Emlyn started to speak again. 'I saw ... I watched him ... I didn't mean ...' He stood, swaying, hunched in the dim light. 'He wouldn't tell me ... I knew, you see. When I heard about Cliff, I followed him. I wanted him to tell me who'd done it. I knew where they lived, Jim and Janette – I followed them. I saw him, that night, fighting with Janette; I saw her leave him. And he was staggering along by the river, and I grabbed him. I asked him, tell me, why did he die? Why did Cliff die? And he wouldn't tell me. He said he didn't know ... and then I was angry, and then I saw him fall into the river, and I watched him ... He kind of sank, then floated again, then sank, out of reach, and it was like I was staring into the tunnel again, into the black, black like coal ...' He began to cough again.

Venn took a step forward. 'You killed my brother.'

Emlyn looked up at him. 'And you killed mine.'

Venn was staring at him.

'Cliff was my brother,' Emlyn said. 'And you killed him.' There was an echoing silence. Emlyn spoke again. 'He was going to tell you, the night he died. But you killed him.'

The silence was broken by a distant rumble of a train, rising and fading away. Emlyn addressed Venn. 'When I found him, it was like the lifting of a burden. My past ... a burden, lifting. I felt it was what my dad would have wanted, to have his sons together. And we had those weeks, good weeks they were. And I met his daughters . . .' His eyes sought out Claire. 'And he was coming off the drink, wasn't he? – And he was going to find some work . . . It would have made my dad's heart gladden to see it.'

'How did you find him?' It was Agnes who spoke, and again, Emlyn strained to see her in the darkness.

'I tracked him down.'

'But how?'

'My dad, see, he loved Cliff's mum. Your nan,' Emlyn said, turning to Claire with a flash of tenderness. 'She was lovely, Denise.'

'But you can't have known her,' Agnes said. 'She ran away, before you were born.'

'I found out where she was living, in London. I wanted to know why my dad had died. And she told me about my half-brother, two years older than me, he was. But she said, don't try to find him. He doesn't know. She begged me, don't track him down, not till I've gone. So I kept that secret, like all my other secrets that I've carried all these years. But they weigh you down, these secrets, they begin to bury you alive. And so one day I went to find Cliff. And now I wish I'd never gone to find him, never told him. It was the death of him. Instead of me being buried, it was him instead.'

Another draught came from the tunnel, and Emlyn seemed to sway in the movement of the darkness.

'It wasn't your fault—' Agnes said.

'He wanted to start a new life. I made him ambitious for himself, I gave him ideas . . .' Emlyn glanced towards Rosanna, but she looked away, shrinking into the darkness, avoiding his gaze. 'He brought me to your club,' Emlyn went on, addressing

Venn. 'I tried to warn him off, tried to talk him out of it. It made it all worse . . .'

'We didn't want him there,' Venn said. He looked towards Rosanna, who glanced up briefly, her face tense, her eyes blank. Venn turned back to Emlyn. 'Shame for him he never kept away.'

'Shame for us all,' Emlyn said. He took a stumbling step towards Venn. In the dim light Agnes could see his face. He looked dishevelled, confused. 'It's over now,' Emlyn said. 'When I saw Jim by the river . . . I didn't mean to . . .' he held out his arms. 'It's done now, see.' He stood unevenly on the platform. 'I've carried the past all this time. It should have stopped with me. I should have been strong. But I was weak . . .' The last word was a sob.

'It's too late—' Venn began, his voice harsh, but he was silenced by a hiss from Rosanna.

'I saw him die, my dad,' Emlyn said suddenly. 'I saw him die, Venn. After your da had taken an iron bar and swung it at him, and then let the trucks roll over him. We were called to the pit, my ma and me, we were with him. An accident, they tried to call it, but we knew.'

Venn stood, uncertain in the flickering shadows. Agnes waited.

'History, see,' Emlyn said. His hands began to pull at his clothes, his fingers nervous and clumsy. 'The sins of the fathers.' He seemed to smile, a flash of white teeth in the darkness. 'Your da, and my da, Venn, they loved the same woman. Denise. Only, my da, he won. She chose him. And then she found she was carrying his child, out of wedlock, and she ran. Ran to London, all those years ago. And my da, he married my mam. And no one knew, about his other love. And she sent no address. No one knew what had happened to her. And then one day, years later, your dad, drunk one night, starts telling my da about Denise, about how she was the love of his life. And my da says, but she was mine, Lewie. She was mine. And this is too much for Lewie, and the next night, on the shift, he's drunk. On purpose, stoking himself up with drink because he knows what it'll do to him, like it does for his dad too, and his dad before him. And with the heat of the drink running through his veins, he takes his revenge on his little brother, for having nicked his girl, all those years before, even though they were both married now, both with boys of their own.'

Venn looked round at Agnes, then spoke. 'I don't see what this has got to do with—'

Emlyn appeared not to hear him. 'When I saw my dad lying there in the tunnel, dying, I knew I had to get away. I looked down into the darkness of the tunnel and I thought, all I have to do is walk the other way. I waited till my dad was buried and then a while longer, and then I packed my things and walked. I walked to London. It took me weeks, sleeping rough, eating what I could find, and all the time I thought, here I am, leaving it all behind me. I thought it was like a burden lifting, but I didn't know then. I didn't know that I was carrying it still. I didn't know then that it was just a matter of time.'

Claire had gone to sit down, leaning against the dusty concrete of the wall, and now Rosanna went to sit next to her. She took one of Claire's hands in hers, massaging her fingers to warm them. Venn stood, rooted to the spot, stooped and cold. In the distance they heard the rumble of a works train, approaching, fading away.

Emlyn looked up, at Venn, and Agnes, and Marky, at them all staring at him, waiting for him to speak again. He smiled, crookedly, and began to laugh, an empty, hollow laugh. He shook his head. 'Gypsy's curse,' he said, still laughing. 'The sins of the fathers.' Venn tried to speak, but Emlyn went on, 'Your da and my da. And then me – and Cliff – and you – and Jim . . . Cliff didn't know, did he? How could he know, when he fell for your girl, how could he know that it was the same old story? He had no idea. And then I tell him . . . I tell him that he and you . . . flesh and blood . . . and that's why he was in such a hurry, that night . . . when he came to see you.'

Venn began to speak. 'He seemed so angry, that night . . . He never said . . .'

'I couldn't stop him.' Emlyn appeared not to hear him. 'I was working that night. I knew something was up, when I finished work. I was looking for him . . . It was my fault . . .'

'I didn't realise . . .' Venn seemed bewildered.

'My fault,' Emlyn repeated. 'If I hadn't . . . If I'd never . . . then he'd still be here.'

'So that was why he . . .'

'And then I saw Jim.' Emlyn's voice stopped abruptly, and he covered his face with his hands.

Venn took a step towards him. 'Jim,' he said, like someone waking from sleep. 'You . . . you killed . . .'

Rosanna looked up at him, then glanced across to Agnes. Her face was blank with fear.

'All these stories,' Venn was saying. 'But he was my brother.'

Emlyn took his hands away from his face, and straightened up. In the dim light there was a flash of metal, and Agnes realised he was armed.

'You killed Jim.' Venn took a step forward.

'Venn—' Rosanna's voice was level, but he ignored her.

'Yes,' Emlyn said. 'I killed him.'

'Jim didn't deserve to die.' Venn's words reverberated through the concrete.

'No,' Emlyn said. 'No one deserves to die.' He opened his

arms wide, an odd, clumsy gesture, as if he was about to embrace Venn, his pistol like a dart of silver in his hand.

Agnes looked across at Rosanna. 'He's armed,' Rosanna whispered to her. 'Venn. He brought a gun. Stupid bastard.'

Claire was still sitting on the ground, with Marky next to her.

'Claire—' Agnes tried to keep her voice calm. 'Marky – get her out of here. Both of you, get out.' They jumped to their feet and ran back into the tunnel. Emlyn was shouting something, and then Agnes saw Venn move towards him, and then Agnes heard Rosanna yelling, 'Get down – *down*!' and then, 'Stop them – for God's sake . . . Oh Christ, get down . . .' Agnes threw herself to the ground as a shot rang out, and another.

In the hollow, echoing silence that followed, Venn slumped to the ground. Emlyn had moved a few steps forward and was now standing under the lamp. His face seemed swollen by the flat white light, his eyes shadowed into empty sockets. He was holding his gun, and now he lifted it towards his face and stared at it. 'I . . .' he began to say. 'I . . . walked. When I saw my dad, lying in the tunnel, dying . . .' He looked up, as if seeing everyone for the first time. 'I knew, if I stayed there, I'd kill.'

'Put the gun down,' Rosanna said, getting to her feet. Agnes sat up. Emlyn dropped the gun. Rosanna went to Venn and took hold of his wrist. 'There's a pulse,' she said. 'Not great, though.'

Venn groaned, and she slid one arm under his shoulders and held him, her face near his. 'Baby . . .' she murmured to him. 'My honey . . .'

Emlyn spoke again. 'The sins of the fathers,' he said, staring at his gun where it lay at his feet. He looked towards Venn, who groaned again, and briefly opened his eyes.

'He killed my brother,' Emlyn said.

'No,' Rosanna said. 'He didn't. He's killed in his time, don't get me wrong: there's blood on his hands, although heaven knows, them souls he's taken out, they ain't going to be missed, not even by their own mothers . . . But not Cliff. Not him.'

'Yes . . .' Emlyn shifted from one foot to the other in distress, and his hands flapped at his sides. 'Yes.' His voice became shrill. 'Venn killed Cliff, that's why I . . .'

Rosanna was shaking her head. 'No, baby. Not him.'

'But how do you—'

'How do I know? How do I know it wasn't my sugar here? Because, honey, it was me. I killed Cliff.'

Venn stirred, and called out her name in a whisper.

'Yeah, sugar, I'm here. Baby, I'm here . . .' She began to murmur to him, stroking his face. 'That's it, baby, keep breathing. Marky'll have gone for help. Not long to wait . . . You're going to be okay, sugar . . .' Her voice was low and mellow but Agnes saw that her face was wet with tears.

Venn struggled to speak. 'Rosanna – don't tell them . . . Signed. By me. In the safe. Confess . . .' he collapsed, exhausted by the effort.

'Baby . . .' Rosanna was slapping his face. 'Sugar, don't leave me . . . Honey, I'm here. I'm with you, baby . . .'

Then everything changed. Alarms shrieked, there was a rumbling noise, and footsteps echoed overhead. The sudden chaos stirred Emlyn, who looked up at them all. He stared at Venn, at Rosanna, at Agnes. 'I walked away,' he said, and his voice rang out above the noise. 'I walked away from my destiny. But it turned out all this time I've been walking right into it.' He turned, his back to them all, and began to disappear into the shadows.

Agnes stood up, uncertain. She and Rosanna looked at each other.

The alarms were still ringing, and now they could hear shouting, feet running, and a group of men appeared, armed, uniformed. 'Police,' one shouted.

'Stop him—' Agnes tried to say. She could see Emlyn in the distance, illuminated in a single beam of light, walking into the darkness of the tunnel. 'Marky said through there it's live . . .' She was shouting now, but no one seemed to hear above the alarms and the barked orders of the police, who seemed to be trying to get Rosanna to stand up.

'Look—' Agnes cried out, pointing, stupidly, shouting out to Emlyn by name, her voice lost in the chaos. And then there was another noise, a low, rumbling crescendo, merging discordantly with the shrill ringing of the alarms.

'There's a man—' Agnes yelled, but the rumble was getting nearer, louder, and there was the grind of rails. 'He went down there,' Agnes shouted above the noise. 'He shot this man here and then walked—'

'Down there?' One of the officers yelled across to her, but she could hardly hear above the sudden fizz of current, the screech of wheels; and then the lights of the works train flashed past inches away from them, the wheels sparking in the darkness. In the midst of the noise she thought she heard a single cry, sounding faintly, drowned by the rush of the train. The alarms stopped. The sudden quiet closed in, so heavy it was difficult to breathe.

'Down there?' the man repeated, whispering.

Agnes nodded.

The men looked at each other. One of them took a few steps into the tunnel, turned back to the group, expressionless. He shook his head.

'He worked down here,' Agnes said.

'Then he'll have known . . . He must have known . . .' the policeman shrugged, appalled, helpless.

In the odd, suspended silence Agnes realised that the laboured breathing had stopped. It had been replaced by a quiet sobbing. Rosanna was collapsed across Venn's body.

'He's dead,' she wailed, and her voice rose to a howl, endless, unfettered, echoing through the deepest reaches of the tunnels.

Chapter Twenty-Five

They came back to the surface through a maze of tunnels and staircases, escorted by the police. Venn's body was carried into a waiting ambulance, and Rosanna went with the ambulance too.

Agnes emerged into the cold night, into a police car. The clock on the wall of the police station said five past two. She sat in a warm, windowless room under fluorescent light, and gave her account of the night's events. Yes, she'd realised Emlyn was dangerous. No, she didn't see the gun until it was too late. Yes, the two men were cousins. Yes, Emlyn shot Venn. Yes, Emlyn must have known that the lines were live in the other tunnel. Are you saying he intended to kill himself, madam? Yes, Agnes nodded. Yes.

Outside the interview room she found Marky and Claire. Then they were outside the police station, and the night was no nearer dawn.

'It's 21 December,' Claire said. 'The longest night. Won't be light for hours.'

My soul waits for the Lord. More than the night-watch for the morning.

'Did you say something?' Claire turned to Agnes.

'Did I?'

There was a ringing noise, and Marky took his mobile phone from his pocket. 'Yeah?'

At the same time, there was a sounding of sirens as two

police cars screeched out of the gate behind them, fracturing the night's silence.

Marky put his phone away. 'It's Ian. Asking if I knew where you were. Prison's on fire.'

They ran through the streets, under the railway arches, skirting the station. They could smell smoke as they approached the prison gates. A crowd milled outside. The yard was cordoned off, and a row of police were keeping people out. Agnes saw Eleanor run across the yard and speak to an officer. Then Eleanor saw Agnes, and ushered her through the cordon. 'East Wing,' she shouted, above the noise of fire sirens, the water hoses, people shouting. 'Healthcare. We're evacuating the surrounding wings. Everyone's over in D wing. Someone's gone in to get Amy.'

'How did it start?'

'I wish I knew. I know Lise is behind it, but how she did it I don't know. Stupid thing is, I knew it would happen, I knew something was up. There was a silence about the place all day—' Her mobile phone rang. 'Yes? Sure. Fine. Okay.' She rang off. 'Where was I? Oh, yes, it was Amy, of course. I'd warned everyone. I knew if I didn't get Amy moved something would happen. I've been saying I can't keep her any more – either I segregate her or she goes to a hospital. I knew this would happen. And now – look . . .'

Women were trooping out of the other wings, flanked by ranks of officers. Behind them smoke poured through the windows of the hospital wing.

'And Amy—'

'She's still in there. Someone went in a minute ago.'

'But how—'

'There was an upheaval in D wing, this afternoon. Alarms, bit of a hen fight, usual stuff. It must have been a diversion.

333

Meanwhile, someone got into Healthcare with stolen keys, started something smouldering—'

'But – how—'

'Lighter fuel? Glue? Really, I don't know.'

Agnes looked at the smoke. 'How can they hate someone so much?'

Eleanor shook her head. 'It's not personal. It's just hatred. It's there all the time, spilling around the prison.'

Agnes saw a figure, running fast across the courtyard, heading towards the smoke, ducking under the cordon, shouting, pleading . . . 'Get her out. For God's sake, get her out . . .' It was Ian. Agnes saw him stop, suddenly, staring towards the burning wing. A fireman appeared out of the smoke, carrying a woman in his arms. Agnes and Eleanor ran towards them.

'Amy,' Ian shouted.

Amy was conscious, and she fought free of the fireman, struggling, and crying out, 'No, not me, get my baby, please, save my baby. My baby's in there. She's all I've got.' Her face was streaked black with tears and smoke, and between shrieks she coughed, then started again, on her feet now, fighting the fireman, who was restraining her. 'Let me get her. I must go back. You don't understand, my baby's in there . . .'

Ian was beside her, and she turned to him. 'Please, you understand, don't you? Get my baby. Don't let her die. Oh God, for pity's sake . . .'

Agnes looked at Ian. He had tears rolling down his cheeks. He took Amy's hands. 'Amy . . .' he began, but Amy broke free from him and dashed back towards the smoke. She was stopped by two firemen, who brought her back and held her. She flung herself from side to side, making bursts of noise, piteous animal yelps.

Ian stood next to Agnes. He dashed tears from his face with

the back of his hand. 'It's a photograph,' he was saying, his voice raised above the chaos. 'A fucking photograph. How's it going to survive this? It's all she has . . . It's all she had left . . . It'll kill her, Agnes . . .'

Above the shouts of the firemen and the shouts of the prisoners watching through the windows, Agnes could still hear Amy's grief. Nearby she saw Eleanor, striding amongst her staff in her smart heeled shoes and pleated skirt. Everyone was coughing, their eyes watering, but Eleanor was upright and calm, issuing instructions. She was speaking on her phone again.

'It'll be at least thirty women . . . I'll need vans . . . Yes . . . okay. Thanks. You're telling me. Containment?' She laughed, hollowly. 'Yes, I know. Thanks.' She switched off the phone, then Agnes saw her freeze. There was a man walking towards her. He broke calmly through the police lines and came up to her.

'Richard . . .' Eleanor's voice shook.

The man was smartly dressed, with neat spectacles, and short dark hair, slightly greying. 'You didn't come home,' he said.

'I told you, I phoned you . . .'

'You should have come back.' His voice was even, expressionless.

'I couldn't.'

'I've been worried.'

'I'm sorry.'

'But I've been worried. I haven't been able to sleep.'

'Really, I'm sorry. Please . . .'

'You know you mustn't worry me like that.'

Agnes listened to the tone of his voice. She found she was shaking, although perhaps it was just the smoke.

'I know, Richard. I'm sorry, it's just . . .' Eleanor waved an arm weakly towards the chaos behind her.

'You should have phoned again. To reassure me.' Agnes glanced towards him. His eyes were narrow behind the thin frames. His arms were at his sides, and he was clenching and unclenching his fists.

Eleanor was standing in front of him. She tried to speak again. 'Richard . . .'

'I don't want your excuses.'

'Richard . . . this is my prison.'

'I had my dinner at the pub,' he said. 'As you weren't there.' He looked down at her. 'Look at me,' he said.

She stood, rooted to the spot, unmoving.

'I said look at me.'

Slowly, she raised her eyes to his.

'I'll see you later,' he said. He turned on his heel and walked away, and the line of police closed in his wake.

Eleanor was staring after him.

This is my prison.

Agnes went up to her. 'Are you all right?'

'What? oh, um—' she cracked a brittle, empty smile. 'My husband,' she said, and tried to shrug.

'I know. I was married to one like that,' Agnes said. 'Look, my hands are shaking just like yours.' Agnes held out her fingers. 'It's the way they say "I'll see you later", isn't it? And you know then exactly what's going to happen when you get home. It's funny,' Agnes said, watching her outstretched hands, 'it can still do this to me.'

Eleanor was staring at her. Then she looked at her own shaking hands, and held them next to Agnes's.

'Even after all this time?' she said to Agnes, barely audibly.

Agnes nodded. 'So it seems.'

'He's a difficult man,' Eleanor began, trying to keep her voice light. 'It's because he cares . . .'

'Of course.'

'No, really, he loves me.'

'Oh, yes, he loves you. He loves you so much he has to own you. To impose all his fear on you. God knows they mean it, these men. They love you enough to hurt you really badly. They think that's what love means.'

Eleanor was gazing at her. 'He's not a bad man. You don't know enough about him.' Agnes met her eyes. 'I tried to leave,' Eleanor went on, looking into the distance. 'Once or twice. It just makes everything worse . . . Now that Chris has left home, my son, it's easier, you see.' She glanced up at Agnes.

A shout came out of the smoke. Men ran towards the blackened building. Agnes and Eleanor turned to see what was happening.

'It's Amy.' Eileen approached them, breathless. 'She broke free from her guard. She's run back into the wing. That boy's followed her, Ian . . .'

The fire was out. They stared at the smoking prison, the charred walls, the cracked glass of the windows. The hoses had stopped. Firemen ambled around their engines. Agnes began to walk towards the building. She walked past a group of firemen, and calmly stepped over the threshold of what had been the hospital wing. No one stopped her. The floor was littered with debris. Puddles of water shimmered in the darkness. There was no lighting, only black walls, black beams, blackened doors hanging from their hinges. Above her they could see patches of the night sky where the roof had collapsed.

Agnes picked her way through the darkness. 'Ian?' There was no answer. She turned into the next corridor, coughing against the smoke. She heard an answering cough. 'Ian?'

'Agnes?'

'Where are you?' She followed his voice.

'Here.'

She stumbled into a corridor that she now recognised, through one door that had been forced open, into Amy's ward. Ian was standing there. He took her arm.

She stood blinking. It was light, illumined by candles, candles everywhere. Amy was moving softly around the wreckage of the room, lighting candles, sticking them on what was left of the window ledges, digging them into the broken glass, humming to herself. She was in her nightdress still, and seemed to float among the charred ruin of her cell. She looked up, and smiled. 'Look,' she said, 'my baby, she's safe.' She held out her photograph. It was perfect, its corners still white, the baby pink and spotless at the centre. 'It was just here,' she said, tiptoeing over to the centre of the room. She pointed at the floor, at the epicentre of the fire, now blackened joists. 'It was just in the middle there. Jesus saved her, like he said he would. Jesus kept her safe. He told me he would. In all the flames, she didn't burn. It's a miracle.' She turned to Agnes, smiling radiantly. 'See? A miracle.'

Ian went to her. 'Amy, it's not safe here. We must go. Now you have your baby.'

'I'm lighting candles to the Lord,' she said.

'And now you're free,' Ian said.

Above them Agnes could see the skeletal beams of the roof; the glittering stars.

Amy allowed Ian to take her arm. 'A miracle,' she said, clutching her photograph to her chest. 'You just have to have faith.'

Chapter Twenty-Six

They led Amy out into the night. Eleanor was there, speaking on her phone. She turned to Ian. 'There's an ambulance ready for her,' she said. 'Will you go with her?'

Agnes breathed again, away from the intense smoky darkness. The sky was now softened with grey, with the breaking of dawn. The longest night is over, Agnes thought. She yawned.

'I don't suppose you've slept for ages,' Eleanor said.

'No. I don't suppose you have either.'

'Oh, I'll manage.'

'Eleanor—'

'Don't say it.' Eleanor's gaze was fierce. 'These things are never simple. It's a marriage, after all.'

'If I'd stayed put, I – I wouldn't be here today.'

'He's not a bad man,' Eleanor said. 'Don't judge him just on – on what you saw.'

Agnes looked beyond her, to the scene of the fire. Only one fire engine remained, and the crowd of onlookers was reduced to just a few stragglers. At the other gate there was renewed activity, as vans arrived to take women to other prisons.

Agnes turned back to Eleanor. 'This is your prison,' she said.

Eleanor smiled. 'I've work to do,' she said. Briefly, she grasped Agnes's hand, then walked away. Agnes saw her at the gate, issuing instructions, organising inmates into groups.

Agnes yawned again, gathered her coat around her against the chilly dawn and headed for home.

She knelt in prayer as the sky lightened. She thought of Venn, dying in the tunnel, Rosanna by his side. She thought of Emlyn, trying to avoid his destiny only to walk right into it; and then, in the tunnel, walking into the path of an unseeing train. She could hear once again his faint cry in the darkness. She shivered.

Darkness is not dark to you, O Lord. Darkness and light to you are both alike.

And then there was Rosanna, Agnes thought. Rosanna had killed Cliff, she'd said, throwing her confession out into the echoing expanses of the tunnel, where the only witnesses were Venn and Emlyn. And me. I'm the only living witness to that truth. If it is a truth. And what had Venn tried to say, something about a safe, and a signature?

Nothing was over. Emlyn had tried to end it, to put a stop to it, by ending his own life. And the tragedy was, he'd failed. Nothing was resolved.

As the cold morning light seeped through her curtains, Agnes got into bed and fell into a deep, exhausted sleep.

She woke some hours later. She sat up, blinking in the midday sun. She wondered what day it was. Tuesday, she thought. There was a lot to do. Janette's case needed to be sorted out. She must phone Ian. And there was Mal. And Claire. Claire, she thought, realising there were several questions that still needed answers.

She showered and dressed, and was just making a pot of coffee when there was a buzz at her door. She picked up the intercom.

'It's me. Rosanna.'

'Come up.'

A moment later Rosanna appeared at her door. 'I been thinking,' she said, walking into the room. 'Thing is, Sister, there's only you who knows.' She went and stood by the window.

'Would you like some coffee?'

'And I ain't come here to plead. I want you to understand that here and now, Sister. I ain't pleading for my life – you understand?'

Agnes poured herself a cup and sat down. She looked at Rosanna, who was framed by sunlight.

'Last night,' Rosanna began, 'after the hospital, the police, all that, I went home. I opened the safe. I found Venn's confession. He must've written it the day after – the day after Cliff died. The day after I shot him. He must have known one day I might need it. I dug it out of the safe, just like he said, and I read it, and I read it. I didn't go to bed till daybreak. It don't say much – he wasn't one to be poetic. But I sat over it with tears pouring down my face. The coppers were lucky there was any ink left on the page.' She laughed, then grew serious again. 'I loved that man. The only man I ever loved.' She turned away and looked out on the street for a moment, then turned back. 'I will have that coffee, thank you. Black, with sugar.'

Agnes went and fetched a cup. Rosanna sat down at the little table. 'So you see,' Rosanna said, as Agnes poured her coffee and sat down opposite her, 'this is my life sentence. I killed Cliff and Emlyn killed Venn. This is my prison.' She stirred sugar into her coffee.

'People might say,' Agnes began, 'there are worse prisons than that.'

'People would be right.' Rosanna nodded. 'That's what I'm saying to you; that's why I'm here. If you want, you can have me locked up. I've killed a man, as the Lord is my witness. I had my reasons, but only the Lord can sit in judgement on us.'

'Except now you're asking me to.'

Rosanna looked up and their eyes met. 'I have nothing to plead in my defence,' she said.

'So – why? Why did you do it?'

'He was – he was a bad man.'

'He loved his daughters.'

'He drank. That's what made him bad.'

'And do all drunkards deserve shooting?'

Rosanna touched the corner of the table. 'There's bad. And there's bad.' She turned back to Agnes. 'Cliff raped me. A few months ago.' She ran her finger along the polished wood.

'I'd heard it slightly differently . . .' Agnes stopped.

'What had you heard?'

'From Des. A friend of Cliff's—'

'What did he say?'

Agnes hesitated.

'I know what he said,' Rosanna said. 'He said Cliff and I had some kind of affair, didn't he? Thing about Cliff, see, is that the booze had addled his brain. He got to the point, see, where if he wanted something, he took it. He helped himself. And when he wanted me, God knows, he claimed he loved me . . . He couldn't see there was anything wrong with what he'd done.' Her eyes narrowed at the memory. 'That night, the night he came for my Venn, I didn't know before I pulled my gun that I was going to shoot him dead.'

'Were they working together?'

'Yeah. There'd been a deal. Cliff was acting as courier for Venn, selling stuff on, cocaine. And Cliff had tried to keep some back and resell it.'

'And Mal?'

She nodded. 'He was involved too. Trying to keep Cliff and Venn sweet. Then he got that work, down the tunnel, and tried to get out of both deals. But you see, Sister, that's not the real story. The real story is what Cliff did to me.'

'Why didn't you tell anyone—'

'About what he'd done to me?' She sighed. 'I'll tell you, Sister. I'd met Claire by then. A sweet voice she has, Claire. I was growing fond of her. And her sister, before she got her share of trouble . . . and I thought to myself, if I tell Venn, Cliff's a dead man. And I thought, those girls need someone. Even if he's a loser like Cliff. He's still their dad. And then that guy, Venn's cousin . . . I'd met him before. He came to the club. He told me Cliff was sorry for what he'd done to me. Told me he loved me, stuff like that. I said if you love someone you don't do to them what Cliff did to me. He said, that guy, that guy in the tunnel, he said, it'll all be different now. He said it was all the drink, and that all that was over now. I said he could blame the drink all he liked – it wouldn't take away what that man had done to me. Sister, you can't ever know what it's like . . .' She glanced up at Agnes, then shook her head. 'Of course you know.'

'You could've told the police—'

Rosanna looked at Agnes. A smile broke across her face. She shook her head.

'I see. So, that night—'

'That night, Cliff found out. About his family. Emlyn must have been to see him, told him, about them being half-brothers. And Venn being his cousin. And he must have known then what Emlyn said in the tunnel, about the feud. And he's about to tell all this to Venn. He comes to find him in the club, but Venn ain't in no mood to listen. He knows that Cliff has been trying to screw up the deal, and he's angry with him. So Cliff says to Venn, I'll be at home when you want me. And off he goes. And later, Venn says, we're going round there. So we get there, and he tries to tell Venn that they're cousins, but Venn wants to talk about the money. And Cliff gets all agitated, and he's trying to tell Venn the truth, and Venn won't listen, and then I see Cliff looking at me, and I know what he's going to say. And he starts to say all this shit about us being lovers – lovers?' She spat the word. 'Like I can't tell the difference between love and hate? Between pleasure and pain? And Venn's looking at me, and even then, I have no idea I'm about to kill the man. But I look at Venn and at that moment I see a shadow of doubt cross his face, and I think, it's Cliff's word against mine. I watch the doubt in my baby's eyes, and then he looks at me, Venn does, like I'm damaged goods. That look in their eyes – you know what I'm saying? That wounded masculine pride. And then I feel this rage, like I'm thinking, how dare he doubt me? After what I suffered, how dare he look at me like that? And this rage is rising in me, this white heat, like looking into the sun – and I hear this loud noise, loud, loud noise, like an explosion, and I find I'm holding my gun. And Cliff's lying there. Dead. It was only when I saw him, lying there, I realised what I'd done.' She shifted in her chair, picked up her cup, put it down again.

Agnes poured them both more coffee. 'And Mal?'

'Claire and Mal, they'd been at the club, earlier. When Cliff had come in. Claire could see something was up. She'd got worried. So she and Mal, they followed us. They walked in. Cliff was still warm. And Venn, he's holding the gun by then; he's taken it off me. And he hands it to Mal. And I'd wrapped my scarf round my fingers, and Venn's wearing gloves – and Mal ain't.'

'Mal took the gun?'

'It was loaded.'

'So Venn threatened him?'

Rosanna was silent.

'And how did you feel?'

Rosanna got up and went over to the window. She looked out at the street. 'It's a nice day, Sister.'

'Yes. It is.'

She smoothed the folds of the curtain. 'Do you think we choose who we fall in love with?'

'I really don't know.'

'With Venn, it was like a whirlwind, a tornado, an earthquake, all the things they say. It was the end of one life and the beginning of a new one. And the new life, it was like nothing I'd ever known before. It was like having to learn the rules all over again. Threatening people was normal. Handling guns and drugs was normal. Sewing up gunshot wounds with my own hands to keep it from the law – that was normal. All the rules had changed.' She turned away from the window and came and sat down. 'And now that life's over. So I'm about to start another life. New rules. All over again. And all I can think is that he's gone. I can look out of that window at the sunshine, and I can think, it's a nice day. But it means nothing, Sister. I'm already behind bars.'

'Did Venn believe you, in the end? About Cliff?'

Rosanna nodded. Her eyes welled with tears. 'The crazy thing is, Sister, I didn't have to kill a man to prove I was true to him. Venn knew I loved him. He always knew that.'

Agnes glanced at her. 'If I tell the police—'

Rosanna shrugged. 'It's up to you, Sister.' She stood up. At the door, she smiled. 'I'm glad it's you, Sister. If anyone's going to pass judgment on me, I'm glad it's a friend.' She kissed her on her cheek, and then was gone.

Agnes was left alone. She paced her flat, pausing by the window to stare out at the sunshine. Behind bars, she thought. Cloistered, enclosed, imprisoned. But then Julius would say we're all imprisoned. Only faith can set us free.

Agnes glanced out at a group of teenagers gathering by the bus stop. She remembered what Ian had said about Amy being free. Perhaps he was right, she thought. Perhaps Amy really is freer than any of us.

She picked up the phone and dialled Marky's number. After a long while, he answered. 'Yeah?'

'Were you asleep?'

'Yeah.'

'Is Claire there?'

'Yeah.'

There was a pause, then Claire came on. 'Hi.'

'Can we meet?'

'Sure. When?'

'This evening?'

'Earlier?'

'Okay. Five?'

'I'll come to you.'

'Okay. Claire?'

'Yes?'

'Thanks.'

Agnes hung up. She looked at her watch. She put on her coat, went out and caught the bus to the community house.

'Agnes, how many more times do we have to go through this?' Catherine paced her study. Agnes sat, silent and miserable, in a wide wooden chair by her desk. Catherine was still speaking. 'I'm sure you have your reasons. But it seems to me, until you can stop running away, there'll always be a reason not to be here, with us. I've had Sister Christiane on the phone every day since you vanished. She's not pleased. It would help if you could tell me where you've been.' She sat down and looked across at Agnes, her gaze soft and questioning.

Agnes thought about the descent into darkness, about the

lamp swinging in the tunnel, about Emlyn in the shadows, about the fire at the prison, and Amy and her miracle. 'It was the longest night,' she said. 'But now it's nearly over.'

Catherine sighed. 'Between you and Imelda, we've had very little peace recently.'

'I'm sorry.'

'And what about your mother?'

'If I'm permitted, I'll go back and see her soon.'

Catherine's frown smoothed into almost a smile. 'Funny you should think of asking permission.'

'When all this is over—'

'You'll be a good nun?' Catherine was smiling.

They sat in silence a moment. Then Agnes said, 'You're very kind to me.'

'I can afford to be.' Catherine stood up. 'I'm not your official superior. Thank goodness.' Agnes opened the door for her, and they went through to chapel.

'How deep I find your thoughts, O Lord, how great is the sum of them.' Agnes stared up at the Advent painting. The shadow of the cross, she thought. 'If I were to count them, they would be more in number than the sand . . .' And Jesus, the infant, sleeping peacefully within the wooden angles.

'Search me out, O God, and know my heart. Try me and know my restless thoughts.'

Agnes found she had tears in her eyes.

Afterwards she went into the kitchen. Imelda was alone, standing by the window, staring out at the garden, at the sunset.

'Imelda?'

Imelda jumped. She stared anxiously at Agnes.

'How are you?' Agnes asked her.

'You've been away.'

347

'Yes.'

'You ran away?'

'Sort of.'

Imelda came over to her, and gestured to her to sit down. She glanced at the door, then turned back to Agnes, her grey eyes intense. 'How did you run away?'

'By sheer disobedience.'

Imelda shook her head. 'I have none of that.' She looked thinner, and her face seemed to have aged. Her hair was scraped back and roughly pinned.

'Where do you need to go?' Agnes asked.

Imelda shook her head. 'I can't.'

'Imelda – you can't go on like this.' Agnes took a chance. 'Your child—'

Imelda opened wide eyes and stared at her. 'How do you know?'

'Because you told me. In the prison. And you told Amy, in a way, too.'

Imelda's fingers went to her cheek, moving in nervous, gouging movements. 'The nuns. Where I was sent. They took him away.' Her eyes filled with tears.

'Imelda—'

Imelda jumped to her feet, shaking her head. 'No,' she said. 'There's nothing I can do. There is no child.'

'Has something happened? Something to make you think about it after all this time?'

Imelda stared at Agnes, her eyes wide with fear. Her lips moved, but no words came.

'Imelda, if you need any help . . .'

Imelda's eyes held hers for a moment. Then she turned to go, walking carefully to the door. At the door she turned back to Agnes. She opened her mouth to speak, struggling with the words. 'Christopher. I called him Christopher.' The sound of the name reverberated through the room. She fled out of the door, her hand across her mouth.

Agnes checked her watch. It was time to go back and meet Claire.

'I can't take it all in,' Claire said, lounging cheerfully in Agnes's armchair. 'That guy Emlyn, he killed Jim? And it turns out that Venn killed my dad. I knew that anyway – I just didn't dare tell anyone. We're all better off without Venn, except Rosanna, and no one can tell her that he wasn't worth it. And the weird thing is that Marky and me are cousins. Isn't that strange? We were trying to work it out.'

'Second cousins,' Agnes said, handing her a mug of tea.

'It's funny, 'cos we've always got on well. It's like we've always felt like family.'

Agnes sat down opposite her. 'Is that why you sent Des to see me? Because you wanted someone to tell me it was Venn?'

Claire's expression clouded. She nodded. 'I felt terrible, Agnes. I knew it was Venn, and if it hadn't been for me, Mal would never have got into it . . . I was desperate. I could see it was all going Venn's way, and I felt really trapped. I knew he'd kill me if I told anyone . . .'

'They warned Des off, you know.'

She nodded. 'I heard that Doc and the others had been down there. I felt even worse then. But . . .' She shook her head. 'I didn't know where to turn. I thought, Des'll know the truth.'

'Yes,' Agnes said. 'The truth.'

'I told him where you lived.'

'I know.' Agnes sipped her tea. 'And what about you? What's going to become of you?'

'What do you mean? I'm okay.' She giggled. 'I'm a survivor, me.'

'Surviving has its price. Like, for example, what you do for a living.'

Claire's expression suddenly hardened. 'It ain't none of your business.'

'No. Maybe not.' Agnes lightened her voice. 'So, how come it was your fault that Mal ended up at the scene of the crime?'

Claire sighed. 'We were in the club, when Dad came in. I knew he was involved with some deal with Venn, and he was in a weird state, my dad, different from normal. Not drunk, not in the same old way. It kind of scared me, like something was up. He said he wanted to talk to Venn. And, see, I've seen what Venn can do. I mean, what he could do. And Venn let him go, but then I heard him say he was going to sort Dad out. I was scared, and I told Mal. Mal was working the club that night, and we thought we'd try to stop it. We were stupid, I was stupid . . . And we got there, and I walked in and I saw . . . my dad . . . he was dead. Like I told you. But I never told you this bit before, 'cos I was scared – I didn't tell anyone. Venn and Rosanna standing there, right. And Venn smiles at me. Like he's really pleased to see me, which of course he is. 'Cos he's holding the gun, right, and he's wearing gloves, and he hands it to Mal. And he goes, take the gun. And Mal refuses, and Venn holds it to his head. And he says, you can take it, and get rid of it, or I can kill you. I was so scared, I can't tell you. So Mal takes the gun. And he runs then, runs out of the flat. He said later he'd thrown the gun over the wall, but the cops ain't stupid, are they?'

'Didn't he wipe his prints off the gun?'

'Yeah, but by the time they find the gun, everyone's saying it's him, aren't they? And the coppers knew they couldn't pin anything on Venn in any case.'

'And after Mal took the gun?'

'I was left there. With my dad still warm. I said to Venn,

you killed my dad. And he laughed. And he said, do you care? He was a bastard, that Venn. And then I said, Mal's my sister's boyfriend. And Venn said, so what? Do you care about your sister? And – and I said, no. 'Cos I didn't then. I was so wrapped up with Venn, and him saying he'd look after me and make me a singer . . .' Claire's eyes filled with tears. 'But I do, you know. Now it's over . . . I just keep thinking, she's all I've got. I want me and Cally to be how it was when we were kids. Before Mum died. Before it all went wrong.' She burst into a fit of sobbing.

Agnes stood up and put an arm around her shoulders.

'Can I see her?' Claire asked. 'Can I visit her?'

'She's due out next week. Before the New Year. If she's managed to convince everyone she's clean, which I doubt.'

'Look at us, eh? Me and Cally.' Claire sat up and wiped her eyes with a tissue. 'It didn't used to be like that.' She looked up at Agnes, her blue eyes still welling with tears. 'Will they let me in to see her? At the prison? It's Christmas, after all.'

'Of course.'

'If she wants to see me, that is.'

'I'm sure she will.'

'She hates me.'

'I know. You said.'

' 'Cos of my dad. 'Cos of it all going wrong.'

Agnes picked up their empty tea mugs and carried them through into the kitchen. She came back into the room and sat down. 'It wasn't your fault,' she said.

'I hated him, Agnes. I wanted to kill him sometimes. We both did, me and Cally. We'd talk about it. When she dreamed it was me who'd done it, it was like she was saying the truth. It could've been either of us.' She shrugged. 'It's over now.' She stood up. 'I'd better go.'

'Are you working this evening?'

She nodded, staring at the floor.

'Claire—'

Claire met her eyes, suddenly defiant. 'Listen, Agnes, you can sort out me and my sister, and you can get my sister out of prison, and you can tie up all the loose ends of my life, but you can't do everything.'

'It's no way to make a living—' Agnes began.

'Yeah? Well, that's where you're wrong, Sister.'

'But—'

Claire stood in front of her, straight-backed, her face flushed. 'It's not for you to judge me. When I've made enough, I'll retire. I'll set myself up in some other business – dressmaking I was thinking of, something straight. And the singing, I'll do something with that. Or maybe I'll get married and have kids.' She looked down at Agnes. 'I'm a call girl, Agnes. Do you have a problem with that?'

Agnes sighed. She got up, and went to open the door for her. 'No,' she said. 'My mother did exactly the same thing.'

Chapter Twenty-Seven

'You see, Julius, I'm the only one who knows. I'm the only one who knows it was Rosanna and not Venn.'

'You and God, then,' Julius said. He sat down at his desk and switched on the lamp. 'And me, now,' he added, and smiled at her as if the idea amused him.

'I really don't know what to do.'

'That makes two of us.'

'And God.'

'Three, then.' He laughed. 'Except only two of us are floundering around trying to make a moral decision.'

'I feel terrible, Julius. I've felt terrible for days.'

'You've had a pretty awful time, Agnes.'

'It was the tunnel; it was the way the whole thing just played itself out, as if I was helpless to do anything. The policewoman who took my statement – I kept saying I could have prevented it, and she said it's quite normal to feel like that if you've witnessed something. But I wasn't just a witness, Julius, I knew. I knew why Emlyn was hiding down there. And I knew that Emlyn and Venn were heading for something terrible, and yet . . . when it came to it, there was nothing I could do. I keep thinking there must have been a moment when I could have got Venn out of there—'

'Would he have listened to you?'

'Or I could have got the gun off Emlyn before he used it—'

'How could you have done that?'

Agnes looked at him. 'I don't know. I just keep thinking I should have intervened.'

Julius took off his glasses, looked at them, and put them back on.

'Two deaths,' Agnes said.

'But a whole history behind them,' Julius said. 'A whole history that's nothing to do with you.'

'What do you mean?'

'Maybe the policewoman's right. You were a witness. You happened to catch the ending of a story. But it wasn't your story, you had no part to play in it. Maybe it was right that you did nothing.'

'How can it be right to stand by while people kill each other?'

'Simply, in this case, as you just said, there was nothing you could have done. There wasn't a moment when you could have put a stop to it.'

Agnes sighed. 'I don't know. I suppose not.'

He picked up a biro and started to doodle.

'Perhaps there's a lesson in all this,' Agnes said.

Julius's biro was making scratchy marks on the paper. He picked it up and frowned at it. 'Why do these things only last five minutes?' he said.

'A lesson about stories,' Agnes said.

He looked up, and patted her hand in a vague sort of way. 'Yes,' he said. 'Perhaps there is.'

She looked at him and smiled. 'Silly old Julius,' she said.

That evening, Agnes sat at her desk and dialled Yvette's number. She spoke in French for a few minutes, then said goodbye and rang off.

She sat by the light of her anglepoise, staring at the phone. Two, three weeks at the most, Yvette had said. She's holding on by sheer willpower, Yvette had said. 'She's waiting for you. She can't say so, but I know she is. She's waiting to say goodbye.'

Tomorrow's Christmas Eve. I'll be there in four days, Agnes thought. If I can find a flight.

' "And the angel said unto her, fear not Mary: for thou hast found favour with God. And behold, thou shalt conceive in thy womb and bring forth a son and shall call his name Jesus . . ." '

Agnes glanced across to Imelda. She was staring up at the sister reading the lesson, and her lips were silently mouthing the words. Afterwards, as they filed out of chapel, Imelda took Agnes by the arm. 'Come with me,' she whispered. She set off up the stairs of the house, towards her room, Agnes following. 'I haven't told anyone,' she was saying, more to herself than Agnes. 'They said I mustn't tell, so I didn't. I want you to see this,' she said, as they reached her door. Her room was sparsely furnished. She went to her desk, opened a drawer, and pulled out a letter. 'I don't know what this means.'

It was a brown, official-looking envelope, addressed to Sister Imelda at the house. Agnes held it in her hands.

'Read it,' Imelda said.

Agnes hesitated, then opened the envelope. It was from a social services department in the West Midlands. It was dated October. She read its contents. She looked up at Imelda, who was waiting, her eyes fixed on Agnes, her face working, unable to contain any longer all the grief and the anger and the loss and the sorrow. And the hope.

'You've had this for weeks,' Agnes said.

'I didn't know what I'd done.' Imelda spoke quietly. 'I didn't know it would make a child. We were kept in such ignorance. My father sent me to the nuns, to live there until . . . and then he was born, and he was beautiful. Beautiful. I held him. I nursed him – they let you feed them. I had six weeks with him. And then one day he'd gone.' She choked on the word. 'Gone . . .' She began to sob. 'In the night. I thought I'd die.' Tears were pouring down her cheeks. 'For weeks I waited to die. I prayed to die. The nuns let me go home, but I wasn't wanted there any more. Eventually I realised that you couldn't just decide to die. So then all I did was look for my baby. I followed prams, I followed women with babies, I waited outside nurseries . . .'

'How old were you?'

'Seventeen.'

'And the father of the baby?'

'He was a nice boy. Jerry. My father lied to him, told him I'd gone away. I wrote to him from the nuns but he didn't get the letter. He married someone else, had a family . . .' she stumbled over the word. 'After a while, I realised it was my punishment. I realised I'd done wrong, and this was my punishment. So I went back to the nuns, and told them I'd learned my lesson. And asked if I could . . . asked to join them. I realised there was no other life left for me.' Her eyes were dry now. 'I felt I'd turned to stone. In a way, I had. After that, everything went on just as it was, for years. I made my penances. I realised that God had let me glimpse happiness, and I should be grateful for that; I should give thanks for having known my boy . . .' She burst into tears again.

Agnes took her hand. She spoke gently. 'Your son. He wants to trace you. That's what this letter says.'

Imelda's mouth moved, struggling to form the word. 'My son,' she said at last. She shook her head. 'It can't be. I don't understand.'

'That's what it says. Your son. And he's married, with three children. You're a grandmother, Imelda.'

Imelda looked up at Agnes, her eyes swimming with

bewilderment. 'But it says Robert.'

'They used to change the babies' names. When they were adopted.'

'It says Robert. Not Christopher.' Her fingers dug into her cheek. 'He can't want to see me,' she said, as if it was obvious.

'I think he's worked very hard to see you. To get your details from the nuns must have taken some doing.'

'It can't be him. It was in Ireland.'

'People adopted from all over the place in those days.'

'He'd be thirty-three. His birthday was in September.'

'Yes. That's what it says here. Look, this is his address. The letter says he'd like to hear from you but he didn't want to upset you. That's why he's left it to you.'

Imelda was staring at Agnes. 'When I got that letter, I didn't know what to do. I didn't understand why God should give me another chance. So I left it and left it. And all the time I was remembering, things I thought I'd forgotten. The nuns were so cruel, you know. I didn't know why they should treat me so badly when I'd brought this lovely beautiful boy into the world. I was waiting for Jerry to find me. I thought, he'll come and find me and we'll get married and it will be all right. And he never came. My father had lied to him. I didn't know at the time. My father said I'd gone away and wasn't coming back.'

'You must see your son,' Agnes heard herself say.

Imelda stared at her.

'There's nothing to stop you,' Agnes said. 'You can write to this address here. They'll pass him the letter.'

'I'd better ask permission.'

'From the order? Imelda, you'll do no such thing. Don't give any more nuns the chance to interfere. Write first, ask permission afterwards.'

'But . . .' Her lips were working. 'What if . . . after all this time . . . He might think . . .'

'He wants to see you.'

'But I gave him away.'

'No. He was taken from you. You loved him for six weeks.'

'I've loved him for ever.' Imelda's eyes filled with tears. 'Every day, I've thought of him, I've prayed for him in every office of every day . . . Robert,' she said suddenly. 'I haven't prayed for Robert. I've prayed for Christopher.' She bit her lip, her face tight with anxiety.

'It's the same person.'

Imelda sat still, thinking. Then she looked up at Agnes. 'Yes. He's the same person.' She went to her desk, took out some notepaper and a pen, and sat down, the pen poised in her hand. 'He's my son,' she said. The tension had left her face. 'Grandchildren.' Her cheeks flushed a soft pink. 'How extraordinary!' Agnes stood up, rested her hand gently on Imelda's shoulder for a moment, then left.

Agnes left the community house and went straight to the prison. The burnt shell of the hospital wing was cordoned off, but the main gate was functioning normally again. Eleanor was sitting at her desk, crisp and efficient, as if nothing had happened. She looked up as Agnes came into the room. 'How are you?' she said.

'I've brought you some coffee,' Agnes said.

'Just like old times.' Eleanor smiled, but it was edged with tension.

'You should take a break.' Agnes handed her a paper cup. 'It's Christmas, after all.'

Eleanor looked at her. 'I like being at work,' she said.

Agnes met her eyes. 'It's no answer,' she said.

'It'll do for now.'

'I got out,' Agnes said.

'Only when he nearly killed you.'

'Do you have to wait till then?'

Eleanor shook her head. 'He isn't like that.'

Agnes stirred her coffee. 'I used to think there were degrees of violence. Measurable, like a kind of points system.'

Eleanor sipped her coffee. 'That's what prison is,' she said. 'That's how sentencing works.'

Agnes was silent. After a moment, she said, 'Ian phoned. I'm having lunch with him on Boxing Day.'

Eleanor breathed again at the change of subject. 'Amy's been moved, of course. She's in a semi-secure unit, a halfway house. Ian says he's very pleased with it. It's what I'd been asking for, for weeks. She's even allowed outside, when supervised. Her case is being heard in the New Year. Ian's optimistic. She's served so much time already. And Cally's due for release next week, in time for New Year. Why they can't do it for Christmas I don't know. She's improved enormously now that Mal's been released.'

'Already?'

'Yes, the case is closed.'

'And Janette?'

'She's due out today. Christmas Eve. Crazy time to release someone like that, but we can't hold on to her just because she's incapable of functioning in the outside world. And what are you doing for Christmas? You will do our Christmas service tomorrow, won't you?'

'Yes, of course. And then after Christmas I'm going to see my mother.'

'Again?'

'It'll be the last time.'

Eleanor looked at her. 'It must be very difficult.'

Agnes picked up her cup, put it down again. 'In a way. The odd thing is, it's all changed now. I was so angry with her;

even a week, two weeks ago, I was angry with her. And now, when I think about it, I can't remember what I was angry about. Now I just feel sorry for her.'

Eleanor listened. Then she got up and threw her empty coffee cup in the wastepaper basket. 'That's how it is with Richard, you see,' she said. 'I feel sorry for him. He finds life so difficult . . . He – he needs me, you see. There've been times when he's begged me to stay.'

'But—'

Eleanor sat back down at her desk. 'Don't say it's different.'

'My mother wasn't violent.'

'She still did you harm. And you still forgave her.'

'Eleanor – forgiveness isn't like that.' Eleanor looked down at her hands, but said nothing. 'Forgiveness isn't about putting up with something that does you harm,' Agnes said. 'My mother was my mother. I didn't choose her. But you can choose to leave.'

Eleanor spoke quietly. 'You don't know the whole story.'

Agnes opened her mouth to speak, closed it again.

Eleanor sat, calmly. 'One day I'll go, you see. When I'm ready.'

Agnes looked at her. There was nothing more to say.

Agnes got home that evening to find a note from Sister Christiane saying that she had permission to go to France, but that they'd expect Agnes to do no more travelling for some time to come. There was also a message from Athena on her answering machine. She sounded subdued and monosyllabic. Agnes dialled her number.

'Oh, Agnes, hi.'

'Are you all right?'

'Sort of. No, not really. Are you busy?'

'I've got midnight mass later.'

'Can we have dinner first?'

'Athena, I'd love to.'

The tapas bar was full of noise and celebration. There was a Christmas tree, and the lights above the tables had been decorated with shiny gold stars.

'We were lucky to get a place,' Athena shouted above the hubbub as Agnes joined her. 'I've ordered some bread and olives and stuff.'

'Hardly the place for a quiet chat,' Agnes said.

'It'll do. It's nice to be out, actually.' Athena poured Agnes a glass of wine.

'So?' Agnes sipped her wine, then looked up at Athena.

Athena sighed. 'I don't know. Don't ask me.'

'What's happened?'

Athena brushed a lock of hair from her face. 'Well, Greg and I are over. I told him. And Nic and I are – whatever we were before. An item, I think they say. And he claims he can forgive me, although I think that's just his therapy-speak and really he's hopping mad, but we'll see. And he won't insist we live together, and he accepts that things are fine with us living separately, although he tried to make a joke about having to keep an eye on me, but you could see he didn't find it funny.' She sighed. 'And that's it, really.'

'And are you happy?'

The waitress came over and took their order. Athena turned to Agnes. 'Happy? Sweetie, I don't know. We all think we know what happiness is, we all go chasing it, and actually, we've no idea what we're looking for. Greg made me feel happy, I know that. But I've had to accept it was a false happiness. And there's you, nodding wisely like that—'

'I wasn't.'

'You were. Just because you nuns don't have to bother with

all this. You see, the worst thing is, it makes me feel old. I used to live in a world where that kind of Greg happiness was enough. Where it was enough to fall in love and have fun, and have fantastic sex, and be vain, and spend half a day choosing underwear . . . and now look at me. None of that works any more. It was fine for a few weeks, but in the end I had to face the consequences.' She sipped her wine. 'And the thing is, sweetie, the greatest irony is, Greg is really keen now. Typical, isn't it? As soon as I get all sensible and commit myself to Nic – you see, I must be old, I'm even using the C-word – then Greg is keener than ever. Phoning me, most days – "Just wondered how you were," kind of thing . . .' She shook her head.

'And what have you told him?'

'The truth. That Nic means more to me than I realised.'

'And does Greg accept that?'

She nodded. 'Yes. I think at first he was relieved, because of all that stuff we'd got into, of me being upset if he didn't ring, all that stuff. It was making him feel trapped. But now I've become something he can't have. Really, sweetie, every time I find myself face to face with just how simple men are, it surprises me. You'd think I'd know by now. Greg couldn't bear me to need him. And now I don't, he wishes I did.' She laughed. 'And yet they give such a passable impression of being part of the human race. We're fooled every time. Crazy, isn't it?'

'Not all men are simple.'

Athena looked thoughtful. 'No,' she said. 'Nic, for example. He's been wonderful.' Her eyes filled with tears. 'And I've been such an idiot.' She blinked, tried to smile.

'A learning curve, Athena. There's no point regretting it.'

'That's what Nic said. Through gritted teeth.'

Agnes laughed. 'I almost forgot. I brought you a Christmas

present.' She reached under the table and brought out a large, circular object tied with gold ribbon.

'Sweetie, you shouldn't have.' Athena pulled at the ribbon and tore off the paper, revealing a blue china plate.

'I got it from a market stall,' Agnes said. 'The man who sold it to me said it would last for years.'

'He couldn't have known you'd give it to me,' Athena laughed.

'The end of our crockery-throwing days . . .'

'Now we're old and mellow.'

Agnes raised her glass. 'To commitment. And forgiveness.'

They clinked their glasses together, and the wine shimmered with gold in the light from the star above their table.

Agnes left Athena at her door, promising to see her before she went to France. She caught a late bus, and arrived at the community house in time for midnight mass. The chapel was full of flowers and candles, poinsettias and lilies, and trails of holly pricked with bright red berries. Imelda had taken her place right in front of the painting of the infant Jesus.

One of the sisters went up to the lectern. ' "For unto us a child is born, unto us a son is given . . ." '

Imelda was gazing up at the image of Christ with rapt attention, her eyes shining.

' "And his name shall be called Wonderful, Counsellor, the mighty God, the everlasting Father, the Prince of Peace." '

As the bell tolled midnight, the nuns moved softly along the pews, shaking hands, murmuring, 'Peace be with you.' When Agnes reached Imelda, Imelda grasped her hand and smiled. 'I posted my letter,' she whispered.

Agnes woke next morning to a dull, drizzly day. Christmas morning, she thought. It could at least have snowed. She dressed quickly and made a quick cup of tea, as she was due at the prison within the hour. Her intercom buzzed.

'Hello?'

'It's Claire. Are you going to the prison?'

'Come up.'

Claire appeared at the top of the stairs, breathless, clasping a huge gift-wrapped parcel. 'Will they let me in?' she asked anxiously.

'Come in. Have some tea. Of course they'll let you in. It's Christmas Day.'

'I hope she'll want to see me.' Claire sat down, her face lined with doubt. She took the mug of tea that Agnes handed her. 'I've brought her a present and everything.'

'She's due out in a few days.'

'Where will she go?'

'I don't know. Mal's out now – maybe he'll look after her.'

Claire frowned. She sipped her tea. 'I was thinking, see, it's part of my plans to buy a place soon, somewhere nice, somewhere with a garden. Me and Cal could live there together.'

Agnes smiled at her. 'Come on, we should go.'

They went to the main gate, and the officer let them in and filled out a form for Claire. The women were sitting in the association room. The walls and ceiling were criss-crossed with decorations, but their shine was dulled by the heavy gloss paint. Agnes stood in the doorway, Claire by her side. Cally was sitting with Nita in one corner, and she looked up and saw her sister. Her face looked blank. Claire took a step towards her. The chatter ceased, as the other women sensed a scene. Cally opened her mouth to speak. 'Claire?' She stood up, and began to walk towards her. Claire held out her arms, awkwardly, trying to hang on to the parcel at the same time. Cally reached her as the parcel fell, landing in her arms. She giggled.

'Happy Christmas,' Claire said, laughing too.

'But I ain't got you nothing,' Cally said. She sat down, Claire next to her, and began to unwrap the present. 'I'll owe you now,' she said, ripping the unwieldy paper.

'No,' Claire said, as the paper fell away to reveal a huge, old teddy bear. 'No, girl. You don't owe me nothing.' Cally looked at Claire, then hugged the teddy, her eyes welling with tears. Then she hugged Claire.

A thin sun broke through the clouds, and suddenly the tinsel flashed with colour, and the room flickered with red and green and gold. Agnes closed the door softly behind her.

Chapter Twenty-Eight

Of course, Agnes thought, it would choose now to snow. Boxing Day, just when I have to catch a plane tomorrow, and it's freezing outside, and sleeting, and they'll cancel all the flights. No wonder the English complain about the weather. She went to her suitcase and added a large woollen jersey to her packing.

I wonder what the weather's like in France, she thought. She opened a drawer and looked at her swimwear. I might even get to the beach, she thought, as her intercom buzzed.

'Sister, it's Rosanna.'

Agnes pressed the buzzer, and opened the door for her.

'Any chance of some coffee?' Rosanna beamed at her, then she noticed the suitcase. 'Hey, what's this? Running away, are you?'

'I'm visiting my mother. In Provence.'

'You nuns. Having it all, or what?'

'Hardly having it all. She's dying.' Agnes surprised herself by starting to cry.

Rosanna came to her and took her hands. 'Dying? Sister, you never said.'

Agnes found some tissues, and wiped her eyes. 'She's been ill for ages.' She went to the kitchen and put on the kettle.

Rosanna settled into the armchair. 'That grim reaper, he sure is working overtime these days. I've shed tears for my Venn. Thought I'd drown in them.'

'I've tried to be calm. Death is inevitable, after all. Part of God's will. We might as well accept it.'

'Accept it? Rosanna sat up straight with indignation. 'It may be inevitable as far as your God is concerned, but what does He know? When I see that grim reaper walking those streets out there with his mean face, what am I going to do? Invite him in to tea?'

Agnes tried to smile, fighting back tears.

'No, Sister, acceptance is for later, as far as I'm concerned. When Death came for my Venn, in the darkness, it was like he was standing over me, and I lifted his black hood and looked into those hollow eyes, and I was ready to holler and fight, I was, feeling my man's life blood draining out of him, I was all set to stamp and shout . . .' She brushed a single tear from her eye. 'You can tell me it's your God's will, you can tell me that Venn's death was his final destiny, playing itself out, an eye for an eye . . . but that's not going to stop me railing against it, screaming and shouting and shaking my fists. And I know you, Sister, and I know that a woman who can dance like you, you have to grieve as I do, girl, you have to lay yourself down and roar. Then you can talk about acceptance.'

Agnes rested her head in her hands, and Rosanna went and stood by her, her hands on her shoulders. After a while Agnes dried her eyes. 'I was angry, you see. For years. Angry with my mother.' Rosanna sat down in the armchair again. Agnes went on, 'I was so angry I couldn't think about her dying. And now I'm not angry.'

'So, now it's time.'

Agnes sniffed, nodded.

'Now, how about that coffee? You tell me where things are. I'll make it.'

Agnes smiled, got up and went to her kitchen.

'And here I am,' Rosanna went on, 'come here to invite you to hear me sing tonight.'

'At the club?'

Rosanna shook her head. 'That's all closed down now. Venn left debts.'

'So how does that leave you?'

'Me, I'm no fool. I might have handed my heart over to Venn, but not my money. And now this old friend's just got in touch with me. He's got a venue in the West End. He's booked me for this evening. And I'd love you to be there.'

'That would be lovely. Can I bring my friend, Athena?'

'Sure. Bring the whole world. It may be the last time I ever sing as a free woman.'

Agnes looked puzzled. 'Why?'

Rosanna burst out laughing. 'You forgotten already? I make you the guardian of my future, and you don't even remember?'

Agnes smiled. 'I'm not going to hand you over. Not yet, anyway.'

'You mean, one day. One day when I've annoyed you in some way, like I've forgotten your birthday, or I've said something which implies you've put on weight, then off you'll go, walk up to the nearest friendly policeman and shop me.'

Agnes laughed, and shook her head.

'Seriously though.'

'Rosanna, I've been thinking about it. I can see that according to the law, I should let the authorities know. But they might not even believe me. They've got their man. And Mal's free. And who's going to listen to my evidence?'

Rosanna looked suddenly serious. 'It's not about getting away with it, you know. Because I haven't.'

'Anyway,' Agnes said, 'you can't sing in prison.'

Rosanna shook her head. 'You know what they say about caged birds. It's the bars that make the song. I sing because

I'm caged. When I sing, then my spirit flies free. It's always been that way.'

Agnes got up and went to the kitchen. 'Still, there are different kinds of cages,' she said.

Rosanna nodded. 'Okay, sure, I'd rather be out than in. But don't expect me to be eternally grateful to you. It ain't my style.' Agnes brought a tray of coffee through to them, and Rosanna smiled up at her. 'Tell me, Sister, when is your birthday?'

'Happy Christmas.' Ian stood up from the café table and kissed Agnes on the cheek.

'Happy Christmas,' Amy echoed, sitting quietly beside him. She was wearing jeans and a navy sweatshirt, and her hair had reverted to its natural nut-brown colour, cut into a short, layered style.

'It's nice to see you out in the world,' Agnes said to her, as Ian went to the counter to order some sandwiches.

Amy gave her a shy smile.

'How's your new accommodation?'

'Okay.' Amy's voice was barely audible.

'Better than Silworth?'

Amy nodded. Ian came and sat down next to her again, and Amy touched his arm, her thin fingers resting on his sleeve. 'Cottage cheese all right for you?' he said to her, and she nodded again, and smiled at him, and her eyes seemed to sparkle.

'Bit of a coup, getting her out for the day,' Ian said. 'I had to plead all sorts. But it's a different regime there, more flexible.'

'I gather your case comes up next week,' Agnes said to Amy, who looked at Ian.

Ian nodded. 'We've got a good defence, and anyway, no

one's going to argue about her staying where she is now for a few more weeks. And then all being well she can stay at your hostel for a while until we—' he blushed, and looked up at the waitress, who approached with a large plate of sandwiches. Then Ian busied himself distributing them.

'Until you what?' Agnes said, picking out a ham and mustard on brown bread.

Amy glanced at Ian. 'We thought we might get married,' she said. 'It was his idea,' she added, as if Agnes might not believe her.

'But—' Agnes stared at Ian.

'I'll leave my job, of course,' he said.

'But—'

Amy looked at Agnes, and now her gaze was level. 'I know I've been – I've been somewhere else, in my mind, for a while. Like I was crazy. But I needed to be there. And now I'm here. I know what I'm doing.' She got up, and leaned over Ian. 'You tell her about it,' she said. 'I'm going to the loo.' She disappeared down the stairs at the back of the café.

'Don't look at me as if I'm mad,' Ian said.

'But – but getting married . . . ?'

'That's the whole point.'

'But she's – when you think what she's been through—'

'But she's come through it. It's like, if you think of the flame that burns in all of us, the spirit or whatever you want to call it . . . She can still laugh, you see. She can still hope.'

'But to get married—'

'That's just what I mean. It's about hope. Like any marriage.'

'But the way you met—'

'We're taking our chances. Like any other couple.' He looked up and smiled as Amy rejoined them.

'Have you convinced her?' she said. 'Or does she still think we're stark raving mad?'

'He's convinced me that you're no more stark raving mad than anyone else who decides to get married.'

Ian laughed. 'That's the most we can hope for.'

'You see,' Amy began, 'what I meant was, since the fire . . . since all that . . . Jesus doesn't talk to me any more.'

'Is – is that a good thing?' Agnes watched her as she thought for a moment.

'I think – I think if you go looking for Jesus, you find him. But I think, you have to, kind of, go away. Go somewhere else. And then he's there.' She smiled at Agnes. 'But I came back. I came back here.' She glanced up shyly at Ian, then turned back to Agnes. 'I can't explain it very well – I'm not clever like you.'

'It's not about cleverness,' Agnes said.

'He hasn't left me, though. I know he's still there. It's just he's not there in the same way. You know, like in parallel universes and things, like in them films? It's like that, maybe.' She giggled, in a small, quiet way. 'You know more about it than me,' she said.

Agnes shook her head. 'All I know,' she said, 'is that what seems true to you is true. Although I'd watch out for Ian here – he'll tell you it's all an illusion.'

'No, I won't—' Ian protested.

'You said all feelings were illusions.'

'I've moved on since then.'

Amy squeezed Ian's arm. 'Well, all I know is that my life's never been more real than it is now.'

They came out into the street. The sleet had settled into dirty puddles. A nearby pub had shed some of its afternoon customers, and people straggled along the road. Agnes noticed someone waving, and realised it was Janette, on the arm of a large grey-haired man who was wearing only a T-shirt despite the cold. Janette crossed the street and came up to them, and took hold of Agnes's hand in a warm, clammy grip.

'I wanted to thank you,' she said, her speech slurred. 'It was you what done it, weren't it? You told them about my Jim – how it weren't me, it were that cousin of his.'

Agnes nodded. The man towered over her, looking down at her in an unfocused but vaguely hostile way. She noticed he had a gold earring in one ear.

'This is Warren.' Janette smiled adoringly up at him. Warren nodded at her, and managed a thin smile. 'And this is my friend Agnes.' She appeared not to see Ian and Amy, who stood at a distance.

'Come on, doll,' Warren said. 'They said at the Green Man they'd be opening today.'

'Nah, wait, I want to tell her . . .'

'Tell her what?'

'Our news, babes. You can be the first to know.' She grinned at Agnes, breathing whisky fumes.

'Now wait a minute, gel—'

'Nah, Warren, you said, you did, he did.' She turned to Agnes. 'He proposed to me, just now, in the pub. My Christmas present, you said, di'n't yer?' Warren swayed slightly on his feet and glared at her. Janette turned back to Agnes. 'We're goin' to get married.' She smiled, a wide happy grin that showed the gaps in her teeth.

'I'm very happy for you,' Agnes began, but Warren had grabbed Janette's arm.

''S'enough of your rubbish,' he said. 'I never said nothin' about getting married—'

'You did. Just now, in the pub, you said you was giving me the best Christmas present a girl could want—'

'I never meant marriage—'

'What's this, then?' Janette showed her ring finger, on which sparkled a cheap, ill-fitting diamond.

'I never said wear it on that hand, did I? Anyway, I can't marry you.'

'Why ever bleedin' not?'

''Cos I'm already married.'

'You lyin' bastard—'

'I told you. Suzy—'

'You said that was over. Last night, you said that was finished two years ago.' Janette was distracted, ignoring Agnes, caught up in her new drama.

'Yeah, but she don't think so, does she? Come on, your friends here don't want to listen to your bleedin' rubbish . . .' He pulled her away, down the street, towards the traffic lights at the main road. Their voices were still audible, raised in anger.

'Well,' Ian said, looking after them, 'it's just as I said. Taking our chances. Like any couple.' He looked down at Amy, and they both laughed.

'Sweetie, this is much better than that old underground dive. Decent booze and everything.' Athena raised her glass of chilled white wine.

Agnes looked towards the stage, which was busy with activity. 'Proper stage crew too,' she said.

'It's the West End, isn't it, sweetie? Better class of venue here. I mean, south of the river is always going to be a bit second-rate in comparison.'

'Thanks very much.'

'Poppet, don't be silly. I didn't mean you.'

Agnes poured herself some more wine. 'And how was your Christmas?'

Athena looked wistful. 'Okay. I think.'

'Were you at home?'

'Nic and I went away, overnight. Got back this afternoon. A lovely country hotel, straight up the A1 somewhere. I'm not sure where. Nic did all the driving.'

'And?'

'Oh, I don't know, poppet. Yes, it was lovely. He gave me these earrings. Look, they're absolutely perfect – must have cost him a fortune.'

'And what did you give him?'

'A tie, Italian silk. Pictures of luggage all over it. He said he liked it. But that's just it, sweetie, I can't tell. I can't tell what he's thinking, and I think it's all my fault, and now I'm here about to listen to some jazz and it'll remind me of Greg and all I can think is that I feel a fool. A complete fool, sweetie. I've never regretted my behaviour in the past, and now I do, and that makes me feel old, and then I get a sense of loss for the carefree person that I used to be, and Nic knows all that. He can see it, he asks me about it and listens when I tell him, and he's lovely, really, lovely, and all I can do is think that I've wrecked it.'

'Does he think you've wrecked it?'

Athena looked at Agnes over the top of her glass. 'And that's the strangest thing of all, sweetie. He doesn't. He says he was wrong to try to change the way we were, and take me for granted, and he says we're all on a learning curve although it feels more like a bloody roller coaster to me, but anyway – I really don't deserve to have him, sweetie.'

There was a smattering of applause as Rosanna's band appeared on stage. 'I think you have to try,' Agnes said.

'Try what?'

'Try to deserve him.'

Athena met her gaze. She nodded. 'Yes. That's what I think too.'

A burst of applause heralded Rosanna's entrance.

Something had changed about her, Agnes thought, watching her. She had the same power in her voice. The numbers were the same, most of them. But perhaps it was the more professional lighting, or the severe black drapes of the stage, against which she seemed to stand out, sparkling in the glitter of her dress. Or perhaps it was the way she seemed to scan the audience, her eyes searching, searching through the songs of love and loss, as if looking for something from the audience but never finding it. It lent an edge to her performance, a restless energy, as if the stillness that Agnes had seen in her before had sharpened in intensity.

As the last song came to an end, Agnes recalled Rosanna's words. It's the cage that makes the song, she'd said.

'She is fantastic,' Athena said, shouting above the loud applause. 'In fact, she's better than before. It must be because she's not tied down to that gangster any more. Don't you think?'

'Sorry?'

'Sweetie, you're not listening. I said, it must be good for her to be free of that villain.'

'Oh. Yes.' Agnes watched Rosanna take a last bow and leave the stage.

'Anyway, sweetie.' Athena raised her glass. 'To Us. To not running away. Any more. Ever.'

Agnes lifted her glass. 'Except I am. This time tomorrow I'll be in France.'

'Yes, but you'll come back. Won't you?' Athena's eyes widened in panic.

Agnes laughed. 'Yes. I'll come back.'

'Promise?'

'Well, unless the prospect of my inheritance proves too much. My own large house in Provence, complete with acres of grounds, and a beach not too far away . . . I could grow a vineyard, keep horses, bees – actually, I've always wanted to keep bees. What do you think?'

'When's the flight? I'm coming with you.'

Agnes laughed, and shook her head. 'I'm sure none of it's mine. My father left debts, and my mother's care hasn't been cheap. No, Athena, we're old and wise now. No more running away. We've learnt that where we are is where we're meant to be.'

Athena nodded, then looked glum. 'Shame about the beach, though.'

Agnes unfastened her seat belt and accepted the plastic cup of gin and tonic that the air hostess offered her. She looked out at the bright sunlight, at the crisp blue of the sky. Thank God my mother waited for me, she thought.

She leaned back in her seat, and breathed deeply. It was strange, she thought, to feel so calm, so free. Liberated by the truth, she thought, by knowing the story of my mother's life.

Agnes swirled the ice around in her cup. She thought about her mother, refusing her destiny, rewriting her story. Perhaps Athena's right, she thought. Perhaps I am like my mother.

Agnes smiled and looked out of the window. The clouds below made soft icy peaks in the dazzling sun. This is my story, she thought to herself. This is the beginning of my story.

If you enjoyed this book here is a selection of other bestselling titles from Headline